The PEN/O. Henry Prize Stories 2009

SERIES EDITORS

2003–	Laura Furman
1997–2002	Larry Dark
1967–1996	William Abrahams
1961–1966	Richard Poirier
1960	Mary Stegner
1954–1959	Paul Engle
1941–1951	Herschel Brickell
1933–1940	Harry Hansen
1919–1932	Blanche Colton Williams

PAST JURORS

2008	Chimamanda Ngozi Adichie, David Leavitt, David Means
2007	Charles D'Ambrosio, Ursula K. Le Guin, Lily Tuck
2006	Kevin Brockmeier, Francine Prose, Colm Tóibín
2005	Cristina García, Ann Patchett, Richard Russo
2003	David Guterson, Diane Johnson, Jennifer Egan
2002	Dave Eggers, Joyce Carol Oates, Colson Whitehead
2001	Michael Chabon, Mary Gordon, Mona Simpson
2000	Michael Cunningham, Pam Houston, George Saunders
1999	Sherman Alexie, Stephen King, Lorrie Moore
1998	Andrea Barrett, Mary Gaitskill, Rick Moody
1997	Louise Erdrich, Thom Jones, David Foster Wallace

The PEN/O. Henry Prize Stories 2009

Chosen and with an Introduction by
Laura Furman

With Essays on the Stories They Admire Most by Jurors
A. S. Byatt
Anthony Doerr
Tim O'Brien

ANCHOR BOOKS
A Division of Random House, Inc.
New York

The editor wishes to thank the staff of Anchor Books, whose energy, skill, and enthusiasm make each new collection a new pleasure, and Domenica Ruta for her good thinking and hard work.

For K, M, T, *story lovers all, in memoriam*

An Anchor Books Original, May 2009

Copyright © 2009 by Vintage Anchor Publishing, a division of Random House, Inc. Introduction © 2009 by Laura Furman

Permissions appear at the end of the book.

Cataloging-in-Publication Data for *The PEN/O. Henry Prize Stories 2009* is available at the Library of Congress.

Anchor ISBN: 978-0-307-28035-0

Book design by Debbie Glasserman

www.anchorbooks.com

Printed in the United States of America
10 9 8 7 6 5 4 3 2 1

A BRIEF HISTORY OF THE PEN/O. HENRY PRIZE STORIES

Many readers have come to love the short story through the simple characters, easy narrative voice and humor, and compelling plotting in the work of William Sydney Porter (1862–1910), best known as O. Henry. His surprise endings entertain readers, even those back for a second, third, or fourth look. Even now one can say " 'Gift of the Magi' " in a conversation about a love affair or marriage, and almost any literate person will know what is meant. It's hard to think of many other American writers whose work has been so incorporated into our national shorthand.

O. Henry was a newspaperman, skilled at hiding from his editors at deadline. A prolific writer, he wrote to make a living and to make sense of his life. He spent his childhood in Greensboro, North Carolina, his adolescence and young manhood in Texas, and his mature years in New York City. In between Texas and New York, he served out a prison sentence for bank fraud in Columbus, Ohio. Accounts of the origin of his pen name vary: one story dates from his days in Austin, where he was said to call the wandering family cat "Oh!

Henry!"; another states that the name was inspired by the captain of the guard in the Ohio State Penitentiary, Orrin Henry.

Porter had devoted friends, and it's not hard to see why. He was charming and had an attractively gallant attitude. He drank too much and neglected his health, which caused his friends concern. He was often short of money; in a letter to a friend asking for a loan of $15 (his banker was out of town, he wrote), Porter added a postscript: "If it isn't convenient, I'll love you just the same." The banker was unavailable most of Porter's life. His sense of humor was always with him.

Reportedly, Porter's last words were from a popular song: "Turn up the light, for I don't want to go home in the dark."

Eight years after O. Henry's death, in April 1918, the Twilight Club (founded in 1883 and later known as the Society of Arts and Letters) held a dinner in his honor at the Hotel McAlpin in New York City. His friends remembered him so enthusiastically that a group of them met at the Biltmore Hotel in December of that year to establish some kind of memorial to him. They decided to award annual prizes in his name for short-story writers, and formed a Committee of Award to read the short stories published in a year and to pick the winners. In the words of Blanche Colton Williams (1879–1944), the first of the nine series editors, the memorial was intended to "strengthen the art of the short story and to stimulate younger authors."

Doubleday, Page & Company was chosen to publish the first volume, *O. Henry Memorial Award Prize Stories 1919.* In 1927, the society sold all rights to the annual collection to Doubleday, Doran & Company. Doubleday published *The O. Henry Prize Stories,* as it came to be known, in hardcover, and from 1984 to 1996 its subsidiary, Anchor Books, published it simultaneously in paperback. Since 1997 *The O. Henry Prize Stories* has been published as an original Anchor Books paperback, retitled *The PEN/O. Henry Prize Stories* in 2009.

HOW THE STORIES ARE CHOSEN

All stories originally written in the English language and published in an American or Canadian periodical are eligible for consideration. Stories are not nominated; magazines submit the year's issues in their entirety by May 1.

The series editor chooses the twenty PEN/O. Henry Prize Stories, and each year three writers distinguished for their fiction are asked to evaluate the entire collection and to write an appreciation of the story they most admire. These three writers receive the twenty prize stories in manuscript form with no identification of author or publication. They make their choices independent of one another and the series editor.

The goal of The PEN/O. Henry Prize Stories remains to strengthen the art of the short story.

To Bernard Malamud (1914–86)

Bernard Malamud, author of *The Magic Barrel, The Assistant,* and other classics, taught at Bennington College in the 1960s.

One practical piece of advice he gave was that in fiction the writer should never use the names of movie stars; in time, the stars would be forgotten. The astral reference used in a student description of a character's jaw was Kirk Douglas; surely he would be recognizable forever. The years have proved Malamud right, though his point, like any fixed rule in art, is up for argument. What Malamud taught of lasting importance was that the writer must not consider pleasing anyone, not even the reader. Only the work's integrity mattered in the end. In a talk he gave at Bennington in 1984, two years from his death, he said, "I have written almost all my life. My writing has drawn, out of a reluctant soul, a measure of astonishment at the nature of life. And the more I wrote well, the better I felt I had to write."

Through the example of his careful attention to our work and the work of writers he admired, Malamud demonstrated to his students the passion and devotion required to be a writer. He wasn't devoted to teaching or to us but to literature. For the moments we were in his presence, reading and writing, we were part of literature too.

Contents

Introduction

NINETY YEARS ago, The O. Henry Prize Stories was created by William Sidney Porter's friends and colleagues to honor him and the form in which he wrote.

Since 1919 there have been a few years without the publication of an O. Henry Prize Stories collection, but still, in an industry where many books enjoy the longevity of a mayfly, lasting for ninety years is a superb accomplishment.

Our annual collection is an institution among writers and readers, who look for it each spring. For a writer beginning what might or might not be a career, inclusion is both recognition of the particular story and warm encouragement to keep writing. One of the collection's first stated goals was to "stimulate younger authors," but even for writers who have long and distinguished careers, inclusion in *The O. Henry Prize Stories* is meaningful and even "gladdening," as one of this year's authors, John Burnside, said.

The O. Henry's recognition of quality extends to the magazines that publish the prize story. *The New Yorker,* committed to publishing fiction since its beginning, has a large readership, and a smaller journal such as the *New England Review* only a fraction of that number. What matters in the long run is that a magazine continues to publish excellent fiction in its pages, stories that readers are challenged by and sometimes love.

For its readers, our prize collection is a faithful yet exciting friend. Each spring *The O. Henry Prize Stories* offers a renewed engagement with the immediacy of the short story. This is what O. Henry's friends and colleagues hoped when they conceived the unique idea of publishing a book annually to draw attention to an outstanding group of short stories and short-story writers.

In the ninetieth year since its founding, the O. Henry Prize differs from its first iteration. Instead of a committee choosing the stories, as in 1919 and for many years following, the series editor does so alone. Since 2002, the criteria for stories have widened; now the prize is open to any story if it's originally written in English and published in a North American magazine, regardless of the citizenship of the writer. The prize stories thus come from a broader range of voices and countries—witness our current group of authors, who live in Scotland, England, South Africa, Singapore, and Canada, as well as the United States. The original system of awarding first, second, and third prizes was eventually abandoned. All twenty stories are equally prized, though separate recognition comes to the stories picked by the jurors as their favorites. There have been nine series editors, and each has tweaked the book's form. What hasn't changed is fidelity to the mission of The O. Henry Prize Stories stated by its founders ninety years ago, "to strengthen the art of the short story."

Starting with this 2009 volume, the collection is to be retitled *The PEN/O. Henry Prize Stories* in recognition of a new alliance with the PEN American Center.

PEN is an international organization devoted to the stimulation, support, and sustenance of writers and literature. Bernard Malamud, the story master to whom this year's PEN/O. Henry is dedicated, was president of PEN from 1979 to 1981, and he wrote: "I believe in a fellowship of writers, more or less formally constituted, aware of how deeply and complexly we are concerned with, and foster, a literature as a civilizing force in an unstable world; a literature that gives flesh and bones and perhaps a brain to the politics that assails us; a literature that entices us to understand and value life."

PEN American Center, founded in 1920, lives out its ideals in a number of ways: by defending writers who are imprisoned or in danger of imprisonment because of their work; by offering coveted awards for writers, editors, and translators; by supporting public discussion of current issues of literature and freedom of expression; and—most relevant for *The PEN/O. Henry Prize Stories*—by "mentoring teens through the PEN Writing Institute, which brings underserved public school students and professional writers together to discuss literary craft." *The PEN/O. Henry Prize Stories* will be used in the Readers & Writers Program to strengthen the art of the short story and to stimulate younger authors. And readers, young and old. We hope for a long and happy working life with PEN.

For the 2009 collection, our three jurors are A. S. Byatt, Anthony Doerr, and Tim O'Brien, all authors of past O. Henry Prize Stories. All three have very different concerns and hallmarks as writers. Tim O'Brien's canonical stories of American soldiers in the Vietnam War and its aftermath have defined that war and its era for many readers; the ways in which war haunts its veterans as effectively as any ghost has long been a subject for O'Brien. But subject matter has only so much importance in any story. O'Brien generously calls his favorite "a very wonderful story about war, though in exactly the same way and to exactly the same extent that 'Bartleby' is a wonderful story about office life." Byatt's work reaches brilliantly into the life of the mind, and she creates a fictional world where the imagination controls the commonplace, another kind of haunting. Byatt's essay explains a great deal about her own view of the short story, as well as of her also demonic favorite. The troubled, shape-shifting relation of Doerr's characters to the natural and man-made world is central to his work. The loving, detailed attention to the tangible that's the hallmark of Doerr's fiction stands in contrast to the big, emotional narrative he chose as his favorite. The three jurors served in the usual O. Henry antijury, without consultation with one another or with the series editor.

Byatt and O'Brien chose the same story as their favorite—Graham Joyce's "An Ordinary Soldier of the Queen"—and both writers speak eloquently of the choice (see pp. 381 and 386). Joyce's skilled combination of the moving ordinary and the frightening extraordinary gives the story its energy. "An Ordinary Soldier of the Queen" contains elements of both the demonic and the realistic war story; its narrator could hardly be more reassuringly a savvy military man, but his tortured perceptions of his shattering wartime experience make him a tragic figure.

Anthony Doerr chose Junot Díaz's "Wildwood" as his favorite, for reasons he gives beautifully in his essay (see p. 383). "Wildwood" is narrated powerfully and seductively by a young woman who is hellbent on getting away from her mother, an all-too human demon, and on escaping her mother's sexual ideas by leaping into her own destiny, guided in equal parts by love and fear. The story's larger-than-life mother and the narrator's own disasters and escapes will be recognized by many women, though most of us don't have stories to tell of such mythic proportions.

The twenty PEN/O. Henry stories are gathered over a year's reading, May to May. When they come together in a single volume, they develop a semifamilial relationship not apparent when they're individual stories written by authors far-flung and published in, this year, fourteen different magazines. For the reader, resonances are heard of subject matter, if not of voice or technique; these remain individual.

Some of this collection's stories are about the experience of being a child or the impossible relationship between child and parent. Others concern love, thwarted or triumphant. Others concern disasters, imagined or real. Two are about stories themselves and how we live through them.

In Nadine Gordimer's "A Beneficiary" the daughter of a famous actress must cope with her capricious mother's final secret. In doing so, she must make decisions about her own identity in a way that separates her forever from her mother.

L. E. Miller's "Kind" might be read as a companion piece to "Wildwood" and "A Beneficiary," for it brings the perspective of age to a young, unformed woman's experience of mirroring—or choosing not to mirror—an older woman. In "Kind," the narrator is on a plane when she meets by chance the daughter of someone from her distant past; she remembers the woman who taught her at least two shades of the idea of "kindness," that is, similarity and active sympathy.

In Paul Yoon's lovely Korean War story, "And We Will Be Here," the past haunts the main character in her overwhelming wish for the return of a brother orphan who, when they were children, became everything to her. She knows nothing about herself, not even her date of birth, but she clings, as one would to family or to self, to this boy—another identity-less being—who is gone forever.

The founding disaster for the heroine of Yoon's story is that she has no family; on the other side of the world in postapartheid South Africa, the adult daughter in Alistair Morgan's "Icebergs," an accomplished and successful artist, is doing her best to rid herself of hers. "Icebergs" is narrated by the daughter's lonely widowed father, himself adrift without his wife, captive of a pricey home meant for their life together in retirement. The daughter shatters his unhappy peace and breaks with the security and stability he offers her.

Candy, as a nurse's aide in a VA hospital, looks on terrible wounds and deprivation, while the reader of Marisa Silver's "The Visitor" wonders when Candy will feel something aside from clinical interest. Throughout the story, Candy wants to pry a reaction from her latest patient, a soldier who "was three-quarters gone. Both legs below the knee and the left arm at the shoulder." Her own mother proved graphically to Candy that love was weaker than an addiction to drugs. The heroic figure in "The Visitor" is Candy's grandmother, never a visitor to her emotions, willing to make impossible decisions.

The story sticks closely to Candy's point of view while simultaneously pulling the reader far enough away to see what made her the way she is and what might spring the trap.

Karen Brown's story "Isabel's Daughter" circles around the child of the title but lands on the character of the narrator. It's possible to see all first-person fiction as being about the narrator in the end; in this case the sweeping generalization seems true. The delicacy with which Brown handles the narrative gives the reader the ability to see the child's life through two different perspectives at once.

Two stories about mothers illustrate the grip of love; in both, the mothers knowingly distort the child's fate. Caitlin Horrocks's character in "This Is Not Your City" has left her country, language, family, and friends behind to better her life and her child's. But her bargain with the devil—an arranged marriage with an old man about whom she knows nothing and whose language she doesn't understand— teaches her daughter not about love or survival but about selling herself. In one arresting moment, the mother borrows her child's underwear to pose for a provocative photograph in order to find a new life. Yet the lesson of survival proves stronger than the example of self-degradation, and perhaps in this case maternal love will conquer the child's righteous anger.

"The Nursery" by Kirsten Sundberg Lunstrum is a story that grows on you, especially in repeated readings, until its full quiet horror is apparent. The idea of mothers as monsters reminds us of Medea, perhaps of Joan Crawford and her hangers. The mother in Lunstrum's story doesn't believe in the possibility of trust, and relies only on security she can provide. When she betrays her son, she's left with her life of raising plants that will mature in other people's gardens.

E. V. Slate's main character in "Purple Bamboo Park" is a woman who provides child care, but it is the caregiver who's more vulnerable than the child here. Slate's moving story is about power and how differences of class, money, and education—but mostly money—make a helpless child of an adult.

Manuel Muñoz's "Tell Him about Brother John" is a layered story about the nature of love, how it pulls you toward it as strongly as it pushes you away. The narrator grew up on Gold Street in California's Valley, Muñoz's fictional locale as Winesburg, Ohio, was Sherwood Anderson's. On his annual visit home from Allá, from Over There, he's told to visit Brother John, abandoned as a boy, who lives next door. John also escaped to Allá but returned to Gold Street, battered and brokenhearted. He is open about his pain, which the narrator in his closed, closeted heart can't bear. In the narrator's complex life on Gold Street, it isn't being gay or Mexican American or living Allá that creates his palpable sense of danger, it's being human and having a heart ready to be broken again, and of acknowledging the truth about his life or his neighbor's.

"The House Behind a Weeping Cherry" holds a world of exploitation, helplessness, and forbidden hope. Ha Jin's love story about a factory worker and a prostitute has a weird cheerfulness as they rise above the enormous difficulties of their lives. The story shows us the rarity of freedom and what some few individuals do to try to bring it to their lives.

In Judy Troy's "The Order of Things," adulterous lovers who are interwoven in their community and families plot to join their lives. Troy's story is as much about spiritual faith as it is about romantic and sexual love, though it's convincingly about those emotions too. Troy's clear, straightforward prose ensnares the reader in the lovers' complex perceptions and decisions.

The title of Mohan Sikka's "Uncle Musto Takes a Mistress" sets a comic tone, and the characters' melodramatic emotions and relationships are written broadly enough that for much of this young writer's fine story the reader sits back in amusement. Then the story's comedy reverses course; what was comical or silly seems poisonous and destructive. A harmless, even useful love affair becomes the cause of division and isolation in a family.

John Burnside's "The Bell Ringer" brings to its reader a taste of desire and of disaster. In a small community a lonely woman decides to come together with others in the ancient activity of music making, in this case, bell ringing. Perhaps it is her initial willingness to join one group that opens her to other possibilities for communication and even intimacy. Part of the story's strength lies in the writer's respect for his character's compromises and her range of feeling. The beauty of the story lies also in the writer's language and his ability to describe both characters and place so that we're involved emotionally before we know it.

In Andrew Sean Greer's "Darkness," three old friends are fleeing a disaster; two are lovers, the third an acute observer of human behavior. The story's form of short sections imitates the characters' journey and reveals the internal shortcomings and triumphs of human love and friendship.

Viet Dinh's "Substitutes" begins before the fall of Saigon. Narrated in first-person plural, the story traces the changes Communist rule brings through the substitute teachers the students endure. Their most significant lesson is about their own future, and how they must learn to behave in order to survive peace.

Paul Theroux's "Twenty-two Stories" and Roger Nash's "The Camera and the Cobra" demonstrate the place of stories in our lives. In the latter, a new doctor is posted to an Egyptian village on the edge of the Sahara and the Great Bitter Lake. He brings with him a camera through whose lens he learns to understand his position as a doctor and the ever-changing, ever-stable nature of the world around him. In a new place, assuming grave responsibilities, the doctor uses his camera to contain and reframe his experience. One disease looks like another. A fox and a hawk are mistaken. He asks, "Was this, after all, how life had to be, with events—even lives—overlapping like crabs and presenting as each other?"

Paul Theroux's "Twenty-two Stories" can be read as twenty-two separate offerings or as one whole with twenty-two pieces. The reader is free to choose how many stories to make of this one, and to find the places of congruence and difference, framing and reframing the experiences Theroux so economically delineates.

What is obvious for Theroux's story is true of all the stories in *The PEN/O. Henry Prize Stories 2009.* It is up to the reader to participate—to decide what each story is about, or how many things the story is about, and to discover how the writer created the singular world that is the story. In the end, the art of the short story is sustained by its reader.

—*Laura Furman*
Austin, Texas

The PEN/O. Henry Prize Stories 2009

Graham Joyce

An Ordinary Soldier
of the Queen

I'M GOING to ask the Queen. I'm going to tell her what I know and ask her what is true, and if she winks at me, well, there will be trouble. This is me, Seamus Todd, born in 1955, ordinary soldier of the Queen and very little else, and this is my testament, which is honest, true, and factual. If I haven't seen it with my own eyes, then I have left it out. There's more than enough cheap talk and I don't want to add to it.

I joined the army at eighteen. I done my twenty-two. I started off as a private in the Staffordshire Regiment and I worked my way up to color sergeant. Three tours of duty in Northern Ireland, then joined the landing assault as a battle casualty replacement in the Falklands.

I had the tip of one finger shot off in South Armagh bandit country on patrol, while another soldier was telling me a joke about three nuns out picking mushrooms. Wedding finger, left hand. Lucky for me the IRA sniper was a shitty shot. Also broke my leg in the Falklands, but this was in a game of football after we'd taken the islands back from the Argies. Slipped on sheep shit. That's the only injuries to report out of all my combat experience.

When the Gulf War kicked off in '91 it was just another posting for me, except that now I was well seasoned and babysitting a platoon of boy soldiers. It was my job to tell them how normal everything was. Most of my lads were pink-nosed puppies, boys of eighteen or twenty-one. I was their big angry daddy, and I looked after every one of them. They all said I was hard but fair. I stand by that. I looked after my boys, and they knew it. I told them: "Loyalty and a sense of humor is what I want, but you can fuck the sense of humor." That always got a laugh.

War is normal. That's why it's a paid job. You don't ask, Why are we in the Gulf? Why are we in Ireland? Why are we in some sheep-shit South Atlantic island that no one's ever heard of? You don't argue with the Queen. You form up. Move out. Press on.

We knew we were going to war long before Christmas that year. They haven't told you but you hear the drum. I can't explain. You're on active duty and there's a drum beat, an echo, maybe it's your own heart beating very quiet, and it thuds on until something happens or until you're stood down. Hear the beat, get the order.

With the heavy armor already at sea we were to be airlifted after Christmas so I was able to tell my boys: Shag your girlfriend and kiss your wife and get ready to go. It's what I always said and it always got a laugh, too. But the family men, those of them with little sprats in the homestead, there was always a quick switch off behind the light in their eyes. Yeh, better get the lad that new bike this year. Yeh, better get that little gal a big teddy bear.

Within a few days the tinsel and the Christmas cards and the Brazil nuts were all just another check box on last year's calendar and we were in the Saudi desert, lined up against Saddam Hussein's Iraqi cohorts to drive them out of Kuwait. Saddam was saying it was going to be the "mother of all battles" and his saying that put the wind up everyone. But that's not how it turned out.

Now, the desert held no fear for me, but it wasn't the kind of fighting I was used to. Street to street, house to house, urban shadow— that's me. I learned my p's and q's in Ireland, and that education served me well in Bosnia when I was the blue hat, and before that over the bog fields of the Falkland Islands. Give me rough cover, coarse terrain, half a shadow, and I'm your man. But the flat trackless desert: not my arena.

Tanks for the desert is the thing. Line up your tanks. Get your air power to fuck over as many of the enemy's tanks as you can before you roll him up. It ain't complicated. But then when you do hit a settlement or defensive position you've got to have your infantry—that's me—keeping pace with the tanks in armored Warriors so's we can dismount and engage at the battle line, mopping up with bullet, grenade, and bayonet. That's where I'm happy. Don't get to use that bayonet very often but I do love to keep it shiny and sharp.

But what's a bayonet's length when for the first time since the First World War there was serious threat of gas and chemicals? We drilled and drilled and drilled, fixing those spooky chemical hoods in place. Stinking. Hear yourself heavy breathing. All your buddies bug-eyed, trying to see your face behind the mask. Get your jabs at the ready. That's not fighting. But you got to do it.

And it's the fucking boredom of it that can get to you.

We'd finished up the drill one evening and I was standing, dripping with sweat and getting my breath back from bellowing at the lads from behind the mask. The lads were dismissed and I was standing with my hands on my hips looking out at the sky over the flat desert sands.

"What you looking at, Color Sar'nt?" This was a lad called Dorky. Good lad but wouldn't shut up. Used to follow me round like a little dog. Always asking questions: What's this? What's that?

"Come 'ere, Dorky. Look out there. What d'you see?"

"Nothing, Color Sar'nt. Nothin' there. Desert, only desert, Color Sar'nt."

"Look again, son."

"Can't see anything. Nuffink."

"Look at that sky. You ever seen a sky that color?"

"No, Sar'nt."

"Not Sar'nt, Color Sar'nt, you little toe-rag. What color is it, Dorky?"

"Pink color, Color Sar'nt."

"It ain't pink, you fucking muppet. Look again."

A few of the other lads trudge by, clutching their sweaty chemical masks, wanting to know what we're looking at.

"Dorky says it's nothing," I says to 'em. "Then he says it's pink, but I says it ain't pink. What color is that sky?"

"Lavender," says Chad, a Black Country kid. "Innit."

"No, ti'nt lavender," says Brewster, a Liverpool scally, good lad in a fight. "Ti'nt lavender."

Next thing there's seven or eight lads looking into that nothing, trying to decide what color that nothing is. The truth is I don't know what color it is. It's the most beautiful sky I ever seen in my life and I don't know what color to say.

"See that sky, lads? That's why you joined the army. It ain't just to have it out with the Iraqis. It's so you'll see miraculous things. Like that sky."

And I walk away, leaving them scratching their heads. They don't know if I'm taking the piss. I don't know either. Though I do remember thinking: look at the sky now 'cos it's gonna get dark.

Waiting, drilling, waiting, drilling. Saddam had used chemicals against the Iranians and the Kurds and the marsh Arabs, so we're expecting him to fling it in our faces. Real Soon Now, as they say. But it doesn't come. There are a few more sunsets while the air assault makes softening-up runs over the Iraqis occupying Kuwait. It turns out the enemy has no decent air assault to answer with and I'm already thinking this might be a short war.

I never like it when it's too easy. If it's too easy, it ain't worth it. This is supposed to be the biggest army in the Middle East. What are they doing? The waiting is getting our boys nervous.

There are a few duels with the artillery but our only attackers are helicopters. The Multiple Launch Rocket Systems are pumping out rockets and with these little bug things—unmanned RPVs—whining in the sky to send coordinates back to our computers so we can throw still more rockets I start to think to myself: *That's it, mate. Your type of soldier is redundant, get cashiered, hang your boots up.* See—there's nothing coming back. One-sided war if they don't have the technology. Then, at the end of January, the Iraqis stir. They move across the Kuwait border and into Khafji. That don't last long. We're getting rumors that the Iraqi prisoners picked up in Khafji have no stomach for the fight.

Nobody is more relieved than me when they tell us we're on. We're going up the Wadi el Batine and then swing right into Kuwait City, and even though my lads are looking a bit sick, except for Brewster who is well up for it, I'm laughing and singing, *Wadi, wadi, we're going up the wadi,* and my boys are going: *You're cracked, Color Sergeant, you are.*

Not cracked. It's just that when I know that I'm doing what I'm supposed to be doing, that's when I'm happiest. Form up. Move out. Press on. Twenty-fourth of February, 1991, and the British 1st Armoured of which we are a part is rolling. Hear the noise of war engines. It's overcast, cold, and raining. British weather in the desert. Staffs ride in the hull of Warriors, just behind the tanks—we're moving. Into the desert we bounce.

After sunrise I begin to hear the gun reports of tank engagement. What I don't know is that the Yanks and the French have struck north to slam the back door on the Iraqis. The enemy have no air reconnaissance by now so they can't have known this. No reinforcements and no way out. They've been popped in the oven and we're just about to turn it up to Mark 200.

It isn't until later in the first day that we swing back eastward to engage Iraqi armored troops around the Kuwait border. I have the strange feeling that the war is already over after the first day because we just keep going. Black puffs of smoke drift across the sands and the crump of engagement ahead isn't getting any nearer. We stop to mop up a couple of emplacements, but besides a few rounds fired off the resistance is feeble. We pick up some of their troops—conscripts, kids trying to smile at us—and they are all passed back down the line as prisoners of war.

There is no conflict. We can't find it. Just deeper into the desert and thick black smoke billowing around, and a weird stench. I can see the smoke, I can hear the guns, but where's the war? Not that I'm hungry for it, like some of the kids looking for action. I'll do it if it's there to be done, but I've learned enough about the bookkeeping of war. You don't want to get yourself in the red column just by staying too long.

We roll on for hours, past burned-out shells of tanks and beetled armored vehicles, all Iraqi. Flame is still licking from some of the gun turrets, smoke unwinding from the guts of engines. Metal is buckled and bent. Vehicles are lodged in the sand, caterpillar wheels buried deep, and dust covers them like they've been there for years. It all has the feel of a battle long over. The only thing that makes you certain it's recent is the occasional burned corpses of soldiers flung from a bombed vehicle. Or half a corpse still in a vehicle, like the bit of the sardine you can't get out of the corner of a can. We put rounds into every burning tank we pass anyway, with either the 30 mm Rarden cannon or the chain gun. Just to be sure. Well, not even that—more out of frustration of having nothing to shoot at.

I'm in the turret with the gunner. Phosphorescent flashes keep popping from miles up ahead, and they're followed by what I want to call a flutter; it's like your eye goes aquiver for a moment. And there's a smell in the air, nothing like the usual reek of burning and high-ex. I don't like it. When it comes to combat I don't much like anything I haven't seen or smelled before.

That's what I'm thinking when we come under fire. Mortar and small arms.

"Ragheads, 'bout five hundred yards, quarter left," goes my driver

Cummings, a snippy hard-case Bristolian with shit tattoos all over his neck.

"Shove into that dip, quarter right."

There's a dune we try to snuggle in behind. Our vehicle stops dead in the sand and the engines power down. I drag my knuckles across the side of Cummings's head.

"Do not, repeat, do not let me hear you refer to the enemy as ragheads towelheads sand niggers or any other fucking thing other than the fucking enemy, right Cummings? Right?"

"Color Sar'nt!"

They should know that by now. I won't have it. Not in the middle of combat. Down the pub, in the mess, or in the whorehouse they can call 'em what the fuck they like. But not here. Won't have it.

"Why not?" I ask him. "Why fucking not?"

Another mortar falls and there are a couple of pings as bullets strike our AV. The boys in the back think I'm mad. We're under fire and I'm giving them parade-ground drill. But I know the mortars are well short and the bullets are spent when they hit the sides of the Warrior. "Come on! Let's hear it!"

"Underestimation of enemy, Color Sar'nt," says Brewster at the top of the class.

He's going to say more but I cut him off. "Under-fucking-estimation of enemy! I don't know what we've got here but sitting just behind them is the Iraqi Republican Guard. More fucking highly educated than you are, Cummings. Crack fucking soldiers, you cunt. Loyal to Saddam. They are not towelheads, ragheads, or sand niggers; they are the fucking enemy and you will respect their capacity to blow your fucking balls off, right Cummings?"

"Color Sar'nt!" goes Cummings, red in the cheeks. Another round of bullets ping the Warrior.

"These fucking people invented reading and writing while we were still living in mud huts and dancing 'round Stone-fucking-henge with a blue face, you got that Cummings?"

"Color Sar'nt!"

Well, that's enough of that. All the lads in the back are looking at me, so I swing down and give 'em a nice big smile, like I'm just lemonade. "Good lads. Now then, what we got?"

Turns out there is a little emplacement dug into the sand, still active behind our front lines. This is just what we're here for. Clean up. Mrs. Overalls. Get the marigold gloves on, out with the bleach and polish, make the world shine. Our infrared should be able to tell us how many bodies they have dug in, but it's on the fucking blink, which is normal. All this gear works fine until you need it to run with sand in it; though I suspect these phosphorescent flashes might have something to do with the malfunction. Doesn't matter. Our AV is well equipped to take the enemy out.

The terrain suits us. There's a slight rise on our eastern flank so I can get a couple of lads out there to attack the position while we give covering fire with the cannon. Brewster and Dorky volunteer, as do one or two others. I give them the nod, and then for some reason—I don't know why—I decide I'll go and hold their hands. It's not that they need me.

I order the driver to power up and move on fifty yards to fire a couple of white phos grenades to make a smoke screen so's we can drop out and flit over to get behind the rise, hopefully unnoticed. When we reach the rise we can see a burned-out Iraqi tank on the sand maybe just another hundred yards away. We scope it out. There are bodies lying around it. No life. It's all clear. It's a bit of useful cover and we go up behind it to set up our gear to help the Warrior make its fire on the Iraqi bunker.

"Fucking hell," says Dorky.

He's looking at a torso nearby. Or at least I think it's a torso. It still has its arms and legs, but it's a weird shape. Shrunk. Nasty.

"Never mind what's around you," I bark at him. "Get operational!"

But Brewster and Dorky are paralyzed by this thing. It's an effort for them to look away.

"Come on, lads," I say, a deep low growl.

Training kicks in, they go to it, fumbling a bit, fidgety, hyper, but they set up. And I look at this thing out of the corner of my eye because I don't want the lads to see I'm freaked by it, too. It's a corpse—of a kind—of an Iraqi soldier spilled out of the tank. Part of his head's gone but most of the rest of him is there. I can't see hands and feet. None of that bothers me. I've seen enough bits of bodies in my time, and after a while it's no different from what's in your burger. But this thing: it's a body, but it's shrunk to maybe a third of the size it should be. It crossed my mind that it might be a kid, but it's bearded and anyway it's not like it's a kid, it's like the whole thing has twisted like a plastic bag when you set fire to it. And it's left a spooky shadow behind, a man-shaped shadow on the sand.

The boys are set up and ready, but I've got to shift this bloody mess. I step over to the thing and I try to side-foot it under the tank, out of eyesight, but my foot passes straight through part of it. Nothing turns my stomach. My guts are cast iron, but for the first time in years and years my bowels soften. Some of the thing sticks to my foot. I scrape sand and debris and push as much of it as I can under the tank.

I turn back. Dorky and Brewster are watching me now. "All set up, lads?"

"Color Sar'nt!"

Brewster radios the Warrior and we watch the slow elevation of the cannon before it locks. There's a pause before the Warrior launches its bombardment of the Iraqi emplacement. Dorky watches the results through binoculars and reports what's happening. I have to make a mental effort not to think about this goo stuck to my boot.

"Give 'em a strafing."

"Chain gun!" Brewster tells his radio.

There's not much more. After the cannon and chain gun has softened them up they come out and all we have to do is point our weapons. These are not Republican Guard. These are conscripts;

they've had enough and they're stumbling out with their hands on their heads. They seem to think we're the Yanks. Their idea of being a prisoner is to try to talk to us in Iraqi.

Later, after the prisoners are passed back down the line, the mopping pattern is repeated a few times. The only thing that's changed is the dust. The tanks and the armored vehicles are kicking up so much sand that it's getting hard to see farther up ahead. We're proceeding pretty much by radio coordinates and infrared activity. We stop a couple of times to check out a destroyed tank or other vehicle and we keep spotting these shrunk plastic bodies with their shadow casts, and all the time I'm thinking: what weapon is it that shrinks a human being but doesn't destroy a tank? I mean the tanks are burned but the shell is intact. I have to break up little groups of boys who stand mesmerized over these shrunk bodies.

"Don't look at it, lads. Press on."

Another few miles ahead we get radio directed to another clear-up. Same as before: a few salvos to loosen the sand around them then in we go. The Iraqis are pouring out like ants from a poisoned nest, but I don't want my boys to get complacent. There are always diehards, and I want no rush. By the book, me. I'm dedicated to bringing all my boys home with their trousers on.

The dust and the sand are being swirled around by a strong breeze coming from the east. It smells of spice and engine smoke, and it's choking so we have to go in now with scarves over our faces just to stop our noses and mouths filling up. This time I peel off with five of my boys, Dorky and Brewster among them. From somewhere up ahead there's sniper fire coming at us, bullets flying blind in the dust. We get down behind an escarpment.

They know the drill. I'm going out very wide; they're going to crawl on their bellies at spread intervals but stay in visual range, using the dust storm as cover. Meanwhile I've got my other boys noising up the Warrior's chain gun to draw fire and support our attack.

I yomp off maybe three hundred yards wide. I can hear the report of the sniper as he fires on the Warrior, but I can't see him. The dust gets thicker. There's a strong breeze picking up and I can't tell how much of this dust is generated by vehicle movement and how much is a natural windblown storm, but it's swirling and lashing about like a sand lizard's tail.

I look across the line. The dust is so strong I can barely see Brewster, who is my nearest support. I wave at him. He sees me and I point to my eye, warning him to stay in visual range with me and the next man. I don't want to be shot by my own troops: happens all the time in combat. Brewster gives me the thumbs-up to show he understands.

We make slow progress toward the Iraqi emplacement. They're still firing, infrequently and wildly. I have an instinct there's only one or two of them, maybe three hundred yards away. I'm going on my belly.

Then the dust whips up again. The sand is turning aggressive spirals in the air, a whip-o'-will, a dark thing, like a live creature, part smoke, part sand. The dust is so thick I've lost sight of Brewster, but if he remembers his training he'll stay exactly where he is until we reestablish visual range. I can't see more than maybe ten yards ahead of me in the gritty yellow fog. We're all radio disarmed: nothing like somebody squawking through your set when you're on your belly six feet away from the enemy. Maybe I could use the radio safely with this wind and racket going on but I don't want to risk it. We wait. Behind the wind I can hear our artillery pounding the Iraqi dugouts a few miles ahead. Then I can't even hear that.

After a while the sandstorm begins to ease. I have a thin cotton scarf over my mouth and it's almost stiff with the dust logged in it. My eyes are stinging and sweat is dribbling along the curve of my spine. I'm scoping out the spot where I last saw Brewster, but even though the dust is clearing I can't see him.

What I can see is the Iraqi dugout, and I'm way nearer to it than I should be. There's no activity. The dugout has taken a direct hit and there are bodies spilled. But I'm exposed and there's still no sign of Brewster.

I have a white phosphorous grenade. I decide to use it because as well as clearing anything within fifteen yards of where it lands it makes a good signal. I chuck it at the dugout and get down, keeping my eyes averted from the flash to avoid the after-dazzle. The thing goes off and the smoke rises pretty quickly. Anything coming out of the dugout is going to walk straight into my line of fire.

But there's nothing there.

I hang in, still waiting to make eye contact with any of my boys. Visibility in the dust is fluctuating at between maybe twenty to thirty yards, no more than that, and after the shock of my phos grenade everything is quiet. I can't even hear the artillery up ahead and the fly-overs have stopped altogether. I decide to wake up the radio.

My radio, like all of them in our unit, is a piece of shit twenty years old and it's fucked and we've reported it fucked and got no replacement gear. I have to make several calls before someone in my Warrior picks me up.

"Who's that?" I ask.

"Fox." It's Corporal Middleton. Fox is his call sign; normal names are prohibited over the radio. "Where are you, Cobra?" he asks.

"I'm at the dugout. Where's Echo and Valiant?" These are the call signs for Brewster and Cummings.

"They've lost you, Cobra."

"Did you see my flash?"

"Flash?"

"Phos bomb, you idiot. You couldn't fucking miss it. If you can't raise Echo and Valiant send me two other lads to clear this dugout."

This is bad radio procedure. Normal conversation is also prohibited but we're on a closed net at short range and I'm getting mighty irritated with everything.

"No flash, Cobra. Give me your last coordinates."

I sit back and wait. The thick yellow cloud of sand and dust is like a gas, a sulfurous fog, and I still can't see more than about thirty yards.

I wait for half an hour, and then I do what I tell my boys never to do: I make a solo approach to the dugout. Not because I'm feeling brave but because I'm bored. I'm in the middle of combat and I'm bored, and when I'm bored I start thinking too much and that scares me more than the enemy.

The dugout is well sandbagged and there is a big, black, broken gun blasted halfway over the sandbags. I can smell the oil and the ripped steel. I approach slowly from the rear. The dugout is clean: no live enemy. Plenty of dead ones, though. Nothing done by my phos grenade—these are all shrunk, shriveled bodies like I've seen before. Shrunk with their original shadows scorched into the dust.

I kick over the mess cans and check round. There's nothing of useful intelligence and I need to return to my unit. The problem is I don't know where my unit is and my radio is still on the blink. I go outside the dugout to climb the rise to see if I can get a better signal. Maybe ten yards from the sandbags I hear a sharp, metallic click.

You've seen those war movies, maybe Vietnam, where a soldier steps on a mine and they cut to the expression on his face as he realizes what he's done. There's a pause. *Boom!* Nah. Never happens like that in real life. You step on a modern mine and there's no pause and you've no face left to have an expression. You know nothing about it.

But I step on something and there's a loud click. I don't know what it is, but I can feel a metal plate under my foot. I've trodden on something and I've triggered a spring-release mechanism.

I have no idea what this is. It may be a mine, it may be an improvised booby trap. But I know that if I don't keep my foot down on it, it's going to blow my leg off and maybe a lot more. I'm stuck. I'm not going anywhere.

With the yellow smog, visibility is still down to about twenty yards or so, but should any Iraqis come stumbling through that dust I'm a dead man. Should I lift my foot I'm a dead man. I can't see what it is I've trodden on but I can certainly feel the hard metal shape under my size-nine boot. Maybe it's a mine that has malfunctioned. Maybe it's some old piece of crap the Iraqis had left over from their desert war with Iran, and it's not going to blow. I don't know.

A maggot of sweat runs along my spine. My mouth is full of dust. Keeping my foot in place, I get on the radio. Miraculously I get a signal and patch through at the first attempt. Middleton answers again.

"Cobra, where are you?"

"Listen carefully. I've stepped on a mine."

"Fuck! Are you all right?"

"No, listen. It hasn't gone off. I've got my foot on it and I can't go anywhere or it will detonate."

"Fuck! Don't move your foot."

"You dickhead! I'm not moving my foot anywhere. But I need you to find me pronto. I need someone to work out how to get me out of this."

"What are your coordinates?"

"Exactly what I gave you last time."

"Can't be, Cobra. We've been all over there looking for you."

"Speak with Brewster. He was the last man I saw."

"Exactly what we did, Cobra."

"Well fucking do it again! I'm getting a bit fucking warm out here, Corporal!"

"Color Sar'nt!"

"I'll fire three rounds, wait fifteen seconds, and then fire another three rounds. You listen for me."

"Won't be easy in this noise, Color."

I'm thinking, what noise? There is no noise. The desert is completely silent. Then I realize at the back of Corporal Middleton's radio voice I can hear artillery booming. I end radio contact and I fire three rounds into the air. I count to fifteen and do the same again. I try to radio Middleton to get confirmation but all I get on the airwaves is angry static.

Hoping they can locate me from my gunfire I wait, my hot foot on the mine. In the heat and dust of the desert, in full combat gear, with the sweat trickling inside my helmet, my vest, and in my groin, I wait and I wait.

And no one comes.

I'm on alert and my automatic rifle is primed in case an Iraqi might turn up out of the dust and spot me standing there. I think about getting down on one knee to give my limbs a break; but I'm afraid that the slightest easing of pressure from the spring mechanism will detonate the mine. Eventually I have to do something and I do lower myself on one knee, but only by resting my gun arm across the thigh bearing over the mine and forcing my entire weight down on that leg.

I stay in this position for over two hours. The radio crackles with static but nothing else. At one point I lose my patience and bellow out loud. "Brewster! Where are you, you little shite-hawk? Brewster!"

Nothing. No one. Not even a sound. My leg is cramping up badly so I return to my standing position. By now I've run through every possibility for getting myself out of this. I have the fifty-pound weight of my pack, my equipment, and my weapon, but I can't risk manipulating it all onto the mine in the hope that it is heavy enough. I even try to make a calculation, but I have no way of knowing what force I'm currently bearing on the mine under my foot. I reckon that if and when the boys turn up they will have the gear to clamp the mine, or to weight it, or to get me out of my boot somehow without the thing triggering.

I take off my helmet. Even though my head is shaved it's caked in sweat and grit. Weird sensations are running up and down my leg. A horrible feeling of lightness is in my foot, as if it's threatening to float up quite against all my intentions for it to stay bearing down on that metal plate. Then a red admiral comes by. One of those beautiful ones you sometimes see in an English country garden. I didn't even know you got butterflies in the desert and I think, well, there ain't much green round here for you, is there? I'm glad to see it. It takes my mind off the situation for a few seconds as it flutters by. Then it turns back toward me and it settles on my wrist. Is this the last thing I'm going to see? I do believe it drinks the sweat from my wrist. It opens its wings and just stays there quite happy, drinking sweat from a man with his foot on a mine.

That's not bad, I think. If that's the last thing I'm going to see, a red admiral. I can think of a lot of things lower down my list. But these insects are strange. They look like they're looking back at you. Like they're holding this cloak open for you to see. Rubbish, I know, but I start to think about keeping the red admiral alive. "You don't wanna stay there too long, old pretty. You're in the wrong place. You don't wanna stay there."

I flex my hand, gently, but the red admiral doesn't move; it's still drinking my sweat. Then it beats its wings and flies away. I track it for several yards, to the vanishing point where the yellow dust closes in around it. But it seems to stay, fluttering in the air, the tiniest red dot; and then the red dot changes and the red dot I'm looking at isn't the tip of a butterfly's wing at all; it's the red dot of an Arab's *shemagh*, a traditional head scarf, and the Arab wearing it is making his way toward me.

I instantly sight my rifle on him. He doesn't miss a stride, but he does raise the palms of his hands toward me to show me he's unarmed. He certainly isn't dressed like a regular soldier. He wears a long flowing black dishdasha thing and he's barefoot. But I guess the Iraqis have auxiliary soldiers or a militia; whatever he is, I'm ready to drill him if he even looks at me wrong.

His red-and-white *shemagh* shrouds his face. He wears it over his head and high over his nose and mouth against the dust. All I can see are his eyes. Still showing me a clean pair of hands he draws up about five or six yards away, not looking the least bit worried by my rifle trained on him.

I say I can see his eyes—that is, his one eye, an eye of the most piercing blue I've ever seen. The other eye is stitched closed. The stitches are clumsy, angry black threads. His robe is dusty and his *shemagh* is smirched and dirty. He peers hard at me with that one blue eye. Then he looks around him.

The Arab seems confused. He puts a hand to his forehead, as if trying to remember something.

"On the floor!" I bark, gesturing at the sand with my rifle. "Get down."

He laughs. Just a little snigger, before peering hard at me again.

"Down! Now!"

He shakes his head quizzically. Then he lowers himself to the sand. He takes a squat position, clasping his hands in front of him. But I want him down on his ass and I bellow at him some more. "Down! Get down!"

"If you wish," he says, as if this is a game.

"Speak English? You speak English?"

He looks confused. Then he nods a yes, before looking round quickly to all points of the compass, as if expecting reinforcements or something.

"What's your unit?"

"Unit?"

"What's your company?"

He shakes his head, making out he doesn't understand.

"Are you a soldier of Iraq?"

He shakes his head.

"I'm holding you prisoner. You understand? Prisoner."

He seems taken aback. I mean he does that thing of jerking his head back in surprise at my words. He takes the *shemagh* from his mouth and he smiles at me.

"Prisoner," I say again.

Again he looks puzzled. There is an expression on his face that makes me think of men I have seen who were concussed. I wonder how long he's been wandering in this state. He certainly doesn't seem to know where he is or what is at stake here. Maybe he's retarded.

Finally he gestures at the mine beneath my boot. "You are in some difficulty."

His English is very good, though he speaks with a thick accent, like he has sand in his throat.

"You let me worry about that."

The Arab makes to stand up again.

"Get down!"

He sinks back down to the sand and spreads his arms wide. "I was trying to think how I might help you."

"Like I say, I'll worry about that. I've got people coming."

He laughs. Quite loud. "Who? Who is coming?"

I flick on my radio and make the call. Still nothing but static. I give him a cold stare. "Where are you from?"

Again he looks around him, all points compass. Though there is still nothing to see beyond the twenty-yard radius to the dust curtain. "I don't know."

"You don't know. Dark when you left, was it?"

"Pardon?"

"Never mind. Joke."

"Ah! Joking is good . . . in your predicament."

"Where did you learn to speak English?"

He rubs his chin. "I can't remember."

"Funny fucker, incha?"

"Inshallah."

I'm only asking questions to establish the upper hand, to show him that I'm in control. Given the situation I don't feel in control and he seems to know that. "Name. What's your name?"

He looks at the sky. "You couldn't pronounce it."

"Try me."

"It's many. And many don't like to repeat it."

He turns his one eye on me when he says this, and I don't know why but my skin flushes. I mean my skin ripples like the sand does when the wind moves it.

"Funny fucker," I say again.

We spend the next half hour staring at each other in silence. My wristwatch tells me I've been there with my foot on the mine for seven hours. Soon it will be nightfall.

The Arab makes no movement. But something about him has me scared. And I'm the one with the gun.

He breaks the silence. "Perhaps you should tell another joke."

"What?"

"To improve your situation. Perhaps one of your jokes."

"Perhaps I should put a bullet through your head. That would make me laugh."

"Then how could I help you? I'm thinking of how to help you, but this is all I have come up with so far. And you should not underestimate the power of levity. Your situation is grave. You must work against it."

"Excuse me, I don't know why, but I don't feel like telling any jokes right now."

"The war you are in the middle of is only part of a larger war, which is the war declared by levity on gravity. Indeed gravity is what placed your foot in this difficult situation. Levity is what will raise you out of it."

I twist my lip into a sneer. "Are you taking the piss, you fucking raghead?"

He blinks at me with his one eye. "I don't understand this expression."

"No? Well fuck off."

I try my radio again. I'm starting to suspect the batteries are failing. The static makes me want to toss it into the sand, but I keep my head, and I keep my gun trained on the mocking Arab. I'm thirsty. My throat is choked with dust, and I need a piss pretty bad. My cramping leg by now is in a desperate state. I can't feel my foot at all and I'm afraid that the slightest gust of air will lift my foot off the mine and release the spring underneath it. Worse, a kind of involuntary tremor has set into my calf muscle. My shirt and my combat trousers are saturated with my own sweat. For the first time I begin to wonder how long I can hold to this. At some point I know I'm going to lose concentration and remove my foot. I keep my full weight on the mine, tapping the sand with my free left foot, bouncing lightly, just to work some feeling into my leg.

It's no good. I have to manipulate my cock out of my combat pants and take a piss on the sand. All while keeping the weight of one foot on the mine and leveling my rifle at the Arab. He watches this operation with great interest. My piss foams and sizzles on the sand. Finally I manage to put my tackle away. I'm exhausted.

"It's difficult for you," he says. "Very difficult. I really think a joke would help."

I raise my rifle and aim it right between his eyes. I'm close to pulling the trigger. I want to. But it's against my principles, though he doesn't know that. He doesn't seem the slightest bit worried. He just keeps talking. "You know, God laughed this world into existence. He saw the night and he laughed. His very last snort of laughter was to create man. We were made from the snot in his nose, from his laughing too much. Do you know what the prophet said? *Keep your heart light at every moment, because when the heart is downcast the soul becomes blind.* Even now in your difficult situation, this is good advice.

"Levity is the only thing we have in the face of the absurdity of death. Laughter is the cure for grief. But you know all this because you are a soldier and you have seen death. You have also killed. I know this, you see."

He talks this way for an hour or more. I listen because it takes my mind off my situation. And after a while his voice becomes a kind of murmuring. I don't know how it happens, but without me seeing him get up he's on his feet and he's whispering these things in my ear. I must be tranced out because I don't see him get up—wouldn't allow him to get up. But there he is, an inch away, whispering, and I can feel his breath in my ear as he speaks. The sky has turned dark. Dusk is coming to the desert. I look at my watch. I've been standing on the mine for more than ten hours.

"I've decided I'm going to help you," he says. "If you will let me."

"Who are you?"

He steps back, shakes his head. "I don't know. I've been trying to remember. All I can tell you is this: there was a white flash in the desert, an explosion, and a terrible wind and there I was, wandering. And then I found you. I can give you a wish."

"Yeh, you're a fucking genie."

He claps his hands and jumps, laughing. The laughter takes him over for a moment. His black dishdasha flaps as he laughs and in a split second of dizziness I hallucinate him as a black bird hovering near me.

"There, a joke! A good one! It will help. If I am a djinn I can summon up a wind. But if I help you, you will never be rid of me. You understand that?"

"Get me out of here."

All at once the Arab is gone and in his place is the fluttering red admiral. The butterfly settles on the sand where the Arab has been, and within a second a black crow flies down from the sky and eats the red admiral, and I know it is the same crow that I hallucinated a moment ago. It eats the butterfly and it grows before my eyes, twelve feet, thirty feet in the air and I can smell the stink of its hot black feathers and its bird shit and I see its yellow claws scrabbling the sand near my foot on the mine; I want to shout, No! But already a screaming is coming across the sky.

"Incoming!" I shout to no one. It's a mortar or a rocket and it lands maybe thirty feet away and the blast lifts me up high into the air and blows me clean across the desert. I'm already flying backward when I hear the mine detonate safely, and then I'm dumped on the desert floor.

When I come round, I am in a field hospital with about two hundred beds. I've been unconscious for nearly three days and the fighting is done and dusted. The Iraqis have retreated and we've torched their entire fleeing army on the Road of Death. I've missed it all.

I get a visit from the brass and later that day Brewster comes by. "I'd heard you were awake."

"Brewster! Who brought me in?"

"They said you'd stepped on a mine. The whole unit was out looking for you. We lost radio contact. The unit had to press on but the major left three of us behind to try to find you. Hours it was. Then some friendly fire came in. After that we found you."

"Friendly fire?"

He smirks at me. "Yeh. It blew half your uniform off. We found you on your back giggling like a fucking drain, Color."

"I don't fucking giggle."

"You was giggling like a fucking loon. There wasn't a scratch on ya but your tongue was 'anging out and you were giving it the big tee-hee-hee."

"Fuck off, Brewster."

"I'm tellin' you, Color. And you had this rag on yer head."

He turns away and steps over to a cabinet at the end of the tent. Takes something out and brings it to the bed: a neatly folded, red-checked *shemagh*. I take it from his hand. "What happened to the Arab?"

"Arab?"

"The one who was wearing this. What happened to him?"

"No, *you* was wearin' this."

I sink back into my pillow. The last thing I can remember is the Arab whispering in my ear, and then the blast of the incoming. That's it. Lights out.

Brewster is looking at me strange. "What happened? Where d'you get to?"

"My fucking head is killin' me, Brewster."

"You want the medic, Color?"

"Nah, just a bit o' peace. All the boys sound?"

"All present and correct. All relieved you're OK."

"Good boys, good boys."

We clasp hands and Brewster leaves the medic tent. Leaves me holding the *shemagh*.

I didn't know it then but my army days were already numbered. It was true that the blast hadn't left a scratch on me—physically. But after what had happened I couldn't sleep properly and never have been able to since that day. I've taken all kinds of medications. Useless. And the lack of sleep led me to have headaches. I took even more medication for the headaches, and that brought on bad dreams—so bad that I didn't even want to sleep.

My job relied on me being as fit as a flea. I couldn't ask any boy to do what I couldn't do. I hid it from myself for a while, but I suppose inside I knew it was all over. About a year after the Gulf War, the colonel called me in one day and started to talk to me about career counseling and all the wonderful opportunities that can lie ahead of a man when he leaves the forces. There was counseling; there was retraining; there was a house-purchase scheme. This wasn't like the old days when you used to get dumped out of the army with nowhere to go, he said. I listened to it all in stony silence. When he'd had his say I stood up, saluted him, and marched out of his office.

I wasn't discharged or cashiered or anything like that. I retired with full honors and with an army pension. I got work, mostly in security. I was happy to take on night work since I couldn't sleep anyway. That lasted for about three years.

I don't know how many times the Arab visited me before I dropped to who he was. That was his way: he would take over someone, maybe for just a few hours, or maybe just for a minute or so. But he'd let me know. There would be something in what he said to me. Sometimes he would be quite open; sometimes he would give just a little hint or a word or two to remind me of our moments together in the desert. Sometimes he would play games, you know, fuck with my head. He liked to wink. That would be like a reminder of his one eye, the wink. The trouble was that you do get people who like to wink at you in the middle of a conversation, and I would think: Ah, he's here. But I might have got it wrong, and it was just someone winking. He knew that. He knew he was fucking with my head. I'd be in an interview for some shitty job as a night watchman for this or that corporation and the suit interviewing me would say I looked right or whatever. And then he would wink. I would have to look behind his eyes. But I'd have to make sure the suit couldn't see me staring. So I didn't like people winking at me.

It wasn't just winking. I'd go into a bar and there might be someone drinking alone there, you know, leaning against the bar, staring straight ahead, pint half-supped, fags and lighter lined up just so, and he'd say, "Ever seen a red admiral?"

"What?" I'd go. *"What?"*

And the fucker would look at me and then look away. And I'd know it was *him,* see. But I couldn't challenge the drinker at the bar, because it would be his way to leave immediately. Go from behind the eyes. In and out as fast as you like.

Sometimes he would stay long enough to have a conversation. But I could never be sure. The thing I could never work out: was the Arab riding these people, or was he riding me?

My headaches were getting worse, my sleep was a mess, I had pains in my liver. When I told my quack about the sleep disorders and the nightmares he arranged for me to see a shrink, but it didn't go well. The first thing I said to the shrink was, "Don't wink at me, I don't like being winked at."

"Why ever not?"

"It don't matter why not, just don't wink at me and we'll be all right."

"I assure you I'm not the winking kind of psychiatrist."

"Good. We'll get along fine. What are you writing down?"

"Notes. We make notes, it's one of the things we do."

"Listen, I'm not an uneducated squaddie, right? I'm a color sergeant. Was. So stop with the notes, because I know that if I tell you what's on my mind I know exactly what you'll say, so there's no point to all of that, right?"

"Oh? And what will I say?"

"Don't fuck me around. You know, I know, we all know."

"Seamus, how can I help you?"

"Just give me the medication. Just give it to me."

I wasn't going to tell him. It's a short road from telling what happened to getting sectioned and put away. I'm not stupid. I never told him, never told the army doctors nor the quacks on civvy street. There are some things you do not talk about.

My piss started to burn. Well, I hadn't had a girlfriend in a long time but I went down to the clap clinic anyway. Embarrassing thing was the doctor was a good-looking bird, sort of Arabic herself, I don't know. She shoved that metal cocktail umbrella down my pipe and I nearly hit the roof. She winced herself, closed one eye, and I thought: *Is it you?*

Nothing. Clean as a whistle. Just burning. I couldn't even have a J. Arthur Rank without my spunk burning. There was something wrong with me but they couldn't find out what it was.

I lost my job with the security firm. The lads called me Winky behind my back. I didn't mind that, but when one of them tried to take the piss out of me one day I broke his jaw. And his arm. I faced charges and I had to do time. I was helped by an army lawyer and my previous clean record helped but I still had to do a stretch in Winson Green.

The Arab used to come to me in prison too. He'd come as a guard, come as one of the other cons. There was another bloke in there from the Gulf, Otto. Ex-para, hard case, clever bloke. In the nick we ex-army boys used to stick together. No one would fuck about with us. Otto used to talk a lot about the Gulf. Why we were there. Opened my eyes it did. At first I wanted him to shut up, but he wouldn't let it go.

"It gets better."

This is how he used to talk. He'd always say "It gets better" when he was about to tell you something he thought you didn't know. We were in the exercise yard one day.

"It gets better. Wait till you hear this. So Saddam Hussein is the big Western ally, right? We've equipped him, sponsored him, trained him up, right?"

"Give it a rest, Otto."

"I've heard of Arabs," says Nobby, ex–tank battalion, biggest thief on the planet, inside for fraud, *"who could steal the bedsheets from under your sleeping body . . ."*

"Yeh, listen Nobby, 'cos it gets better. So you all know about the PR firm that sold the war to the American Senate? They make news videos to make it look like reporting. They sell it like it's a bar of chocolate. They even fake a story with a weeping fifteen-year-old girl who says she saw Iraqi soldiers dump hundreds of babies on the stone-cold floor to make off with the incubators."

"That's old stuff," I say. "We've heard all that."

"What they do," says Nobby, *"what they do is get a giant fevver, right, a fevver, and they tickle you while you're sleepin' . . ."*

"Yeh, but what you haven't heard is this: that girl, that fifteen-year-old girl is a member of the royal family! Her dad is only the Kuwaiti ambassador to the United fucking States!"

"They start on the right side of you wiv the fevver, and when you roll over they lift up the sheet on that side . . ."

"It gets better. The Senate was persuaded by just five votes, right?"

" . . . then they nip round the other side of the bed with the fevver and they start working on you from that side . . ."

"One senator's a Bible Belt Christian and they've got him stitched up with a beautiful Kuwaiti boy; another is having a long-term affair with a Kuwaiti princess, not the one who sobbed about the fake incubators, another one . . ."

" . . . so then you roll away from the sheet that side . . ."

"And a third senator admits he voted the wrong way because he had a terrible headache that day."

"*. . . and that's it, they fuck off, you wake up hours later with no sheet underneath you. Fucking brilliant it is . . .*"

"This is all true, I'm not making this up, no fuckin' need. One PR job, two fucks, and a headache. That's it. You see what I'm saying? Yanks go, Brits follow, *baaaaaa baaaaa* and we're out in the desert heavy breathing depleted uranium."

Otto didn't wink when he said this, but he pulled one eyelid down with his forefinger and looked at me with one blue eye, and I knew who it was talking to me. I didn't know how long he'd been there, inside Otto, but I knew it was him all right.

"You all right, Seamus?"

After that I slipped. I got paroled out, lived in some odd places. Hostels. Squats. Derelict buildings. Stone me, I even washed up at the Sally Army more than once. The Arab showed up in these places more than ever before. He told me it was easier in these places for him to get inside someone for a minute or two. I always knew when he was about to take over someone, maybe a fellow inmate at the hostel, maybe the Salvation Army hostel director, maybe some tattooed psycho sharing the squat. A fuzzy gray shadow would appear, like soot everywhere, there's no other way to describe it. Then their faces would go luminous for a passing moment, and the Arab would be there—maybe dropping me the wink, talking, always talking, like he was trying to teach me things. Even tried to teach me Arabic, he did.

I see Otto sometimes. He got a payout for his arthritis and sank the money into a toy shop. He says he wants to see happy faces. I go there sometimes and lean against the boxes of molded plastic soldiers on the shelves. He hands me a few quid to help me get by. But I wonder if he's dead too. Died in Desert Storm like I did, and this is limbo. It would add up. I don't know. A beer doesn't taste the same. A cigarette doesn't taste the same.

I was a soldier of the Queen. I am a soldier of the Queen. I have wept for myself in the dark.

As I look back over the last few years, I don't know how I've lived.

I can't remember most of it. It's a half life. Sometimes I wonder if I died that day in the desert. Took my foot off the mine and died, and this is me dragging on my way over. I've no markers, you see. No coordinates. I'm adrift.

Yes, sometimes I wonder if I am dead, and sometimes I wonder if I'm still in the desert with my foot on the mine. It could happen. I'm well trained. Maybe I've just been there for twenty-four hours and I'm still waiting for my boys to find me. Like I'm tranced out but I'm still covering that mine, muscles locked into position, holding down that spring. It could be. It really could be. I don't know.

I know this: you can't trust the Arab. Every time I see him now I think he's on the brink of telling me something even worse, that he's going to pull the loose flap of skin under his one good eye with his forefinger and say, *Seamus, there was no mine.*

But I won't take the bait. I know he's just out to get a rise from me. Because I know that Arab is a liar.

Only the Queen can straighten it out for me. If I could find a way to talk to her she would make it all make sense. I'm going down to Buckingham Palace. They can change the guards all they like. I'm going to chain myself to the railings and I'm going to ask the Queen to come down and have a little chat.

Kirsten Sundberg Lunstrum

The Nursery

AFTER THE accident it was decided that the boy would spend the winter working at the nursery, hauling bags of soil, doing the hard labor and handy work his mother assigned him. The nursery was hers—Beth's. Thirty acres of land just beyond town, on which she had installed a series of crude, glass greenhouses and some raised beds, several small stands of pines and birch trees still root bound in burlap sacks, and a pretty grove of Japanese maples that colored a flaming red in the fall. From the far side of the property the Cascades were visible on days when the fog disappeared, and from the road the fray of strip malls and housing developments that bordered the town of Woods Creek could be seen. The town had taken over the stand of trees it had been named for in the years since she'd built up the nursery, but the creek still ran at the edge of the property in the winter and the spring, a narrow, silty vein of the Snohomish River where she had taken the boy to play when he was young, his small clenched fists hovering over the water, above the darting bodies of salmon, smelt, and bullheads.

The boy's name was David, and he was seventeen now and short but stocky. On his first day at the nursery he wore a T-shirt, even though the weather was cold, and a pair of muddy, worn jeans, which he cuffed above his rubber boots. He woke up with the alarm, ate the egg Beth fried for him, and took a cup of coffee that she watched him taste and then douse with milk and three spoonfuls of sugar. This early in the morning, he had the look of a child still, his eyes swollen with sleep and his hair mussed.

"You all right with this?" Beth asked him. She got up and took his empty plate from him, stood at the sink washing their dishes and laying them out on a towel on the countertop before moving to the back door for her coat.

"I'm not missing much anyway," he said.

They walked together down the pathway David had made one summer. There was a fine icing of frost on the rocks, and where the path sloped, he lost his footing for a moment. She reached for his elbow as if to stop him from sliding, but he shrugged away from her hold.

There was frost on the plants she kept outdoors, and as Beth walked she stopped to finger the branch of a birch, touching the small buds where leaves would appear in a few months. "It'll warm up in another hour, and you can water them then," she said. "Just a little water on the roots." She toed the burlap ball in which the roots were packed. "Don't overdo it."

David seemed to be listening and nodded at her directions, followed her as she moved down the rows of saplings and listed the other chores he would have for the day: load topsoil into the back of the truck and make the three deliveries she had scheduled; relevel the small parking lot with the gravel that had been dropped off the day before.

She took him into the one-room building she used as a shop. There was a window on each wall, and a peaked A-frame roof David had helped nail down several summers before. Beth turned on the space heaters she kept there, tugged the chains on the three bulbs that lit the place, then collected a pair of leather work gloves for him, a shovel, one of the coiled green hoses he could use to do the watering.

She handed him the keys to the truck and the list of delivery addresses, and he nodded at each instruction, kept his eyes on his feet.

"Hey," she said, and she put her hand on his shoulder. "You remember to be polite when you drop off the soil." She smiled at him, squeezed the meat of his arm, and motioned for him to get started.

All day she watched him. As she worked in the shop building, figuring orders and organizing receipts, she glanced up and saw him through the window, his frame bent while he watered the line of dogwoods and poplars. Later, she moved into the greenhouses to tend the stock she kept there—rhododendrons and azaleas, blueberry bushes and spirea, as well as annuals and perennials and several varieties of fruit trees. She clipped dead leaves from camellias and trimmed a boxwood back into shape, watered the flats of white, pink, and red poinsettias she hadn't sold over the holidays. Through the glass, beyond the greenhouse, David loaded the topsoil and took off in the truck, and in an hour was back and began on the gravel. Beth could see the packed muscles of his shoulders beneath the fabric of his shirt, the ropes of tendons on his forearms and at his neck when he strained with the shovel at the pile of gravel. She wondered at his strength, at how quickly it seemed he leveled that gravel and the single-mindedness with which he attacked the task, his body moving in deliberate rhythm as he dug the shovel's blade into the pile and lifted it again in one easy arc. He had red hair, like his father, though he wouldn't have known that, and his father's eyes, too—close and blue and sometimes hard in a way that made Beth feel quiet around him, kept her from saying what she thought a mother might have at the end of the day: Good job today, Son. Nice work. Instead, David waited while she shut off the lights and the heaters in the shop, walked around the grounds locking up the greenhouses, and then they made their way together again toward the house for dinner, for a little television before going to bed.

.   .   .

At school, David had been an athlete. As a younger child, he played in the town's youth baseball league and then ran track for a season in high school before settling on wrestling. Beth hadn't been sure about this. She had seen wrestling only on television—the sort of dramatized play fighting that sometimes shows in taverns on a Friday night. She had enjoyed the game of it—grown men in superhero costumes and makeup throwing one another against the walls of human-size cages, beating each other with folding chairs while an audience cheered. It was funny enough, and she had nothing against wrestling of this sort because it was like a soap opera or a circus. Nothing but an act. She wrote David a check for the uniform and the team registration, and she went to his first match and sat in the bleachers with the other parents in the gym she remembered from her own high school years—the smells of floor wax and young bodies, the stale popcorn a girl sold for 50¢ a bag at the gymnasium door.

Two pairs of boys wrestled at a time on two mats laid out on the gym floor. David was in the second group, and when he got up from the bench, he looked for her on the bleachers. She lifted her fist in the sort of salute she had seen audience members use on TV. David, a freshman, was smaller then, not quite 120 pounds, and in his singlet he looked fragile—thin legs and scrawny arms, his rib cage pronounced under the tight-fitting fabric. The other boy was smaller still. David checked his headgear, took his stance in a squat, and waited facing the other boy for the call to start.

The boys put their heads together, locked bodies, and pressed against one another. Beth could see David's grimace when he turned for a moment, a look that surprised her, that at first seemed to be pain and then rage. From the bleachers, she could hear both boys breathing, grunting to keep their footing, and then David was down, the other boy on top of him, and the scorer hollered time.

Before the next match Beth went out into the corridor and bought a bag of popcorn, stood eating it, and looked out at the parking lot. Inside the gym, the next match had begun, and there was the sound of other parents calling out their boys' names, the voices of the boys yelling encouragement to their teammates.

She thought about the look on David's face and the press of the two boys' bodies against each other, the way their foreheads had met, their noses close as in a kiss, the way they had turned their heads into one another's necks in a violent crush. She didn't like the other boy's look, his expression when he pulled away, as if he were eyeing her son.

She waited outside the gym until the evening ended and David appeared with his athletic bag thrown over his shoulder, his jeans and sweatshirt on, and his hair still damp with sweat.

"I didn't win," he said. He was a boy again, his face puffy where it had hit the mat, his eyelids heavy and tired. "I was bigger. I should've won."

"It doesn't matter," she said. She reached out and put her arm around his shoulder, led him back to the car to take him home.

Beth liked having David around the nursery, close to her, just as he had been when he was small. They fell into a routine, and although whole days often passed without much conversation between them, she liked that she could raise her eyes from her own work and find him out in the nursery lot.

She left the house early most mornings, setting out an opened loaf of bread and a jar of peanut butter on the countertop, a short note of jobs for him to take care of at the nursery. She put on her coat, tucked her yellow work gloves into the pocket, walked the short distance from the back door of the house to the nursery grounds, and began what she thought of as her rounds. This was the best time of day—not quite dawn, when there was just the narrowest halo of blue above the mountains and the nursery was still dark, the leaves of the maples beaded in small gems of dew, and the buds in the greenhouses closed like the mouths of sleeping children. There was a certain scent in the greenhouses at this time of morning as well, not yet the heavy green odor of late afternoon, but the individual plant perfumes of the junipers and the laurels and the wintering roses, cut back to barbed skeletons but still smelling somehow of summer. Beth moved through the rows of trees first, tugging free any dead leaves, noting any changes in the stock, and then walked inside and began the day's watering. By midmorning David passed beyond the greenhouse glass. He looked up at her and nodded, tipped his chin in acknowledgment. She smiled and nodded back, and then returned to her watering, dragging the coil of garden hose behind her as she attended to her plants.

In the evenings, she closed the nursery at five, packed the day's receipts and profits into a money bag to count at home, and walked back to the house along the gravel pathways David had tidied during the day. She liked the way the evergreen boughs brushed against the legs of her jeans as she passed them; her jeans would smell like them later when she undressed, put on her nightgown, got into bed with her paperback. She liked that time of day as well—the hour or so before falling asleep.

David stayed awake in the front room, the television on, long after Beth had washed their two dinner plates, milk glasses, and forks, and had gone to bed. From her bedroom, even with the door closed, she could hear the muted voices of a sitcom and now and then his laughter or a grunt of approval. She didn't mind his staying up so late because of the comfort in hearing him in the other room. She remembered what she'd said to her son when he was a boy: *You're my man of the house.* Hearing him there, on the other side of the wall, Beth felt easy and safe, and she could read until her eyes drifted, could turn out her light and fall asleep without trouble.

In time David had become a better wrestler—the best on his team—and it seemed to Beth that he was obsessed with the sport, unhealthy about it, in love with it. She rarely saw him anymore. He spent the summer of his freshman year in the high school gym, lifting weights and running laps on the outdoor track so that when he did come home—too late for dinner and without apology—he came smelling of work, his track suit and shorts stained, she noticed when she did the wash, the armpits and crotch yellowed with sweat. She started doing his wash in its own load, keeping her things separate, leaving his clothes in a basket for him to fold rather than going through them herself in what seemed suddenly too intimate a chore.

In the fall, he wrestled for the team again, and Beth sat in the bleachers and watched. David always held back at the beginning of a match, waiting for the other boy to take him, to get him down, back to mat. But then a look crossed his face—perhaps only Beth saw it—and in the last seconds David took the upper hand. He wrapped his arms around his opponent's shoulders, twisted the other boy to the mat, pinned him. This was sneaky, some of the other boys' parents suggested, but reversals became David's best move, and the coach encouraged him to keep at this strategy, to keep winning.

The victories unsettled Beth—the cheering of David's teammates, the sour smell of boy sweat in the gym, the animal noises she recognized as her son's when he locked another boy to the ground, when he knew he had won. At first, she turned her eyes away when he wrestled, and eventually she completely stopped going to his matches. Beth had missed all the matches and the state championships that David won as a junior. She'd missed the practice during which the accident had happened.

"There's been an accident," the coach kept repeating when he called her. "It was an accident. You should come to the school."

Beth noticed news vans from Seattle parked in the school bus lane when she arrived. She recognized a reporter for the *Woods Creek Monitor* and saw several women and men in suits, microphones in their hands, standing as near the gymnasium as the police would let them. She had to push to make her way through the crowd, had to convince an officer to let her into the gym. Inside, the boys stood around in their practice uniforms. A group of parents sat on the bleachers in coats and hats. A radio tuned to a rock station played for a few more moments until someone shut it off.

The boy had been taken to the hospital, though it had been clear from the beginning that he was dead. His body was flaccid when they tried to wake him, his arms limp at his sides, his head lying at a funny angle on the mat, crooked, out of line with his neck. And there was no breath. The coach had got down on his hands and knees above the body. He had pressed on the boy's chest and breathed into the boy's mouth for fifteen minutes while they waited for the ambulance, but there was nothing there to resuscitate.

All of this Beth heard from the coach several days later. He drove over to the house, sat on her couch, and spoke to David as she made coffee in the kitchen and slid a few Oreos from a bag onto a plate. She hadn't been expecting him, but it was a relief to see the coach when she opened the front door—someone to break the tension in the house, someone to talk to David so that she could disappear for just a moment, relax enough to take her eyes from him, and sit at the kitchen table listening to the coffee percolate. Her son sulked and would not speak to her. He moved from room to room, getting up in the morning to lie on the couch, then returning to the bedroom to spend the afternoon in a deep sleep that worried her. She found herself looking in on him every few minutes as she had when he was small, standing over him as he slept, holding the palm of her hand close enough to his mouth to feel the wet condensation of his breath on her skin.

Once, he had awakened to her face close to his.

"Mom!" he yelled, startled and angry. He pulled the quilt up over his bare shoulders. "Get out of my room."

Beth felt as if the wind had been knocked from her. "You ought to get around today," she said. "You ought to get up and have a shower." Her voice came out sounding accusatory, bitter, and David looked away from her until she had left him and closed his bedroom door.

Now, she could hear the coach talking to David in the front room, explaining the situation, the school's decision that he should be suspended for a while at least—for his own sake—that he should take the free time to think about what had happened, to prepare for whatever the other boy's parents decided to do about a lawsuit.

She got up, put the cookies, coffee, and two mugs on a tray, carried it out to them, and smiled. "Coffee, Coach," she said, her voice bright. "You take coffee, right? David, I thought you might get yourself a pop."

"I'm fine," David said. "I'm leaving." He grabbed his coat from the rack, and let the door slam behind him without saying good-bye.

"I'm sorry," Beth said. She sat, poured coffee, and nudged the tray of Oreos toward the coach. "He knows better than to act that way."

"He's upset," the coach said. "He should be."

Through the window she could see David standing at the far edge of the lawn. He kept his hands in his pockets, and he didn't move but held his back to the house and seemed to look at nothing—at the line of spruce that made a boundary between the yard and the open field beyond it, at the sky. He kicked at the grass, and Beth saw chunks of sod fly.

"I heard what you told him," she said. "I can keep him at home as long as need be. I run a business." She nodded toward the back of the house and the nursery. "He can help me. He'll be better off here anyway."

The coach sat back against her couch, his knees open and his hands clasped in his lap. He took in and let out an audible breath, and then told her what had happened that day, before she arrived at the gym, before she came to collect David.

It was a practice match—boys from the same team wrestling each other to improve their holds, to work specifically on reversals. The coach put David in charge, then told the other boys to line up, let David wrestle each one in turn.

The boy who died kept fighting, though, lying on David, anchoring him. And when David finally moved the boy and got an arm around the boy's neck in a sort of clumsy chokehold, something happened to the boy, something within him collapsed. At first it was unclear what was wrong. The coach had been standing right there— he had been watching. He thought maybe David had just knocked the breath from the boy, winded him. But it was certain in a moment that the boy was dead. And now his parents were distraught.

The team blamed David; they might not be so easy on him if he were allowed back to school. The other boy had been popular. He had been in the homecoming court just a month back. He was liked. He did not have David's reputation for being distant and standoffish, a loner.

David should stay home for now, the coach told Beth, sitting farther forward and setting a hand on her knee in what she understood as a gesture of pity. They should get an attorney. They should wait.

Outside, David had walked through the spruce and into the field where she couldn't see him.

The coach replaced his mug on the tray and stood. "I like your idea," he said. "You could put him to work, just for a while, until this is all figured out." He smiled and reached out again as if he might touch her shoulder or take her hand, but Beth didn't stand.

"I think this is the best place for my son," she said. "I can look after him."

"Beth," the coach said, picking up his coat. "I'm not saying our Dave's a bad kid. I'm saying it was an accident. I'm sure of it." She walked him to the door, and held it open for him, thanked him for stopping by.

Most of the year, Beth could handle the nursery by herself, keeping the grounds during the day and taking the books home at night. In the springs and summers, though, when the weather cleared and people began to think about their gardens, she employed a boy or two part-time to deal with the new stock and the deliveries and to allow her more time with the customers, who tended to want help selecting their purchases—help from someone who knew which shrubs would thrive in shade or sun, which fruit trees needed companion plants for pollination, how to take care of particularly finicky roses. The boys were usually David's acquaintances—teenagers old and responsible enough to drive the delivery truck and guaranteed to return to school in August. This last season, though, Beth had hired Uri and had kept him on for the fall and now the winter, not because she needed the help but because he needed the job. She pitied him and his loneliness, and she couldn't see who would hire him if she let him go.

Uri was past middle age, she guessed, older than she was by a decade at least, which placed him around fifty. He was wiry and thin and smoked while he worked. At the close of his first day, Beth found the butts of his cigarettes littering the nursery grounds—half-smoked stubs crushed between the rows of forsythia plants in the greenhouse, the wet sawdust of tobacco spilling from the broken wrappers onto her dirt.

"No smoking," she told him the following morning. "I should have said it before."

"You worried about your plants? Because I don't think it's a problem out here." He'd been shoveling and spreading new topsoil near the shop and had dug the blade of the shovel into the earth when she approached him, kept the toe of his boot propped up on it, and leaned against the handle. "It's open air out here."

"There's just a rule," she said. "Sorry."

He nodded, seemed to smirk. "I'll just finish this last one, then, if that's okay." He turned away from her, and she could hear him humming beneath his breath as she left.

After that, he stood at the entrance to the nursery in the mornings, smoked one, then another, and then a third cigarette quickly, before his shift, dropping the butts along the road. He insisted on a break before lunch and one after, and when he drove deliveries, the truck came back smelling of his Winstons, the yellow odor of smoke as heavy in the upholstery as it was on his skin and in his clothes.

He kept his graying hair long and pulled back in a ponytail beneath his baseball cap, and he hobbled a little, because of arthritis of the knees, he said. He took medication for it, he'd told her once—tablets with codeine that he had to drive into Canada to get once a month—and now and then a little weed.

"You can't use that here," she said. "I can't have you coming to work that way either."

He looked at her for a moment—that smug look again, like the half smile of an untrustworthy boy. It was a look that made her embarrassed to have said anything, as if she were prudish, acting like a woman. "Gotcha," he said. "Good thing you let me know." He turned his back to her then, returned to watering the dogwoods.

Later, inside the greenhouse and watching Uri through the glass, Beth wondered how he got the marijuana and pictured him parked outside the high school in his little white pickup, waiting for some sixteen-year-old to open a backpack and pass him a Ziploc. She imagined his apartment downtown—a one-bedroom in the brick building across from the bakery and down the street from the post office. There would be an unmade bed, a thrift-store couch, a stained coffeemaker on the kitchen counter. She felt she could see all the wrong turns he had made, even if he could not.

When David began at the nursery, Uri didn't ask any questions. There had been articles in the paper, but he didn't mention them, simply nodded to David that first day as if he had been there all along. Later, the two of them took their lunch together, David sitting on the opened tailgate of the truck bed with his thermos of orange juice, his peanut butter sandwich and apple set out on his lap, and Uri on an upturned five-gallon bucket, smoking. Beth watched them through the window of the shop where she ate her own lunch—leftover lasagna warmed in the narrow microwave she'd bought for the place and a mug of fresh coffee. She had imagined David might come in and eat with her, that they would talk and joke in the easy way coworkers sometimes do, but she could see, now that Uri had befriended him, that David would take his lunch outside. Beyond the window, David laughed at something Uri had said, nodded in agreement. It was something crude, no doubt. Uri was teaching him to be rough about work, about women, about her, maybe, because she was the boss and the mother, the authority around the place.

Beth nudged the last of her lasagna around on its plastic plate, dumped it in the trash, and got back to work.

In the evening, fog settled over the valley and hung low above the nursery, obscuring the tops of the taller saplings, clouding the glass roof of the greenhouse, and tempering the last of the daylight. There were no lamps inside the greenhouses, and so Beth looped the hoses into neat bundles and locked up early, gathering her coat and closing the shop before starting toward the house. In the distance, she heard the chortle and start of Uri's truck.

Behind her on the path she heard David's footsteps. She stopped and waited for him to catch up so they could walk side by side. She reached out to touch his arm, but he shrugged away from her grasp.

He smelled of sweat and the air outdoors—gray and damp. Under his arm, he carried the cloth lunch sack he used to take to school, and he had to slow himself to walk in pace with her, his stride longer and more deliberate than hers.

"Good you're getting along with Uri," she said. And then, in a lighter tone: "Lesson one of the working world—making do with your coworkers."

"He's a good guy," David said. "You're hard on him."

"Well, I can see how it might seem that way to you," Beth said. "This is your first job. You don't know the experience of another boss yet, and you don't know Uri."

She listened to the sound of their feet on the gravel path, the crunch of the rocks rolling slightly and rubbing up against one another beneath the movement of their steps. Above them, the fog muzzled the dusk and drowned the bit of moon that might have already been visible in the eastern corner of the sky. The fog seemed to drift in wisps, to hang from the low, blue boughs of the spruce trees and the bare branches of the alders just beyond the house. Beth would turn on all the lights when they got inside, put on the TV as she cooked dinner. She liked the idea that from the outside the house would look bright and warm.

At the back stoop, she stopped and tugged off her muddy boots, then stood. "There are things I've been glad you never had to learn, not having a man around," she said. She stood a moment facing his figure in the dark, then turned and opened the back door, flipped on the porch light so David could take off his dirty shoes before coming inside.

David had his father's build and his easily flushed complexion, his manner of walking, of holding his mouth a certain way when he spoke and of speaking only rarely. These similarities struck her—the pure products of genetics, no different from the way a pea plant would grow to resemble its mother plant, leaves and flower and stalk all biological facts long before the seed had sprouted.

When she met David's father, Beth was young. She had left home after high school and moved into an apartment near the boatyard in Everett, worked as a waitress for a couple of years before entering junior college to take classes in anatomy and biology. She had liked science in high school—the way it made the world seem ordered—a series of knowns one could memorize and count on—but also startling and lovely. She remembered a heavy book the teacher had kept on the back lab counter. Inside were photographs taken by tiny cameras within the human body. The lungs opened on a double-page spread, pink and netted in a delicate bronchial lace. Hormones bloomed in pink, green, and blue like the crystals she had grown in Mason jars as a child. And the brain lay soft and gray on the book's last page, a knotted mass of earthworms.

As it turned out, Beth had no stomach for anatomy classes, so she took horticulture instead, found a part-time job at a wholesale nursery near the navy base, not far from her apartment, where she worked Saturdays, Sundays, and afternoons.

David's father appeared one day at the nursery, which was nothing more than a flat plot of land and a trailer that served as a shop. It was Beth's job to deal with customer orders, and when David's father came into the shop, it was Beth who took him out to the rows of birch trees and quaking aspens, to look over their stock and decide on his order.

He kept close to her side as they walked, and she could smell tractor oil on his skin, saw its black grime in the creases of his hands when he reached out to put his fingers to the plants, to touch them. He pinched a leaf from an alder and rubbed it hard between his thumb and forefinger, so that the green smudged and the leaf tore.

"We'd prefer you didn't," Beth said, and he smiled, nodded politely, dropped the ruined leaf, and moved on ahead of her toward the pines. He had a heavy step, and his shoes left pocked prints in the soft soil of the tree lot.

Later, after he had been back to pick up his order and Beth had helped him load it into his truck and agreed to meet him sometime, to have dinner maybe—after they had gone out to their dinner and driven back to her apartment and found their way to her bed—she held his hand up against the light of her bedside lamp and saw that the oil there was part of his skin, inked into his palms and the fine lines of his knuckles like a tattoo. He kept his nails short and had thick hands, and she thought of him crumpling the alder leaf, of the way it had rolled in on itself and had left a pretty stain between his fingers.

They were happy for a time, and then they weren't. There weren't fights, but there was often the threat of one—a silence between the two of them that made Beth think of the way a lake or a river expands when it freezes, and the way the earth underneath it must crack from the sudden cold, with the weight of the frozen water. She believed one day he might hit her. His anger was stiff and still, and she found herself waiting for a break in that stillness.

When she became pregnant, though, he left. She quit her job and moved back to Woods Creek, worked checking groceries at the Safeway, saved her money, and bought her land.

Now, looking at her son, at the force of him behind a shovel, the violence with which he swung the heavy plastic sacks of topsoil into the truck bed, and the stern set of his jaw when he spoke to her sometimes, Beth thought of his father and doubted that David was different. She hadn't seen the accident herself, but she could imagine David struggling on the wrestling mat beneath the other boy's body. She remembered the look on his face during that first match, his teeth bared and clenched, and it was not a great leap to imagine him hurting that boy—wanting to hurt that boy.

The thought settled in her, and she began to believe it was the truth. If she ever mentioned it to David, she would not talk about it as a weakness or a sin but would say that we cannot manage ourselves the way we can manage the faults out of plants, hybridizing a perfect rose or a hardy, tall poplar. She rehearsed this conversation in her mind and believed herself to be forgiving, because wasn't it also her burden? Wasn't she somewhat to blame, having picked a father for David in the careless way that she had? Having allowed David to wrestle in the first place? She might have told him no when he wanted to join the team—told him that it was unnatural and dangerous, boys on boys that way.

Some things are beyond our control, she would say, and she would mean it.

In February, the spring stock arrived at the nursery: three dozen buddleia already beginning to flower; several lilacs, quince, and deutzia; flats of snapdragons, chrysanthemums, and impatiens. Room needed to be cleared in the greenhouse near the shop for the annuals, and the shrubs would be stored outside, arranged at the front of the lot where customers could see their early blooms from the road.

Beth asked Uri to come in on a Saturday, and she and David met him and began the work of moving the unsold winter stock to the far greenhouse, repricing it, bringing in the new plants. The weather had warmed, the sky overcast but white, sharp, and glaring; as the morning went on, Beth took off her coat and sweatshirt and worked in short sleeves. Beyond the greenhouse, she could see that Uri was crossing the lot to the back of the property with a wheelbarrow of poinsettia plants wearing only his dirty jeans, his T-shirt wadded into the back pocket like a handkerchief. He had the sort of barrel chest she would have expected to see on a much older man. His ribs were distinct beneath his skin and working with his heavy breath. A cigarette hung from his mouth.

He had taken David out the night before; she didn't know where. After work, the two of them had stood talking near Uri's truck, Uri tapping a new packet of cigarettes on his palm, shaking one free. She watched him offer it to David, watched David decline, and she smiled to herself. But in a moment David looked up and hollered to her where she stood near the shop. "I'll be back," he said, and he turned away and got in Uri's truck.

Beth closed up the shop and locked the greenhouses, walked home by herself and made macaroni in a pot on the stove, sat eating it and drinking a glass of wine in front of a sitcom. Outside, the light had gone out of the sky, and the homes up the valley were lit—small and distant needle points of light visible through the trees. She got up and pulled on a sweater, stood outside on the front stoop and tried to listen for sounds from those other houses, but it was quiet. Beyond the edge of her land, there was the sound of cars on the highway near the strip mall—a sound that she might have mistaken for wind if the spruce had not been so still across the lawn. There was the sound of the creek if she listened hard enough, if she held her breath in her throat and listened past the noise of her own pulse. The cold water riding out the narrow course of the stream, eddying and swirling and wearing down the gray backs of the stones in the creek bottom, the muddy banks. The creek water slowly destroying its own bed.

Beth went inside and put the porch light on for David. She was still not asleep when she heard him unlocking the front door, and saying something to Uri from the stoop before his figure appeared in her bedroom doorway, looking in at her. She lay still, and didn't acknowledge him, didn't lift her head when he closed the door again, didn't ask him when she woke up in the morning where he and Uri had gone.

Today, David worked beside her in the greenhouse, raking out the dead and fallen leaves from the winter stock, tidying the gravel underfoot. Uri returned with the empty wheelbarrow, began sorting and settling the next load.

Beth dug her fingers into the soil surrounding an impatiens that needed repotting. She lifted the plant and shook dirt from its roots, sunk it into a new plastic container. "Late night for you two," she said without looking up. "You must be tired."

"No different than any other day," Uri said. "I don't sleep, at least not without help. Sleep aid, I guess you could say." Beth believed she saw him wink at David.

She dug her hand into the bag of soil she had lifted to the shelf beside the flower flats, brought up a fistful, and pressed it in around the roots of the impatiens. There was condensation on the roof of the greenhouse, water running in beads down the sides of the glass and dripping now and then on her scalp. "David sleeps, though," she said. "On a Saturday, it's all day sometimes. All day the rest of the week, too, if I'd let him. His father was the laziest man I ever met. But I won't allow that in David."

Beth finished with the plant, set it among the others, and heard David drop the rake behind her and leave. At the other end of the greenhouse, Uri laughed. He had the wheelbarrow nearly full. His belly was flat and hairless. Beth wanted to argue with him, tell him to shut up his laughter, but she returned to the plants, pinching withered leaves from their stalks, tugging browning petals from their heads, and lining up the plastic planters in neat order.

"If you think you have to know," Uri said, "I took the kid out to eat. He said he hadn't had a burger in months, and I felt bad for him, trapped here all the time and almost eighteen. I took him to eat, and we saw a movie downtown, and then I drove him right back here, where I knew you'd be waiting with your face pressed up against the glass. I've met women like you before," he said. "I know how you all end up." Uri set the last poinsettia into the wheelbarrow and pushed it forward and then back, turning around, leaving her in the nursery alone.

Beth brushed the dirt from her hands, wiped the back of her wrist against her warm forehead. She twisted the air from the opened bag of soil and knotted it, carried it back to the shop.

At home that evening, she made dinner and set the table. David had come in from the nursery after her and disappeared into his bedroom. When she called to him, he came out to the kitchen, sat down at his place across from her, and began eating without a word. She had made spaghetti—his favorite—and had driven down to the Safeway for garlic bread and soda, for a gallon of strawberry ice cream that she would tell him about later, once he'd cleaned his plate.

They ate without speaking, their chewing and swallowing too loud and the low voices of the radio David had left on in his bedroom audible from their quiet table.

"He took me to eat and to a movie," David said finally.

"I know." Beth nodded, and when David was finished she told him about the ice cream. He dished himself a bowl and started toward his room with it.

At the doorway he turned toward her. "What you said earlier— you're wrong. You're too hard on him. You've always been." He started to look away from her and then met her eyes. "And you should be nicer to Uri. He's alone, just like you are." David turned and left, and in a moment Beth heard David close his bedroom door, heard the sudden pitch of his music against the silence in the house.

She cleared the kitchen table and shook the crumbs from their place mats into the sink, washed the dishes and the pots, and went to bed. Her arms were tired after the day of lifting flats, her back sore. When she lay on the bed, her shoulder blades against the mattress, it felt as though she were trying to relax a metal rod, and she had to turn to her side and lie with her knees up against her chest and her back curled around herself like a child.

She pictured David and Uri at a table at the Denny's downtown, plates of burgers and fries in front of them, the cigarettes in the center of the table where they could be shared after the meal. Anyone watching would have believed Uri and David to be father and son, maybe. The waitress would believe she saw respect in the boy's eyes when he looked across the table; the people in the next booth would look for resemblance. Beth could understand why Uri would want to spend time with her boy.

In the low light of her bedroom, Beth read from her paperback until David's music quieted in the other room, then she turned out her light and slept.

It was only a week later that the coach called. David was out with Uri—bowling, Beth thought she'd heard them say as they left.

"It's late," the coach said. "I should have waited until morning to call, but I thought David would want the good news."

Beth was in her pajamas, her hair still wet from her bath and wrapped in a towel on top of her head. She tipped her chin now and let the towel fall and unravel itself, land in a heap on the floor at her feet. In the reflection on the front room window, she could see herself—bare ankles and drawn face, her hair wild until she reached up with her free hand to smooth it. "David's not here," she said.

On the other end of the line, the coach's voice was boisterous. "You can just pass the good news on when he gets home then. The Fosters have had a change of heart. Their boy can't be replaced by ruining David's life—that's what the mother said to me. Beth, if you can believe it, that's the end of the whole thing."

The coach went on about the discussions between the school and the other boy's parents, about the wrestling team, about what David had missed.

Beth sat down. She rested the phone in her lap for a moment, so that the coach's voice was dulled by the sounds of the house around her—the washing machine churning a load in the laundry room, the heater kicking on and off. When she picked up the phone again, she said, "So he should be back to school, I guess. Soon."

"Monday," the coach said. "You both can rest easy now and have a nice weekend." He wished her a good night, and she hung up, sat with her hands in her lap and her eyes fixed on the frail reflection of the room visible in the dark front window—the blank television screen, the couch, her own figure. She imagined Sunday night, David home instead of out, his sack lunch packed already and sitting on the top shelf of the refrigerator, and his knapsack slumped at the front door and full with books again. And then Monday morning. The walk to the nursery on her own.

In a moment there were headlights beaming through the window from the driveway, the sound of a car door shutting, and then David stomping his feet on the doormat outside before coming in.

"It's raining," he said. His hair was wet, and he held a plastic cup from the bowling alley in his hand, the straw bent where he had bitten it. He looked up at her and smiled. "Good for the trees, though, right? Less watering for me to do in the morning." He shrugged off his coat and left it draped over the back of the recliner, walked down the hallway to bed.

Beth went to the kitchen for a glass of wine, then moved back to the couch, and turned on the TV, and stayed awake staring at the news. When she counted forward, she figured only ten weeks left of school, including spring break and the week of senior activities the high school always held before graduation—a skip day when the kids drove into Everett to the water park or the arcade, a senior picnic, a day of graduation practice and gown fitting. So many wasted days, and David already far behind his class. Even if he returned on Monday, he would need summer school, a tutor. And wrestling season was over.

Beth turned off the television finally and got up, smoothed the sleeves of David's wet raincoat, and hung it in the closet where it would dry. She locked the door and turned out the lights. In the kitchen she put out pancake mix, two oranges, and a bottle of syrup. She set the table, folding paper towel squares into tidy triangles beside a plate for David and one for herself, lining up each fork and knife, settling the butter dish and the tub of peanut butter in the center of the table. As she did these things it occurred to her that she didn't need to make any decisions tonight. All she needed to do now was sleep and then get up in the morning and make her son this breakfast. She would get up early to cook for him, and they would eat together before walking down to the nursery. They would spend tomorrow working, just as they spent every day, and Beth could decide about the coach's call another time. This thought quieted her, and she finished setting the table, shut out the light, and went to bed easy.

The following week there was a string of sunny days—skies blue, enameled, and fragile enough, it seemed, to crack against the green tips of the highest evergreens. The nursery bulbs sent up shoots and then bloomed, camases, crocuses, and hyacinths blooming beside the purple-black heads of tulips, the spotted tongues of the lilies. Beth had ordered extra flats of petunias and bleeding hearts, pansies and primroses, and had decided to try herbs this season as well, and so received a shipment of chives and basil, lemongrass and mint plants. She potted a few of these in oversize ceramic planters and kept them in front of the shop, where all day the sticky scent of the mint, the sting of the chive drifted in to her as she worked, burned in her nose pleasantly.

She had altered the daily routine, scheduling herself in the shop for most of each day to keep up with the extra sunny-weather business and asking David to help her out in the greenhouses, to pick up the tasks she could no longer look after. David's touch had become sure with the plants in his months at the nursery. He recognized each species by sight now, and could name plants in conversation, stepping into the shop to tell his mother that the exochorda in the far greenhouse was withering, that he believed he had seen aphids on the American Beauties. He wore a pair of rubber-fingered gloves, had taken to buckling a carpenter's belt around his waist in which he kept a short-handled trowel, a spade, a pair of gardening sheers. His hands, Beth noticed at dinner one night, were callused and rough across the palms from lifting flats, and there was dirt etched into the fine creases of his skin.

Several times Beth had thought to tell him about the coach's call—had almost done it, but stopped herself. She had a sense of what she was saving him from: the other students and what they inevitably thought of him, the pressure of fitting nearly a whole year of missed study into just a few months, and what existed beyond graduation—the empty space of his life that David would fumble to fill. She wasn't certain who her son would become in the face of so much undefined time, what difficult choices he would make and what errors. She knew him better than anyone, she was sure of that. She was his mother. She'd been charged with keeping him intact—with keeping this family together, no matter the struggle. And so she did not tell David about the coach's call and did not think about the risk in her choice. She did not allow herself to worry.

On Saturday Beth and David took the truck out on deliveries. All the way up the hill beyond the nursery Beth watched the bright leaves of the roadside alders and birch and quaking aspens shattering sunlight in her rearview mirror. All the way back, sunburned now across her cheekbones from the day of delivering and planting, she kept her window rolled down. The late afternoon temperature was warm, and when they reached the nursery and climbed out of the truck, she noticed the pungent scent of the air—the smell of the grass and tangled blackberry bramble and leggy undergrowth in the trees beyond the property line overgrowing, smothering itself. The choked sound of the high-running springtime creek.

Uri stepped out from around the nearest greenhouse, a rake in his hands, and stood waiting for her. He tipped his head as David walked off toward the shop.

"What is it?" Beth said. She'd asked Uri for only a half a day's work while she and David made the deliveries. She'd had to pay him overtime to convince him to come in on a weekend. Now he stood before her with his dirty gloves still on his hands, his weight leaned against the slim rail of the rake handle, and that look on his face again—a look that embarrassed her, made her feel as if he'd seen her bare. "What is it?" she asked again, impatient.

"Your friend the coach stopped by," Uri said. "He was looking for David." Uri let the rake fall to the ground at his feet and slid off one glove, searched in his jeans pocket for a cigarette, a lighter.

"Don't do that here," Beth said. "I told you."

"Coach said David's missed his chance now. It's too late for him to finish out the year."

Beth looked away as Uri lit the cigarette and drew in a breath. "I appreciate that you're passing on the message," she said. "I'll have a word with David."

"Come on, Beth," Uri said. He dropped his cigarette but didn't put it out, and Beth watched the thin tongue of smoke lift from where it lay in the dirt. Uri stepped toward her—close enough that she could smell the smoke still on his breath, the unwashed smell of his long hair beneath his cap, the scent of the chives he'd touched earlier still strong on his hands. "You're strangling that kid," he said.

Beth stood still. In her ears, she could hear her own pulse and, beyond her, the sound of the creek. She had seen the creek flood before. The first spring she owned the property, the water had risen so quickly that the creek ripped down its own banks, the mud still too soft with snow melt, the earth too weakened and spongy to withstand the water's force.

She heard the sound of the creek moving—a small torrent to match the sound of her blood—and she reached up and struck Uri across the face with the wide plane of her opened palm.

Uri put his hand to his cheek. She had left a welt; she could see it. She had split the skin near his eye in a tiny fissure so that a skein of blood ran down toward his jaw line. When he took his hand away, there was blood on his fingers. He looked at her.

"I'm sorry," Beth said. She held the hand that had hit him close to her body, against her stomach, her fingers curled into her palm.

"You've wanted to do that from the start," Uri said. He looked at her over the cup of his hand at his cheek. "You can only control things so long." He crossed the lot then, and in a moment there was the sound of his truck starting up and driving off.

Within the week, Uri had come for his last paycheck, and David had packed his things into his old gym bag and left. Beth believed at first that he'd gone back to school, that the coach or one of his old friends was housing him, but then it occurred to her that he wouldn't go back now, that she'd closed that possibility for him, and that he was with Uri. She imagined the two of them in that one-room apartment in the brick building downtown. The two of them lying on the dirty couch all day in front of the television, smoking Uri's cigarettes and his marijuana, driving around in his little truck to kill the afternoon.

She started driving into town herself in the mornings, stopping at the bakery across the street from Uri's building, where she could get a cup of coffee and sit at the wide front window before the sun was completely up. The light over the valley was thin, gray brown, and as limpid as creek water, and then slowly, the sky burned blue in a polished glare. Uri's truck was often parked in front of his building, but no one ever appeared to drive it. She never saw David.

One morning, as she sat with her face toward the window, there was a hand at her shoulder, a tap. It startled her, and she spilled coffee on her wrist as she turned.

"Well, shit," the coach said, and handed her his napkin, moved to help her.

"Don't," she said. "I've got it."

He stepped back, sipped at his own coffee as she pushed the wet mess of paper napkins across the glass of the tabletop.

It was June. School was out for the summer, and the coach wore shorts, a T-shirt, and sandals. His hair was uncombed. He pulled out the chair across from her and sat, and when Beth told him that she didn't need company, he simply drank his coffee, looked at her with an expression of pity, sorry for her pride and for her parenting.

The sun had risen since she'd first sat down and was full in the window. It fell in a flat band of light across the window ledge, the table, and caught the glass lip of the bud vase where a slip of baby's breath and a pale carnation stood soaking in an inch of water.

"So he's gone," the coach said. "He came to see me a couple of weeks ago. He said he was leaving." The coach shook his head. "He didn't say where he was going."

Beth nodded. She hadn't heard that, but she had imagined that David would, in time, go.

"I wouldn't have predicted it, Beth," the coach said. "All those seasons working together, getting to know him and you—I never would have pegged Dave as the kind of kid to skip out. Go truant just when he had the green light to come back."

The coach reached across the table and laid his hand over Beth's. He looked worn and older than she remembered, his skin tanned but dusky and deeply creased, and she understood suddenly that his pity was for her loss—that his regret was David's behavior, not hers. He believed her the mother of a runaway. He believed David had betrayed her, had abandoned her without reason or good-bye.

Beyond the window, the sun slid behind a thin cloud, and the square of light on the table disappeared for a moment and then unfolded again across the glass. There were stone pots of begonias and alyssum in red and yellow on the sidewalk that she hadn't noticed before. A matching set across the street, in front of Uri's building, and another in sight down the block. She hadn't imagined this reversal of blame—that David would take it. That he would let go of her so completely.

She wanted to believe that she would see David again one day—bump into him on the street here in town, or maybe in Everett. He might have gone there for work—a bigger city, but not so big. She would recognize him, she was certain. She would see something familiar in his eyes, in the way he moved and held his mouth—something in his face that resembled her own. The wear of fear, maybe, or regret. The set of contrition. The nearly visible softening of mercy.

E. V. Slate

Purple Bamboo Park

AYI WAS small, a small and stout ayi. Her eyes were very close together and when she wore her spectacles she knew she looked like a pig (in spectacles), but that was all right, since she was born in the year of the boar and had always kept her nose down, looking for treasures in the mud. Sundays were her only day off. Usually she would rise at dawn and cycle over to Ritan Park to hug trees, swing her arms around and around, and jog backward down the ancient paths. Then she would stop by the street market on her way home to buy vegetables for the coming week. In the afternoon she would clean her own rooms and wash her broad white underpants at the communal faucet, where she loved to gossip with Old Yang, who lived next door to the sink, and peek in through the windows at Yang's grandson stretched across the width of three chairs, watching television. Often Yang invited her in for supper and Ayi would sit crowded in with the family around the fold-out table, slurping her noodles and watching the cross talk on television, laughing in such a funny way, with tiny bits of noodle sometimes flying out of her mouth, that everyone else laughed with her and she felt like a real granny. But lately, she often came up with excuses not to join them, and even if Yang insisted, pulling her by the sleeve, Ayi found that she couldn't even follow the rapid cross talk, such was her dread of going back to her empty rooms.

This Sunday, though, her employers the Zhangs have asked her to join them on an excursion all the way across the city, to Purple Bamboo Park. Ayi was so excited during the night that she kept jerking awake, wondering if it was time to get up. Finally, at four thirty, she heard a pot clanging next door: all the ladies her age across Beijing were beginning to stir, and so Ayi too sprang out of bed and set her hair in curlers. She cooked porridge in her biggest black pot and steamed a batch of egg and chive dumplings. There was only one dress to choose: the dark-blue silk hand-me-down from Husband's mother, and of course anklet nylons and the pair of pumps she had found at Lan Dao for only forty yuan. The pink ribbon that the salesgirl had used to tie up the shoe box Ayi now wound around the lid and pot. She wedged the tin of dumplings beside it in the basket on the carrier of her bicycle and she was ready to go. Pushing through the cluttered alleyway leading to the street, she finally had to stop and catch her breath. Sweat trickled out from her curls and dripped off her earlobes. She felt a little pool forming between her breasts.

It was only half past seven, but this was August in Beijing. Ayi was very good at guessing the time and the temperature, and she would have been able to tell that it was nearing thirty degrees centigrade, but that didn't take into account the humidity, or the muddy tint of smog that obscured the sun, or the lack of a breeze, of the winds that plagued Beijingers in the springtime, whipping their faces with grit from the Gobi Desert. Her neighbors shuffled past her on their way back from the communal toilet, some still in their cotton pajamas, the men in white tank tops pulled up over their pale bellies. *Where are you off to?* they asked. She told them that the Zhangs, who treated her like their own mother, had invited her out on a family excursion. *Oh, they want you to tend the baby!* the women answered. *You should make them pay you for working on your day off. Tending the baby is hardly work,* Ayi told them. *She minds me better than she does her own mother.*

Sunday mornings were the busiest time in the hutong street market. People came not just for the longans and peaches, for the crisp bok choy and fatty slabs of meat that hung from hooks in the stalls, but also for all the extra goods placed along the sidewalks by anyone who had something to sell. Here you could find anything from plastic buckets to oily bicycle parts to piles and piles of pink bras, all the same size. Not many people could push through the crowd, paw among the wares, come up with the last or best of its kind, and haggle for it as ferociously as Ayi could, but this morning she steered her bicycle through the crowd without even looking at the stacks of ripening fruit that, even today, delighted the heart of any Beijinger who could remember the mean times.

She rode past Ritan Park, past side streets lined with delicate shrugging willows, past the gates and fences of the handsome old embassies, guarded by boys in oversize uniforms and shaded by the lusty ginkgo trees that lined the street like sturdier, more befitting soldiers. When she reached Chang'an Boulevard, she put her foot on the curb and wiped her arms and neck with the handkerchief she kept wedged up in her sleeve. After the traffic guard finally turned his shoulders north and south, she crossed the street to the pink stucco high-rise apartment building where the Zhangs lived, next to Sci-Tech, the Japanese department store. Down the ramp she plummeted, her brakes squeaking, to the cool basement parking lot, where she turned the miniature key that locked the back wheel of her bicycle. But really, who would steal this rusty old Phoenix? The same one she had scrimped and saved for, to give to her daughter on her first day at university. Unfortunately, it hadn't been the one that Hua had wanted. She had kept it chained outside her dormitory, summer and winter, and returned it to her mother with a corroded chain, the leather seat cracked and stiff, the day before boarding the train for her new job in her father's work unit in Tianjin.

"Ayi, working on Sunday?" The parking lot guard raised his head from his desk and then slumped back down, resting his chin on his forearms.

"Not work, play!" She lifted the pot and the tin of dumplings and laughed when she saw the boy sit up expectantly. "All right, all right!" she said indulgently. "Don't they feed you at your work unit?"

"Never enough," the boy answered, pulling out a small metal plate and a pair of chopsticks from his desk drawer. "How I wish the other ayis were like you."

Ayi's heart bobbed slightly in her chest, like a little boat rocking back and forth in shallow water, as she doled out six dumplings for him: not enough to fill a boy's stomach, just a snack. "Husband upstairs can eat twenty dumplings in one sitting, but I made a few extra, just in case."

The boy bent his downy face over the steaming dumplings, though he did not lift his chopsticks until he had run ahead of Ayi, punched in the code, and opened the big metal door for her when it buzzed.

She rode up nineteen floors, feeling an upward tug on her intestines, as she did every morning except Sundays, usually. When she reached the Zhangs' door she pulled out the key that hung from the long red string tied around her neck, and then wondered if today she should ring the bell. No answer. Cold air seeped under the door and chilled her toes; just that easily a woman her age could get sick. She waited for her sweat to dry, picking at all the places where her dress clung to her body, and looked out the hallway window at the gray network of alleys and divided courtyards of the hutongs far below. Down there everyone knew your business: arguments, friendships, debts, and favors raced back and forth in the alleyways. Nothing was forgiven, nothing was new. Everything was recycled, from the cardboard patching the roofs to the memory of grudges handed down from one generation to the next—kept alive, always, on the watery nourishment of gossip. Here the neighbors pretended not to see each other. Only the other ayis spoke to her, and from them she learned of the strange eating habits of their mostly foreign employers. And the pay these ayis received, some of them a thousand yuan a month! They bragged to Ayi about how they cheated on the shopping, something the maid of a Chinese family would never be able to get away with. To all this Ayi could only think of one thing to say: just think, they can fire you at any moment! What do they care? Anyway, she told them, she had the best sort of job security: family affection.

"Ayi's come," she called as she unlocked the door. In the living room, the shades had been drawn against the sun; the Haier units on the wall whirled and creaked. Ayi hurried into the kitchen and closed the door behind her. This room was always hot. Even if she had wanted to open the door to the balcony, she would have faced the hot blast of exhaust from the air conditioner.

"Here so early?" Wife opened the door and leaned against the door frame in a silk nightgown the color of a ten-fen coin. Bought at Sci-Tech, no doubt, where Ayi and Old Yang had gone together on the day of its grand opening, along with everyone else in the neighborhood and much of East Beijing, to walk the aisles and marvel, clutching their hands or burying them in their pockets, as if to reassure the glaring salesgirls that no, they would not be touching anything. "It's so hot in here! Blah! What is all that?"

"Porridge and dumplings, Husband's favorite."

"Who's hungry on a day like this? Put all that away, right now, into the refrigerator. If Xiao-Geng eats that he'll want to do nothing but sleep on the couch, and you'll have come over for nothing. Anyway, Ayi, I want to ask you something. Come out here so I can close the door. Listen, have you been running the air con?"

"Only in the afternoon, when Baby fusses. She gets so irritable and rashy when she's hot, and then she won't take her nap."

"Then take her over to Sci-Tech or to the park! She'll fall asleep in the stroller. You run it so much we can't afford to use it on the weekends. Xiao-Geng gave me hell about it last night."

Ayi turned to go back into the kitchen. Now she would have to transfer all she had brought into the stackable plastic containers that Wife liked to use. She couldn't let her get the last word, however, so she asked, "If we have to go out every time Baby gets hot, how am I going to get any work done?"

Just then Baby came running into the room, naked but for the plastic American diapers she wore on the weekends. "Yi Yi," she said with a wide smile that showed her three teeth and most of her upper gums. She was not a pretty baby, no prettier even than the beggar children who ran after tourists at the silk market. The main problem was her mismatched eyes: one was narrow and lidless like her father's, the other wide and round, surprised, almost like a foreigner's. It gave Ayi the shivers sometimes when Baby looked at her.

"Come," Wife said to her daughter. "Let's show Ayi the pretty dress you're going to wear today!"

Draped over the rails of Baby's crib was a little gown a princess or a foreign child might wear, of pale yellow linen, with white skirts crowded underneath and pink flowers stitched along the hem and on the puffed sleeves.

"Is the color faded?" Ayi asked.

"Faded! What would you know! It cost two hundred yuan, from my older sister in Shanghai. Ayi, just think, you'd have to work for three weeks to be able to afford this little dress!" Wife never tired of marveling over how long Ayi would have to work to buy all the various things in the apartment.

Ayi sat in the back of the Santana with Baby, who kept trying to crawl over the front seats. Husband drove with one hand and fiddled with the air conditioning and the radio. He was grumpy, Ayi knew, because he hadn't had any breakfast. He hadn't even given her his customary grunt when he came out of the bedroom, buckling his belt. He worked for an American company, and in Ayi's opinion the Chinese people were their new slaves; she had once asked Husband if he at least got lunch vouchers and he had laughed bitterly. Now Ayi stared at the back of his tousled, greasy head and felt as if the warmth of her affection would fill the car and overcome the chilled air. She was excited by her car ride and had hoped that they might drive past Tiananmen Square and see all the kites, the crowds, and the golden roofs of the Forbidden City, but Husband had instead taken the ring road and was driving so fast that Ayi got dizzy whenever she tried to fasten her glance on anything outside the window. In all the years she had lived in Beijing she had never been as far west as she was going now. She wanted to mention it, to express her gratitude, in case she forgot to say a special word to him later, but she was so aware of his moods that she knew now was not a good time.

Baby crawled over Ayi's knees to try to boost herself over the front seat, and Ayi had to stop herself from slapping that padded bottom. When they were alone, Baby would be sure to get a few well-deserved slaps each day. She would cry and cry (she loved the sound of her own voice) and glare at Ayi from across the room. As soon as Wife came home, Baby seemed to know that she could now do all the things that Ayi had forbidden, and she did them with a malicious grin. When Hua was that age, Ayi had had to strap her to her back so she could still go out to the fields, in the midday sun, in the cold and rain, in all the miserable seasons of Qinghai province. The little girl could barely move, but she would sing and talk to herself in her babbling, bubbling language and sleep for long hours of the day, lulled by the heat pouring off her mother's back.

A bamboo fence surrounded the park, and as they pulled into the parking lot Ayi saw the tops of the trees inside, the spears of hanging leaves. These were the first bamboo trees that she had seen live and growing in the ground, and she felt a quick heightening of her senses, the length of one heartbeat; her breathing stopped. *Oh look!* she said to herself, and it was almost like being young again. Now she understood why people went away on vacation. When the Zhangs had gone to Hainan Island, that time, Ayi had helped them pack and repack and all along she kept asking herself, Why all the fuss? Better to stay at home and relax where you felt, well, at home. Now she knew better. But she didn't have more than a moment to admire the trees, or even, once they entered the park, to see how sickly and ill cared for they really were, because Baby began to scream as soon as she was strapped into her stroller, and as soon as she was set free, it was up to Ayi to hold her tugging, squirming hand, to scold her with a forced good humor when Baby tried to pick bits of things off the ground, and constantly to dust and slap and blow the gray dirt of Beijing off the pale yellow dress.

Husband tried to pay for their three-yuan entrance fees with a fifty-yuan bill that the women in the ticket booth couldn't change. They all began to speak at once and laugh and say he was just like a foreigner, until finally Husband zipped up his leather money pouch and said he would collect his change on the way out. *No, no, pay on your way out!* they insisted. But Husband waved their hands away, and Ayi smiled smugly when he got the last word.

Families strolled along the paths: grannies, mothers and fathers, maternal uncles, unmarried paternal aunts all crowded around the youngest member, holding the hand, pushing the tricycle, buckling the sandal. Little cousins were pushed up against trees, gates, even the walls of the WC, for photographs. *Smile or we'll hit you,* Ayi heard one father say, his nose pressed to the camera.

At the teahouse, Husband chose the big round table in the middle of the pavilion. Wife furled her sun umbrella and sank down on one of the metal chairs with a sigh that blew the strands of hair from her face. Her delicate hand waved like a moth in front of her sundress. Sweat beaded like dew on her shoulders. Already she was pouting. The pavilion looked out onto a perfectly round lake, and countless royal ladies must have sat where Wife sat now, tying her fine hair into a knot at the base of her head. Even Ayi had to admit that she was as pretty as any concubine, with her long supple neck resembling so much the smooth forearm of her husband, her small, rounded nose, the bulb of her bright red lips. At first, Ayi had been curious about her mistress and had often opened drawers while she dusted, had even peered into Wife's purse, which was often left in the strangest of places, like under her pillow. She reported back to Old Yang all that she found out: that Wife's family lived in the countryside, Shanxi province of all places. The letters she received from home were barely legible. She routinely kept three hundred yuan in her purse, ate a carton of Parmalat ice cream a week, and sometimes met a blond foreign man for lunch. Ayi had seen them coming out of the New Otani Hotel, had seen how Wife pretended not to see her and Baby.

Husband had bought an egg pancake from a hawker, and as soon as he sat down he began to eat with noisy gusto. Ayi chose a chair across from him and watched with contentment. She hardly noticed the green lake, the jutting hill topped with an ancient-looking pagoda, the swarming, sun-faded pedal boats in the shapes of cars and flying saucers and ducks. Still, she would have been the first to say that Purple Bamboo Park was pleasing. She only had a moment to enjoy it, though, for as soon as Baby saw all of them sitting down she began to scream, and then Ayi was up and following her from table to table, across the breadth of the pavilion, into every dirty cranny and very near the edge of the water, trying to slip crackers, then the straw from a tiny box of soy milk, then an assortment of dried meats that Wife brought out from her plastic bags, into Baby's mouth.

Young lovers sat at the other tables: students from the nearby universities and a few workers dressed in their best outfits. They drank the fancy tea that came on bamboo serving platters and laughed and chatted: getting to know each other—how nice for them! Ayi had felt forced into her own marriage as a means of getting back to Beijing. After eight years in the countryside, both of her parents had died and she had lost her city registration. She was the last of the young people from the polytechnic who had arrived at the commune in 1969, waving their flags and Little Red Books, and even the peasants seemed to have forgotten that she had once been a student. Eventually a young farmer fell in love with her accent and began to sing forbidden peasant songs outside the mud barracks until one day she let him in and tutored him in mathematics. She scraped numbers with a stick into the walls that had once been decorated with posters of Mao and Lei Feng, until they were covered with equations, and the farmer had passed the entrance exam to university after the third try, and they had had two children, and finally, minus one child, they moved back to Beijing.

"Ayi, come drink tea," Husband called to her. Baby was pushing one of the metal chairs across the pavilion floor. Ayi winced, not because of the screeching sound the chair made, but because Husband had called her Ayi, and now everyone who had given her and Baby such fond, indulgent looks would know that she was the maid and not the granny.

Husband and Wife were arguing. Finally he made a sweeping motion with his hand and Wife got up sulkily and came over and took Baby's hand. Ayi sat at the table with a tentative smile.

"Drink your tea," he said, refolding his newspaper and motioning for the waitress to bring over another canister of hot water.

Ayi took a sip from the tiny cup. Husband seemed intent on his paper, so she felt free to admire his handsome forehead, the flabby earlobes that meant long life, the light-blue collared jersey with the creases she had ironed into the sleeves. She wanted to please him, to say something about the lake, to lie about how fond she was of Baby, or even, if things went really well, to complain about the arthritis in her shoulders, which was exacerbated by carrying Baby, but she found all these words sticking like twigs in her throat. She had no idea it would be so awkward to be alone with him, and she couldn't help wondering if it might have been the same way with her own son if he had lived. No! Meager as the affection was between Ayi and her daughter, they always found something to say to each other. Words just came as if propelled up from their toes. And her son had been her favorite from the very beginning. When Ayi put her spectacles on his red puffy face, he had looked just like a suckling pig, in spectacles, and Ayi had laughed and kissed his hands and feet, put the array of pebbly toes in her mouth and tasted him. But then the winter after he was weaned, after his father had ridden off to the city on the commune's tractor to take his exam for the third time, Di Di fell ill, which wasn't unusual. But the more Ayi fed him, starving herself and Hua, and stealing wood from the neighbors to keep the kang bed warm day and night, the farther he sank into the quilts. She told him his father would bring him firecrackers. They would move to the capital and he would get a kite on his birthday, and she would bring him to a square larger than the village fields to fly it. But this seemed to frighten him. She was certain that he hated living in the countryside as much as she did: he shivered and went hungry in the winter, was listless and sallow in the summer, but he had never been anyplace else, and Ayi wasn't able to describe it all to him. Unlike his sister, who ran about with the peasant children, squatting down to defecate whenever the urge took her, Di Di liked to stay at home. By age two he could read more characters than his grandparents. He clung to his mother's leg when someone came to the door. And on the eighth night of his illness, without ever having a fever, when Ayi caught his sister helping herself to the cabbage soup she had made for him, she slapped the side of the girl's head with a loud *whack!* that felt so good, that made both of the children cry, and he had stopped his breath.

Baby ran along the edge of the pavilion, pointing at the pedal boats. Wife trailed behind with her arms folded. Husband looked up from his paper and, as he watched them, a dent formed between his eyebrows.

"What does she do all day?" he asked in a soft voice that Ayi knew she wasn't supposed to answer.

He put down his paper and lit a cigarette. "She wants me to fire you," he said, squinting as he exhaled a plume of smoke. "She said the houses of our neighbors seem cleaner, she said you use the toilet bowl as a bucket when you mop the floor, she said—well, women always find things to complain about, don't they?"

Ayi stared at the leaves in the bottom of her cup. Her ears began to buzz and her throat clamped shut.

"Don't fret. Just pick up a bucket from the market, pick up anything you need," he said, unzipping his money pouch. Then he paused and began rubbing, then picking his nose. "And, ah, well . . . I don't know about the facilities at your place, but we do have three bathrooms. If you want to shower there each day, feel free. We don't even use the one in the guest bedroom."

Ayi couldn't breathe. She averted her eyes while Husband fingered the bills in his pouch. The fact was, she had always admired that bathroom, which held her pride and joy, the Haier washing machine, and Baby's colorful swimming toys. She had often imagined herself showering under the hot blast in winter, cool in summer, and bicycling home all clean and breezy, with bouncing hair. A bath in the hutongs required two or three trips to the faucet, heating the water on the stove, and then sponging down in the kitchen, hoping that some naughty boy wasn't peeking through the chips in the painted windows. But none of that mattered now that Wife had complained about Ayi's smell.

"That's not why she wants me gone," Ayi heard herself saying. She waved away the bills he held out to her. Her voice sounded calm to her at first, though the words got louder as they rose up, and she felt a keen pressure bursting from the hot coil of her intestines. "She knows I saw her with another man, a foreigner, coming out of the New Otani, and she was afraid I would tell you!"

How good that felt! Ayi sat back with a satisfied huff that the Empress Dowager couldn't have matched after ordering an unruly concubine to be tossed down a well.

"A foreigner," Husband said with a strange smile that Ayi couldn't read. "Probably ran into one of our neighbors. We're the souvenir friends on the nineteenth floor. Proof that they're experiencing 'Chinese life.' "

"Then why did she pretend not to see Baby and me, turning her back on her own daughter?"

Husband put the bills back into his pouch. "Keep your voice down," he said.

"Xiao-Geng!" Wife came up to them, holding a screeching Baby under her armpits the same rough way a child holds a puppy.

"Ling-wei wants to go out in a pedal boat! Now. Leave Ayi here to watch our things."

"No," Husband said, grinding his cigarette into the tinfoil ashtray. "She's coming too."

The backseat was wet. The hard plastic of the front seats pressed against Ayi's knees. The sun bore down on the orange roof of the boat, staining the tears on Baby's face. She had the hiccups. She refused to let Ayi hold her. She wanted to stand, she wanted to sit, she wanted to hoist herself up and poke the back of her father's head. She tried to crawl up to the front, but there was no room for her there, and Husband told her sharply to sit down and be a good girl, and she began to wail again. Ayi willed the day to be over. Husband and Wife grimly pedaled the boat. They passed cars and swans loaded down with family members of all ages, chewing snacks, laughing, and tossing Popsicle wrappers into the water.

Ayi thought she must be the only ayi on the lake. She would never have a grandchild of her own. Even if one day Hua found a boyfriend, a husband, and got pregnant, though for some reason Ayi couldn't quite imagine any of these things happening, Hua would poison the child against her with stories of the time Granny had done this or done that.

Husband and Wife were talking, but Ayi couldn't hear the words over Baby's operatic wails. For once, she wasn't curious about what was being said. Wife would be sent back to the countryside, where she belonged. Ayi would take care of Baby, and with Wife's shopping days over, Husband wouldn't have to work so hard; he would come home early and Ayi would shuffle out in her flip-flops to greet him. Ayi wiped away Baby's tears with her thumbs and pointed at all the other boats—*Look at that one, Baby, a duck! Say duck!*—so that Husband could see how well she would be cared for once Wife was gone.

Baby stopped crying and began eating the crackers that Ayi took from the plastic bags that made such crinkling, crackling sounds that Ayi still couldn't catch the words that were dashing now, back and forth, in the front seat. *Have more?* Baby asked after each cracker. It became a game. Baby could eat a frightening number of crackers when she got down to it, and she found Ayi's shocked expressions funny. *Have more?* Baby asked, laughing with her mouth full of soggy swill. *Ayi . . .* Wife said. *No, Ayi said . . .* Husband retorted. Ayi felt very important.

Then Wife turned with a violent twist of her shoulders and cried, "Ayi!"

Whack! The flat of a wooden spoon breaking on her little bottom; running into walls, into table legs before she got her first pair of spectacles; the boards and sticks she and her classmates had used to beat their teachers; the whip of a branch on her cheek, running in the park, panting in the drainage ditch while her best friend struggled under the grinding legs of a Red Guard; the hot flash in her own palm all those times she had laid into Hua; the thump of her head against the bedpost every New Year's Eve when her husband visited from Tianjin; and now the thin whip of Wife's jeweled hand striking her cheek so sharply, so unexpectedly, that Ayi crumpled with her hands over her head, and Baby, who was standing with one foot on the backseat and one on the side of the boat, caught the carom of the slap and tumbled out of the boat bottom first.

Babies would seem to be buoyant little creatures. Their fat bottoms, their pudgy arms and legs—all like built-in floats—though their heads are heavy, even heavy to hold. Ayi had held the head of her son pressed against her neck, his thin body wrapped in quilts, and ran, slipping on the ice, to the village chief, then to the midwife. They all tried to take him from her: *Dead already!* She heard the words as if they were speaking in cross-talk puns: she thought they were saying he was four, *Four already!* when he wasn't four, he was small for two, very small and sickly because his mother couldn't find a way to get back to Beijing, where there was meat and the markets were full of fruit.

Since her husband had taken the tractor into the city, the village chief and midwife had had to come after her with a mule and flatbed wagon, and she was halfway to the next village by the time they caught up with her. She let them take Di Di away and steer her back toward home, with the mule following, with the midwife saying, *Elder sister is hungry, elder sister is hungry,* as if that would bring her to her senses! No, she went with them, had waited for them, because she felt the way his head bobbed against her shoulder as she ran; it didn't feel like him. By the time they caught up with her, she couldn't let go of him soon enough.

Why don't babies float? Why don't they kick and paddle and hold their heads up with the muscles in their meager necks and try to save themselves? Baby was also weighed down by her diaper, by the heavy linen skirt of the yellow dress, but help was coming. Blue cars and red saucers and decapitated yellow swans all swarming toward them, toward Baby, guided by the beacon of Wife's scream: one long exhalation of breath that seemed to last forever. It came from her heels, from the bottom of the lake, from the white, unpolluted fire in the core of the earth. Husband clambered over the front of the boat, tipping it deeply right and left, and then splashed in himself, headfirst. Ayi held Wife's shoulders and pressed down to keep her in her seat.

The story went like this: Mao swam across the Yangtze in June of 1966, at the age of seventy-three. *"I have just drunk the waters of Changsha / And come to eat the fish of Wuchang . . . Today I am at my ease."* Imagine how that feat captivated a nation of nonswimmers! Little did they know that this would be the preamble to the darkest chapter in anyone's life at that time. *"The mountain goddess if she were still here / Would marvel at a world so changed."* But that book was closed. Anyway, Ayi couldn't swim. She assumed that if she ever landed in the water she would sink to the bottom, hold her breath, and walk out. Husband was the grandson of a revolutionary, the son of an army officer, but he sat in a cushioned office chair all day long and liked to eat at Kentucky Fried Chicken for lunch. He also had his shoes on, of course. Ayi watched the gray soles disappear in the water. Other men splashed in, but they could swim, more or less. Some even had the presence of mind to kick off their shoes, to pull off their shirts. They reached Baby easily and lifted her into a flying saucer boat steered by a foreign couple. Wife dangled half in, half out of their boat, reaching out for Baby, but it wasn't clear now which boat held her. Ayi climbed into the front seat and pedaled over to the spot where Husband had disappeared, pointing here, no there, for the men to dive. They went down and then came back up too quickly, whipping the slick hair from their eyes. Ayi leaned over the side of the boat, pressing her face toward the murky water, but she could only see her own reflection—a drowning pig in spectacles—and she clawed and clawed the water until the image disappeared.

John Burnside

The Bell Ringer

HALF A mile beyond the sign for Lathockar mill, Eva Lowe turned off the main coastal road and took the back way through Kinaldy woods. It wasn't the most direct route into the village, but her father had always liked that stretch of road, maybe because it reminded him of Slovakia, and they'd often come this way on their Sunday walks, when her mother was still alive. It was dark, out on the narrow lane that ran past the sawmills, dark and very green, the boundary wall a dim colony of moss and ferns, the shadows under the trees damp and still. To most people, it seemed gloomy, but for Eva it was as close to the landscape of home as she could imagine—especially now, with new snow settling on the pines and on the ridges of the drystone wall, so that the land resembled nothing so much as a children's-book illustration, the snow steady and insistent in a kingdom that had succumbed to the bad fairy's spell and slept for a hundred years in a viridian web of gossamer and thorns. Her father had always loved that story, and she still had the book he had read to her from, the one he'd bought because it reminded him of home. Those pictures were her one real memento of him, page after page of watercolors from a world that, even before she opened the book for the first time, was gone forever, leaf green and sky blue and damson, wiped out by a tide of cattle trucks and unmarked graves.

Her father had been a long time dying, and Matt had lost patience with it all. He would never say what he was thinking, but it was clear that he resented the time she spent at the hospital, and Eva had started looking forward to the days or weeks when her husband was away, inspecting a rig in the North Sea or designing some mysterious installation in Egypt or Nigeria. During the last month of her father's life, Matt had been away more often than not, and that had been fine with Eva. It had given her a space to come to terms with things, a silence in which to remember her father's voice, singing to her in the language of his childhood or reciting those old folk stories that he loved. Later, when it was all over, she had found herself alone in the old farmhouse, with nowhere to go and nothing to do, and nobody to talk to but Matt's sister, Martha, who had started coming to the house on Saturday mornings with cakes and baskets of apples. She never came when Matt was there, but when he was away she would invite herself over. It had become a routine: every Saturday, at around ten thirty, Martha would arrive and they would sit by the Aga and have long conversations. Sometimes *too* long. It was Martha's fault, in fact, that Eva was late now, though she didn't mind that so much: her sister-in-law had been a good friend in those first days, when her grief was still raw. That was how Martha talked about such things, her language straight out of self-help books and women's magazines, but it had worked, and Eva had looked forward to sitting for hours over a plate of biscuits, telling each other the stories people tell when they are trying to remember what it was they were doing before their lives were so rudely interrupted.

Looking back, though, Eva could see that the real interruption had not been her father's death. She had always known he would die, and she had tried to prepare herself for the loss. Of course, as Martha said, you can never be truly prepared for the death of a loved one, especially when it happens so slowly and painfully. Still, the fact was that in the aftermath of the funeral, when it had seemed as if the whole world had fallen silent, what had troubled Eva most was her marriage, not her father's absence. Matt had come back for a few days to assist with the arrangements, and she couldn't help noticing his relief that this phase of their existence was over, just as he seemed relieved to be going back to work once the business of the interment was over. Until then, she had thought it was her husband she was missing when she sat up at night staring out at the orchard and the fields beyond, fields that had once belonged to Matt's people and were now rented out to neighbors. Sometimes, she remembered him as he had been when they first met: his charm, his quiet sense of humor, the little games he had played to amuse her. He would bring her flowers, or fruit from the orchard, and when it became clear that they were serious about each other he had created a long-running joke about their having identical tattoos: hearts, roses, Celtic knots, tiny bluebirds tucked away in the secret angles of their bodies, where only they could see. That romantic phase hadn't lasted past the first year of marriage, but she still remembered it. When he'd started traveling, she had replayed it dutifully in her mind, because, she told herself, surely they had loved each other back then, and if they had loved each other once they could love each other again. Yet all the while she was aware of how deliberate that remembering was, and she knew, when she was alone, that it wasn't really Matt she was missing.

The truth was that she didn't mind being on her own; it was just that she didn't like being alone in that house. If they had lived somewhere else, if Matt had sold up and bought a property in the village—a notion he'd considered for a long time before abandoning the idea—she would have been fine. She could have got by, even when he was away for months, living his separate life, not bothering to phone for days on end and, when he did, making it clear that he had other things to think about, that this was some duty he felt he had to perform. Whenever she put down the phone, she would picture him in some bright room—a conference center, perhaps, or a restaurant—discussing weighty business with colleagues, talking about engineering or politics just loud enough so the waitress would hear. Maybe he would flirt a little, and maybe he would do more. She could see him telling his little jokes, she could see how charming he would seem to the girl, who would be young and bright and eager to please. At such times, the house would close in around her, dark, damp, utterly still, and yet busy with the echoes and memories of those who had gone before, generation upon generation of Lowes, all dark-eyed and stocky and taciturn, watching her from the shadows, listening when she spoke on the phone: listening, watching, judging. Sometimes she even imagined she saw them, though it was never final, never anything as conclusive as a haunting, just phantoms from the stories Matt had told her when they were courting: Old John Lowe with his hurricane lamp coming in from the orchard; the twins, Maybeth and Cathy, sitting on the cold flagstones in the scullery amid a litter of kittens; the stricken, defiantly cheerful Eleanor, lying in what was now the guest room, dying slowly in her midteens. Whenever Eva was alone in the house, they would make themselves known, not quite present but there all the same, and it always seemed to her that they were waiting for something. After a while, she'd find herself talking, not so much to herself as to them, pretending she was somebody else, trying to win them over, and she knew she had to get out.

She hadn't known what to do at first; then, one afternoon when she had finished the shopping, she had stayed on in the village, wandering about like a tourist, taking it all in. The church, the two pubs, the school. The large well-kept green, with its row of chestnut trees on the south side. This was her home, but she had never really felt like a local. Her father had come to the place as a young man; she had gone to the school, and her mother had stood in the queue at the butcher's with all the other women, picking out cuts of meat at one counter, then going over to the kiosk at the back to pay. In those days, the people who prepared the meat didn't handle money, and she had liked that, the way they kept it all separate. The butcher had been a good man, friendly to her mother, always offering a kind word and picking out the best cuts for her, but his wife had been mean and silent as she took the money, and sometimes she had kept it a little longer in her hand, staring at it, as if she thought it might be some kind of foreign currency. That was how they were, back then. They hadn't liked having a stranger in their midst, and they liked it even less when one of their own took it into her head to marry him. Those people were gone now, and the man who served the chops and sausages took her credit card without a second glance.

At four o'clock, the church clock chimed, and she was about to go back to the car when she thought of the community center. There was a café there, and she remembered that they had activities: flower arranging and Italian classes, Toc H, the Women's Institute. She didn't see herself as the WI type, and she wasn't even sure what Toc H was, but she walked to the center anyway, and scrutinized the notice boards in the foyer, the timetables for events and classes neatly pinned out in rows among notices for Brownies and photographs of children in karate whites. She considered yoga, because she thought it would be relaxing, but she quickly dismissed the image of herself in a leotard. On Wednesday nights they had a beginners' class in French, which she'd studied in school but completely forgotten, and she had more or less decided that this was the class for her when she saw a small white postcard, set apart from the rest, announcing that the bell-ringing club was looking for new members. Everyone welcome, it said; no experience needed.

If someone had asked Eva Lowe to imagine a typical bell ringer, she would have pictured some churchy spinster in a hand-knitted cardigan and brogues, or maybe a man in a tweed hat and one of those army-navy-store sweaters that all the keen hikers wore when they climbed the Ben, but, reading that notice, she had a sudden notion of herself in a bell tower, standing in a circle of like-minded souls, the kindly faces touched with a warm, coppery lamplight, the bells ringing out over the stillness of the churchyard as the people of the village settled to their dinners or rose from their beds and made ready for Sunday service. She wasn't a religious person, as such, but she had always liked the church for its own sake, especially when it was lit with candles on Christmas Eve or brimming with sheaves of barley and ripe fruit at harvest time. As a child, she had sometimes walked around the graveyard during lunch break, when the other kids were playing, and she had made a point of reading all the names on the stones. Her father had told her off for that: God was a lie, he said, and Heaven was a myth. Yet Eva thought the place had less to do with God and his angels than with an ordinary, and understandable, desire to have things continue as they had always done. Easter, Harvest, Christmas: it all went round, forever and ever, and nothing could change that. It was a pagan desire, she thought, and it was a pagan place: a dark garden of yews and straggling roses and, at its center, the stone church, with its altar and its font and, above it all, the bells, suspended in the chill air of the belfry, heavy and still, waiting to be brought to life. It surprised her, all these thoughts running through her head as she stood there, reading the postcard. She took out her shopping list and jotted down the relevant contact details.

It turned out that the organizer was someone she had known in school, and though the woman seemed not to remember Eva, she had been very kind, and the other bell ringers gentle and considerate, always ready to help her out, never noticing when she got things wrong. Matt had laughed when she told him. He'd come home three weeks after she started, and after listening to her talk about it for a couple of minutes he'd just shaken his head.

"Well, I'm glad you've found something you like," he said. "To be honest, I think you're crackers, but if it keeps you happy." He'd noticed that she was annoyed then, and stopped talking, but he hadn't tried to undo the damage. He wasn't that interested. Whenever he was home, he would spend hours on the phone or go out to the pub with his old crowd; then he would be off again. Eva hadn't expected him to understand, but she was still hurt that he could be so dismissive. Hurt, and then, when she talked to Martha about it, angry, because Martha had been angry and that had made Eva's anger seem more justified. Martha had been supportive, not just under-standing that Eva needed a hobby but getting it—getting, without having to be told, the whole thing about the lighted church and the belfry and that magical resonance of the bells ringing out over the fields and the village green. But, then, that was how Martha had been from the first. She had understood how Eva felt about the house and, even though she was just as proud of her family history as Matt was, she could see how all that Lowe mythology might make an outsider feel uncomfortable. Eva had been impressed by that, and later, as they had got to know each other, she had been gladdened by the idea that someone she knew, a friend, almost a sister, was on her side.

So it had come as a shock, that morning, when Martha more or less announced that she was having an affair. She hadn't intended the revelation to be shocking, of course; she'd even tried to make light of it as they sat in the kitchen over a glass of wine. Eva didn't normally drink in the daytime, but, maybe because it was so close to Christ-mas, she had fetched a bottle of white wine out of the fridge, instead of doling out the usual coffee and biscuits, and Martha had opened up after her second glass, talking about how unhappy she was with James, and how tired she was of being taken for granted.

"I'll pretend to other people," she had said. "But I won't go on pretending to myself." She wasn't terribly upset; she wasn't even that emotional. Most of the time, when people talked about their prob-lems, Eva thought, they were working things out as they went along, looking for the reaction that would justify whatever decision they were hoping to reach—but Martha wasn't like that. She had thought it all through beforehand, and was now simply confirming what she had decided. "A person can die from lack of . . ." She considered a moment.

Eva was worried, afraid she was about to hear something embar-rassing, but she didn't say anything. She didn't want to interrupt.

"Contact," Martha said at last, with grim satisfaction. She gave Eva a curious look, as if she wanted to ask her something, then she let it go. "I'm not talking about sex here," she said. "Or not *just* sex. I'm talking about *contact*. A hug, a touch—that's all." She thought for a moment, and gave a soft laugh. "All right," she said. "I am talking about sex."

Eva laughed, though she wasn't amused. "But what about James?" she said.

Martha waved her hand. "To hell with James," she said. When she was annoyed, she looked older, and not so attractive—something she obviously knew, because she bowed her head. Then, after a moment of quiet, she spoke, her head still bowed. "It's not as if it's going any-where," she said. She looked up, and her face was calm again, com-posed. "It's just one of those things. I didn't plan on it. It just happened."

Eva didn't know what to say. She remembered Martha telling her once that James was constitutionally mean, and she wondered whether he suspected anything. He was a big man, with large hands and a cruel mouth, a man used to getting his own way, at any price—a man like Matt, in fact. Casual and charming, but careless of others, steeped in quiet judgment and long-term calculation, his life a fixed agenda that, no matter what happened, would continue on its set course, to whatever end he had decided he deserved. If James found out about the affair, he wouldn't go out with a kitchen knife looking for Martha and her lover; he would find much finer ways—legal ways—to make their lives miserable.

Martha smiled, but she was far away, lost in her own thoughts. "It's not as if it's going to change anything," she said, more to herself than to anyone else. It was a minute or so before she looked back at Eva. "You only live once, right?" she said.

Eva shook her head and stood up. Suddenly, she had to do some-thing. She knew Martha would take it badly, but she needed to be out of the house, away from the ancestors in the walls, listening in on Martha's confession, away from the thought of Matt and of what he would think if he knew what his sister was up to. Worse, what he would do if he discovered that Eva had known about it from the start. She picked up her glass and carried it over to the sink. "My

God, look at the time," she said, aware of how awkward this diversion was, of how inconsiderate she was being. She turned and gave Martha a quick glance. She felt guilty, but she was annoyed, too, because she didn't want to be in on this secret—or maybe it was because she didn't want to have to think about all this, about contact and affairs and things that just happen.

Martha looked more surprised than upset. "Is there somewhere you have to be?" she asked.

"I'm sorry," Eva said. "I just . . . I'm going to be late for bell ringing." She looked away quickly, blinking back tears that she hadn't expected—and the fact that she was about to cry was somehow the worst of it all, a self-imposed humiliation.

Martha's expression didn't change; if anything, she appeared to be more concerned for Eva than with her own problems. "I'm sorry," she said. "I shouldn't have told you about it. It's not fair." She looked at her glass and saw that it was nearly empty. She sat back, and smiled ruefully. "Some secrets are better kept secret," she said.

Eva shook her head. "It's not that," she said. "I hope you'll be . . . happy."

Martha laughed. "Well, I doubt that," she said, with just a hint of a hard edge in her voice. She gave Eva a long look, then she shook her head and laughed again. "I doubt anybody will come out of this *happy*," she said.

Before Eva could think better of it, she had spoken, and though she didn't mean it to sound dismissive, she wasn't sorry when it did. "Well, there you go," she said.

Martha froze for a moment and stared at her. Then she laughed again and raised her glass. "There you go," she said, without a trace of mockery or dismissal. "There you go, indeed." She tossed back the wine and poured herself another glass. "And God bless us, every one," she said, as she rose, fetched her coat from the hat stand, and made herself ready to go.

.   .   .

When Eva arrived at the church, the others were already there, though she wasn't as late as she feared, and they had not begun without her. Nobody said much, but then they never did. Nobody inquired about family or work. She knew these people only as they were in this place, a group of like-minded souls, equals in discretion, united by a common tact. The world outside and what they did there was another matter altogether. Richard, Catherine, Grace, Simon, John: as soon as they put on their coats and scarves and—yes, it so happened that some of them, at least, fitted the image she'd had of them that first day—their tweed caps and bicycle clips, they seemed to dwindle away, the light going out of their faces, their secret selves discarded for their return to the outside world. It had come as a surprise to her, those first few weeks: the reason she had joined the group had been to make new friends, but now she was grateful that nobody here wanted to do anything but gather at the appointed time, ring the bells, and go home.

The one exception was Harley. He was the newest member of the group, and he was nothing like the others. He'd been a welcome addition to the company: young, casually dressed, and very good-looking, he was an American student from Illinois, or Iowa, or some such place. No doubt, he had come along the first time out of curiosity, because bell ringing struck him as quaint and Olde Worlde, like warm beer or clootie dumpling, and thus one of the experiences it would be a shame to miss while he was over here. He'd taken to it, though, and the group had accommodated him easily, in spite of his youth and his accent and his fondness for sweatshirts with oddly unsettling slogans printed across the front. Catherine was particularly considerate of him, bringing in brown paper bags full of apples from her garden and Tupperware containers of mince pies to share with his housemates. She was old enough to be his mother, but Eva wasn't so sure her attentions were wholly maternal. Harley was always polite with her, in the way that Americans are: doggedly courteous and, at the same time, utterly remote, like the landing party in an old episode of *Star Trek,* curious and well-meaning and occasionally bewildered, but sworn not to interfere in the everyday life of their hosts.

For her own part, Eva was as scrupulously polite with Harley as he was with her—and just as distant. Yet there were times when she imagined—not sex, of course, nothing so vivid, but a shared moment of some kind. A picnic, say, on Balcomie Law, or a long walk in the woods by Lathockar. In these imaginings, they never touched—not because Harley didn't excite her but because she'd suddenly discovered that she was superstitious, and she was afraid to imagine what she most desired, afraid even to wonder what it might be. As soon as she did, it would fall away into the realm of the impossible. That afternoon, however, she couldn't help thinking about what Martha had said, and as Harley moved back and forth in the dim space of the bell tower she noticed how beautiful his hands were: fine, almost delicate, not large and heavy, like other men's hands, but strong nevertheless, like a pianist's or a dancer's. Of course, as soon as the notion entered her mind she did everything she could to extinguish it, because she didn't want to think about him in that way. Yet she kept coming back to him: to his dark eyes, to the way he carried himself, and, time and again, before she could stop herself, to the beauty of his hands. Hands she wanted to feel on her skin, light and slow and graceful; not heavy, never heavy, but gentle the way a bird is when it alights on a branch or a stone, resting for a moment but never entirely settled, always light, always about to take off.

And all this time, as she thought about Harley, the bells rang out over the snowy land. The bell ringers were continuing a tradition that had once been central to the life of the community, and she liked to think that only a generation ago, whenever these bells had rung out over the fields and the streets, everyone had known what they were saying. A call to worship, a royal wedding, an armistice, an enemy attack. Everyone would have understood those signals, because those were the public events, those were the facts. Yet surely there had been something else, another music inside the public proclamations, and there must have been those who could hear more than the facts, gifted listeners who could pick out the subtleties in the way one bell worked against the others, say, or in the pauses when one ringer stopped, weary or undecided, or touched with the knowledge of imminent mortality. Now the bells were nothing but background— pure atmosphere, a little local color—but perhaps there were still souls in this very parish who could decipher the inner workings of a bell ringer's mind, just by listening. If such souls existed, they might know everything about her: the lie of her marriage, her secret thoughts about Harley, her half-formed plans to get away. With every pull on the bell rope, she might be confiding everything to some old man in the almshouses at the far end of the village, or to some dying woman in one of the cottages out by the woods; some seasoned listener who would set aside a book or a pile of darning and listen awhile, wondering who it was that was giving herself away. It frightened her, that notion, but it pleased her, too, because she wanted to proclaim the truth, she wanted to reveal who she really was: not the good and faithful wife she pretended to be but someone else, someone interrupted. That was what she wanted to say—not to confess but to proclaim to all the land.

It was snowing again as she left the church. Over the green, the lights had come on in the shops, the usual gold and white mixed with the Christmas decorations, red and green and a pale, otherworldly blue around the doors and windows of the butcher's and the greengrocer's. Eva was dreading Christmas now: James and Martha would come over, as usual, and she would have to sit in that house with them, pretending everything was normal, drinking sherry while the men talked, passing round the mince pies and trying not to be offended by Matt's jokes about her baking. This year, she decided, she would buy mince pies from the new delicatessen, the one that sold Polish sausage and French cheese, just to see if anybody noticed the difference. Better still, she would just disappear, maybe go out for a walk in the woods by herself. She would leave a trail of footprints in the snow, and when she got to the end of the track she would look back, the way her father had always done on their winter walks when she was a girl—and it struck her that she'd never really allowed herself time to go back to the woods, or out to the meadows where her father had sometimes led her, in the dusk of a summer's evening, to look at moths, naming them, first in the language he had been obliged to learn as a young man, the only language Eva knew, and then in his mother's tongue, being careful to match the two, even though the moths they found, ash gray and soft on the barks of the trees and the stones, were local to this place and only distantly related to those he had known as a boy.

"You OK?"

Eva turned and saw Harley in the shelter of the porch behind her, his coat buttoned up to the neck, a thick woollen crew cap pulled down over his ears. She remembered that he'd told her once that he was accustomed to cold weather, where he was from. She wished she knew what kind of region it was, whether it was prairie or forest, or just mile after mile of suburb or strip mall, like the America on television crime shows. She nodded. "I was just thinking we'd get a white Christmas this year," she said. "But then I suppose you're used to that, where you live."

He grinned. "Oh, we get plenty of snow, all right," he said. "Masses of it." He paused for a moment, and Eva thought she saw something in his face: a memory, or maybe a trace of homesickness. It made him seem preoccupied, like someone who knows he has lost something and can't remember what it is. Maybe it was a girl. There would be a girl, of course; a pretty girl in Illinois, or Iowa, a girl with long dark hair and reading glasses that she wore only when she wanted to look serious. Pretty and smart, and funny. A smart, funny girl who talked more than he did, which was why he loved her, or maybe why she loved him.

"Will you be going home for Christmas?" she asked.

He looked puzzled, as if her question were terribly personal and inappropriate, then his face brightened. "Oh, no," he said. "I'm planning to travel around, maybe go to Paris."

"Paris?" For some reason, the idea shocked her. She had wanted to think of him at home, with his family and his girl, not alone in some foreign city, among strangers. "Really?"

He laughed. "I don't know," he said. "Maybe Paris, maybe somewhere else." He poked his head out from under the shelter of the porch and looked up into the falling snow. "Maybe I'll just stay here," he said.

Eva shook her head. "Oh, don't do that," she said. "Go to Paris. Go skiing or something, but don't stay here."

Harley laughed again, then he saw how serious she looked and he nodded. Eva tried to smile then, because she knew she had given something away, but she couldn't, because she suddenly felt sorry for him, and for the pretty, smart girl in Iowa, with her books and her reading glasses. She knew how ridiculous that was, and she wanted to shrug it off, to stop being such a fool—and maybe Harley sensed that, because he touched her, his hand alighting on her coat sleeve and lingering for a moment before he took it away. "I have to go," he said. "Have a nice evening, OK?"

Eva nodded, and this time she did smile, but Harley was already moving away, loping off toward the gate in his winter coat, the snow clinging to his coat sleeves and the wool cap as he stepped out onto the pavement and headed across the green. Eva knew that she should go, too, but she couldn't bring herself to drive home to her husband's house, and she lingered in the porch awhile, watching the snow as it fell through the shop lights on the far side of the green. Harley was gone; he had vanished suddenly and she was surprised, because he'd just been there, crossing the green, heading to the row of shops opposite. She didn't know where he lived, but she knew it was in a shared house somewhere outside the village, probably on the west side, out by the woods. It would be a half mile or so, maybe more, and it struck her that she should have offered him a lift. But he was used to the cold and, besides, it would have been dangerous to get into a car with him and drive up through the Kinaldy woods in the snow. Out there alone with him, in the dark, with snow falling all around them, she might have said something she would have regretted.

But then he didn't appear on the far side of the green, and she wondered where he'd gone—not because she wanted to give in to the temptation to catch up with him and drive him home to his warm house but out of simple curiosity. That was what made her step out into the snow and walk to the gate. It was like watching a conjurer perform a magic trick, when you shouldn't really care, because you know it's an illusion, but you just have to figure out how it's done. Only she couldn't figure it out, because Harley wasn't there. He was gone. The others were gone, too, all but Catherine, who was putting something into the boot of her car twenty yards farther along, and there was nobody in the shops opposite but the people who worked there—the girl in the greengrocer's, come round from behind the counter to stare out at the falling snow, the butcher in his white coat, clearing away the slabs of beef and lamb after a busy day. Eva felt cheated, as if Harley had tricked her on purpose—and the thought scared her, because, if he had, what reason could there be except that he knew how she felt about him and was mocking her? Or maybe he'd *wanted* her to look for him, maybe he'd wanted that lift, but couldn't ask, because she was a married woman and he was an outsider. That was ridiculous, of course. The sad truth, surely, was that he'd already forgotten she existed and was on his way home, trudging happily through the snow: a young man, used to the cold, heading for home in a place he would never see again. Surely that was it, Eva told herself—yet she looked for him still, expected him to come back and resume the conversation because he had seen something in her face, something he'd looked for all along.

She stood at the gate, the snow lining the creases in her coat, her face and hands already numb with cold, and she waited to see what would happen, because something would happen—she knew it would. And just as that thought came to her, as if on cue, a familiar car appeared on the far side of the green. It was moving slowly, and the driver's-side window was wound down, so Eva could see that it was Martha, her hair damp from the drifting snow, her face attentive as she gazed across the green toward the trees by the church. For a moment, Eva was annoyed. She assumed that Martha had come for her, and even though it made no sense, even though she didn't want to be drawn back into that morning's conversation, she lifted her hand, lifted it without thinking, and waved. She waved, and then she waved again—but Martha didn't see her, and at that same moment, a few yards off to the left, a dark figure detached itself from the shadow of the big chestnut tree and hurried across, a dark figure that Eva knew from somewhere, though at first she couldn't place it, because it didn't make any sense: a dark figure who became Harley, running around the car and getting in on the passenger side with an air of having done this before. As soon as he was in, the car pulled away, heading out of the village and west, toward the lower woods, where the snow would be thick all night, thick and heavy and, even on the road that ran up to Kinaldy and Lathockar, completely unmarked, except for a line of tire tracks that would soon vanish into whiteness.

Mohan Sikka

Uncle Musto Takes a Mistress

U NCLE MUSTO had hired the services of a female secretary. In
our slow-paced colony, news like this gave the street a charge,
with its hint of juicy developments, its premise of slowly revealed
impropriety. The secretary's name was Rose: a Goan lady, dark com-
plexioned, with two pigtails tied in bouncy red ribbons and looped
on top of her head, the arrangement embellished with rhinestone
brooches and Little Mermaid hairpins.

"Trimmings suitable for a girl of thirteen," Grandma remarked at
dinner with a sniff. She'd seen Rose when she'd paid a bedside call on
Uncle Musto's wife, but there'd been no introductions. "Skitting
about here and there like a doe, eyes made up with too much kohl,
Sir this, sir that, running circles around our Prince Musto. She has
taken up quarters in the room above their garage, rent free!"

"Why are we discussing Musto's affairs?" Grandpa said gruffly,
over his plate. "He works hard to put food in many mouths. Leave
him alone and eat your own meal."

Grandma cracked off the end of a radish. "*Arré?* His welfare is our
welfare. I don't say he shouldn't have an assistant. But *that* sort of person? And live-in? How does it look?"

I was ten and living with my grandparents (my mother and father were abroad). Musto was my mother's cousin and lived two streets over from my grandparents. Since Musto's own parents had passed away some years before, he often came to seek Grandpa and Grandma's guidance on matters both personal and professional. The two households, his and ours, were known in the colony as the junior and senior Chopras respectively.

Recently, Grandpa had helped Musto make a series of useful business connections—Grandpa was retired from the Ordnance Corps of the Indian Army—and Musto had clinched a large deal to make special field radios for soldiers.

After dinner it was time for my glass of warm milk with almonds in the kitchen. Grandma stood by to make sure I downed every drop. Meanwhile, Dheeraj, our servant, scraped vegetables with gusto from the bottom of a steel skillet, his unruly thatch of hair flopping over his boyish face. "Mataji," he piped up, "it is not my place to meddle in big people's affairs, but the market talk is that Musto Master and this Sister Rose are taking long evening walks. What should I say when I hear such words against our family? It makes my steam rise."

"Those who cast aspersions on decent folk should look inside their own black hearts," Grandma snapped. Any other day, she happily ate up the tidbits of street news Dheeraj brought, clucking her tongue at colony shenanigans. "Sister Rose is Musto's office assistant. If they are walking, they are discussing strictly business, okay? Tell your friends to stop their impudence."

"But, Mataji, not only servant folk, the whole colony is whispering."

"Who speaks this rubbish? And who listens? Give me their names, servant or sahib."

"Why raise your voice at me? There are things I have not said out of respect. Some I witnessed with my own eyes—lip to lip in the park! For two days my mouth was too ashamed to open."

"Then you should have kept it closed, rascal! Did I ask for this broadcast?" She stuffed the free end of her sari into her petticoat.

"What's happening in the kitchen?" Grandpa called from the living room. "Why this commotion? Dheeraj Singh!" He was watching TV with his one seeing eye. His ears were still sharp, though.

"I'm scolded for speaking the truth," said Dheeraj in an injured tone. "Check for yourself if you doubt me. Master is upset, so I'll get on with my cleaning. From now on I will only chant the Holy Name." With a clatter he dropped his skillet in the sink, muttering *Hari, Hari.*

Grandma glowered at him while he worked up the soapsuds. "Clever man," she said, as though he wasn't there. "Arrived from the village prepackaged with city wiles. Shows me his temper; takes the Name of the Lord. *Very* clever." With a loud huff she took my hand and escorted me from the kitchen.

I was sure Dheeraj's mood wouldn't last the night. He was too genial to hold rancor. When Grandma was out, I sometimes sneaked up to his modest quarters above the garage, and he'd say, "Hey, hey, Sanju brother. Ready for a game?" He would take out a beat-up board of Snakes and Ladders and we'd sit cross-legged on his scratchy *charpai* and play. He showed me photos of his family and pointed out who was who: That is my dear mother, this short one is my wife, these are my children, my aunts, my cousins. Dressed in starched clothes, they stood in pairs and groups and stared gravely at the camera. On an especially good day, he liked to tell me tall tales: His grandfather owned so much land it took an entire day to walk its perimeter. Inside the property stood an entire forest, with monkeys and wild deer and foxes. In season there was such a bounty of sweet peaches the entire valley ate until they couldn't stand another peach. I must have glanced then at his paltry belongings, because he laughed. "Yes, Sanju *bhaiya.* That was before my father befriended two devils—Liquor and Dice." He made a monster's face and claws. "Slowly they ate up all our groves and farmland. After that even my mother had to go to work." His mother, I knew, had been Grandma and Grandpa's maid at one time. "Life's Ferris wheel." He shrugged.

"Someone goes up, someone goes down." With a wink he added: "If you are patient your turn at the top comes again."

In contrast, Grandma tended to burn on a much longer fuse. After her exchange in the kitchen with Dheeraj, she put on her polyester nightie and came and sat with folded arms on the living room couch. Her small brow stayed overcast all evening. On the other end of the couch, Grandpa leaned forward on his cane and watched TV, although he glanced at Grandma now and then. With her dyed black hair braided for the night, she looked like a jowly, overgrown child, grumpy about her approaching bedtime. Later, after she'd tucked me in and put out the lights, she began her *khuss-puss* with Grandpa. As usual, their whispers carried clear to me in the adjoining room.

"A man of Musto's class cannot be seen taking strolls with a Christian secretary. Dear, you *must* say something. Being a Romeo at eighteen is one thing . . ."

"Exemplary, Sushma!" Grandpa replied, in a pooh-pooh voice. "An army wife chin-wagging with the servant class. Encouraging pernicious chatter."

"In your good moods Dheeraj is more reliable than a son. Now he's a tattler."

"Tomorrow, for his reliability, I'll give Dheeraj a royal dressing down he'll never forget."

"Yes, yes, punish the messenger. Meanwhile, the real offender carries on unchecked. We are partly to blame, of course. We've coddled Musto too much."

In his drawer Grandpa kept a cutting of the feature on Uncle Musto that appeared in *The Indian Express*. MADE-IN-INDIA RADIOS FOR OUR FORCES, read the headline. DELHI CONTRACTOR BEATS RUSSIAN COMPETITION. There was a photograph with a caption: *Musto Chopra on the shop floor of his Gurgaon factory.*

"What was he before the leg up we gave him?" Grandma went on. Even I knew the answer—a secondhand car-antenna salesman. "One newspaper article and Musto Sahib thinks nothing can touch him. A self-made man. A hero who supplies the entire army—"

"He *is* a self-made man. It *was* his hard work."

"Look how he repays our confidence. Public walks with that wench while his wife is sick in bed. Servants watching and passing comments. I tell you in his arrogance he'll go further yet. Like his father, Pammo, before him, whose own tendencies when he was alive—"

"Enough!" snarled Grandpa, smacking his wooden bed frame and making me jump. "Follow your advice to Dheeraj and learn when to lock your tongue!"

I pulled the covers tight over myself. For a minute the only sound that floated through the house was the *thug thug thug* of the night watchman's stick outside. Then a creak from the other room was followed by the flip-flop of unsteady rubber slippers. To my surprise, Grandma's portly profile trundled through my doorway. Breathing heavily, she crossed over and plopped herself beside me. "He's like the shah who plays chess while his palace burns. The buffalo that chews its cud under a tree in the lightning. Musto can paint our faces black in the *mohalla,* no matter. We'll see about that! There is Someone Above who knows all."

Rallying around near and dear ones was one of Grandma's lived virtues. Every month she dragged me to visit a widowed aunty who lived in a tiny flat, forcing money into the lady's hand. Two years earlier, when my parents moved to Kenya for work, she wouldn't hear of them leaving me in boarding school. And, of course, many family weddings were arranged in our house. She told prospective in-laws considering a Chopra boy or girl: "Unlike other families, we have never given the world the chance to point fingers—except at our children's merits."

"Good night, Grandma," I said, and she said: "Hardly good night!" and kept up her muttering. Despite her agitation, I was secretly glad for her company. Sleeping alone was the thing I hated most since my parents' departure.

Outside, the watchman blew a long, mournful whistle. By and by Grandma quieted down. Eventually, she let me snuggle up to her plump upper arm (which made a nice pillow). "Still my baby boy," she said with a sniffle. She sounded very much the aggrieved party despite all the close-range shots she'd been firing.

The next evening, Dheeraj was out running market errands so I had no one to play carrom with. Grandpa preferred bridge, but wouldn't teach me ("It's not a game for children"). Grandma was at prayer. I climbed up to the roof and pretended to shoot over the parapet at enemies who had kidnapped my parents—in my story line, they were being held captive in the fort across the street. As the time for Musto's walk-by approached, I heard Grandma plodding up the steep back stairs. By the time she reached the roof she was wheezing and looking pinched and pained. She leaned her doughy body against a pipe to catch her breath.

"Uff," she said. "Sanju *beta,* come here. Good boy." Then, more crossly: *"Come here!"*

I walked over, blowing smoke from my imaginary barrel. She grabbed my arm with a ferocious grip, still panting. Using my support to counteract her fear of heights, she propelled us toward the water tank in the far corner of the roof. From the side of the tank we could watch the street without being visible from the ground. Below us, servants in pairs ambled past, on their way to buy milk and vegetables. Other groups of men in loose white pajamas and singlets gathered at the corner cigarette stand smoking and laughing, draped over each other's shoulders in familiar fashion. A cricket game played by rough boys shared time with passing cars and auto-rickshaws. Their shiny cork ball flew viciously through the air, with many near misses of a car window or a person's skull. I preferred the safe solitude of the roof.

Uncle Musto and Rose appeared around the corner. All heads turned to them as though they were royal eminences. Tall and erect, Musto, with his proud hazel eyes, did seem like a prince on his daily walkabout. His right hand held a cigar, and as he strode forward he sent up spinning saucers of smoke. Jaunty Rose kept pace to his left with occasional hop-steps, her head turned slightly in his direction. A plastic shopping bag hung from her free arm. You had to squint a little because of the way Rose's *kameez* fell, but yes, it was quite clear they were holding hands.

"The sorceress!" Grandma spat out. "He's caught in her spell!" Her tubby face glowed darkly, like its own small evening sun.

"What if they see us?" I said, pulling away.

"Wait, wait." She pushed us right against the parapet.

Musto and Rose were two houses from ours when, as if on cue, they dropped their clasped hands and moved apart. Musto extinguished the stub of his cigar under one of the heels of his bright white walking shoes and threw it into the ditch.

"Hmm," said Grandma, her fleshy mouth collapsed and trembling. "Office assistant by day, personal attendant by night. Holy Holy Jesus in the a.m.; roly-poly mistress in the p.m. *Ay Khuda,* I had to live to see this day."

"Grandma, let's go," I insisted.

"Why do *me* the favor?" she said hoarsely to the street. "If you can display such depravity before the whole colony, why hide it in front of my house?"

They were directly below us now. They couldn't have heard Grandma from that height, but still, Rose said something to Musto, and he glanced up. Spotting us, he smiled and waved.

Grandma froze, her clammy hand still clasping my arm. The lines around her eyes vanished, the skin stretched taut by alarm.

"I think they're coming in," I said. Indeed, they had entered our driveway.

Grandma exhaled. "Why darken my home? *Hai, hai,* take me down quickly, my sari is a mess."

Downstairs, Grandpa received the guests while Grandma dressed. Grandpa was always pleased when Musto stopped by. Dheeraj Singh had also returned; his curious face kept bobbing into view in the serving window between the kitchen and the dining room.

Musto stood before Grandpa, one arm akimbo like a hero. "Please give us your blessings, Papaji. With Waheguru's mercy, my days are so busy that I need a dependable person to manage my diary." The diary planner looked at Musto with a gratified smile, showing *paan*-stained teeth. "Rose!" he commanded with a chop of his hand, as if she'd forgotten a trick.

Rose collapsed in a heap at Grandpa's feet. "Enough, enough," Grandpa said, shaking his big, bald head. "Get down. I mean, get up. Have a long life! I don't like all this." But he didn't sound annoyed. He knocked the end of his walking stick twice. "Dheeraj Singh! Bring tea and some snacks. Right away. For Musto Master and Miss, uh, Rose."

The couple sat side by side on the couch, Musto very straight and Rose gazing down, her hands clasped on her ample lap. The shopping bag lay between them. Grandpa sat across from them on the love seat.

Uncle Musto and Grandpa began talking army politics. The article about him in the paper had made enemies, Musto said with odd satisfaction. Since he was the first Indian vendor chosen to supply radios, hostile elements inside the forces were claiming he had disclosed classified information in his press interview. The reporter had foolishly mentioned a few technical details, Musto agreed, but he wasn't the source. He very much wanted to defend himself.

"Don't worry," Grandpa said. "I know a man well positioned at the Ministry of Defense. He was my aide during my Frontier Army days. Loyal chap. He'll clear this up." Musto nodded slowly.

"People are jealous of a winner, that's all," Grandpa went on, crossing and uncrossing his bony legs and taking in Rose with his good eye. Sitting on a corner stool next to Grandpa, I also examined her.

Her clothes were cut very modishly, but they were a size too small.

There was a growing circle of sweat under each packed armpit, and a damp mustache over her upper lip. Her cheeks were a high color—from makeup or from sitting in our stifling house, I couldn't tell. But if she was too warm, she didn't say a word about it while Uncle Musto and Grandpa continued their discussion. The ceiling fan blew air around us ineffectually.

At one point Musto turned to me with a grin. "So, Sanju my boy, how is my African sister?" That was his joke about my mother ever since my parents left for Kenya.

"Fine, Uncle Musto," I said politely, while inside, a bomblet of anger went off. She was only gone temporarily, so why wasn't she Indian anymore?

"Such a brave lad," he said to Rose. "Living far away from his mother and father at a young age."

Rose's gaze steadied on me. The pupils of her kohl-marked eyes flickered open. I saw some fleeting play of light and shadow inside, her first display of independent feeling. Her wide features softened and a smile of great tenderness appeared on her lips. As she tipped her head a small pang of sympathy wrung across her face. I felt a hook snag inside my own chest. Flustered, I glanced away.

"Sir—," she began, but just then Grandma rolled in from the back of the house.

"Why, Musto!" Grandma declared. "Are *we* not Sanju's parents also? Is this not his own home?" Her hair was combed into a serviceable bun, some slapdash powder and lipstick on her face.

Musto got up to greet Grandma with folded hands. "Of course, Mummyji. I did not mean to imply otherwise." He paused while Grandma's eyes narrowed for an instant on Rose. "Supporting others, charity to all—these are lessons you and Papaji have always exemplified."

Rose stood, too, and tried to touch Grandma's feet, but missed because Grandma brushed past to Grandpa's love seat.

"You make it sound like we run a public service, Musto,"

Grandma scoffed as she lowered herself down. "Our love and support is not for any *erra-kherra* off the street."

"Dheeraj, where is the tea?" Grandpa bellowed. To the guests: "Why are you standing?"

"Yes, sit, sit," said Grandma. "So what was the reason you came today? Can Papaji be of further assistance?" But her expression wasn't charitable at all.

The guests subsided again. Musto smiled. "Mummyji, for once I'm here not just with my begging bowl. I have good news: The new wing of the factory finally became operational this morning. We've brought small tokens to mark the occasion. Rose, open the package!" Rose bent and retrieved from the shopping bag a neatly folded silk sari, a bottle of Johnnie Walker, and a box of sweets. Even I could tell that the sari, with its contrasting border and golden *zari* embroidery, was expensive.

While Musto was speaking, Dheeraj Singh had appeared. His stocky form stood on the side with the tea things, all bug-eyed, entranced by Rose and the presents. He was wearing his household uniform—striped drawstrings and a sweaty undershirt.

"What are you gaping at, Dheeraj?" said Grandpa. "Next time put on clean clothes for guests! Come on, leave it now and go."

Dheeraj placed the tea tray on the center table. Grandma scowled at the sari and made no attempt to serve the guests. Nobody moved or made eye contact. Finally, Rose picked up the gifts and, one by one, put them back in the bag. She then reached forward and poured a cup each for Musto and Grandpa. She didn't take any for herself. "Mummyji?" she said, and Grandma twitched at the word. "Tea?"

It was plain Grandma wasn't going to say anything about the gifts. Grandpa cleared his throat. "There was no need for all this."

"Not at all," said Musto. "You are *my* second set of parents as well." He got up and took two steps in my grandparents' direction. In the endless ritual of feet-touching, it was his turn.

Grandma came back to life. She put out one pudgy hand to stop him. The other clutched at her chest, where heaving sounds began to emanate.

"Musto," she blubbered, "this, ah, affront could have been a mark of respect—if delivered from the hands of your *wife*! Why must you grind your boot in our faces, when Papaji has done nothing if not aid and assist you at every turn?"

Grandpa's eyes popped out. "Sushma, cease and desist!"

"It's okay, Papaji." But a look of distaste had replaced Musto's earlier affability. "Neeta wasn't well enough to come today, Mummyji," he said evenly. "We suspect severe heat exhaustion. She asks your pardon and your good wishes."

We all knew Aunty Neeta had been ill for some weeks, but Grandma was having none of it. "You forget I saw her yesterday, Musto. I don't think it's the weather she is suffering from. Oh my poor Neeta Rani, my little innocent one." Her hand was still at her chest.

"It *has* been oppressively humid," Grandpa said. "*Khuda* knows when the monsoon will break."

"Take them back!" Grandma cried. "These poison presents. Tell Neeta I will come to *her* house and receive them from *her* hand. Tell her to phone me when she is better and I will come. The joints of my legs are swollen in pain, but I'll come. No one can stop me from collecting what is my due." And she challenged Rose as if Rose were a three-headed monster who had to be stared down to enter Musto's palace.

But Grandma was mistaken. Rose was neither a sprightly doe nor a mythic beast, but instead, a giant turtle in human form. Her broad back, her small-stepped gait, her ready compliance to Musto's every direction, all were evidence of this. At this moment, she had pulled back into her carapace, sitting stock-still.

The muscles on Musto's face, on the other hand, were twitching with a response he was having trouble keeping at bay. He collected himself with an effort and said, in his best molten voice: "As you wish, Mummyji. In this colony, you have two houses and many children. Please come as your convenience allows. Let me know and I will even send the driver to pick you up." He nodded curtly at Rose, who sprung out of her immobile state with surprising swiftness and followed Musto as he moved to leave. The bag of presents was in Musto's hand this time.

Grandpa had found himself sidelined during Grandma's display. Now, holding his cane, he stumbled after the departing pair. "Musto!" he said, his voice cracking. "I am a superstitious man. Don't leave offended. Here, I'm happy to keep the whiskey." He snatched the bottle and gave Musto an awkward, bony hug. "You make the family proud! May you have an even brighter future, son." Musto stopped, silent. "The knives are unsheathed, Musto," Grandpa added in a low tone. "The world tries to pull down a rising star. That is what is upsetting Mummyji, nothing else. Look after yourself, okay?"

That night the heavy artillery was out in my grandparents' room. Shells were launched, grenades thrown. In the aftermath Grandma slept in my bed once more, holding me for comfort.

The following Sunday, Grandpa dozed in the afternoon while Dheeraj massaged his legs. Instead of joining him for a nap, Grandma made me put on a clean shirt and combed my hair. We were going to Uncle Musto's.

It was a hot, sticky day. Grandma held up her black umbrella in a gesture of rebuke to the sun and complained about her knees the entire way. When we reached Musto's house, we found it in its usual state of disarray. The air-conditioning was blasting on the ground floor. Some aunties and uncles were eating a late lunch, filling the trapped air with the tang of heavily spiced meat. Servants brought steaming dishes out of the kitchen. One cousin had his homework spread out on the carpet, another her toys. They screamed at each other for taking up too much space. A houseguest wandered in and put on the TV. Musto's older brother, Jaggu, a known wastrel according to Grandma, was sitting on a divan with his hairy white legs exposed, demanding to know why his diabetic diet had not been prepared. The telephone rang incessantly. Rose and Musto were out at the factory site, where shifts went on around the clock.

I stayed right behind Grandma as she hauled herself up to a room on the second floor. Its door was partially open, and as we let ourselves in, we saw a woman lying on a small cot. It was Musto's wife, Neeta Aunty. The curtains were drawn to keep out the sun's glare. There was no air-conditioning here, only a table fan rotating from side to side, making a loud clicking noise at the end of each turn. The dark room smelled of urine and incense.

Neeta slowly raised herself on one elbow to greet us. She was a pale version of the brisk, no-nonsense aunty I remembered.

"*Aiyo,* Neeta Rani," Grandma panted. "You look worse. What have you done to yourself?"

"I am well now," she replied, so softly I had to strain to hear. "My favorite mother is here to take care of me. And who is this—has my little son come, too? I want to pinch your cheeks, but you must stay away from Aunty today." The skin around her eyes had darkened in a band, making her appear raccoon-like. "Over there is a comic book," she said, pointing to a trunk covered with rumpled clothes and knickknacks. "The children left it. Take it, Sanju *beta.*"

"Such a showman with everybody else," Grandma said, "but won't install an AC for his own wife. Shame!"

"Of course Musto Sahib would provide anything I asked, but I am too cold, Mummyji. Even the fan makes me shiver." When Grandma called Uncle Musto *Sahib* I knew it was a jab, but from Aunty Neeta's lips, it sounded respectful, even tender.

Neeta motioned to side-by-side rattan chairs a few feet from the bed; I wasn't sure either was sturdy enough for Grandma. "Please," she said, trying to sit up. "Should I ring for lemonade?"

The space was as bare and inhospitable as the inside of an ashram. The solitary portrait mounted on the wall above Neeta's head was a rendering of her personal guru, a man with a buzz cut wearing a saffron dhoti. His burly arms were crossed over his chest and he watched over the patient with an expression of genial self-assurance.

A garland of flaccid marigolds hung sadly around one edge of the portrait. Incense sticks stuck into the frame had burnt themselves out.

"The bed, the bathroom—everything reeks, Neeta. Why is no one coming to clean?"

"While I am in bed I don't want servants bustling around. Till last week I could manage by myself. Now Rose takes care of what I need."

"Did they call Dr. Mukherjee again? Or do you not even deserve medical attention?"

"Doctors! He says more tests. But I had Rose mail an entreaty with five hundred and one rupees to Guru Baba, and his response will be arriving any day. Then I have full confidence I will be up and about."

A servant arrived to take instructions for dinner. Neeta gave him detailed orders for each child and adult in the household, altogether fifteen people. She was especially concerned about what her elder brother-in-law would eat. Rose had a request, too—mutton cutlets. When the servant left, Neeta lay back down, exhausted. Just looking at her made me feel tired, too.

Grandma appeared far from being done. She pulled her chair in closer. "The less you mention that wench's name, Neeta, the sooner your mystery sickness will subside. Her black magic has caused this. Tomorrow I am returning to fetch you, my daughter. I will look after you in my house till you are well."

"Who will organize things here, Mummyji? Musto Sahib depends on me. Don't worry. Guru Baba will send his gracious blessings and I will be back on my feet, you'll see."

Grandma put her hands on Neeta's head. "My child, in a way you are right. This sickness *is* related to the spiritual state of this house, the things that are being allowed here. And you are also implicated. I say confront Musto, put an end to this Rose business. Is this any way to treat the woman who makes his home?"

Neeta lifted her eyes at me pleadingly, as if I had the power to intercede. I wanted to tell her it was no use: when Grandma was fired up, there was no derailing her till she got satisfaction. Once she showed up at my school unannounced. She pulled me out of class and took me to the office of the PT instructor, a skinny, narcoleptic man fond of keeping his door closed. "Sanju is small for his age," she baldly told the bleary-eyed gentleman. "Is he on the field during sports period? You have a big name for all-around education, but he is doing physical activity neither here nor at home. What will his parents say when they see he hasn't grown?" The PT instructor and I both gazed at the floor, conscious of each other's exposure. After that I had to participate in cricket matches at school, standing on the edge of the ground praying the batsman wouldn't hit the hard, horrible ball my way.

When Neeta spoke, it was with practiced resignation. "Mummyji, what can I say in my condition? With Musto Sahib just now enjoying success after so many years of financial struggle?"

"He came to my house and brought the witch and made her give us presents."

"Please don't call her that! Your sari is in the cupboard. It will make me sad if you leave without it."

"Neeta, these Chopra men can't help their appetites. But these aren't the days of kings and sultans, when husbands camped in borderlands and saw their wives once a year after battle. I know how to deal with this kind of situation."

Neeta smiled. "Yes, I am aware what our menfolk did in olden times." She looked directly at Grandma. "But this is more mutual. Musto Sahib and I aren't man and woman with each other any longer. Perhaps you suspected. There is nothing left to fight about."

"*Chee, chee,* Neeta. What are you saying? It is your own fault you have not maintained yourself." Grandma gave me a stern glance, but I pretended to be engrossed in my comic.

"No, it's for the best. At least we're friends now. I have my home, my children. He has the business. Rose and I are becoming like sisters."

"*Hai,* don't throw dirt in my ears!"

"She has a sad story. Her husband beat her. She left her baby in Goa. She has an aunt in Old Delhi who helped her find the employment agency that Musto Sahib uses."

"You are too good-hearted, Neeta. You believe anything. She probably gave her own chap trouble. She's like the washerman's dog—pariah in the house, pariah on the riverbank. May she meet an ugly fate for snatching another's man, the husband-eater!"

"No, No. You can't mean that. . . ." But she was sounding progressively deflated, as if less and less air was reaching her lungs. "*Hai,* Mummyji, I am so tired! Forgive me, I can't talk much longer."

Seeing Aunty Neeta's condition, I wanted to grab Grandma and usher her out of the room. I said: "We should go, Grandma," my voice coming out high and insistent.

But Neeta didn't help her own cause. "No, no. Stay a little, please, and drink and eat something. I am so happy to see you."

In a minute she was asleep. Grandma stroked her forehead and bent down to check her breathing. Then she leaned back in her chair and sat for a while in silence. She pursed her lips and slowly kneaded her dimpled elbows. She stared at the picture of Neeta's guru, who stared jovially back. When the lemonade came, she barely sipped any. I drank mine and most of hers.

"Finished?" she said, and I nodded. "Let's go, then. I've heard enough."

"The sari," I said. "Aunty Neeta—"

"Hush! What kind of woman do you think I am?"

When Grandpa returned from his bridge game that evening, Grandma gave him a dire account of her visit: how Musto was absconding with Rose at all hours, how he showered her with gifts while criminally neglecting Neeta in her time of need. ("The backyard hen is only good for laying eggs. The *market* chicken makes the master's roast!") She declared that she would not step into Musto's house again "until some action is taken regarding that woman."

Grandpa said nothing, only coughed dryly from time to time. For the rest of the day Grandma wore a righteous expression. When Grandpa was watching the evening news, she went into the back verandah and gave Dheeraj another report in *khuss-puss* tones. It was funny to see Grandma and Dheeraj's roles reversed.

Two days later I was on the roof again, firing at my imaginary enemies. Negotiations had failed. It was time to storm the fort and release my captured parents. As Musto and Rose strolled by right on schedule, a group of pajama-clad men broke off from their huddle at the corner cigarette stand and fell into step behind them. One pair approached Musto from the right and asked him for a match. Musto stopped and amiably offered his silver lighter. He appeared to exchange pleasantries with the pair. Meanwhile, two others sidled up to Rose from the left, pinched her hard on both substantial buttocks and fled.

"Aaeeee!" screamed Rose hideously, rubbing her bottom in a most unladylike manner, as the feinters on the right also absconded, taking Musto's lighter with them. The cricket boys stopped their game to gape, unable to believe their luck.

Musto's expression was something to see. Surprise and impotent fury took turns playing out on his smooth, lean face. He attended first to the needs of his lady. Then he conducted a grim assessment of the street. By now the cigarette stand was deserted.

"The sons of whores who have done this mischief will pay, mark my words!" he shouted, at no one and everyone. "You think I don't know who you are, you fatherless bastards! Who dares to laugh?" He looked like he would shoot the nearest person if he had a gun. The cricket boys assumed sprinting positions.

I should have ducked away from the parapet but I was too enthralled. Musto glanced up.

"Sanju! Sanju *beta*! Come down this second!"

"I saw nothing, Uncle Musto, I swear," I shouted, and ran across the roof and down the back stairs, my heart beating faster than a steam engine. I thought about telling Grandma, but didn't in the end—I felt party to the misdeed I had witnessed.

The entire colony now had permission to punish Rose. When she took an auto-rickshaw to the market, the driver sang movie songs: *Darling, why keep this distance when we both have the love fever? One kiss from those ruby lips and I'll be your slave forever.* If she told him to stop, he felt her up before he drove off, leaving her crying by the roadside. Boys threw pebbles from behind trees when she sat on a park bench. A brick shattered the window of her room. Letters full of curses were dropped in Musto's mailbox, addressed to Ms. Rose, Whore of Goa. Old widows, hobbling to the community milk booth, spat on the ground when they saw Musto and Rose together. A gold chain was snatched from Rose's neck by men wearing pajamas who sped away on bicycles. The next day her purse was taken. These reports came back to Grandma's ears from Dheeraj's sources. Dheeraj couldn't stop grinning as he narrated each new offense.

Oddly, Grandma wasn't upset about any knocks the family name was receiving as a result of this abuse. "The fruit of her own misdeeds," she said to Dheeraj. "The she-devil! It is only a matter of time now."

One night, after dinner, Grandpa announced: "Dheeraj has asked me for leave. He says he has to settle a property dispute in the village." In the past, Grandma had complained bitterly about housework falling on her old bones in Dheeraj's absence, but this time she replied: "Let him go, poor man. He hasn't seen his mother or wife in almost a year."

Before Dheeraj left, I heard Grandma telling him: "Come back quickly, my son. The news of the shrew's departure will be waiting."

"Can I start my driving lessons on my return, Mataji?" Becoming a part-time driver was one of Dheeraj's dreams (mine, too; I was promised free rides).

"We'll see," said Grandma. "Once there are good tidings, everything is possible."

But while Dheeraj was away, no reports of any kind arrived from Musto's house. Grandma held to her vow and did not visit there. When she called on the phone she was told Neeta was too weak to speak. Grandpa went to see Musto once or twice, but never told us what they discussed. Musto and Rose weren't seen on our street anymore, nor did we run into them elsewhere in the colony. I asked Grandma about it, and she said, her whole face puckering with pleasure: "Perhaps the message penetrated her thick skin. She may have packed up already, with God's grace."

Then, one day, a man in uniform rang our doorbell. He was Musto's height and build, very dark and fit. He wore a cap and carried a leather briefcase.

"Major General Chopra," he said, after Grandpa received him in the living room, "I am sorry to cause this inconvenience." He retrieved a slim file from his briefcase. "We are conducting an inquiry regarding Mr. Musto Chopra, your relative from Block A." Grandma watched, suddenly vigilant, from the dining table, where she sat darning a shirt.

"Yes, yes," Grandpa said, thinking this was about the newspaper affair. "My brother's son. A fine, upstanding citizen. Any accusations against him are false. As an ex-Ordnance man, I assure you that nothing quoted in the press has any national security implication."

"Sir, I'm not sure of your meaning. I am with Delhi Police. The inquiry was launched *by* Mr. Musto. His employee, good name Miss Rose, has been attacked several times. Her necklace and purse were robbed in the colony in broad daylight. The other day, a sharp object was thrown as she left Mr. Musto's premises, causing a temple wound that required six stitches."

Grandma jumped in from the dining table: "If that's true, Inspector, it was a bad thing. On one point, though, Mr. Musto has misled you. Miss Rose is a common prostitute posing as an employee, and that kind of individual provokes a reaction even among law-abiding citizens. *She* is the one you should investigate." Her chin twitched with indignation.

"Sushma!" Grandpa said. "Not another sound!"

"Indeed, madam," the inspector replied. "I will complete a thorough review, not to worry. The thing is, some rough types we have questioned have identified one Dheeraj Singh as an instigator in these assaults. Is a servant of this name currently in your employment?"

"What?" started Grandpa, while Grandma promptly shifted her attention to her darning. "Yes, we have a Dheeraj Singh, but he is visiting his family in Jammu right now. He is an utterly trustworthy chap. He has served us faithfully since he was a boy. You are mistaken, Inspector. You shake rotten trees and of course bad fruit falls. The thugs you have caught will say anything to stave off a beating."

"As you say, sir. Nevertheless, would you give us permission to examine his quarters?"

"Under no circumstances," Grandpa said sharply. "On principle I could not. A servant is a human being too. If the police break down honest people's doors when they're away, well then, we should look to thieves to protect our homes."

"I didn't mean to offend you. In any case, would you mind sending your man directly to the station the day he arrives? We have one or two questions for him. What date is he due back?"

Grandpa summoned Musto after the inspector's visit. Musto arrived in his chauffeur-driven car, wearing a white suit and brown patent-leather shoes. Grandma stayed in the bedroom with a migraine.

Musto removed his jacket and reclined on the couch. He stretched out his legs and rubbed the ring stone on his left forefinger that matched his green-gray eyes. From the breast pocket of his shirt he took out a silver cigar case. Something jangled inside. Grandpa remained standing, watching him.

"Smoke if you like," Grandpa said, and Musto smiled and shook his head.

"Out of respect I could not." Then Grandpa massaged his saggy gullet, until Musto said: "Papaji, what is the matter?"

Grandpa sat down next to Musto, his cane by his side. He placed a sinewy hand on Musto's arm. "Why didn't you confide in me? Mummyji and I had to hear the entire sordid story from that inspector. He had the temerity to point fingers at Dheeraj."

Musto calmly acknowledged making the police report, but claimed he hadn't implicated anyone by name. "Suffice to say, Papaji, we have been under siege. I didn't want to alarm you. Of course, it never occurred to me that the perpetrator could be from *this* house."

Grandpa turned quite red. He picked up his stick and began to twist it with both hands. "Stop this *tamasha,* Musto," he said quietly. "You know better than to trust these colony policemen. They are merely casting about."

Musto was unmoved. "Let Dheeraj tell them what he knows and the matter can be brought to a close in five minutes. I'll give him fifty rupees for the blemish on his honor."

Grandpa saw me hovering close by. "Go away and play!" he said. "*Now,* Sanju!"

I didn't budge, made rash and bold by Uncle Musto's cavalier demeanor. Grandpa scowled fiercely at me. With a crimp in my gut, I waited for him to raise his cane and demand compliance. When he abruptly resumed the main debate, I knew that something had shifted between us.

"Consider carefully the implications, Musto. Your own prestige will suffer in the end. Maybe there is a more prudent path. Perhaps it's time to help Rose find another situation."

"With due regard, Papaji, I made a promise of protection to a woman, a loyal employee. I intend to keep it. And you know getting the police to take a case seriously requires capital. I can't simply abandon my investment."

"What are you hoping to discover?" Grandpa said, his voice shaking. "The inspector wanted to search our servant quarters. Can you imagine the insult to an army household?"

"I beg your forgiveness for the intrusion. They want to match the writing on the dirty notes Rose received. Her snatched property has not been located either." Musto still made a show of appearing unruffled, but his tone crackled with malice. "We've faced every sort of humiliation, Papaji, let me tell you. My suspicion is that my business rivals have paid someone off to harass us."

Grandpa clutched and unclutched his stick. With a dismal face he said: "So are you saying a sample of Dheeraj's handwriting would clear his name?"

"It might," said Musto with a cryptic look, and on that note he and Grandpa went out, presumably to find what they needed in Dheeraj's room above the garage.

"I taught that boy his letters," Grandpa said later, when Grandma appeared from the bedroom with her darning. "I opened the lock on his door and broke my own principle." He watched TV with a wretched expression, his bandy legs restless. Grandma worked her needle, her lower lip jutting out.

After Musto's call, the waiting for Dheeraj sat heavy in our household.

"Will that fool return on his due date?" Grandpa said.

"You know his village situation better than I do," Grandma responded. "After all, you brought that *manhoos* into our lives. He would never have been *my* choice as either servant or support for my old age. Too impressionable as a boy. Too little character as a grown man."

Grandpa was unable to hold back. "Your poor training is the real reason. From the start you and he have talked rubbish about Musto. Tell me the truth now: Is he mixed up with the Rose situation?"

"You've become a foolish old man. You cannot see through Musto's countermove. He wants to intimidate us so he can continue his fancy dance with his girlfriend."

"Why do you *care?*" Grandpa broke out. "Why does Musto stick like a mango seed in your throat?"

"A *rotten* mango seed," shot back Grandma, "that grew in the fruit of a rotten mango tree! Where do you think Musto learned this from, this bold-faced sense of license? Over my dead body will I see these behaviors tolerated in another generation, you hear?"

These words lit up Grandpa like dry kindling. He stepped toward her with his cane. "Disrespectful woman! I'll teach you to keep digging up the past."

"Strike me, then!" she said, cowering a little. "But I won't be quiet. Have you been swapping Frontier tales with Musto lately? Of conquests with army maidservants while wife and children are sent away?"

The stick flew up and stayed there, suspended. Spasms passed through the atrophied muscles of Grandpa's arm, as if the cane were a great weight. But in the end he could not strike, perhaps because he wasn't able to steady his raised arm. His grip slackened, and the stick fell to the floor with a clatter.

When I went to my room that night, I was startled to find Grandma standing like an apparition by the ironing table, her head covered by a gray shawl, staring out of the window at the moonlit driveway. I put on the light, and she shifted slowly around—pale cheeks, pale lips, eyes bleary and bloodshot. "Grandma!" I said, but she shuffled away without a word.

Grandma and Grandpa hardly spoke till Dheeraj arrived the following weekend. I was playing in our driveway in the morning when he stepped out of an auto-rickshaw with his luggage. "Hello, Sanju brother," he called cheerily. As he opened our front gate, three policemen who'd been loitering close by dashed toward him from the street. He made a half-witted attempt to dodge them, but they easily caught him and dragged him into the driveway. In their arms, he shook as though he were having an attack of malaria.

The inspector stepped out of a nearby car, strode up to our doorstep, and rang the bell. The pajama men and the cricket boys gathered at the gate to enjoy the unfolding carnival. Since Musto and Rose's disappearance there had been so little excitement on the street.

"What are you trying to prove by this underhandedness?"

Grandpa demanded, once he'd appraised the situation with his seeing eye. "Didn't Musto give you the writing sample? I'm going to have it out with your superior, you two-bit policeman!"

"Sir!" said the inspector, unperturbed. "I ask for your patience." The hard edge in his voice was so different than the day he sat in our living room.

Grandma came bustling to the front door in her nightie and rubber slippers. "What is happening? Has Dheeraj Singh come? Why are these men holding him?"

Dheeraj began bawling for the mother he'd left behind in his village. "Ma, Ma, save me. I have done no wrong. Protect me in my time of need, Ma."

"Shhh, don't worry, *beta,*" Grandma called to him from Grandpa's side, one stocky arm half-raised in uncertain assurance. "Sahib will sort it out. Quiet down and say nothing." Her other hand, white-knuckled, was balling up the lace on her nightie's neckline. The corners of her mouth were turned down, her face grim.

Some of the police, meanwhile, had seized Dheeraj's key and climbed up the back stairs to his room above the garage. As we watched from below, figures appeared now and again in his window—a vigorous rummage of his possessions seemed to be underway.

Presently we heard a cry from the search crew. A young policeman came sprinting down the stairs. When he reached us, he smartly saluted the inspector. "Sir," he said, "we found one of the items." He held up a gold chain with an unmistakable rose-shaped pendant. Its petals were inlaid with dark red stones.

The inspector took the necklace and examined it. "Very good taste, my man," he said, malevolently displaying it before Dheeraj. "A gift for your mother, perhaps?"

Dheeraj cowered as though the inspector were brandishing a baby scorpion. "This is some black magic," he blurted out. "I already gave the necklace to my wife." Then, realizing what he was saying, he shut his mouth. His eyes darted this way and that. I glanced at Grandma from the driveway: she appeared to have stopped breathing and shrunk in size.

The inspector gave Dheeraj a sharp, backhanded slap across the face. Everyone jumped. "Then you must be the magician," he said. The policemen holding Dheeraj took this as their signal to start pummeling their captive. The crowd from the street also muscled in. Surrounded by a circle of fists, Dheeraj dropped down on his haunches, wailing, *"Hai, Hai."* He removed his shoes and held them aloft, a sad and inadequate protection from the beating. I waited for Grandpa to step forward and command that the violence cease, but Grandma and Grandpa just stood in the doorway, stunned and immobilized. I felt an awful clenching in my groin.

The ringleader of the pajamas planted a vicious kick on Dheeraj's shin. "See?" he said to the inspector. "I told you he was the master-mind. He paid my men to pester that nice lady. He said she was a whore."

On every side the neighbors were at their windows. The inspector turned to my grandparents. "We have witnesses who swear this man personally organized the assaults on Miss Rose. Sir, madam, you had a poisonous snake living in your home. We had to ferret him out for your own safety. At any time he could have attacked and robbed you in your sleep."

That roused Grandma. She lurched down the front step, moved to intervene, I thought, by this grossly unfair description of Dheeraj. But she, too, railed at him: "Liar, conniver, two-timing bandit. Lock him up, Inspector. Who knows what else he has stolen?"

At Grandma's words the beating grew more intense. Dheeraj's shirt tore in several places. He dropped his shoes and waved his hands above his head. One side of his face was inflating like a dark balloon. Blood flowed from his mouth. Frightened by its bright color, I ran and hid by Grandma's side.

"Master, Master," Dheeraj cried between raps. "I never saw this chain before. I take this oath in my dead father's name. Someone put it in my room while I was gone." When Grandpa didn't respond he made a final entreaty to Grandma: "Mataji, tell them whose idea this was. Mataji, it hurts. Make them stop—" But Grandma pressed her lips together and averted her eyes. Dheeraj fell facedown and was kicked from all sides.

All of a sudden Grandpa shouted: "Stop! The boy will die." He rushed past us into the circle surrounding Dheeraj and a few punches caught him on his gizzardly head and shoulders.

"What are you doing?" Grandma shrieked after him, still holding the front of her button-down nightie. "Get back before you get hurt."

Grandpa ignored her and flopped on the battered Dheeraj Singh, enclosing him within his skinny arms and legs, shielding him from his persecutors with his body. The unusual sight of an elderly gentleman collapsed on top of a servant brought the thrashing to a rapid halt.

"My boy, my boy," Grandpa wept, hugging and cradling Dheeraj. "I promised your mother I'd shelter you. I have failed her. I have let you down." And he kept rocking back and forth over the comatose Dheeraj, moaning, "My boy," over and over. The crowd stared at this fresh spectacle, astonished.

I thought Grandpa was overcome by Dheeraj's wounded state. After all, he had served him for so many years. But then I noticed Grandma's condition. The pouch of flesh beneath her chin was quivering uncontrollably. Her color was that of dry, old dust. Her arms fell loosely by her side and the top of her nightie parted open most immodestly. She took a step back and squatted in a heap on the low front step, like the colony washerwoman. For a moment she sat very still. Then she swayed gently from side to side. In a raspy, shredded voice she cried: "The old man's mind is mush from the shock. He speaks rubbish, rubbish. . . ."

My hands and feet had gone clammy and cold even though it was a sunny day. I knew the sensation well—I'd felt the same way the morning I woke up and realized my parents were gone.

The crowd had fallen quiet and moved back from the injured Dheeraj. Their gaze turned from Grandma to Grandpa, from Grandpa to Grandma. "Get up, Grandma," I said, shaking her arm as hard as I could. The whole neighborhood was watching.

Rose had a baby girl, her second child. The father, they said, was her old Goan husband, with whom she had reconciled. No one believed this, but the colony didn't dare speak ill of Musto now. Rose continued to live in Musto's house, where Neeta slowly recovered from her illness. Rose and Musto's evening walks resumed.

I saw Rose at close quarters in the market once, her baby in a pram. She was dressed in a fashionable white and magenta pantsuit, and her hair was styled very short around her broad face. Before I could hide she approached me. "How are you, Sanju *beta*? What news from your Mummy and Papa?" The *paan* stains, I noticed, were gone from her teeth. She looked at me so kindly I smiled back without thinking. I was about to answer when I remembered what Grandma had called her: *common prostitute.* I made my face hard and walked brusquely past on the sidewalk. From then on I was careful to cross the street whenever I saw her wheeling her pram.

Dheeraj Singh was sentenced to prison for two years despite Grandpa's efforts on his behalf. Grandpa wrote and received a lot of letters at this time, and made a long trip (I wasn't told where). After the trial was over, he spent his time reading books on improving his bridge game, even though he rarely went out to play anymore. Grandma and Grandpa talked to the TV when they had something to say to each other; they would nod yes or no at the news announcer.

As a result of these events, Grandma lost both her ally and her target. She, too, left the house much less frequently now, so Aunty Neeta had to come to our place when she wanted to see her. Musto never came. Grandma became noticeably fatter because of her lack of exercise. She stopped dyeing her hair, which grew out stark white. No one threw rocks at us, as I had feared, but on a rare winter afternoon when she and I were out for a colony stroll, an old lady passing by made ugly eyes at us and muttered a curse. Grandma squeezed my hand mercilessly as she dragged me back home.

"What crime have *I* committed?" she said many times under her breath. It sounded like old Grandma, but the bark was gone from her voice.

That night, like so many to follow, she crept into my bed. When I woke up toward morning, she was fast asleep and shivering. Strands of stringy hair were stuck to her forehead. Somewhere in the dark her comforter had slipped off.

L. E. Miller

Kind

YEARS LATER, Ann saw one of the daughters. She ended up seated beside her on a flight from New York to Chicago, the odds who knows how many millions to one.

As strangers will in transit, they began talking. Ann learned that the woman taught high school English and was just now trying her hand at playwriting, that she had never married but had lived with someone off and on for years. After a while, exchanging names seemed beside the point. Ann wondered why this woman seemed familiar, but now that she was seventy-seven, almost everyone she met reminded her of someone she used to know. Still, there was something about her: an expression that was both discerning and compassionate, those pale eyes of no identifiable color, those graying curls poised to spring from their clip. When the flight attendant came by with honey peanuts, Ann's seatmate slipped her reading glasses onto the tip of her nose and peered at the list of ingredients on the package. Even this gesture echoed that of someone Ann had known years before.

"I think I won't," she said, and handed the peanuts back to the slightly flustered stewardess.

"By the way, I'm Bianca Sunderlund," the woman said, an afterthought as the plane angled toward its descent.

Sunderlund. With that name, everything came back in a rush: a lobby in an apartment building, once elegant but fallen into disrepair; a dark painting shot through with streaks of color; the vertigo Ann had felt at twenty-two, living alone for the first time in her life.

Before she quite knew what she was doing, Ann grasped her seatmate's forearm. "Was your mother Edith Sunderlund? Was your father Hugh Sunderlund, the painter?"

Bianca's eyes widened, but her long career in the public schools had left her practiced at hiding any shock she might have felt. "Hugh Sunderlund, the painter." She chortled. "My father spent his whole life waiting for somebody to say that."

The Sunderlunds had lived in the apartment next door. Bianca and her sister had become in Ann's memory a tumble of curls and wild races down badly lit hallways. It was their mother, Edith, who shone most brightly in Ann's consciousness back then, and, later, their father, Hugh.

"I was your neighbor on Columbus Avenue," Ann exclaimed. "Your mother and I were friends. When I met your parents, I'd never met anyone like them. I always thought of them as the first original bohemians."

"*My* parents? That's rich."

"I remember you and your sister very well," Ann pressed on, a gambit to keep the conversation afloat. A skeptical voice bubbled up and queried: you and Edith? *Friends*? Yes, Ann thought. We were.

She felt Bianca looking at her, taking measure of her thin white hair, held back by two barrettes, her no-iron pantsuit and—her one vanity—her carefully tended hands. Ann knew she looked every inch the faded Connecticut matron; though she had not been born to that life, it had become hers. Bianca had been only ten or eleven when Ann was already a young woman living on her own, but her shrewd gaze cut through the decades. Ann felt anxious, culpable.

There was no reason to feel that way. Nothing had happened. It was all so long ago.

"Hmm," Bianca said. "I don't remember you at all."

It is such a familiar story it is almost a cliché: a girl comes to the city in the 1930s or '40s or '50s with two suitcases and half-formed artistic or vocational or intellectual intentions. There were thousands upon thousands of such girls then, eating lunch at a corner coffee shop, passing through turnstiles in the subway, stretching their typist's or bank teller's salary to afford leather gloves or tickets to the opera, but each girl believed she was unique. Each believed she had embarked on a journey that was nothing short of revolutionary. At the time, Ann believed it about herself.

She was from Waverly Falls, Massachusetts, in the western corner of the state, twenty miles from the Vermont border. The Eagle Paper Mill loomed over the steeply pitched streets, employing all the town's men of working age. The stench that belched from the plant's brick smokestacks defied description, eluded metaphor. On humid days, the yellowish air clung like a film, stinging the eyes, burning the inside of the nose and throat. Ann coughed and coughed, but she could never rid herself of that smell. Waste dyes poured from open pipes into the river. From the time she was small, Ann was drawn to the river. She was drawn to the jeweled colors that eddied around the rocks and to the stories: the daredevil boys who had gone over the falls in barrels, the desperate pregnant girls who had jumped. She believed in ghosts. Standing at the river's edge, she heard the drowned whisper, *go, go, go.*

She was a smart girl; she earned good grades. She won a scholarship to Marymount, and when she graduated, she moved into Manhattan, known to her chiefly from a few tightly budgeted shopping trips she'd made with girls from her dormitory. In dizzying succession, she found a job with Travelers Aid, she rented the apartment on Columbus at Eighty-fourth, and, stunned by her own audacity, she bought a double bed on layaway. With some foreboding, she stopped attending mass and spent lonely Sundays wandering through the corridors of the Metropolitan Museum. She lost her virginity to a man she met at a play-reading group, whose personality was a patchwork of strong opinions. Although the experience fell short for her, she realized the moment she agreed to go to bed with him was the moment she truly left home. Though she continued to answer her mother's weekly letters, almost everything she wrote was a lie.

She wrote, for example, that the apartment building was "classy," an adjective her mother assigned half cynically to things that lay beyond her reach. In truth, whatever grandeur the building had once had was gone; tiles were missing from the vestibule's mosaic floor; the carved stone grapes over the entrance had turned black with grime. Despite the exterminator's weekly visits, cockroaches scuttled along the bathroom floor, caught in the sudden light. Back then, in the early 1950s, the neighborhood was like that, run-down in a genteel way. A single girl just starting out could afford to live there, though she'd likely feel she was biding her time until she could live elsewhere: on the East Side or in Westchester if she married well.

Although Ann would have said that marriage was the last thing on her mind, her future seemed nonetheless tied up in men. Therefore, it was Hugh she noticed first of the four Sunderlunds. He was extraordinarily tall; she guessed at least six feet five. He slipped though the hallways with the silent watchfulness of a crow. His tan coveralls were smeared with grease, and Ann thought at first that he was the building super. When she realized that the deep greens and earthy browns on his clothes were oil paint, that Hugh was an artist—and not a Sunday hobbyist—she flushed with an old, provincial embarrassment.

Hugh was the most intriguing of the Sunderlunds, but Edith was the most accessible.

"Tell me your secret. How do you stay so slim?" Edith asked Ann whenever she saw her, giving Ann's waist a squeeze. "As you can see, my interest is strictly anthropological."

Or she'd press a worn paperback edition of Freud's *The Interpreta-*

tion of Dreams or Ibsen's *A Doll's House* into Ann's hands. "You *must* read this. It will change your life."

Ann had never met anyone with so little vanity. Edith's hems drooped; her heavy-framed reading glasses slid down toward the tip of her nose as she rushed through the hallway, her tread heavy in the boxy leather sandals she wore all year. Her curls, threaded with gray, defied all attempts to rein them in. Every few weeks she came around, collecting for one local family or another that was facing misfortune or for "our Negro brothers and sisters in the South." Each cause seemed so urgent, Ann always dropped some money in the jar. She really had none to spare, and the petty economies she had to practice for days afterward left her resentful and ashamed of her ungenerous heart.

"When we married, Hugh and I chose a life of voluntary poverty," Edith told Ann one day. They were standing near the mailboxes in the vestibule of their building. Ann had just donated a dollar to help send a girl from Harlem to college, and Edith was eating hunks of bread torn from a loaf tucked away in her canvas tote bag. Although the sweet, buttery smell of the bread made Ann's stomach growl, she shook her head when Edith held out the ragged loaf, shy of making her hunger so visible to the world.

"I was twenty," Edith continued. "So young, it breaks my heart to think."

Voluntary poverty, Ann learned, meant the Sunderlunds made one another birthday gifts from fabric scraps, the funny pages, cigar boxes that the man at the tobacco shop put aside for them. Voluntary poverty meant that the girls attended the Ethical Culture school on scholarship. (What was Ethical Culture, exactly? Ann couldn't bring herself to ask, to reveal her ignorance on yet another topic.) In exchange, Hugh cleaned the school building once a week.

Ann learned that Edith was a social worker in Harlem. "We should hang our heads in shame, the way people live up there." Edith closed her eyes, as she was liable to do when overcome with strong feeling.

She learned that Hugh was indeed a painter. "A painter, *not* an artist. He *hates* being called an artist. He finds the word so . . . effete."

Ann told Edith about her job with Travelers Aid. She was only a caseworker, the bottom-of-the-barrel position, but she knew she was lucky to have a job beyond the usual typing and filing, a job with a higher purpose. She met the boats at the West Side piers and helped the disembarking passengers find their way to their final destinations. The boats arrived from Trieste and Marseille and Lisbon and Rotterdam. It was so exciting when a boat came in, families crowding on the pier, the dock workers' cries for coopers and interpreters and doctors. But each arrival was tinged with sadness, she told Edith. Many arrived with nothing more than a cousin's friend's address. They'd lost everything in the war.

As time went on, she told Edith about growing up in Waverly Falls, the fourth of seven children and one of twenty-one first cousins. She told Edith how she and all the others roamed from one apartment to another in the triple-decker for meals and play. But there was no privacy ever, she added defensively, anticipating the usual pieties about how warm her childhood sounded. She described the narrow rooms, left unlit through dusk to save on the electric bill. The only art on the walls, she said, were images of Jesus and Mary. Even in the bathroom, they hung there, witnesses to the basest bodily functions.

Ann didn't quite feel she was speaking as herself but rather that she was performing, turning a childhood that was no more unhappy than anyone else's into a grotesquerie for Edith's amusement. She burned with guilt, but Edith simply clasped her hand. "Metaphorically speaking, it is necessary to kill one's parents in order to leave home."

Edith herself had grown up in a German Jewish family on Central Park West, in a ten-room apartment with a maid. ("I could never enter into that kind of relationship with anybody now," she told Ann, "to tell someone to do what I can easily do myself.") When she met Hugh, a gentile from Washington State, her parents made her choose between him and the family into which she'd been born. Edith chose. Her mother, not normally a religious woman, said the Hebrew prayer for the dead.

"When the girls were being born," Edith told Ann on another occasion, "I had no anesthesia. I wanted to feel it all. It was easier the second time, but you still think you'll split in two. You just don't believe your body can open up that way. Motherhood is just the same. It rends you every day the same way, but your love is fierce. It's irrational."

Did Edith forget how young Ann was, closer to her daughters' age than her own? Edith's candor warmed her, but it also unsettled her. To know such personal things: What might she owe Edith in the way of confidences or allegiance?

Several months into their friendship, Edith invited Ann to dinner. "I can't cook to save my life, but the conversation's always lively."

"Look at you. You *are* the spirit of fall."

It was Hugh Sunderlund who answered the door the night Ann came to dinner. His speech seemed both intimate and staged, lacquered with irony and innuendo. Ann was dressed in her tan skirt and rust-colored blouse. The outfit had stood out as the best choice out of the limited selection in her closet, but now that she was standing beneath Hugh's appraising gaze, it seemed a desperate grasp at sophistication. She regretted the sugar cookies she'd bought at the bakery—she should have gone for the babas au rhum—but all she could do now was hand him the string-tied box.

Edith appeared beside Hugh in a robe of coarse white cloth. "Oh, Ann. You didn't have to bring anything."

Hugh said, "Strictly speaking, it's 'take.' You'd say she didn't have to *take* anything to us, since her action is away from herself."

"Give. Take. It doesn't matter."

"Of course it matters. Why be wrong if you can be right?"

Edith surprised Ann with a sharp laugh. "Darling. It doesn't matter in the slightest. Are you planning to serve Ann her dinner in the hall? Ann, please come in."

Hugh hit his forehead in mock self-abasement. "Excuse my boorish manners. I was, in fact, brought up in a barn."

The Sunderlunds' apartment was a mirror image of Ann's own. Her bedroom likely shared a wall with Hugh and Edith's, off the living room behind French doors. Her own place was spartan; she relied on one rya rug purchased on clearance and Impressionist postcards tacked to the wall to distract visitors from the fact that she owned neither a sofa nor a proper bed frame. The Sunderlunds' living room resembled all the overstuffed rooms where she'd spent childhood Sundays. Like those rooms, this one was crammed with faded rugs and tables carved with dust-catching knobs. But here at the Sunderlunds', a woman on the phonograph sang in a mournful foreign language. Here, the bookcases sagged with the weight of double-shelved books.

"When I was a child, we had a Bechstein," Edith said. "Piano. I was the only one of my siblings who played. I was good. I practiced for hours every day. My sister has it now. She still can't find middle C."

Edith's smile seemed to Ann forged with great effort. As was often the case with Edith, her statement, delivered with such matter-of-factness, flickered with an ever-shifting backdrop of emotions Ann struggled to grasp and name. Did Edith expect a response from her? If so, what was she supposed to say?

She was delivered by Hugh, who boomed out, "Come eat," in his languid *basso profundo*.

Ann did her best with the fake meatloaf made from lentils and the gelatinous mushroom gravy. She did her best with a stringy, bitter green vegetable and a chewy brown grain. Two skinny cats skulked around the table, pausing to nose up at the plates. They were Persians with singed-looking fur.

"Quit begging, you mangy beasts!" Bianca, the younger girl, shrieked. She had come to the table in an untucked blouse and rumpled kilt.

"What do you think this is, a welfare state?" Edith picked up one of the cats. Cradling it in her lap, she stroked it behind its enormous ears.

"Ma, do you *have* to wear that housecoat all the time?" the older girl asked. Her name was Imogene.

"It's not a housecoat. It's called a djellaba. It happens to be very comfortable," Edith replied with what sounded like a practiced patience. She turned to Ann. "A friend of ours brought it back from Tangier."

"Our rich, successful friend." Hugh spoke for the first time since he had sat down at the table.

"Tom sold a painting to Peggy Guggenheim for five hundred dollars," Edith said. "That hardly makes him rich."

"That makes him five hundred dollars richer than us. You poor dear. When you married me, your fortunes fell precipitously."

"But they rose in other ways." Edith smiled gamely and patted Hugh's arm. She turned to her daughters. "Ann has a fascinating job, girls. She meets the ships that come in and helps the war refugees get settled. Maybe you'd like to hear about it."

The daughters exchanged lightning-quick smirks. "We'd like to. Very much!" Imogene said.

Across the table, Hugh added in his unfathomable voice, "Yes. Tell us a story from your job."

A story? Most of the refugees managed to create a life of one sort or another. Once in a while someone could not, and his life took a terrible turn, but that was not the type of story she could tell to entertain people at the dinner table. There was one incident, the closest thing to a story she had. With the Sunderlunds' eyes on her, she began. A young German woman had disembarked the month before. After landing in New York, she would travel on to a town called Hastings, Minnesota, to meet up with her fiancé. Ann was supposed to bring (take? she wondered now) the woman to her train. However, the woman did not know that there was also a Hastings, New York, and Ann did not think to clarify which Hastings was the woman's final destination. She accompanied the woman to Grand Central rather than Pennsylvania Station for the Westchester-bound train she believed the woman wanted.

"Oh, no," said Edith. "What did you do then?"

When she discovered the mistake, Ann had hailed a cab and gotten the woman across town to Penn Station; she'd managed to shove some bills under the ticket seller's window and load the woman and her suitcases onto her west-bound train just as the whistle started to blow. She hoped in her telling to seem resourceful, heroic. She didn't tell the Sunderlunds how the woman had hissed, "You stupid, stupid girl," just before she boarded. How Ann stood on the platform perilously close to tears.

Hugh reached for one of her cookies and munched it, scattering crumbs. "If she'd gone to the other Hastings, she might have married someone else entirely. She might have become a torch singer or a racehorse breeder. Her life could have turned out completely different." Ann noticed that the skin on Hugh's face was pitted, perhaps with scars from a childhood illness. A girl with skin like that would never have a chance, she thought. Still, he had a certain rough appeal, with his broad Swedish cheekbones and silvering hair. His other features were surprisingly delicate for a man of his size. His eyes were the color of a frozen lake.

Imogene and Bianca glanced at each other. "May we be excused?" they asked in unison.

"Yes, you may," Edith said. "And I am going downstairs to give Mrs. Neville her soup. Thank you so much for coming, Ann."

With more than a little relief, Ann realized there would be no awkward lingering over coffee. She had been released.

. . .

"Perhaps you could settle a dispute."

Caught in her efforts to free her pocketbook from a tangle of scarves on the table near the front door, Ann startled at Hugh's voice. Edith had left to see the elderly neighbor. The girls had gone to play a game; their screams and laughter carried over from the next room.

"This will only take a minute. One minute. Scout's honor."

"What is it?" Ann longed to slip her left foot from her pinching pump. Edith had eaten dinner barefoot. She'd slipped on her sandals to leave with the soup and then only as an afterthought.

"I'm wondering if you'd look at a painting of mine. It's been the cause of some dissension here."

"I . . . really don't know anything about painting," Ann stammered.

"But you seem like a perceptive girl. I'd value your opinion."

It occurred to her that Hugh might try to make some sort of a pass, but she dismissed this thought as soon as it entered her mind. She was not the kind of girl to whom such things happened. And Hugh did not seem stupid enough or desperate enough to attempt it with his wife just downstairs and his daughters not twenty feet away. Ann followed him back into the living room. She waited by the dining table, still littered with the remains of the dinner, while he moved into the darkness and turned on lamps. He reached behind a bookcase and pulled out a large, paper-wrapped canvas. He moved bed pillows and a blanket from the sofa and piled them onto an end table. Hugh and Edith slept on that sofa, Ann realized. The girls shared the room behind the French doors. Hugh hoisted the canvas onto the sofa. He untied the knot and slipped the string off the paper.

"Come here. You can't see a thing back there."

At first all she saw was black, the paint so thickly layered, he must have applied it with a knife. But as she looked longer, she began to make out a great, mossy foot and leg, cut off at the knee. Knobbed toes twisted out at the bottom of the canvas, reaching toward the viewer. They were brown, midnight blue, deep forest green. Looking longer still, she saw streaks of gold running through them. She saw blood red.

Hugh pointed at the tunneling limbs. "This is the area under discussion."

It was a test, she believed, of her perceptiveness, her discrimination. "They're roots. Roots of a tree," she finally said. "Aren't they?"

"Sitka spruce. They grow out west. When I was a boy, I slept out in the woods whenever I could. I never brought a tent. The summer I was fifteen, I read the *Oresteia* by moonlight. Anyway, my wife thinks they look like phalluses. I'd be interested in your opinion."

So he was attempting a more subtle ambush: to expose her as the uptight Catholic schoolgirl she feared she might always be. Did he think so little of his work that he'd use it to such cheap ends?

Ann turned from the painting. She forced herself to hold his ice-blue gaze. "I don't think so. The ones I've seen don't look anything like this."

After the dinner, Ann felt anxious every time she saw Edith in the hall. The most basic rules of etiquette dictated that she return the invitation, but dinner for the Sunderlunds was not just dinner; it was feints and parries; it was anger masquerading as jokes. There were practical considerations as well. She didn't own enough plates to invite the four.

"Please don't worry about inviting us," Edith said one day at the mailboxes. "I know we're a lot to take on."

But the two continued their hallway conversations. Ann learned that Hugh was working on a new series inspired by the atomic testing in Nevada earlier that year. He was waiting to hear about a commission for which he was in the running, a mural about the march of science for the lobby at Pfizer pharmaceuticals. Ann thought the subject wrong for Hugh, but she said nothing. He would be paid three thousand dollars, Edith told her; enough to keep them from the edge of the cliff for another year.

. . .

One wintry night, a few months after she went to the Sunderlunds' for dinner, Ann heard a knock on her door, a jaunty "shave and a haircut" beat. She was just back from meeting the boat from Trieste. She had bundled her passengers into taxis and onto subways, off to the flophouses and cold-water rooms where each would sleep his lonely, fractured sleep. It was nine thirty, late for company but not yet the hour when a knock signaled an emergency. When she peered through the one-way mirror in the door, Hugh's face blinked back, distorted through the lens.

It would have been wise to ignore his knock entirely. It would have been wise to leave the chain on, open the door a crack and find out what he wanted. But to be cautious would have exposed the visceral unease he stirred up in her. It would have kept her just where he expected her to remain.

She opened the door and let him in. "To what do I owe the pleasure of your company?" She meant to sound bold, but her voice trailed off uncertainly.

Hugh swept the air with his arm. "I was in the neighborhood. Just looking for that clean, well-lighted place." He removed a six-pack of Ballantine from a damp paper bag.

Ann took an instinctive step back. "Where's Edith?"

"Out helping the lame and halt." In an offhand yet fully intentional way, Hugh looked her over. His gaze was like a touch, much more exciting than any of the maneuvers attempted by the man from the play-reading group. Ann wrapped her bathrobe more tightly around herself.

Hugh shook his finger at her, playfully scolding. "You remind me of someone. There's a painting at the Modern of a movie usherette. You have something of her self-containment."

Ann laughed uneasily. "I guess I'll take that as a compliment."

"Please do."

Several years later, Ann would see the painting again, a famous Edward Hopper. The usherette, who stood alone in the dark in the corner of the canvas, looked shockingly young. Ann would remember Hugh's comment with puzzlement. She had nothing in common with this girl. She had recently married. She believed herself protected from such vulnerability.

"Here's where you say, 'Hugh, can I take your coat?' "

Ann held out her arm, and Hugh draped his coat over it. The sleet crusted on his collar had begun to melt and drip onto the floor. She hung the coat over the knob of her front door. To hang it anywhere else, she believed, would send an engraved invitation for trouble.

"I don't have any clean glasses."

"No clean glasses! Now *that's* a catastrophe of the highest order!"

Hugh had been drinking already. His oversize, sloppy gestures gave him away. His coat smelled of it, too. Nonetheless, she had let him come in. When he opened a can of Ballantine and handed it to her, she took it. Was Hugh so commanding a personality that she abandoned all common sense? She was feeling homesick that night— the sound of sleet against the windows made her miss Waverly Falls, whispering in the dark with her sisters. What made her crave his company, such potentially dangerous company? She couldn't say. Many years later, she still couldn't say. She showed Hugh into the living room, to the one upholstered chair. She sat across from him in a straight-backed wooden chair. She felt a thrilling turbulence, sitting so close to him; she could perceive him only in fragments: the sliver-moons of paint around his fingernails. His finely chiseled brow and nose. His eyes so light they were almost no color at all.

"Chin chin." He touched his can to hers.

"What are we drinking to?"

"Pfizer pharmaceuticals." He pulled out a rumpled paper from his pocket. "*After careful consideration, the Committee has selected an artist whose vision is more consonant with that of the company.* . . . So here's to me. Bottoms up."

"Oh, gosh. That's a real blow."

"The money would have been nice, too."

"You were really counting on it?"

Hugh laughed bitterly. "That money's been spent many times over. Christ, I'd do better by my family selling pencils on the IRT."

Ann took a nervous sip of beer. She thought she knew something of the disappointments of women, but whatever failure or grief men experienced they worked out . . . where? At the bar, perhaps. On the ball field. At the Franco-American Social Club. "What does Edith say?"

Hugh slipped into a higher, mournful register. "Oh, Hugh. Those Pfizer men are philistines! They wouldn't know art if it hit them in the face!"

He closed his eyes with histrionic empathy. How ugly he was, Ann thought. How cruel. But he looked just like Edith then; he sounded just like her. Ann felt her mouth tug itself into a smile.

She said, "Edith is very kind."

"Edith is a saint. We mortals are lucky to kiss the hem of her skirt. Tell me this. Any poor slob can pick up a paintbrush and call himself an artist. But if you're not selling your work and you're not getting shows, you're not an artist. You're a loser. And if that's the case, what's all the heartbreak for? What is my fucking, two-bit, son-of-a-sawmill-worker's life for?"

Ann thought herself a modern girl, but she blushed nonetheless when he said "fucking." She thought of her father and uncles at the paper mill, who believed they worked good jobs for decent pay. She thought of all the stonemasons and cobblers and butchers who poured off the ships, hoping to take up their old lives or a semblance of them.

"There are many ways to have a meaningful life," she said.

"How did you get to be so smart?"

"I'm . . . not, really," she stammered.

"Sure you are."

He reached across and took her hand. He stroked her fingers, squeezing and releasing, squeezing and releasing. His touch was teasing, tender, hungry.

"I should go," he said, but he did not let go.

"Yes." The word stuck in her throat like a fish bone.

"No. I really have to go." Hugh dropped her hand. As he went to retrieve his coat from her doorknob, Ann told herself it was all for the best. Whatever flimsy spell he had managed to cast was now broken.

Later that night, Ann awakened to pounding on her door. It was very late. Only someone in desperate straits would show up at that hour. Someone who wished her harm. Hugh again? She lay in bed and pulled the covers up over her head. Maybe if she just lay still, he would go away. But the knocking continued, frantic, impossible to ignore. She padded out to the front room. With trembling fingers, she slid away the brass plate and looked through the peephole. Edith's face goggled back. In the one-way mirror, she looked pop-eyed, wild.

"Ann?

"Ann? Are you there?"

What were you doing with my husband? If Edith were to ask her that, how would she reply? In a literal sense, the answer was drinking beer. Talking. Nothing.

Edith rapped again. "Are you there?"

Ann felt she had no choice but to open the door.

Edith rushed inside. Her overcoat hung open over her nightgown. Released from their daytime pins, her curls spilled down her back.

"Do you know where Hugh is?"

"No, I don't." Ann's heart raced. In her befuddlement, she had forgotten to put on her bathrobe. She felt naked in her nightgown and her bare feet.

"He hasn't been home all night. I thought you might know."

"Well, I don't."

Edith's face crumpled. The right thing to do was make her a cup of milky tea, but all Ann could think was, *Leave, just leave.* The moment passed, like a skip on a record. Edith's face was smooth again. She clasped Ann's hand and said, "I forgive you."

"Excuse me?"

"My husband is a magnetic creative personality. Girls are drawn to him all the time. I understand and I forgive you."

Ann slipped her hand free. Could Edith read minds, discern the attraction that had flickered momentarily between her and Hugh? "I'm sorry. I don't know what you're talking about."

"Men are different from us. They think they're strong, but they're actually very weak. You go around the block a few times, you learn things. Long ago, I decided I have no room for jealousy in my life."

Ann's heart pounded with confusion, with guilt, with anger, with fear. "Nothing happened between me and Hugh. I haven't even seen him tonight. And I don't think of him, you know, that way."

"I see. Well . . ." Edith buttoned her overcoat, then raked her hand through her hair. "Good night, Ann. Have a good night."

Much later, Ann heard rising and falling voices through her bedroom wall. She heard a woman weeping.

"Did your parents stay in that building? Are they still alive?" Ann asked Bianca. They had just touched down in Chicago. Soon she and Bianca would disembark, claim their baggage, part ways.

"Of course they stayed. Even after my father died in 1982, my mother stayed. She fell down the subway stairs a couple of years ago. She won't say it, but she was really pushed. She lost her pocketbook, so she had to have been pushed. Anyway, she was fine until then, but right after that, things took a downward turn and we moved her out."

Ann could have asked Bianca a thousand questions, but all she said was that it often happened that way: a fall was the beginning of the end.

"You could go see her. She won't know you from Adam, but she likes having visitors."

Ann said she would try. She wished Bianca Sunderlund well. She edged toward the aisle and the line of passengers filing past.

.   .   .

"Hel-lo there."

After that night, whenever he passed her in the hallway, Hugh had greeted Ann with the smoothness of a radio announcer.

Edith, as always, rushed through the hall with her overflowing tote bag, those unflattering glasses perched on the tip of her nose. "We must get together. You must come over for dinner again," she called to Ann over her shoulder, never waiting for a reply.

Did Edith believe nothing had happened? Did she believe the ugly exchange between them had been a dream?

Edith left things at Ann's doorstep: a pot of soup; a handmade collage, a whirl of razored bits of wrapping paper, for her birthday. The design was beautiful, terrifying. Ann ended up throwing out the soup and leaving the washed-out pot by Edith's door. She ended up throwing out the collage. She believed Edith was trying to buy her allegiance, to draw the two of them inside a circle that excluded Hugh. Hugh was right about one thing: after a while, you couldn't live with someone like Edith. After a while, she exposed everything dark within you. Ann stopped returning Edith's hurried hellos. She pretended not to see her.

That summer Ann met the man she would marry. She and her husband followed the geographic aspirations of the time, moving first into a larger apartment on the East Side, then to Connecticut. They had their children. Years passed. The poisoned river was implicated in a cancer cluster in Waverly Falls. Rod Arsenault, Davey Daigneault, Gerry Dohr, and even Ann's own brother, Roland, succumbed. Ann and her husband divorced. She forgot about the Sunderlunds until articles appeared in the newspaper about the vanishing forests of the Pacific Northwest.

After Ann returned home from Chicago, she dropped the paper Bianca had scribbled on into a basket on her desk. Star of David Home Convalescent and Care Center. She did not expect to visit. At seventy-seven, she had seen enough friends threaded with tubes in hospitals and extended-care facilities. She had witnessed enough journeys to death.

But one day in the fall, she went into the city for a concert at the 92nd Street Y. Afterward, on a whim, she decided to take a later train back. She wandered over to Park Avenue, then turned south to browse in the shop windows. Everything she remembered was gone: the cafeterias where meals cost less than a dollar, the apartments that could be rented for a quarter of one's take-home pay.

She passed a white brick building, one of many such along those blocks. Discreet steel letters announced its business: Star of David Home Convalescent and Care Center. Although she felt a wave of atavistic anxiety as she entered the pastel lobby, she knew she had been graced by the gift of a second chance, and at seventy-seven, she knew how rare a gift this was.

Edith was tiny now, a parched little leaf in her hospital bed. Someone had tied a ribbon in her sparse hair. Her fingers were twisted, knobbed with arthritis, yet someone had painted her fingernails pink. It was a shock to see Edith so diminished, done up like a doll.

"Miss Edith. There's a lady here to see you." A round-faced nurse's aide leaned over and spoke directly into Edith's ear.

"Ann Beckwith. Ann Cyr," Ann repeated, using her maiden name. "From the building on Columbus."

"*This* ear," the nurse's aide said in her precise Caribbean accent. "She only hears out of her left." The beads in her hair clicked together as she bustled out.

Edith registered neither the aide's departure nor Ann's arrival. In profile, her nose was like a beak, hooked and astute. All her softness was gone. She'd been pared down to sinew and bone. Ann leaned toward Edith's left ear. She told Edith who she was, that they had known each other many years ago. She said she had seen Bianca recently, that she remembered both daughters. Slowly, Edith turned her head toward Ann's voice. Her eyes were milky with cataracts.

"I'm afraid I can't. I never cross a picket line." Her voice came out as clear as it had when she was young—and she had been young back then, not even forty.

On a bulletin board across from the bed, tacked beside a calendar of generic nature scenes, Ann glimpsed a black-and-white photograph. She moved closer to study it. In the picture, a couple stood together on a roof against a backdrop of water towers. The man was fair-haired, his features chiseled and handsome. The woman, short and plump, leaned back against his chest. Her dark curls flared in the breeze. The man's hand rested under her blouse, just above her breasts, on her skin.

"Is that you and Hugh in the picture over there?" Ann said into Edith's left ear.

Edith blinked. Her mouth twisted but produced no sound.

"You two look so much in love."

Again that voice: bubbling like a spring from seemingly dry ground. "I was twenty when we got married. I chose a life of voluntary poverty."

Ann took Edith's hand. "Yes," she said. "I know."

Alistair Morgan

Icebergs

Toward the end of last summer, when I was combating a bout of loneliness after the death of my wife, a new neighbor moved in next door. He arrived at number 16—I'm number 14—late one night. I had seen the color advertisement for the house in the property section of the *Cape Times:* panoramic views of the Atlantic; three-minute walk from the beach; twenty-minute drive from the center of Cape Town; six bedrooms en suite; swimming pool; double garage; price on application.

The FOR SALE signs went down the same day he moved in. Although when I say "moved in," I don't mean that he was accompanied by a moving van and a stream of brown boxes; he came only with his driver, who, I would later discover, was also his bodyguard. If there were any suitcases I never saw them. I was sitting on my pool deck, having a final cigarette before bed, when I heard him step out onto the balcony of what I imagined was the master bedroom. Even at such a late hour he was formally dressed in a suit and tie. His face was in shadow but I could still make out the glint of his glasses. He stood with one hand in his trouser pocket and stared into the darkness for several minutes. There was no sound apart from the waves throwing themselves onto the rocks below us. We couldn't have been more than ten or fifteen yards from one another, and the cool Atlantic breeze was carrying the smoke from my cigarette up toward him. He cleared his throat, and from out of the shadows around his head I heard a crisp, well-spoken voice say, "Good evening."

"Evening," I replied. "Welcome to Llandudno."

"Thank you. It's very pleasant out here."

"You can feel that autumn's on its way, though."

Whatever he said in reply was lost in the pounding of the waves. After a few moments he said, "Well, good night," and as he turned back toward the light of the curtainless bedroom I caught a brief glimpse of a slender, graying man with dark skin.

He stayed for only two days and then I didn't see him for nearly a month. While he was away several vans delivered furniture, still wrapped in plastic, and later I noticed that curtains had been fitted in the master bedroom. I had recently retired and so had plenty of time to watch these comings and goings. Mostly I am on my own. Three years ago my wife was taken from me in pieces: first her right breast went; then her left breast; then her will to fight; until, finally, what remained of her was wheeled away down a corridor. My two boys are in London, and my daughter still insists on living in Johannesburg, in the same house in which we were all once a family.

For many years I ran an advertising agency in Johannesburg. When I sold my shares in it my wife and I bought the house in which I now live. We were lucky because that was just before the property market erupted and I doubt that I could afford the house today. My wife did most of the interior decorating and oversaw the renovations, but toward the end she became too ill to leave Johannesburg and she never did get to live here. She made me promise to move in after she was gone, as she didn't want strangers living in the dream house we had worked so hard for together. So I spend my days alone, although I am constantly surrounded by her.

Most of the houses here are holiday homes. They stand empty for long periods of the year, and in the summer they fill with tourists—

those that can afford the ridiculous weekly rates for a rental—and local people who have either had the houses in their families for decades or were fortunate enough to buy at the right time. Few people move in permanently. Because of this there isn't any sense of community and people rarely acknowledge their neighbors. And so for company I have to make do with the echoes of my wife's voice.

I suppose it was company I was looking for when I invited my new neighbor over for a drink one afternoon. He was just getting out of his car in the driveway as I was walking back from the beach. As usual he was dressed formally in a suit. He nodded at me, and I walked over and stretched my hand out to him.

"Dennis Moorcraft," I said, feeling his smooth fingers tentatively squeeze my hand.

"Bradshaw."

Later I would read in the newspapers that this was his Christian name. He seemed slightly surprised when I suggested he join me for a sundowner or two, and he glanced at his driver, who was scrutinizing me with heavy-lidded eyes, before politely accepting my offer.

From my pool deck there is an unrestricted view of the Atlantic. My wife had designed it so that it would be the ideal spot to watch the sun setting over the sea. With the ocean so near, and the sounds of the waves as constant as a heartbeat, it sometimes feels as though I'm sitting aboard an ocean liner. As my brother, who now lives in Canada, once said when he came out on a visit, "It's like standing on the upper deck of the *Titanic*."

Bradshaw and I sat side by side, facing out to sea, he in a linen suit and tie, me in a golf shirt and Bermuda shorts. My eyes were drawn to his hands, which seemed to hang in the air in front of him as he spoke, as though they were wet and he was waiting for someone to pass him a hand towel. From time to time he would straighten and bend his wrists to emphasize certain points of his conversation. His fingers were long and thin, like the teeth of a comb, and the nails were in immaculate condition. In fact, everything about him and his clothing was precise and carefully measured. Before speaking, and between sentences, he would suck in his lips and it almost looked as if he were checking the words in his mouth, rolling them over with his tongue, before letting them out.

He appeared to be about my age, but his face did not bear the creases and folds that mine had. We made cautious inquiries about one another's background, as strangers do, and how we had come to be living where we were. He kept his questions vague and circumspect, and I got the impression that he wished me to do the same.

It turned out he was not from South Africa. He was, he said, a businessman from a neighboring country. From what I could gather he was involved in imports and exports. However, he was gradually phasing himself out of his work and he hoped to be fully retired within three months. When I asked him about his family he shrugged and said, "They may visit from time to time." I thought it odd that he would move all this way on his own, particularly when he had such a large house, but then I realized that I was in a similar position and I ushered the conversation on to a less personal subject.

We discovered that we had both spent some time in England. He had studied at the London School of Economics, and I had spent several years working in advertising in London before coming home to start up my own agency. We were drinking Scotch on the rocks, and by the time I'd refreshed our glasses for the third time we were both sitting a little lower in our chairs. Bradshaw's hands became more animated as he spoke.

"A few months ago," he said, "I had to entertain some English businessmen. At the end of their stay I asked them how they liked my country and one of them said, Well, it's not England, and I replied, Oh, so you like it then?"

We both laughed out loud at this, and he reached over and squeezed my forearm.

After reminiscing about our experiences in England, we fell into a contented silence. Perhaps it was the Scotch, but I hoped that Bradshaw and I might become friends. We seemed to share a lot of common ground and, although neither of us mentioned it, I think we both realized that, on the whole, life had been good to us, and we shared a sense of common relief at having got to where we were. No doubt we had very different lives to look back on, but somehow we had ended up together, as neighbors, each retired and alone in a cavernous house.

Later, as I walked him back to the front door, he stopped to study some of the paintings hanging in the hallway. There were seven in total, and they ranged in size from two feet by four feet to six feet by eight feet. They were mostly abstract, although they were composed around natural forms—the rings of a seashell, the bark of a tree, the veins of a leaf. Sometimes parts of the actual objects were mixed into the oils to give the paintings added texture. The lines of the shape were then repeated over and over again, like ripples in water, and by the time these ripples reached the edge of the canvas the original form had evolved into a series of reverberations of itself.

With his glasses in his hand Bradshaw pointed to the largest canvas, which depicted an intricate series of lines around the skull of a rat, and asked, "This is an original?"

"Yes, my daughter is a painter. They're all hers."

He squinted at the signature in the bottom right-hand corner and nodded. "Ah, Melissa Moorcraft. Her name is familiar, actually."

"She has done quite well for herself. Do you like art then?"

"Oh yes. I have a little collection. You should come over one night this week and have a look."

"Thank you. Melissa is going to be coming down from Johannesburg soon, so perhaps we could also get together then. I'm sure she'd be interested to meet you."

"I'd be honored to meet such a talented artist."

We said our good nights and he repeated his invitation for me to come over to his house. But after that evening his house stood dark and silent, with curtains drawn, for three or four weeks, and I presumed he'd been called away on some urgent business.

. . .

Melissa arrived during Bradshaw's absence. Ever since the death of my wife, I'd been campaigning for her to move down to Cape Town. But already, at the age of thirty-one, she was set in her ways, and she was determined to keep on living in the house in Johannesburg. It was as if she could not live beyond the walls of the house and its foundations, which were firmly embedded in the past. Perhaps it was because she felt she was closer than the rest of us to her mother and that she was therefore duty-bound to preserve her memory in bricks and mortar.

Two years ago, she had the house converted into a gallery for her work, though her brothers and I had asked her to move out so that we could sell it. I did not impose any time limits on my children with regard to the mourning of their mother, particularly with Melissa, as she was the youngest; but after three years I felt that it was time for us all to close that chapter in our lives and to start looking ahead again. Melissa's visits to Cape Town were constantly shadowed by these issues.

As always, she had come to paint. Two or three times a year she liked to escape her day-to-day surroundings, come to Cape Town, and work on a new series of paintings. She used one of the spare rooms as a studio and after breakfast she'd excuse herself and disappear until I called her for lunch. That was our routine. In the afternoons we'd walk on the beach or take a drive. She always had her Polaroid camera with her and I was used to having to slam on the brakes and pull over whenever we passed something—a rock, a farmhouse, a horizon line—that she thought she could use in a painting.

We had parked on the edge of a forest so that she could capture the texture of the arthritic-looking limb of a pine tree when I mentioned my new neighbor.

"He sounds a bit weird," she said as she waited for a Polaroid of the tree to develop. "Why do you think he's on his own?"

"Don't know. Maybe his family will move down when he's fully retired. Or perhaps he's divorced. Anyway, I'm sure you'll have a chance to meet him one of these days."

That evening was unusually warm, and Melissa and I ate dinner out on the deck. Afterward we drank red wine and smoked as the sea played its usual symphony on the rocks below. Occasionally, Melissa liked to smoke a joint. Although I disapproved I preferred her to do it in front of me rather than sneak around behind my back. She also became very chatty when she smoked, and I enjoyed our after-dinner conversations.

"Uncle Bruce might be coming out for Christmas," I said, referring to my brother in Canada.

"Well, don't expect me to be here if he does," she said. Her knees were pulled up under her chin and she was hugging her shins. "He's never got a good word to say about this country, but he's only too happy to come back once a year and sponge off you."

"He's my brother. I don't consider it sponging. And he's got plenty of good things to say. Why do you think he comes back almost every December?"

"Have you ever experienced a Canadian winter?"

"You're just cynical."

"I'm cynical? He's the one who stood out here last time and said it was like the upper bloody deck of the *Titanic*. If people want to emigrate that's fine. But they shouldn't be allowed back into the country afterward. It's like leaving your husband or wife and only popping back now and again for a quick shag." She plucked a piece of weed from her tongue and flicked it away.

We were silent for a few minutes and then I asked, "How is Jo'burg? Are you still happy up there? There's plenty of room here if you ever—"

"Dad . . . I wish you wouldn't bring this up every time. There's a fat fucking chance of me moving to Cape Town. All my friends are in Jo'burg, my work is there, I love the old house, and, anyway, we'd drive each other nuts. And this place feels like an abandoned holiday resort for most of the year—all these houses like empty seashells."

I must have looked hurt, because she said sorry and leaned over to kiss me. She smoked the rest of the joint and I finished off the wine.

And then she cleared the table and I carried in the cushions from the chairs. As I walked inside I looked up to Bradshaw's bedroom window and thought I saw the curtain moving.

The next day, after Melissa had emerged from her morning in the makeshift studio, we decided to take a picnic down to the beach. Although it wasn't a particularly warm day the sky was clear and the air was still. I think it was the last fair day we had before the winter clouds rolled in. As it was a weekday, we practically had the beach to ourselves. While I unpacked the picnic basket Melissa stripped down to her bikini and briefly endured the sharp Atlantic water. For a moment, as she trotted back to her towel, she could have been her mother. She had the same springy rust-colored hair and pale skin; I could clearly see the blue highways of veins that transported her mother's remaining blood along the contours of her spindly legs. It was only in the eyes that Melissa differed greatly from her mother: her mother's were a life-giving green, whereas Melissa's were the color of an overcast sky.

We ate some ham-and-cheese rolls and then settled down on our towels. I had brought the newspaper with me and Melissa had her iPod. She placed the headphones over her ears, removed her bikini top, and lay back to gather what sun she could. I hid behind my newspaper.

I suppose I must have fallen asleep. When I surfaced again my face was in shadow. A familiar voice floated in over the waves breaking on the beach: "Good afternoon, Dennis." It was Bradshaw.

I blinked, then stood up and shook his hand. He was wearing a long-sleeved collared shirt with no tie and formal trousers, which he'd carefully rolled up over his ankles to reveal his elegant feet.

"You've been away some time."

"Yes," said Bradshaw, his eyes skimming over Melissa's body. "I had to attend to some matters at home. I'm looking forward to some rest now."

"I'm afraid you may have missed the last of the good weather."

"Oh, I don't mind. The beach doesn't really appeal to me."

"Well, when you've had some rest you should come over again. My daughter, Melissa, is staying with me." I pointed to Melissa, but as I did so I remembered that she was topless and I dropped my hand to my side.

"Yes, I noticed. The artist."

"She's been quite busy with some new work, actually."

"Really? I'd be very interested to meet her. I'm looking to add to my collection."

"Perhaps tomorrow night then?"

"I look forward to it."

He wandered off down the beach, and I lit a cigarette. And all the while Melissa lay on her back, with a T-shirt covering her face and the iPod shouting in her ears.

"You should have said something to me," she said later, as we prepared supper in the kitchen.

"How? You were listening to music. And it was awkward with you topless and everything."

"Oh, don't be such a prude, Dad."

"I think he was probably more embarrassed than I was. He didn't stick around for too long."

"I'm sure he's seen plenty of breasts before."

"Maybe," I said, although for some reason it was hard to imagine Bradshaw having been with a woman.

Bradshaw came by as arranged the next evening, and I introduced him to Melissa. They were still shaking hands when Bradshaw began to speak about her paintings.

"I find your work very charming," he said. "Have you ever worked in just pencil or charcoal?"

"Not since I was an undergrad. People know me more for my textured layers than anything else."

And as she spoke I could see the young Melissa emerging from within the invisible layers in which she had repeatedly wrapped herself since her mother's death. I was startled at how easily Bradshaw had pierced this armor. Melissa stood with one leg behind the other, just as she used to do as a teenager when she wanted pocket money or some other favor from me.

"Well, it's easy to see why you're so well known."

"Dad says you have a collection of your own."

"Just a small one," he said with a thin smile. "I don't like to keep too many pieces down here in the sea air: it can be a very corrupting influence."

We went through to the lounge where I had managed to get the first fire of the winter going in the fireplace. Bradshaw sat next to Melissa on the sofa facing the fireplace, and I sat in an armchair to the side. We made small talk about other local artists, where to eat out in Cape Town, wine estates that Bradshaw was curious to visit, books, and generally anything that didn't involve politics or religion. The conversation eventually came round to family. Up until then Bradshaw had divulged little about his personal life, but now, with the help of three or four glasses of wine, he gradually began to let down his defenses.

"My children are working in America," he said. After a pause he added, "It's good for them to travel."

"Are they going to stay there?" asked Melissa.

"Well, they were schooled there and afterward they came back to stay with me. But they had started to see the world differently and struggled to adjust to our African ways. I try to visit them once or twice a year."

"And your wife?"

"We're divorced. She never adapted to life here. America is her home. Atlanta. It's funny, don't you think? I sometimes meet American businessmen . . . sorry, African American businessmen, who tell me how much they love coming back 'home' to Africa. And then I tell them that my wife and children have chosen to leave Africa and live in America. In the South. I can't imagine what their ancestors must think!"

"That is pretty ironic," said Melissa, topping up Bradshaw's glass.

"It is harder these days to try and keep a family together. Geographically anyway," I said.

"Every family is different though, Dad. Some work better when they're split up all over the place. Like ours."

"I don't think we're better off than when we were under one roof."

Turning to Bradshaw, Melissa said, "Dad keeps wanting me to move down to Cape Town to live here with him."

"And you don't want to?"

"I have my reasons."

"In my culture the children are expected to look after their parents when they get old."

"So what about your children?"

"Are you saying I'm old?"

For once Melissa was lost for words.

Bradshaw smiled and then his face went serious again. "I'm not sure if they ever considered themselves to be a part of my culture. They were always closer to their mother."

"God, families can be so complicated," said Melissa.

"From the outside," said Bradshaw, "they appear simple enough: two parents and children. Or sometimes one parent," he added with a glance in my direction. "But it's only once you've been invited inside the family that you get an understanding of all the little intricacies. It's like going backstage at a theater. Only then are you aware of all the ropes and struts that hold the different scenes in place, and how thin and flimsy the painted houses appear, when from the stalls they seemed as solid as brick and cement. I've always enjoyed going backstage. It teaches you about deception."

Then Bradshaw looked at his watch and drained his glass. "I'm terribly sorry, I've been jabbering on without realizing how late it is."

He thanked us and we walked him to the front door. After complimenting Melissa once more on her work, he wished us good night. When he was gone Melissa joined me on the deck for one of her "cigarettes."

"What a nice man," she said.

"He is. There's something very sad about him though."

"Why, because he's all alone with no family to share his big house?"

"You know what I mean."

"He seems happy enough to me."

We smoked in silence until Bradshaw's bedroom light came on. "Come," I said, "let's go inside before he thinks we're spying on him."

"Don't you think it's him who's spying on us?"

"No. But I do think you smoke too much of that stuff."

"Another reason why I'm not going to move to Cape Town."

When the doorbell rang just after ten o'clock the next morning, it took me a moment to recognize Bradshaw's driver, as he was wearing dark shades.

"Is Melissa in?" he asked.

"Yes. What is this about?"

"I have an invitation for her."

"From Bradshaw?"

"He would like Melissa to accompany him to look at some vineyards."

"He would? Oh, well, I'm not sure. You see, she's very busy right now. Painting."

The driver showed no sign of comprehending this information, or perhaps he sensed in my reply a thinly veiled tone of suspicion.

"If you don't mind, I would rather she declined the invitation herself."

We stood and stared at one another for several seconds as I tried to think of a plausible reason why Melissa couldn't accept. But my mind was too occupied with the possible consequences of Bradshaw's invitation, and no convincing excuses were forthcoming. Eventually I muttered a feeble "Right, right. Of course."

I knocked on the door of the room Melissa painted in and repeated the invitation to her.

"What the hell do I know about wine?" she said from the other side of the door.

"Exactly. Shall I tell him you're too busy?"

"Uh. No. It's OK—I'm not being very productive today anyway. It might be fun to do some wine tasting."

"You sure? Don't feel obliged. Your work should come first."

She opened the door. "It's fine, Dad. Tell him I'll be five minutes."

As I walked back down to the front door I wondered why Bradshaw had sent his driver over for Melissa. Was he embarrassed to invite my daughter out face-to-face? Was it less awkward for him like this? Did he think that this was the best way to explain that I wasn't invited?

When Melissa came down the stairs I saw that she had put on some makeup, something she hadn't done in all the time she had been here with me. She was wearing perfume, too. She kissed me on the cheek and then walked away with the driver.

I spent the day trying to convince myself that there was nothing disturbing about Bradshaw's invitation to Melissa. After all, he was a respectable man. It didn't matter that he was a stranger from another country and old enough to be her father: he simply needed someone to buy wine with, someone who knew something about the local estates. But obviously not me. Of course I realized I was thinking like a paranoid parent. If I was to prove to Melissa that we were capable of living together like two adults, I would have to show some constraint by not interfering in her personal life. But I couldn't ignore the parent in me.

At four in the afternoon I tried phoning Melissa to find out where she was, only to hear her cell phone ringing in the bedroom where she'd left it. I pretended to take a stroll down to the beach, even though it was cool and cloudy, just so that I could walk past Bradshaw's house to look for signs of life. Nothing. I didn't have Bradshaw's cell-phone number, in fact I didn't even know if he had one, and his home number was not listed in the book. Already I had begun to regret introducing him to my daughter. I wondered what my wife would have done. She and Melissa had been very close. Two girls against three boys. She had dealt with Melissa during her difficult teenage years, while I had spent my days and most of the evenings at the office, working for a comfortable retirement. For this.

It had been dark for some time when I heard the front door open and close. Melissa appeared in the lounge as if she'd only been out for five minutes. Her cheeks were flushed.

"So? How was it?" I asked as nonchalantly as I could.

"Cool! I feel like I've been on a grand tour of the Western Cape though. He bought a shitload of wine. And then we had dinner and he's just shown me around his house. Did you know that he has three original Chagalls?"

"Oh? Wow. Where did you have dinner?"

"La Colombe. Pretentious as all hell. But at least he insisted on paying."

"That's nice."

She flopped down on the couch next to me. I noticed that her teeth were tinted purple from wine. Then: "Guess what?"

"I don't know, what?"

"Bradshaw asked me to paint his portrait."

"Portraits aren't really your thing are they?"

"For a hundred and twenty thousand rand they fucking well are."

"You're kidding. He's going to pay you that for a picture?"

"Why do you sound so surprised? I've sold paintings for more than that before."

"I know, I know. I'm just . . . when does he want it by?"

"He says I can take as long as I like. So, if it's OK with you, I may extend my stay a bit."

"That's great. Stay as long as you need. That's really good news, Mel. Well done."

And so the next morning, instead of going off to the spare room to paint, Melissa took a sketch pad, pencils, and her camera over to Bradshaw's house. She returned at midday with rough compositions and a series of close-up photographs of Bradshaw's polished hands. That's where you capture the essence of a person, she said, in their hands. She spent several days working out a composition and she repeatedly tried to convince Bradshaw to consider wearing something other than a suit and tie for the painting. In the end they compromised on a white, long-sleeved collared shirt and navy suit pants. I was not privy to any of these sittings or discussions. Often they would go into the city for dinner and to talk about the portrait, and I would be in bed long before Melissa returned home. But she was excited about the project and it made me proud to see how professional and thorough she was. And who knew, perhaps a stint of work in Cape Town would make her feel differently about living here.

For two weeks I hardly saw Melissa. I found signs of her in the kitchen—bread crumbs on the table and soggy tea bags in the sink— and sometimes she'd leave notes asking me to take her laundry out of the washing machine and put it in the dryer, or to buy more groceries. It was clear that our holiday time together was over. The studio she had set up in one of the spare rooms had been transplanted into Bradshaw's house, and it was there that she spent her days, often working deep into the night.

Late one evening I went out onto the deck for a cigarette before bed. I had eaten alone and tried unsuccessfully to watch an old Ingmar Bergman movie on television, but my concentration span had somehow shrunk or been tampered with by the sea air. The wind was gusting up from the ocean and it took four matches to light my cigarette. There was music on the wind: a woman's melancholic voice accompanied by a piano. It was coming from Bradshaw's house. His bedroom light was on and the curtains were drawn. Probably the old boy's lullaby music, I thought to myself. And then the door leading onto the bedroom balcony opened and Melissa stepped out into the night. Whether she saw me or not I can't say, but she turned to go back inside almost immediately and the music was silenced and the bedroom darkened. From my deck it was hard to say what she had been wearing, however, as she'd turned to go back inside, I thought I'd seen, in silhouette, a clear profile of her breasts.

The next morning Melissa's bedroom gave no clue as to whether or not she'd spent the night there. Her bed hadn't been made in days, and her clothes were scattered around the room. After breakfast I went over to Bradshaw's house. Bradshaw's driver answered the door, and I was asked to wait in the marmoreal foyer as he went off to find Melissa. A painting on the wall, presumably one of the Chagalls, depicted a woman floating upside down in a starry night sky. Melissa eventually came down the stairs, barefoot and wearing an oversize paisley-patterned dressing gown.

"Is this what you paint in these days?" I said.

"I worked late and decided to stay over. In a guest room. There's no need to get all excited."

"I came to see how you were doing. If you needed any supplies of new paint or brushes."

"Dad, I'm fine, honestly. I've just got to finish up something and then I'll come over. OK?"

She gave me a hug and pressed her face against my chest. Her hair was oily.

Later, after she'd returned to my house, I asked her how the portrait was going and how soon she expected to complete it.

"I don't know. Probably a week or two more. I've made a couple of false starts but I think the one I'm doing now is working well."

"Is Bradshaw pleased with it?"

"He's not allowed to see it until the end. Neither are you."

"And outside of the painting?"

"What do you mean?"

"I mean what else is going on over there? I hardly see you anymore."

"Dad, I've been working. You see, this is why I could never live here with you: you're constantly watching over me."

"I'm not watching over you. But what am I meant to think when you spend all day and night next door?"

"That I'm working bloody hard!"

And then she was gone again for several more days.

I first noticed the man when I was returning from Hout Bay one afternoon. I had gone down to the harbor to buy some yellowtail for dinner and as I pulled into my driveway I saw a small Japanese hatchback parked a little way up the street. He was sitting in the driver's seat, sipping from a Coke can. It looked like he was waiting for someone. I didn't think much of it at first, and even when I saw him in the same place the next morning I wasn't too concerned. It was only when I saw him again that evening, sitting alone in the car, staring down the street, that I became suspicious and started to look at him a little closer. He didn't seem to care that I was beginning to take an interest in him.

The passage outside my bedroom has a window facing out onto the street, and from up there I had a clear view of the man. He wore a T-shirt and jeans, and his face and head were cleanly shaven. I watched as he answered a call on his cell phone and I noticed that there was a camera on the dashboard. After a lengthy conversation he put the phone down and adjusted his seat so that he was almost in a horizontal position. That was when he saw me. I pulled my head back and felt my face flush with blood. Fool! What did I think I was doing, spying on someone in the street just because he didn't look like the kind of person who would own a house here? I had become like the other people in the neighborhood: people Melissa criticized for living insulated lives behind high walls and security fences.

Feeling like a child caught out, I turned to go downstairs. But then the doorbell rang. I went back to the window and looked out at the car. It was empty. The doorbell rang again. And then there was a loud rapping on the front door. Hard knuckles, I thought. I stayed where I was, thinking how ridiculous I was being, yet at the same time just wanting to be left alone. The doorbell rang twice more and then there was silence. After a minute I heard a car door close. The engine started and I heard what sounded like a can being crushed under a wheel as the car drove off. When I looked out the window again the hatchback was gone. Only a small puddle of oil and a flattened Coke can remained.

The next morning there was no sign of the hatchback and its lone driver. I put it down to one of those strange occurrences that happens daily in cities. Melissa was already over at Bradshaw's house, and I drank coffee on my own in the kitchen. There was no rush for me to do anything—a feeling I wasn't yet sure I was comfortable with in my retirement. I showered and dressed and decided to take a drive into Camps Bay to pick up a newspaper. The ocean was gray, and a south-westerly wind was beginning to push a bank of low clouds in over the sea toward the rocky shoreline. Large clumps of kelp, looking like nests of glistening eels, were washing up in the breakers. As I approached Bakoven, I passed the Japanese hatchback heading in the opposite direction. There were two passengers with the driver.

When I returned home with the newspaper the hatchback was parked outside Bradshaw's house. The three occupants of the car were standing outside having a discussion. One of the men had what looked like a television news camera mounted on his shoulder, and the shaven-headed man was now wearing a suit. As I pulled into my driveway the shaven-headed man approached me. He indicated for me to lower my window. I opened it a couple of inches and he leaned forward and asked, "Do you know the owner of this house?" He pointed at Bradshaw's house.

"No," I said without hesitation, even though I knew my daughter was inside painting Bradshaw at that very moment.

"When did you last see him?"

"I don't keep track of my neighbor's activities."

The man looked back at his two companions and shook his head. It was only when I sat down in the lounge and opened the newspaper that I realized what was going on. An article on the second page reported that Bradshaw Muchabaiwa, sixty-five, brother of his homeland's finance minister, Gideon Muchabaiwa, was under investigation for charges of corruption and illegal dealings in foreign currency. Gideon Muchabaiwa had also been implicated, but through his lawyer he had released a statement defending the dealings as "family investments," adding that he had "nothing to hide" as all of his and his brother's financial dealings were "above board." There was no comment from Bradshaw as he was "currently out of the country on business." The investigations would be continuing, the article concluded.

No doubt Bradshaw had already heard the news. Would he have mentioned anything to Melissa? I went upstairs and looked out the window onto the street. One of the passengers from the hatchback was filming Bradshaw's house while the shaven-headed man stood in front of the camera and spoke into a microphone. I tried phoning Melissa but her cell phone was off. She had to get out of the house before it was besieged by the media. But the last thing I wanted was to be filmed knocking on Bradshaw's front door and asking for my daughter back. And I was sure Melissa didn't need that kind of publicity. Within an hour four more news crews were setting up outside Bradshaw's house.

Melissa phoned me and told me not to worry.

"It's just a political thing," she said. "There's an election coming up and there's a whole lot of mudslinging going on. It'll die down in a day or two when they can't find any evidence. Bradshaw's not that kind of man, Dad."

"Whether he's innocent or not doesn't really matter to me. But you're getting caught up in something that has nothing to do with you. Come home and we'll go away somewhere for a few days. Take a break."

"I'm not leaving Bradshaw on his own."

"He has his driver."

"You don't understand. I want to stay with him."

"What?"

"I'll explain later. Although I doubt you'll understand. But I'm happy, Dad. I'm happy with Bradshaw."

"Happy in what sense? A relationship? Is that what you're trying to tell me?"

"Yes."

"Since when?"

"Not long. But I know it's what I want."

"He could be gone tomorrow, back in his home country, standing trial. I mean, you hardly know him for Christ's sake!"

"This isn't about what the newspapers say, is it. Come on, Dad. Is it his age? His color? What?"

"I'm just worried, Melissa. Can you understand that? Can you understand someone else's feelings for once?"

"Fuck you."

"Please. Melissa. Why don't you come over and we can talk about this properly?"

"I've made up my mind already. This thing will pass in a day or two. It's just rumors. You'll see."

That night the rumors were on television. Bradshaw's house and its worth were displayed across the screen for all the world to see. There were scenes of people queuing for bread and petrol in his homeland, juxtaposed with the sea views from his house next door to mine. A crowd bristling with sticks and placards was demonstrating outside his brother's house in the capital city. Another house, alleged to belong to Bradshaw, was shown being ransacked and looted. I switched off the television and poured myself a drink. Melissa had left several Polaroids of Bradshaw's hands on the dining-room table. The knuckles on his fingers bulged out like full pockets. Once again I noted how well kept the nails were. How, I thought, could a man who paid such close attention to small details get himself into a situation like this? And then I thought of the fingers working loose the buttons on my daughter's clothing and I turned the Polaroids face-down on the table and went to bed.

. . .

The English reporter who knocked on my car window the next day said he was from the BBC. He wanted to know if I knew the woman in Bradshaw's house. I had just returned from buying three different newspapers—two English, one Afrikaans—and had noted that all of them were leading with a story on Bradshaw. One of them had a picture of Bradshaw and Melissa eating out at an expensive restaurant and the caption identified her as "acclaimed local artist, Melissa Moorcraft (31)."

"I'm not aware of what goes on next door," I said.

"Isn't your name Dennis Moorcraft?"

"Why?"

"The woman's name is Melissa Moorcraft. I thought you might know her."

"I'm sorry, I have nothing to tell you."

"No! No, you can't do that!" Bradshaw's driver was striding out from the house toward the reporter and me. Before the reporter could say anything the driver took him by the collar of his shirt and pushed him up against my car. By the time I'd stepped out to try to intervene the driver had turned back to the house and the reporter was kneeling on the driveway, blood streaming from both nostrils.

"Bloody hell," he said. His colleagues came over and helped him back to their car. Someone had filmed the whole thing.

I went over the papers in my lounge. There were calls for Bradshaw to be extradited to face the charges against him. An "unidentified but reliable source" had come forward with new evidence and his brother was said to be "assisting" the police with their inquiries. As I had said to Melissa, it was of no concern to me whether Bradshaw was innocent or guilty; but he had, quite literally, brought trouble to my doorstep and he was involving my daughter in his affairs, even if it was by her own will, and I felt that sooner or later I would have to confront him and ask him what he planned to do next and, more to the point, what his intentions were with my daughter.

The police arrived that afternoon. Two bored-looking constables took a statement from me regarding the assault on the journalist, and I told them exactly what I had seen. I had to lend them a pen as their ballpoint had run out of ink. And then they went and knocked—rather optimistically I thought—on Bradshaw's front door. There was no reply. After a brief discussion between themselves they drove away.

That night was the turning point in the whole matter.

Melissa phoned me a short while before the evening news. Something had happened to Gideon, Bradshaw's brother. He had been returning from a police station, where he had been questioned with his lawyer, when his car was attacked by a mob. The car had been set alight and Gideon had tried to run away. He hadn't stood a chance. His smoldering body was flashed briefly on the news later that evening. Bradshaw was obviously deeply upset, said Melissa, and his driver had not been seen for some hours.

"What now?" I said.

"I'm not sure."

"Come home. This has gone too far."

"I can't just leave him."

"Dammit, Melissa. It's not your business. Let him sort it out. Otherwise you'll be in more trouble than you know."

"We'll think of something."

"Like what?"

"I don't know yet."

I suppose that was the last chance I had to speak some sense to her—when we spoke again there just wasn't enough time. But I'm not sure I could have made any difference. It was like watching a glass topple at the edge of a table and knowing that you will not reach it in time to stop it from falling and shattering. That night I went to bed knowing that I would have to live with whatever happened, and I did not sleep very deeply. As a result the phone call at three thirty in the morning didn't disrupt any dreams. It was Melissa. She was outside my front door. When I went downstairs I saw Bradshaw's car in the road with the engine running. Bradshaw was behind the wheel. He did not look at me. There were no other cars, no television crews or journalists. They would be back at first light.

"We're leaving," said Melissa. "I need to get some of my stuff."

I followed her up to her bedroom. "Where are you going?"

"I'll let you know when we're there."

"You don't have to do this. Do you realize what you're giving up for this man?"

"I've told you. This is what I want."

"I'm going to speak to him then," I said.

"It won't help. He has asked me to stay behind too. It's not his decision that I'm going."

She was picking up dirty clothing off the floor and stuffing it into a tote bag.

"Please tell me where you're going."

"I can't, Dad. I'll e-mail you."

"They'll find you. You're not exactly an inconspicuous couple."

"We'll sort it out."

"They'll freeze Bradshaw's bank account, if they haven't already done so. You won't survive long."

Melissa zipped up the bag. "We've already thought about that."

I followed her out the front door and to the car, which was still idling in the road. Melissa hugged me then and I felt my throat close up and my eyes start to sting.

"Come back," I said.

"Don't worry."

She climbed in next to Bradshaw and I bent over to speak to him. But as Melissa closed the door the car pulled away and I was left standing in the street in my underwear.

That was all last year. I get the occasional e-mail from Melissa. It's impossible to tell if she's in Africa, America, or Australia. She mentions a villa near the ocean. Is it the same ocean I stare out at from my deck? She says she is healthy and happy and painting many pictures. In the end, I suppose, we have to make our own choices, take what we can while we can, so that our final years are comfortable. Isn't that the aim: to build up as much padding as possible in order to soften the impact of death?

After sending Melissa a reply (regards to Bradshaw) I switch off the computer and leave the study. My house is the envy of many people, I'm sure. But my life echoes back at me when I walk through it. I stand in the doorways of the spare rooms and look at the bare beds, their stiff mattresses not yet patterned by archipelagos of stains from spilt bodily fluids. In the lounge I pass the huge yellowwood dining table, a desert plain. I make tea in the kitchen, feeling like a priest pouring wine in an empty cathedral. And then I step out onto my deck and scan the vast horizon.

Roger Nash

The Camera and the Cobra

I

HIS FIRST posting abroad was to Kasfareet, a village in Egypt, at the edge of the eastern Sahara desert and on the shores of Al-Buhayrah al-Murrah al-Kubrā—the Great Bitter Lake. He'd just started work with the aid agency, as a newly qualified doctor, specializing in a giddying, if not somersaulting, variety of tropical diseases. After flying into Cairo at night, he'd straightaway taken a series of hops farther south, by bus.

During a brief stop in the city of Fayid, he'd visited a small bazaar outside the bus station. He was struggling with the unaccustomed dry heat, which whittled at his skin like a first-year medical student somewhat puzzled by a scalpel. This was compounded by his bewilderment at a strange land made doubly strange in being virtually invisible for large parts of the journey. The moonless desert, which presumably stretched back from the road, had been wrapped in astringently scented and mummifying shrouds of darkness ever since his arrival. At best, he could see only a newly qualified doctor staring back at him through the smeared sheen of the window beside him, as though he'd long preceded himself into the desert and was waiting for himself—for anyone—to arrive there.

Luckily, he'd had the foresight to wonder whether there were any last things he might provision himself with, before the bus took him on to remoter parts. He got back onto the bus carrying a small, brown, old-fashioned box camera, which had cost only a few piastres. He settled back into his seat, for the rest of the necropolis of night, and fell asleep eventually. The doctor already in the desert reached for the camera firmly, as it began to roll from his lap. It was obvious that a camera was something he'd long been waiting for in the deserts of his life.

II

In his first weeks at the clinic, patients' symptoms anarchically pursued a life of their own, far from the mountain-cool textbook examples he'd studied in Geneva. An obstructed bowel somehow disguised itself as malaria, malaria as a snakebite, and a snakebite, in an awkward location, as overenthusiastic lovemaking. At times, he felt as if he were present at an overcrowded and overheated masked ball for anatomists, with heavily cloaked symptoms continuously exchanging identities with each other before slipping away down the slow circle dance of the queuing patients.

The brown, vinyl-covered box camera came into its own in these early weeks, in his time off. Taking photographs became a self-prescribed remedy for his confusion and anxiety. With his camera, as in his medical notes, he developed a mania to record and perfect his techniques. It also became something of an obsession to perpetuate whatever changed so quickly and unrecognizably around him. He got up early in the relative cool of the mornings to try and snap the tracks of desert foxes at the edge of the Sahara, even a desert fox itself, before the wind rose and smoothed both tracks and elusive fox back into a shifted and entirely different pattern of dunes. The dunes seemed to lope about as unpredictably as the foxes, and the foxes to ripple about as much as the dunes. They just did so at different paces.

In both the clinic and his time off, he developed a nervous alertness, looking from side to side constantly, gripped by the expectation that something was about to happen that he was in danger of not noticing—until too late. Would the patient's disease turn decisively worse that evening, stalking imperceptibly closer to the kill, like the clinic's cat moving in its strangely motionless sort of way, ears back, toward the chicken roost? Once, through his camera viewfinder, looking for something framable to snap, he noticed a shy cobra before it slid away. Luckily, a colleague was with him and warned him to back off, since cobras can spit venom some distance. He got the photo though, very quickly, aware, on at least this occasion, that the camera in front of his face could be as much a blocking and protective shield as an open lens of perception. That photograph took pride of place in his quickly growing album. In it, the cobra reared up like an ancient hieroglyph, spitting its image straight at the viewer across the intervening centuries.

Film was sometimes unobtainable. In those weeks, undeterred, he carried the camera around empty, scoping out the landscape through its viewfinder. He much enjoyed making life framable, even if it had to remain unrecorded. It satisfied his feeling that, as you can't adequately enjoy anything in the anxious and confusing present, you should at least try to record it, to enjoy more fully afterward. When his camera was filmless, he usually had a pocket full of freshly harvested and sun-dried peanuts, redolent still with the rich loamy smell of the Nile delta, like an expensive and musky perfume in a forbidden street. He'd crack these open and chew them constantly while swiveling his viewfinder around, searching for things to remember. He ate the nuts automatically, and was always surprised when he found his pocket empty. Peanuts were certainly among the things he didn't notice enough to enjoy fully in the present. He was more struck by their annoying absence. Absences weren't a memorable part of photography for him, either. A photograph of empty desert, which for his colleagues breathed deeply with its own beduned spaciousness, was, for him, always a failure: a picture merely of whatever would've been there if he'd snapped in time. Was it supposed to have been a fox or a hawk? He was never sure. For him, there should always be something in a frame.

III

Near the end of his first month in Kasfareet, when his self-medicating passion for photography was at its height, he was particularly frustrated by the lack of film but framed things in the viewfinder anyway. One dawn, he was walking toward the rising slopes of the Sahara, which already shimmered in a haze from the mere promise of a sun still tilting itself above the horizon like a fast-approaching camel train. It suddenly struck him that there was something odd about the camera. It felt heavy for a camera with no film in it, heavy enough to be incorrectly loaded and jammed with several rolls of film.

He knelt down in a narrow valley between two sharp-edged dunes. The valley promptly funneled and tipped light right over his knees, like olive oil spilled from a warmed pan. It almost stung his knees. He opened up the camera. Inside was a nest of honey ants. They swarmed to repel the light, clambered over each other's clambering, in a fist-size ball of rapidly multiplying movements. Their golden, transparent bodies made them look like pieces of animated and highly mindful amber, organizing to protect the distant past from which they'd come, hardening well around their trapped leaves and flies.

He scooped and brushed the ants out quickly, watching them trail optimistically toward a shrinking crumb of shade and burrow under grains of sand. The bulbous ends of their glassy abdomens, where they stored a sticky nectar, were slightly filmy and made him think of grainy and undeveloped negatives. How many times, in the last few days, had the clicking shutter of his filmless camera framed and recorded his life among their precious stores of sweetness? As they moved off in a long wavering line, they unreeled jerkily from his camera like scurrying sepia snapshots.

It was an odd thought for him that, just when he'd consolingly supposed himself most in charge at his viewfinder, shaping things, he'd been more observed by the gathering ants than observing. The thought sent a shiver down his spine that was matched by shivers that flickered down the long, sharp-edged spines of neighboring dunes. A strange wind was blowing up, one that made him nervous. He hurried back to the clinic. Palm trees around the buildings tossed their heads in the wind, clicking loudly, as though tut-tutting in a way that was neither clear approval nor disapproval, but, like an old man's absentminded tut-tutting, was just a resigned acceptance of itself.

As he went in to do rounds, he saw several falcons riding the breeze. They seemed to be gliding to shelter rather than hunting. At a distance, out on the Great Bitter Lake, several feluccas headed for shore at a fair clip, instead of fishing. Their lateen sails strained at such steep angles, even Euclid would've been proud of them. Their wakes tore up deep grazes behind them. There were no clouds of herring gulls in accompaniment. He was mildly surprised, but thought no more of it. He put the camera in a drawer in his room, carefully closed and locked the drawer, then went to open up the clinic.

A grateful Bedouin patient greeted him first, with the gift of a bucket of crabs. He thanked Hassan, and stood for a moment, before starting the day's work, watching the wet and glistening crabs crawl over each other like heavily armored and disorientated tanks. It was impossible to tell one crab from another. He thought of the interwoven honey ants, as impossibly tangled as a large ball of very angry string. The sight of the crabs both intrigued and disconcerted him. The crabs were so excitingly and assertively alive, waving bent lances and gun muzzles at each other. Yet no photograph could possibly sort out one from another. They reminded him of the masquerading symptoms that had worried him. Was this, after all, how life had to be, with events—even lives—overlapping like crabs and presenting as each other? He put the awkward thought quickly aside and moved on to his patients.

IV

The next morning, just before dawn, the khamsin, the spring wind, began in earnest. He was woken by an orderly coming to his room to close the shutters tightly and recommend that he stay inside, even though it was his day off. Made curious, he dressed in a hurry and went outside immediately.

A hot wind was blowing from the southeast. The sky was actually darkening around the sunrise, turning clouds the color and texture of deeply ridged brown corduroy. Thin and ineffectual raindrops were falling that tasted sour on his tongue, like rancid dates or the beginnings of someone else's vomit. Then the light went from the sky suddenly, blotted out behind wave after wave of stinging airborne dunes of flying sand that flailed at his face. He went inside quickly.

Opening the shutters a gap, he peered out cautiously. The wind blew directly from above onto the road outside, so that red columns of sand moved along it in columns that seemed purposeful. They swayed and rotated like the dervishes he'd seen dancing. But where the white-robed dervishes had whirled as gracefully as parasols, or the slowly swirling canopies of drifting jellyfish, the columns on the road moved jerkily, stalks of intent congealed blood. Where the dervishes had danced out an enduring measure of the stars, the columns on the road seemed to whir like the hands of a giant broken clock, its overwound spring driving them round and round crazily. The buildings in the compound, the clinic, the houses, the mosque, all seemed to spin round the columns. At first, it was like an amusing ride on a carousel. But then it seemed as if the world itself was going down a vast plug hole, perhaps being poured back, with the desert and Kasfareet, to become the sandy floor of an ocean. He felt dizzy and closed the shutters tightly.

Sand began to appear everywhere in his room, as if determined to pass beyond mere figures of speech and give "everywhere" its full meaning. He felt it inside his shirt, filing away at his skin, and buttoned his shirt more tightly. It was in his tea when he poured from the pot the orderly had brought him. There were more freshly harvested grains of sand than tea leaves in the pot. When he picked up his fountain pen to write in his diary, it deposited only a few inarticulate blue scabs instead of words on the page, and then dried up. When he read a book to pass the time, he always knew what would happen next: sand slid out as he turned the page. It got in his nose, eyes, and throat, of course, drawing them all together in common complaint. His voice rasped with bloodshot conjunctivitis, his nose smelled only in prickling blurs, and his sight very nearly went dumb. Sand gradually infiltrated the lock on his drawer. Though he tried every key he'd got, none of them would slide back the bolts on the desert. Eventually, there was even sand under his foreskin. The Sahara allowed no one, but no one, not to be intimate with it.

V

It was his first meeting with the khamsin, that hot wind from the south or southeast during the months of March to May. It is so sand laden, it flies rather than blows in as squadrons of airborne dunes: the Sahara as an eternally vigilant pharaonic Air Force, winged chariot wheels spinning vigorously in the red clouds. Hassan explained the Arabic phrase to him from which the anglicized word was derived: "rih al-khamsin," or the wind of fifty days. He began Arabic lessons over a soup Hassan had made from the crabs. He was pleasantly surprised that the crabs, which had overlapped confusingly in the bucket, produced a delicious soup in which savors blended seamlessly with one another. Hassan showed him a secret ingredient his Bedouin mother had taught him to use: a jar of yellow cumin, looking for all the world like a jar filled with very fine sand from the khamsin itself. He enjoyed learning Arabic as much as eating the soup.

His mouth relished both.

The khamsin lasted very nearly the time appointed to it by his

Arabic dictionary, but came and went in intervals, with the free and easy spontaneity of a genuine, though forceful, conversation. He seldom had time off though, or left the clinic, as there was an outbreak of dysentery, followed by cases of typhoid and then smallpox, and he was kept very busy. He did manage one quick trip, by jeep, to explore the ancient necropolis of Saqqara. He had barely stepped from the jeep, slamming its door, when a man on a donkey rose out of a dune, as if sound-activated. "My name is Elias," he said immediately and emphatically, as though there had been some question about this. He offered to introduce some of the tombs. The visit had been memorable mainly because the khamsin had returned with unusual force, and required him to take shelter within a tomb for several hours.

Below ground, in the cavelike tomb, it was almost as cool as springtime in Geneva. Just a few steps away, above ground, they had walked in an endless, whirling oven that seemed unalterably set on broil. The tomb was that of an important landowner. Elias pointed out a well-preserved wall painting at the far end that depicted farming activities on the great man's estate. Servants took long-horned cattle to pasture, gave water to a peaceable bull, and carried geese and other foodstuffs, as well as tools of their various trades, on yokes across their shoulders. The figures were painted in such a lively way, they still vigorously served their master in the afterworld of his endless estate, though they'd been doing it nonstop now for several thousand years.

Very little sand blew into the tomb. He sat on a rock near the entrance. Using Elias's flashlight, and then his own, he watched the figures at their work. The sheer intentness of their labor and his enforced shelter from the storm, drew out a matching concentration in him. He wished he had his camera—now trapped behind a jammed lock—but the scenes drew themselves together for him anyway. The painting did this in such an exact and detailed way that he wondered, at moments, whether the workmen peered out at him as a brief diversion between their never-ending tasks, to try and make out his torchlit gloom.

He could see what the workmen were doing, and see, too, that they knew well how to do it, as masters of their agricultural trades, even if they were slaves of the landowner. Now and again, a thin column of sand blew a short distance into the entrance, interposing itself between him and the ongoing estate work. Then he became uncertain, for a moment, who was doing what. Was that man herding a yoke, watering a coiled rope, or carrying a horned goose? But then the sand sifted down to the tomb's floor, well back from the painting, and the servants' clear musculature, red-brown from their never-setting sun, proclaimed their sweatingly separate activities again. Even in his torch's fuzzy gloom, their wise hands knew what to do. He began to play with the alternating moments of uncertainty and clarity: how the blowing desert covered only to reveal, but revealed only to cover. The sand under his foreskin prickled, and he sensed himself as an intimate part of this process. He looked down at his hands, clutching the flashlight. In the clinic, they, too, were becoming better able to work through the still-recurring moments of confusingly horned geese. He raised one hand in unpremeditated salute to the workers, and then felt self-conscious about what he'd done.

VI

He was back at the clinic two days later, very early in the morning, after driving overnight in the relative cool. Hassan had oiled and cleaned the locks to his door and drawer. The khamsin was not in evidence, and the air lolled about among the palm trees, resting itself. Locals told him the fifty days were almost certainly over for another year. He decided to take a quick walk to the edge of the desert before turning in. He took out the camera from the drawer, which unlocked easily. It needed film, but he'd bought some on the journey back from Saqqara. But, once more, the empty camera felt strangely heavy. He wondered whether ants had taken shelter from the winds, and opened the camera cautiously. A mound of sand fell in his lap. The camera seemed to have been nearly full of it.

How could ants, then sand, have squeezed, with such yogic flexibility, where even the physicist's thin beam of light wasn't supposed to? But the camera was an old model, and some of his photos had always come out spoiled. He'd assumed it was the developing process. He wiped the camera out and found the shutter mechanism was stuck. This was something Hassan would be able to fix. On a sudden impulse, but one that felt quietly sure of itself, he gave both the camera and his recently purchased box of film to Hassan, as a gift. He'd buy a better camera, but there was no hurry. Hassan, delighted, and in the true spirit of hospitality, gave him his mother's jar of cumin in return. Strangely, it looked even more like a jar of fine sand.

After Hassan had left the room, he started to unscrew the top of the jar, to sniff and make sure it was cumin. Then he stopped himself, in embarrassment. How ungracious of him. He was quite, quite sure. Besides, wouldn't it have been fitting, in a way, if it *had* been sand? He looked out at the desert. It was trackless after the khamsin, its smooth dunes unvisited as yet by desert fox, hawk, and herring gull. It seemed to beckon, to make a challenging gift to him of his always erasable, disappearing and reappearing footsteps upon it.

Manuel Muñoz

Tell Him about Brother John

E VERY TRIP back from Over There is a wreck of anxiety. Every trip back, I used to be welcomed home eagerly and with open arms, but today it is only my father, subdued, babysitting the nephews. Over There is "Allá," the way my father says it and then tips his chin at the horizon. Right there. As if the place he means to talk about is either across the street or too far away to imagine. My mother is Over There: she left with another man and packed her belongings, headed for a big city. It's a different Allá, a different Over There, but the way my father tips his chin is the same. It isn't here. I love my mother still, but I wish she would come home sometimes, just so she knows how this feels, this coming back, this answering for the way things are.

My father takes care of the nephews and they start immediately with too many questions about living Over There, the romanticizing of its danger, its enormity. My nephews watch old Charles Bronson movies on television, still popular on the local stations during midafternoons. They ask me if my life is like this: stolen drugs and brutalized girlfriends and guns illuminating the night streets. My oldest nephew is only ten years old.

I started saying Allá too because I was embarrassed about it. "Here," I say, giving one of the lighter suitcases to my oldest nephew. "Put that in the bedroom for me." It pains me to hear my nephews ask such stupid questions, the way their young hearts believe that I'm lying to them and holding back on the details of a life filled with excitement and anticipations. My life is: I'm broke, cramped in my apartment, on edge in the late night–early morning hours, convinced I'm missing out on some unimaginable vitality somewhere in the city. I say nothing to my nephews or my father about my job, but then again they hardly ever ask.

Every year, when the tiny plane descends, bringing me back into the flat arid interior of the Valley, back to the house I grew up in on this street, when my nephews climb on my every limb to welcome me home, I think I might be yearning. But then a fear comes over me, a feeling of being fooled and hypnotized by nostalgia. Sometimes I imagine Gold Street like a living being, an entity with arms waiting. Sometimes I imagine waking up Over There, parting my curtains, and seeing not the shadowy city streets but the plum blossoms and the Chinese elms, the paperboys tossing the morning news, cycling down Gold Street at the point in the neighborhood where you can do a U-turn and not a three-point. All of that imagining gives me a tight, constricted feeling.

"So who's called?" I ask my father, and try to shoo the boys away.

"Your cousin Oscar, your tía Carolina. Your grandpa Eugenio. Your sister wants to show you the new baby." My father shakes his head. "Can you believe it? Seven boys and still no girl."

My nephews run back down the hallway toward me, all of their tiny hands grabbing at a basketball, ready for a game on the dirt driveway. My father has built them a hoop out of a large plastic bucket and a piece of plywood. "Not now," I say, sending them out. "Maybe later." I send them out even though there isn't much to say to my father. My father, as if he knows this too, goes over to the phone and starts making a spate of calls, announcing my safe arrival.

I wait patiently on the couch, looking around at the house that is becoming more unfamiliar, bit by bit, with every trip home. At the back of the kitchen, where the door extends out into the garage and the dirt driveway, one of my nephews bounds back inside. I can hear his voice, already breathless and heated. I can hear the refrigerator door open, the sound of thirst being quenched. He's drinking cherry punch—some things do not change. I can hear my nephew's voice, but I'm embarrassed to admit that I cannot tell which one it is. My father is still on the telephone, but my nephew asks him anyway, "Did you tell him about Brother John?"

Brother John isn't my brother. He isn't anyone's brother, though all of us on Gold Street claim him as one of ours. This is why, whenever I come home, I'm obligated to see him.

Brother John, then and now, is the same person he has always been. He was the boy in town with no parents, no family. He had been held under the care of various aunts and uncles in some of the other small towns, always being shuttled back and forth between Orange Cove and Sanger and Parlier and even Pixley, his clothes carried in a single paper sack. Everyone on Gold Street watched from behind window curtains whenever he was brought back to the neighborhood, staying with the Márquez family, everyone shaking their heads about how poorly dressed he was, how underfed. Long after the Márquez family moved away—back to Mexico, some said—the car with Brother John came back and stopped at the empty house. The two women who had driven Brother John there knocked on the door; then one of them went back to the car and beeped the horn. They kept honking, until one of the neighbors came over, told them that no one was living there, and then claimed Brother John, just like that. Our next-door neighbors, in fact. The car that brought Brother John drove away and, from then on, we were all instructed to treat Brother John like he was one of our own.

I was too young then to know about legalities and I'm too old now to ask something so improper, something that is none of my business. Rumors about Brother John flew all around, but they were not mean-spirited. They were things we asked only among ourselves, and it was understood that we were never to mention our questioning to him. Was he from Mexico? Did his parents abandon him? Were his parents dead? Why didn't his aunts or uncles want him? Was he sick? Did our neighbors get money from the government to keep him? Did we all notice how the neighbors drove new cars every couple of years, ever since they took in Brother John? Why didn't he look like anybody in town, where cousins lived around almost every corner? Did his parents love him?

"You should go next door," my father says to me, "and see if Brother John is home."

I try to think of some excuse to delay the obligatory visit, but there is no avoiding it, not with my father. Even though my mother left him, my father is still a well-respected man in town. He is a war veteran; he marches in all the town parades, holding the American flag. He attends Saturday breakfasts at the Iglesia de San Pedro, where the town elders raise funds. He sits on the town council and reviews applications for new businesses: always *yes* to franchise restaurants, always *no* to the new liquor stores. I can wait only so long before I have to go next door to see Brother John. It's expected, because of who my father is, that I not be arrogant.

I can hear my nephews arguing on the driveway. They are still young. I wonder when my father will start coming down on them.

I knock on the heavy black security door and I hear shuffling in the living room. "Who is it?" says Doña Paulina in her broken English, and when I call out to her that it's me, she parts the curtain as if to make sure. She opens the door and motions me in, but she isn't smiling—I've never liked her. I point to my car next door, as if it were running and ready to go. "Brother John?"

"¡*Juanito!*" she calls out, holding the door open, wiping one hand on her apron. The living room looks much smaller than I remember it.

"Hey," Brother John says, emerging from the hallway. His room is in the back, the same room. We're twenty-six now, both of us, and it flashes through me: why is he still here, when he had a chance to get away? He got away, actually—to Oklahoma—but he came back. "Your dad told me you were coming to visit."

"Yeah," I tell him. "Hey, do you want to get a bite to eat? Just here in town?"

Doña Paulina stands staring at both of us. I know she understands what we're saying and even though I've never liked the woman, I respect her. Brother John is no one's flesh and blood, not on this street, but she raised him when she didn't have to.

"Sure," Brother John says, walking to the door without gathering anything, as if he had been expecting me. He extends his hand and I shake it; it's thick and hot. Neither of us lets go and I'm almost afraid to: it's as if my father were in the room and not next door. I can imagine the town elders talking to my father on Saturday morning. "*¿Y tu hijo?* When is he coming home?"

The trip home from Over There will be only a week long. I will visit my ailing grandfather Eugenio, going to see him between his afternoon naps, and then drive back to my father's house feeling guilty about my grandpa's health. I will supervise my nephews as my father escapes with relief from this daily task my brothers and sisters put on him, knowing he feels too guilty to say no to their demands. My brothers and sisters will go to work, grateful for the savings in day care, but won't say thank you. It will mean an uncomfortable session with my father, a sitting-in-silence that means nothing except that my father is still thinking about my mother and how she abandoned him. Luckily, my high school friends, Willy and Al, will invite me over to Willy's place for beer, and then I will drive home drunk. It will mean running into the girl who had a crush on me in high school, one morning at the grocery store—Lily still not married, still idling in the cul-de-sacs of the men she now wants, parking outside their houses and waiting through nothing. It will mean opening my town's thin paper and whistling at how much property you can get for only five figures, how wasteful and pushed-over I am for living Over There. During the week, I will have to nurse the pulled and aching hamstring from playing basketball with my nephews. They know the small dips and holes in the dirt driveway better than I do. It will mean resting on the sofa with my hamstring wrapped, leg raised, the house quiet, and next door Brother John and the story he told me unable to be taken back.

Brother John knows where the new places are and he directs me to one of the franchise restaurants in town, along the new strip mall that has sprouted on the east side, the painted stucco bright against the fresh parking lot, the cars eager with patrons. Everyone in town comes here now, avoiding the dilapidated downtown and its struggling stores. The strip mall is wide, neon lit, smooth tarred, convenient, sparely landscaped with fledgling trees and shrubs. I would never find a place like this Over There, and part of me is grateful for the proximity of all of this, the wide space, the cleanliness and the order and the newness of everything in sight, everything an enormous city could never offer.

At the restaurant, we sit in a booth with comfortable cloth-covered seats, flower-paned glass, and wide table space. The young waiters circle quickly with hot dishes. I think of all my friends Over There and how they would deny that they come from such places. They feel a particular shame, I think, of coming from towns like this. But I'm glad for it: I think of my father and the town elders planning and hoping, counting the jobs at this restaurant, at the video store across the way, at the giant supermarket and the pharmacy. I wish I could be a little more like them or Doña Paulina, looking out for other people.

Brother John studies the menu, and while his eyes are downcast, I study him: he has waned and his shoulders seem narrowed, his chest caved. Because I've been Over There and know more than just Mexican faces, I see the mystery of his parents through his face. He has the wide face that we all do and the dark skin, but the hair is fine—fine and brown. I don't remember it being brown. Beautiful, actually, the length of it is creeping past his neck. With his face down, his eyes not showing, he could be a white boy, but I have never even tried to imagine who his parents could have been. None of the stories have ever convinced me.

"You look tired," I say to him.

Brother John sighs and closes the menu. "Tough lately." He looks up at me. "Being here." His eyes lock on mine. It's only Over There that people look me in the eye—that I feel okay about looking someone in the eye.

I look back down at my menu and don't say anything to Brother John. Our waiter takes a long time to come to our table, and I put on an act of not knowing what to order. For a while, it works, Brother John with little to say. But as soon as the waiter comes and goes, Brother John starts up, naming names, the people we went to school with. As with my friends Over There, I try to keep as much to myself as possible, only nod my head, try to avoid contributing to conjecture. It doesn't faze Brother John. He tells me that Agustina had a baby a year after high school and could never determine the father. "And word is, Ginger—that teacher's daughter—she had a baby, too, but no one knew about it and she gave it up for adoption. Beto and Patsy got married and then divorced, because Beto was having an affair with Carla—remember her? Carla Ysleta? Now Beto and Carla are married and Patsy's alone with no kids."

Brother John says all this without keeping his voice down, and I can sense people are cocking their ears for gossip. People know people in this town. People know.

"Violeta, of all the ones, never got married or had kids, but word was she couldn't have any and had depression for years. That happened to her sister, Sofía. Remember her? That's why a lot of people think she killed herself. And Emilio Rentería—he hurt himself so bad on night shift at the paper mill that he can't work anymore. But you can see him at the Little League games. He coaches the kids, even though he uses a wheelchair."

A friend of my father passes by our table on his way out and extends his hand. "Good to see you," Señor Treviño says. He beams proudly at me, and behind his smile I can almost hear my father telling his lies to the old men at the Iglesia de San Pedro. "Say hello to your father." Brother John says nothing to him, does not meet his eyes, and it surprises me that Señor Treviño simply goes on his way, giving Brother John only a slight nod.

"What's that about?" I ask Brother John, when the old man leaves the restaurant. "He knows you."

Brother John sniffs. "He thinks he does."

"What do you mean?"

"They're making me pay back the scholarship. Remember that?"

I do remember it. I remember the envy, the luck I thought he had, how the Iglesia de San Pedro had silently pushed their bake sales and Saturday breakfasts and tithing to present Brother John a check to attend a school in Oklahoma. My father had reprimanded me one night when I said something about how unfair it was: "You think about what that kid has been through. All his life. Who does he have to turn to except these people right here at the church?" My mother had been sitting on the couch watching her telenovela. She had rolled her eyes in disgust. That was the year before she left.

"Why are they making you pay it back?"

"I didn't finish," says Brother John, and he looks back down. His brown hair falls a little, but I can still see his face, and for the first time—maybe because I'm old enough now—I recognize what a sad life he has had, all the things he does not know. At least my mother, even though she is not with my father anymore, calls me. "Why are you Over There anyway?" she pleads, and right now, as I think of her and see Brother John's downcast eyes, her pleading is not a nuisance.

The waiter comes with the food, the plates hot, and I shovel the food in. I can sense it coming from Brother John, the need to say something, and I feel sorry for having asked him out to eat. He does not touch his food.

Finally, halfway through my plate, he picks up his fork and starts eating. "Did you think I was praying?" he asks.

I laugh nervously. I remember the school he was sent to, a religious school smack in the middle of Oklahoma.

His voice hushes a little and I have to lean in to hear him. He starts telling me, even while he's eating, but I can understand him. He doesn't swallow the words. "I got there, to Oklahoma, and I had that money. But I ran out real quick after I bought books and stuff, and I couldn't afford the dorms. So I found this room from a family that lived in the middle of town. When I told them I was a student down at the school, they let me stay real cheap. The room was upstairs, like an attic, and I had my own stairwell that ran above the garage. I had to be real careful in the rain. Or the snow. They had used this real cheap glossy paint on the wood and it was slippery. But they never bothered me. I still needed money though, so I started tending bar, without telling them, just to make some extra. Things were going fine for a long time and then . . ."

I resist saying, "What?" and my food is nearly gone, but Brother John takes his time. He pushes the fork around on his plate, takes a few small bites.

"I met someone," he says, very quietly. "One of my classmates. He was from South Carolina."

He is telling me this because I'm living Over There; he thinks anywhere but here will let you live a life never allowed. He thinks Over There is full of people falling in love, people waiting to listen to you while you do the falling. He sees right through me, my moving Over There. But I still say nothing.

"His name was Gary. Gary Lee Brown. I met him and started seeing him a lot. And a few months later I lied to that family and told them that Gary needed help and could he stay with me and they said yes. The father even helped us move Gary's bed up to that room, even though we never used it. We just set it up in case the family came upstairs, but they never did. The hard thing was, Gary was real religious. He believed it, I mean, and even after we'd been together like that for a year, he kept telling me that what we were doing was wrong, that it was a sin. He'd scare me sometimes, the things he'd say, like driving out in the middle of the wheat fields and just sitting, thinking about killing himself. 'You're just out there, thinking?' I would ask him when he'd come home late—real late—two in the morning sometimes. And that's what would scare me, all those hours, being alone at night when I knew what he was thinking. You remember going out to the orchards at night, drinking, how you can see the stars all out? It's pretty when you're with other people, but when you're by yourself . . . And Oklahoma's flat. Flat, flat—flatter than here."

"He didn't kill himself, did he?" I ask him, because the way he's talking is making me nervous, the anticipation of terrible news.

"Nah, he didn't," Brother John says, pursing his lips. "We went on like that for a long time. A long time. Then one day, I came home from school and Gary's things were gone—his clothes, even the bed. He left me a note taped to the mirror in the bathroom, explaining how it wasn't right, saying he went back to South Carolina. Back to his little town."

This is where the tears start and the waiter comes by as if he's been listening the whole time. "Everything all right?" he asks. He must be sixteen or seventeen, young, and he looks like one of the Ochoa brothers.

"Some bad news is all," I tell him, and Brother John holds his head in his hands and I'm grateful that the waiter walks away before he begins again.

"I loved Gary. I really did. And I ran out of money and couldn't concentrate on the studying anymore, so I just came back home," he says, sobbing softly, and if only it weren't here in this restaurant, I would listen. But it's difficult. "It's been real hard to keep inside, ever since I came back. But I don't have anywhere else to go. I don't have family. I only had him. And I remember telling myself, all those times walking home from the bar in that little town, 'This is it, this is it.' How could he go like that? I just couldn't believe it when I read that note, and I haven't heard from him since."

The waiter comes back with a coffeepot and two cups, even

though we didn't ask for it. I'm too speechless to refuse him and Brother John is too busy wiping away his tears, so the cups come down and this is more that I have to sit through, waiting for the coffee to cool down, waiting for the check.

"For the longest time, I thought about going back to South Carolina, to his little town to find him. Call him out in the street in front of all his people and ask him why. But then I think about somebody doing that to me here and I know it would just be mean. At least he didn't kill himself, I hope."

I pour some sugar into my coffee, some of the warm milk and slide the little condiment tray over to Brother John. He takes it calmly, the story out of him, and I figure maybe what he wants is a story in exchange. He wants to know about Over There, what you do when you feel like this Over There, where there isn't an empty wheat field to cry in. So I tell him a little bit, just to say something. But I just talk circles. I say that Over There is tall buildings. Over There is restaurants and the people who eat in them. I say that Over There is the long, high windows by the clean dining tables, the bright candles for the patrons. Over There is side streets with doors always open to the restaurant kitchens, the cooks sitting on the steps to get air. How there are enough restaurants Over There to employ actors and dancers who bend like Ls over the tables, enough work for the Mexican busboys and the dishwashers, how they all split the tips between cigarettes at the end of the long shift. Living Over There is cars and taxis, vans and too many horns, a bus to get you from one side to the other whenever you needed.

I don't offer much more and Brother John sips his coffee, quiet, not asking for more. What city doesn't have those things—tall buildings, too many cars, immigrants in the kitchen, actors and dancers eager for spotlights? His face is done crying and it settles into resignation—he doesn't bother looking me in the eye.

The waiter brings the check and both of us reach for our wallets. I don't want to do the dance of who pays, so I let Brother John put the money down when he insists and get up to leave. We walk out to the car, families going in to eat, the smell of the brand-new tar of the parking lot in the air. When he shuts the car door, before I turn the ignition, Brother John clears his throat. He wants to revive the life in himself and he says, "I loved that guy. Gary Lee Brown. I still love him—" but I interrupt him.

"No more," I say, apologetically. And then, "Keep it to yourself."

During the rest of the week, I think about Brother John next door, and I feel bad about how I left things with him. I nurse my aching hamstring in the quiet of the house, all of my nephews outside playing basketball, tireless. They'll come in filthy later, and it takes a long time to get all of them to wash their hands. I am lying on the couch and I close my eyes, hoping they'll stay out there until my brothers and sisters come back to collect them.

I keep wondering if I did the right thing by not telling Brother John my story, even though I knew he wanted to hear it. But I learned a long time ago to keep things simple. Don't tell much. Don't tell everything. Don't reveal what people don't need or want to know. It makes it easier all around.

Of my father: say no more of what happened to end the marriage. Of my brothers and sisters: nothing of the spider cracks in their own unions. Of my tía Carolina: nothing of the money she stole from her job as the cashier of the mini-mart. Look at the people we went to school with: Agustina, who though she knew the father of her baby, never brought it up. Ginger, whose mother worked with the school superintendent, wore big sweaters to hide the pregnancy. Maybe credit should have gone, then, to Ginger's mother for saving reputations all around. Beto and Carla married at the Iglesia de San Pedro with no one raising a fuss, not even Patsy, alone and with no kids to show for her time with Beto. Violeta never gossips about what is wrong with her insides, never takes her older sister Sofía's tragedy and brings it under the wing of her own misery. Emilio never admits that the accident at the paper mill might have been his fault, might have been caused by the sips of whiskey and the pot during his long breaks at four in the morning. No one needs to know the whole story, I wish I could tell Brother John. No one wants to know what Lily does in her car while she waits outside the houses of the men she loves. No one wants to know about Gary Lee Brown.

But I can't explain it to Brother John without telling him about the Actor. Take the Actor: when the Actor told me he was an actor, I had wanted to know what kind, because *actor* didn't differentiate him from any of the other actors Over There—stage actors, musical theater actors, dancers who did some acting because there was more stage work than dance, improv players, experimental and fringe performers, porn stars, soap actors, commerical hounds, film extras. But it had become apparent that I didn't need to know. All that I needed to know was the Actor's last hour at the bar, that the flirtations with the customers were nothing more than a way to get bigger tips, and that neither of us had to admit that this would be nothing more than a brief, few months of small arguments and jealousies, caught hours and inconsequence. There would be no telling of where each of us grew up and who was the last boyfriend and why we didn't work out. I learned to keep it to sitting at the bar, having two drinks, watching the Actor bend elegantly down, watching the customers admire that elegance. For all his story, Brother John got nothing and I left out my part about the Actor, about dating the Actor, then loving him, sitting at the bar and waiting for the end of his shifts, watching as he stretched over a table to deliver drinks, a sharp L as the customers peered up at him.

"You shouldn't go on the plane like that, hurt and everything," my father says. His voice surprises me and I open my eyes to see him standing over the couch. "Why don't you stay until you get better?"

"I have only a couple of vacation days," I tell him. "I have to go back." I put my hand over my eyes, as if I have a headache, but really it's to ward him off. We have not had our usual session of just the two of us sitting in a room, quiet, until he asks the questions that still eat away at him, the questions about my mother. Each and every time, I refuse to answer. I stay quiet and let him ponder it on his own because I don't know how to relieve his exasperation.

"Why are you Over There anyway?" my father asks me.

"Dad, lay off," I say, sighing, and I rub my hamstring as if he's irritating it. My hand is still over my eyes, but I don't have to look at him to realize that our usual session is here, the two of us quiet. I think about the difficulty of easing anyone's pain with sudden departures, with lack of reasons, with a loss of hope. I can see Brother John in a small room in the wide plains of Oklahoma, the weather battering the thin glass of the windows of his attic apartment, him standing there and trying to ease his own confusion. It makes it easier to picture my father in this house on the first night of my mother's departure, how Brother John's story has allowed me to imagine. But then I realize my father has let go of those questions and those hurts, at least temporarily.

After a long while, I speak. "Dad," I ask, "why did you send me over to Brother John?" my hand over my eyes, my other hand rubbing at my hamstring.

He does not answer. He stands at the foot of the couch. I can hear the clock ticking above the television set, the boys outside arguing, the ball bouncing against the dirt driveway. I still have my hand over my eyes, blind to my father's reaction, and the longer he stays silent, the more I want the pain in my leg to stay fiery and fierce, my hand over my eyes like a blindfold.

Caitlin Horrocks

This Is Not Your City

Her daughter, Nika, is missing, and there are two policemen
in Daria's kitchen. She does not know what to say to them.
"Do you want coffee?" she asks, her voice cracking on the upswing of
the question. It is one of the only perfect sentences she knows, one of
the first she learned. The policemen shake their heads and Daria's
husband, Paavo, makes it understood that he will answer their questions, sign their forms. He lifts his fingers curled around an invisible
pen and signs his name with a flourish on the air. Daria goes to sit on
Paavo's bed. Missing is better than it could be. Paavo had groped for
the word in his dictionary. The policemen looked embarrassed for
them, and Daria remembered why she did not usually open the door
to strangers. The first entry Paavo pointed to meant gone, and Daria
almost died. It was several minutes, terrible gestures, the younger
policeman with his hand like a visor on his forehead, pretending to
look for her daughter under the cupboards, until Daria understood
as much as she did.

  She has left the kitchen still holding Paavo's dictionary. They each
have one, pocket-size, with a larger one on the bookshelf in the living
room. They have not needed the big one yet; their conversation is not

so complex. She turns to *dead* in Russian and rips out the page. She will eat it, she thinks, like an old-time spy, so no one can bring her bad news. She thinks she is joking to herself until she takes a bite of the upper-right corner. She chews and swallows, creases the page in half, tears a bite from the middle. She unfolds it and holds it up in front of the window. It is late evening but the sun is still up. She washed and bleached the curtains a week ago and admires through the paper how white they are now. The page is soft but substantial, good to chew. It has a flat taste like raw oats. She realizes that Paavo would not need this page to tell her that her daughter is dead. He would turn, of course, to the Finnish, and Daria has already swallowed the translation so she does not know what word to rip out. She eats the rest of the Russian page anyway.

Daria hears the policemen leave and Paavo comes into the bedroom, gestures for his dictionary. He sits on the edge of the bed with a pencil and pad of paper, and Daria is relieved that he doesn't notice the missing page. He looks studious, reading glasses pushed down his nose as he writes things out for her, his Cyrillic letters as misshapen as a child's. Nika and Matti, her boyfriend, have not come back from their camping trip. They were due in the morning at Matti's house to return the car and were going to spend the day there. All day Matti's mother tried to call his cell phone. All day nothing, and at dinnertime she called the police. A Russian interpreter will be by tomorrow morning, to explain things better, to ask Daria some questions. Daria nods.

Nika is still missing and Daria still does not know what to do, so she heats the sauna. She strips off her clothes and lets them sit in a heap on the bathroom floor. She fills the red plastic bucket with cold water and pulls the ladle from its peg on the wall. Paavo is always saying he will buy birch, a proper bucket and scoop, but Daria doesn't care. She heats the sauna hotter than she ever has before, and dumps water on the rocks until sweat runs into her eyes and they hurt so badly it's okay if she cries. The steam is searing. She has left her earrings in and she can feel the silver getting hotter, drawing the burn up through the hooks into her ears. They will blister if she leaves them, burn her fingers if she takes them out. She tugs them quickly from her ears and lets them drop between the pine boards to the floor.

When she steps out into the bathroom her eyes are sore and so salted she can barely see. She wraps a towel around herself and walks to the bedroom. Paavo is sitting on the bed watching television, duvet over his legs, his chest bare. He has an old man's body, with small, pointy breasts, white hairs curling around the nipples. Skinny legs and arms, a great melon of a belly. His hair is gray but thick, with a swoop above his forehead; he is not so very old, yet.

"Are you okay?" he asks.

"No. Yes." She mimes sweating, rubs her eyes, says "Ouch." Paavo nods, willing as ever to be lied to.

"Sauna. Still hot. If you want," she says.

Paavo shakes his head. Daria wonders if her body is still hot enough to scald him, wonders what damage she could do if she reached for him now. Paavo turns the channel from Formula 1 highlights, looking for something he thinks she will like better. He stops at an old episode of *Friends* and Daria listens to the laugh track. Someday, she thinks, if she grows old in this country, she will know on her own what's so funny. She has seen this episode already, back at home in Vyborg, the voices dubbed. Chandler is inside a box on the floor, apologizing. She recognizes this much, his apology, and she realizes it is a word that Finnish people never speak aloud. *Excuse me* they say easily, but never this, *olen pahoillani*, a sad man locked in a box. She wonders if Nika knows this word yet, *pahoillani*, if she could say it in their new language and be understood. *Olen pahoillani. Tytärani.* I'm sorry. My daughter, I'm sorry.

Daria puts on her nightgown and joins Paavo in the bed, he under his comforter, she under hers. She lies on her side, facing away from her husband. She hears him turn the television off and put the remote on the nightstand. He puts his hand on her shoulder and she is waiting for it to trail lower, down her spine or over the curve of her hip, when instead he touches her hair. He pets her head like a child's.

"It will be all right," he says, and Daria is grateful but somehow lonelier. Sex is a language they can pretend to have in common; he grunts, he waits for her to sigh, and they can imagine that they understand each other. She doesn't like it when Paavo talks in bed. Her ears know he is a stranger, and if he spoke while he touched her, her skin would know it, her bones would know it, her sex would know that she has agreed to spend her life in a stranger's bed.

The agency promised her no better. She has not been cheated. You have a daughter, they told her. Fourteen years old. What do you expect us to find for you? A divorcée, no less, which seemed to imply to the matchmakers a lack of fortitude, fatally unrealistic expectations. Her first husband did not beat her, she had been forced to admit to them. He was drunk only on weekends when he was in Vyborg, which was only two weeks out of every sixteen. He went to the oil fields in Western Siberia, and brought home money, and how could she be so dissatisfied with someone who was not even there? You wouldn't understand, she said to them. It is what she has been saying for nine years, and what started as reluctance to unburden herself to nosy aunts and cousins has in those nine years become something true. She has forgotten why she staked her hopes on something better, something different, why she was so sure of success. Daria knows that if she thinks about the divorce too long she will be forced to admit that she would not do it again. It is a monstrous realization that she has made a mistake of that magnitude with her life, something that cannot be mended or taken back. If she could choose again she would stay, and it seems like the worst thing she could know about herself.

If she had stayed, she might never have had to go to work at the Vyborg market hall, the building by the bay that still has *Kauppahalli* inscribed in cement above the main doors. In the years after the war, her parents told her, thousands of such signs were scratched out, repainted, rehung. The statelier ones, letters cut into granite or marble, have stayed. So she knows the Finnish for *market hall*, for *train station*, for *bank*. She also knows the Finnish for *chocolates*, and *taste*, and *very inexpensive,* the words she used behind the broad table at the back wall, plastic bins of foil-wrapped candies before her. The teenager at the next table sold bootleg CDs and taught her to recognize the Finns. Terrible clothes and stylish glasses, he told her. Jogging suits and sharp dark frames. That's the look of money.

Daria thinks she will not sleep this night, the sky a starless waking blue, but hours later she finds herself stirring, groggy, the early light pale and confused. When Paavo wakes she has porridge ready, homemade and heavy, a pool of black currant jam in the middle of the bowl. He manages to ask her if she wants him to stay home from work. "Go," she tells him. Paavo works at the pulp factory, and the smell of him after a shift is the smell of the air over the town, the wind off the lake; it smells something like stewed cabbage, and the townspeople have only one joke about it. Smell that, they say, noses in the air. The scent of money. On good days the breeze comes from the other end of the lake, where the Japanese have built a new sawmill. That smell reminds Daria of the forest near Ladoga, picking at bark with her fingernails and opening a divot that bled sap and the pine scent of the tree. She told this to Nika one day when the wind was good, and Nika rolled her eyes. "It's a sawmill, Mom. That's the smell of dead trees. Dead trees getting chopped into little bits."

Not little bits, Daria thinks, not unless the grain is bad. She knows the trees she smells are being planed into boards, long and straight and someday someone's home. But they are dead all the same. She must grant her daughter that, and to explain the rest seems like so much effort. Nika is fifteen now and does not like to listen.

While Daria waits for the interpreter she cleans the kitchen. She cleans the venetian blinds slat by slat because she cannot figure out how to unhook them from the window frame. The thin panels are sharper than they look, and she cuts her fingers in three places. She leaves a streak of blood on a slat close to the ceiling. She likes hiding a part of herself in the apartment, as if it were a claim to the space, a promise that she will not have to leave it, although her entire life has taught her otherwise. She was born in a city that once spoke another language. She thinks the Finns who visited came only to be angry; they kicked the dissolving sidewalks like the tires of an old car they would have taken better care of. This is not your city anymore, she wanted to tell them. It has not been your city for fifty years. Leave us alone.

Daria scrubs the stovetop and wonders if the translator will be a Russian-speaking Finn, or the other way round. She wonders whether to make tea sweetened with jam, or the endless cups of coffee her husband drinks. The doorbell rings and Daria's heart is frantic. Through the peephole there is only a sour-looking man, older than she is, younger than Paavo. "Daria Kikkunen?" he says when she opens the door, and she nods. She listens to his accent and makes them coffee. The interpreter asks her about Nika and Matti, about their weekend plans. Daria is embarrassed at how little she knows. Only the backpack Nika filled, the sleeping bag she borrowed from Paavo and complained smelled like an old man, smoke and aftershave. The borrowed car to drive north of Kuusamo, to celebrate the midsummer weekend.

The interpreter asks about Matti, and Daria tells him what she knows, how one night four months ago they were all sitting in the living room when a car pulled to a stop outside and honked its horn. *"Poikaystäväni,"* Nika announced in Finnish, *my boyfriend,* took her coat from the hallway closet and left. Nika cannot speak the language, had at that time been in the country for all of eight weeks; what kind of a boyfriend could she have? The interpreter gives Daria an ugly look but leans closer, his hands stretching over his notepad and pen, his sleeves sweeping the table. Daria leans back without thinking, then asks herself why she is bothering to be afraid of this man, balding, his skin the white-yellow of new potatoes. Daria tells him that she has seen Matti a few times, that she remembers a boy like a great gold mastiff, giant and eager and mysteriously happy. Dog-boy, Daria says to herself, although she is forced to admit he is handsome in a way that seems terribly young.

Nika thinks they have never spoken, her boyfriend and her

mother, only nodded at each other from the apartment door as she comes or goes. Nika does not know that six weeks ago they ran into each other in the Prisma parking lot. Daria remembers being surprised when she left the store that evening and there was still light in the sky. A cold wind, but a portion of sun: signs of spring. Matti and Daria recognized each other and said "Hello," cleared their throats, shifted their feet. Then Matti said, "Nika is a very nice girl." He said it slowly and clearly and she understood him. He said it a little loudly, too, which embarrassed her, but she could see he was trying. "I like her very much. Do you understand?" he asked, and Daria nodded. "I can take—," he said, pointing at her shopping bags, and before she could protest he'd lifted them out of her arms and begun to walk toward Paavo's car. He waited while she unlocked the trunk and then put them down carefully. He handed her the plastic bag with the eggs and Daria was surprised that he would think to do that. She was surprised that he seemed such a decent boy, so surprised, in fact, that she felt guilty for her astonishment. He took her hand, held it for a moment. "It is good," he said. "That you bring her. That you bring Nika here. It is a happy thing."

Daria knew he was speaking like a child for her, but even so, whatever he said next slipped past her. She smiled anyway, pressed his hand between hers. It was something about "happy," about a "good life," about "welcome." It was something that, standing there in the Prisma parking lot with a beautiful boy as cheerful as a golden retriever, she could convince herself would someday be true.

"He's a decent boy," Daria tells the interpreter. "Truly. Better than I thought."

The interpreter seems impatient, a man who learned her language thinking it would be of more importance than it has turned out to be. The language of diplomacy has turned into the language of sad women in kitchens and too-sweet tea. He asks for her patronymic and Daria doesn't know if he wants to address her properly in Russian or simply be intrusive, make her reveal a name she no longer has any use for, a person she no longer is. Daria Fedorovna, he says, tell me about your daughter, and for a moment Nika feels like someone else's child. The interpreter eats four slices of *pulla,* one after another. It isn't homemade but he compliments her anyway. Daria pulls more pastry from the bag and slices it finer, fans it out on the plate. She pours him another cup of coffee.

Nika hadn't wanted to leave, Daria confesses. There was her school, her home, her whole life. There had been a boy. He was twenty and worked in the post office. Nika was fourteen. Daria forbade her to see him and Nika laughed at her. Now in this country Nika looks too old, eighteen instead of fifteen, but in Finnish she speaks like a child. I don't want. I do. Yes, I like cigarette. Daria is scared that Nika, too, will end up in a stranger's bed, and if that happens this will have been for nothing.

"Do you think she might have tried to go back?" the interpreter asks her, and Daria doesn't know. It seems so monumentally stupid, a kick in the teeth to her mother, to the marriage. It seems like something, on second thought, Nika might have decided to do. But when Daria looks in Paavo's filing cabinet Nika's passport is still there. She shows it to the interpreter. One page has Nika's visa glued in, another is stamped *Nuijamaa,* where Paavo drove his new wife and daughter across the border for the first and last time in a Ford Fiesta. "It looks the same," Nika had announced, crossing into Finland. For thirty kilometers of nothing but forest she was right. The towns, though. Even the villages. So tidy and glossy, pasteurized to the blue-white of skim milk. It was a long drive, and at the end of it was a town so small, so far from the border, it had none of the amenities the agency had suggested she look for: no language classes, no foreign social clubs, no international center where she could sit with other Russian mothers and discuss ways to save their children.

The interpreter thanks her for her time, when it is clear that it is his own that he feels has been wasted. The pad he brought to take notes is mostly empty. She shows him out and then stands on the balcony, watching him unlock his car and drive off. The green on the trees is still pale, the birches fluffy with light-veined leaves. It was a long winter, and patches of snow stayed slumped in the shade of the pine trees until May. Now Daria has not seen stars for weeks and she does not miss them. She has put potted plants all along the edges of the balcony, some balanced on the railing and tied precariously with twine to the rungs, and in the long summer light they are finally starting to grow. The blue nights husband the herbs, the vegetables, which they will have fresh and now not so expensively. The supermarkets here make her nervous. It is sometimes a physical pain, to pay so much for things. In the register lines she sweats and brings the groceries home with damp patches under her arms.

Daria looks in the cupboards, plans dinner. She takes steaks from the freezer to thaw. It is too early to do anything else and the apartment is not big enough to occupy her with cleaning. She did the living room and Paavo's bedroom only yesterday, when Nika was already missing but her mother did not even know. So Daria turns the handle of Nika's door. Her daughter has learned at least one thing in Finnish: *Pääsy Kielletty.* She has written it in black marker on a piece of notebook paper and taped it to her door. NO ENTRY.

Nika's room is a glorious mess, alive with her daughter's things, the smell of her, the perfume Daria suspects she stole, the floor shining with the glitter Nika glues to her eyelids with Vaseline. The top of the dresser is littered with makeup, a dark purple lipstick worn away at a sloping angle, a black eyeliner as blunted as a crayon. Nika wears thick streaks of it every day, doesn't wash it off at night, comes out of her bedroom in the morning looking like a sluggish raccoon. Daria wants to tell her that she must always take off her makeup, that to leave it on will someday make her look ten years older. She wants to tell Nika a thousand things, and practices speeches to her daughter in her head so often they are threadbare before she has the courage to say them aloud, as if struggling so hard in one language has made her mute in every other.

The marriage is a gaping hush, an unraveling hole that cannot be darned. It is growing. It has swallowed the girl Daria was, who spun terrible fairy tales in her school notebooks, about princesses and white horses and the blood-pricked thorns of roses, the icy shards of hearts. It has swallowed the woman Daria was who narrated her days. Who said, this is what happened today. This is who I saw. This is what we talked about. This is who has gotten fat. It has swallowed the woman who asked, How was school today, and worse, the silence has swallowed the daughter who sometimes answered her. Daria has sold herself for nothing, because her daughter is becoming as mute as she is. How was school today, she says in Russian, and Nika has no answer, not in any language, not in the one she was born with, nor in the three she is supposed to be learning. Not in Finnish, or the English she takes three times a week, or the Swedish she is required to take for two, another language she cannot speak, another she does not need, another class she will fail. Paavo has had to put his signature on Swedish tests turned in blank, Nika's name written on the top and every question unanswered. Can't you try harder, Daria has asked her. How do you still know nothing? Speak, Daria has begged her. Just speak. Please.

If Nika writes fairy tales, she has never shown them to her mother. Math was her best subject in Vyborg, and in Outojärvi it is one of the only ones she passed. Her marks would be perfect except for the word problems lurking at the end of every exam. Sometimes she reads them well enough to solve, and those tests Daria sticks to the refrigerator. Nika is a practical child, and has never, as her mother once did secretly, rhymed storm clouds as dark as her soul, or a love that burned like fire. It is just as well, Daria thinks, because the love Daria has known has never burned like fire, and her heart has never broken into shards. It simply beats and that is a language of its own, useless and irrefutable. The heart has one word only, and however wrong or right her life might have gone it would have the one word still.

Daria scoops clothes from Nika's floor into a hamper, puts tissues blotted with lipstick into the wastebasket. The school year ended three weeks ago and Nika's schoolbooks are in a pile in the corner, where she dumped them to empty her backpack for camping. Daria stacks them neatly. Nika's grade report recommended she repeat the year. Paavo said he'd talk to the headmaster again, meet with the teachers, see what he could do. He did not sound hopeful.

"It's okay." Nika shrugged.

"Don't you want to keep up with your friends?" Daria asked, in Russian.

"What friends?" Nika said, then added, because she could, "Matti's graduating anyway."

"And doing what?"

"Looking for work. Staying in town."

"What kind of work?"

"Why do you care? You sold candy. You don't work at all now."

"I work."

"Being Paavo's wife? I guess that's work. I guess that's some kind of work," Nika said, and Daria blushed.

Beneath the stack of Nika's school things there is a folder Daria recognizes, a packet of "Helpful Hints" from the agency. Phrases for courtship, for proposals, for visa arrangements and a life together in two languages: *You are very beautiful. I believe strongly in good family life. My hobbies are to bake and cook. I am sincere and passionate. I like fidelity.*

One of Daria's friends with a PhD in comparative literature and a job managing a florist shop had read it over and laughed. "Full of mistakes. You memorize these and you'll sound even stupider."

The agency had already drawn up Daria's profile with a "1" under language skills: Some basic phrases. Cannot write or talk on telephone.

Daria doesn't understand why Nika would have this folder until she turns a page and reads Nika's notes. There are pages of endearments she has practiced writing over and over, until her handwriting is not so awkward. She has copied phrases out on blank pages to memorize them, inserted Matti's name on the blank lines. *I want to give you the world. Can you speak slower? My heart is like a bird that is ready to zoom up to the sky. Am I deserving for your love?*

. . .

"Sexy," the agency had told her. "These pictures are not sexy."

Daria had borrowed a camera from a friend and asked Nika to go with her to a city park near their apartment. Nika's pictures were head shots, Daria leaning against tree trunks and smiling to show off her straight teeth, shiny brown hair, careful makeup that you could see she did not really need. Daria had Nika when she was twenty-two, was thirty-six when she signed up with the agency. Not so old. She has never smoked and her skin is good for her age, mostly unlined.

"You can't even see your body in these. Who will be interested? They'll think you're fat and trying to hide it."

Daria is slim, almost skinny. She is proud that she does not eat much, that she could wear her daughter's clothes if she wanted to.

"What do you think the men will be looking for? Why do you think they'll pick you? Your teenage daughter? Your '1' in language? We need other photos."

Daria asked Nika to take those photos, too, in her bedroom with the blinds pulled down. Their apartment had only two rooms—Daria slept on the couch in the living room. To be on a bed it had to be Nika's—to wear sexy clothes, those were mostly Nika's, too. There was the shot of her on her hands and knees on the bed, in a short robe, barely covered. The shot she leaned over for, her cleavage at the center of the picture. It was one of Nika's bras that gave the best effect, a padded purple one that pushed Daria's small breasts up and together. Daria knew the bra from doing the laundry and asked to try it.

"Maybe your purple one. That might look best."

"Mom."

"Please. I need you to help me with this. I'll wash it for you after, if you want. It'll be dry by tomorrow morning if you want to wear it."

"Mom."

"Please," Daria had begged her daughter, and Nika had done it. She had fished her bra out of her dresser, pulled her shortest skirts from the closet, the shirts with the lowest necklines. Daria tried to think of the clothes only as costume changes, a whirl of scenery and props as her daughter positioned her in the doorway, on the bed, the nightstand lamp on and then off. She lay on her back, her arms over her head, one leg bent; Nika slit open the blinds and striped her mother with sunlight. "Maybe undo another button," Nika said. "Pull it down a little. Pull the shoulders wide."

The shirt was one Nika had begged for before her first day of high school; she'd bargained for the bra when it went on sale at a department store. The skirt had been a reward when Nika scored highest in her class on a trigonometry exam.

"Do you think this is sexy enough?" Daria kept saying, hating herself but having no one else to ask.

"You're sexy. The pictures will be sexy. Stop worrying," Nika told her. She bent and shaped her mother's limbs like a doll's rubber legs, crooked plastic arms. She lifted a skirt higher on Daria's thighs, the hem pinched between her thumb and middle finger. Daria could feel the tongue of her daughter's fingers not-touching her as the fabric settled over her skin.

"Much better," the agency told them. "Much," and at the time Daria was relieved. Yet if she had to put her finger on the moment it started to spread, the toothed silence between them, she would probably mark it there, that Sunday afternoon in Nika's bedroom with the blinds drawn, Daria dressed in her daughter's underwear. It was a long time before Nika wore those clothes again. The purple bra did not turn up in the wash for weeks. But Nika did not have so many clothes she could afford to be that choosy, and eventually they all turned up again, the skirts and shirts and the short robe. Her clothes are one more way that Nika has not fit in here, but she has refused new ones. Nika and Daria both know that Paavo disapproves. He has copied down Nika's size from the tags inside her clothes and bought her loose jeans and sweaters. She wears them most often when he is not around.

.   .   .

There is the sound of a car outside and Daria wonders if the day has sped forward so quickly that Paavo is home already. In June the light changes so little that it is hard to tell the time. Daria wakes sometimes at four a.m. and doesn't know if it's time to get up and make breakfast or to go back to sleep. She wakes sometimes with Paavo holding her, and when she tries to get up, he tells her again that he does not need a cooked breakfast, that bread and cheese and yogurt did him fine for years, they will do him fine now, that he does not need the things she thinks she owes him.

Daria puts Nika's notebook back under the stack of schoolbooks, arranges them so it will not look like she was spying. She is already worried to be here in Nika's room, to have picked up her laundry. Daria can taste the fight they will have about it when Nika comes home. When. There is a key unlocking the front door and Daria stands with the hamper on her hip. She does not want Paavo to see Nika's room, to criticize the mess. But it is not Paavo who has unlocked the front door, who walks down the hall to the bedroom.

"You're in my room," Nika says.

Daria drops the laundry and takes her daughter in her arms. She has not had the courage to hold her daughter this desperately since Nika turned eleven and started practicing surly looks in the bathroom mirror. Daria holds her now and rocks her back and forth on their feet. She is taller than her daughter, and holds her so hard that Nika is standing on her toes before her mother lets her down and looks at her. Nika's hair is pulled back tight, in a fierce but messy ponytail. She is wearing shorts and a tank top and her shoulders are streaked with red and blue, the pull and press of fingers and nails. There are scratches on her arms, her legs, circles of red around her ankles.

"What happened to you? What did he do?"

"Nothing," Nika says. Her eyes are as red as Daria's in the sauna, sore and tired from crying. "The car. I think I messed it up driving back. I'm not so good at shifting."

"The car?" Daria says. "Where's Matti? Why didn't he drive?"

"I left the tent there. It belongs to his father. I just sat there all day yesterday and then I got in the car and left everything. He'll be mad."

"No one's mad. You're safe," Daria says, touching her daughter's shoulders, just resting her open palms on top of them so as not to squeeze the bruises. "And Matti? Is he safe? Or—not safe?"

"Not safe."

"Does he need help?"

Nika shook her head.

"Is he dead?" Daria asks her daughter, because she can think of no other way to say it, and Nika nods. Daria walks them to the kitchen before she asks her daughter how. She puts on the kettle, looks at the clock. Paavo won't be home for hours. The police won't bother with her while she's alone, unable to talk to them. Which is good because the story, when Nika tells it, takes a long time. Her breath won't come. Her throat tightens, mucus runs over her top lip and she lets it, swipes it with her tongue, until her mother takes a box of tissues from the bathroom and cleans her daughter's face. The story spills out slowly, and Daria can't help calculating the length and breadth of it, the number of words, the way it contains as much as her daughter has told her in years. It is a story that starts with two teenagers in the forest, a midsummer bonfire, a package of sausages to roast on sticks and a case of beer. It was after midnight before the sun threatened to set, sunk rind-deep in the lake they had camped beside. They knew it would slip under and be up again in less than an hour, but there was still a sadness to the moment, that the sun would drown itself for even an instant. They were both full of sausage and beer when Matti suggested they swim toward it, the orange rim above the water. They stripped off their clothes and ran in. The water was frigid. They swam toward the sun, into the middle of the lake, and when Matti started to cramp, Nika was the only thing he had to hang on to. He panicked, thrashed in the water, tried to lever himself onto her shoulders and ended up pulling them both under. He grabbed at her legs, her ankles, and she kicked out instinctively, swallowing lake water and trying to scream to him to stop. He was too scared to listen, unable to make his body obey him. He had had them both under for over a minute, sinking, pulling Nika down with him, when Nika started kicking. She found his shoulder first, then his face, over and over until he let go and she shot up to the surface. Three breaths and she went down again, Nika told her mother, looking for him, to grab him and pull him up. He was twice her size but if he didn't struggle she could have gotten him back to shore. She dived and dived and couldn't find him. The sun went down and the deeper Nika dived the more nothing she found. Her lungs were aching, her feet were numb and sore where she'd kicked him, and when a pressure began to poke at her side, she could think of nothing to do but swim to shore. She swam out two more times that night, until she didn't trust herself to make it there and back again, and found nothing. The next day she spent sitting on a fallen log by their burned-out fire. She started drinking a beer, dumped it on the ashes. Opened another one, took a swallow. Matti's cell phone, still in the pocket of the jeans he'd left crumpled in the mud at the edge of the lake, rang eight times in an hour. On the ninth Nika pulled it out and threw it in the lake. The next night was cold enough. Nika wrapped herself in Paavo's old sleeping bag and must have slept, because she woke up propped against the log, and decided she had to leave. "I killed him," Nika tells her mother. The kettle has burbled and then quieted, the hush before the boil. Daria has picked it up before it could scream but hasn't poured the water. She only stands there, her arm shaking with the weight of the kettle, the burner still glowing.

"You didn't kill him."

"I kicked him and he drowned."

"You didn't have a choice."

"His parents will hate me."

"No one will hate you. It's not a crime. Not being able to save someone."

"They'll hate me," Nika says, and Daria turns back to the stove, sets the kettle down, turns the heat off. She is not sure why this is the thing that troubles Nika so desperately until Nika describes a whole life Daria has known nothing about, helping pick currants off the bushes in Matti's family's backyard and bottling their juice. She has helped Matti's sister braid hair and try on makeup. Matti's father has invited her mushroom picking in the autumn. She has helped Matti's mother tidy the kitchen after meals. His family has a piano and Nika has played a little, only what she remembers from school, since she has never had an instrument to play at home. "His parents," Nika says. "They've been so good to me. They'll hate me now."

"They won't," Daria says, taking mugs from the cupboard, teabags from the tin.

"How could they not?"

"If you don't tell them," Daria says. "If you never tell anyone." She steeps the tea, brings the cups to the table with a little ceramic dish in the shape of a teapot, printed with roses and stained brown from the seep of old teabags. Nika puts her hands around the mug and shakes her head at sweeteners. Daria sits across from her, lets her tea turn almost black and then lifts out the bag. Nika doesn't move and Daria lifts hers out as well, lets them slump soggily in the little dish.

"You will say you were eating, drinking, watching the sun go down," Daria says, as soothingly but matter-of-fact as she can. "Matti went swimming. Only him. He went far out and then you couldn't see him anymore. You shouted and you swam and you dived until you couldn't breathe. It's true. All this is true."

Nika gestures at her scratched shoulders, scraped feet.

"You went as far down as you could, seaweed wrapped around your ankles. You almost didn't make it up. You spent the night leaning against a log. How would your shoulders not be scraped? Besides, you'll change clothes. A long sleeved shirt, jeans. They might never see."

Nika only looks at her, holds her body straighter. She is sore and in pain and her mother can see her trying to figure out how not to show it, how to walk unhunched toward Matti's parents and be hugged without flinching.

"What will it hurt?" Daria asks. "Nothing. No one."

Nika nods, and Daria does not know what it means, whether Nika agrees, whether she trusts herself to speak.

"It's a good story. It's almost true. And it will hurt everyone so much less. Two families. You can spare two families."

Nika looks for a moment as if she is trying to figure out who the other family is, who besides Matti's parents pick berries in their backyard and laugh together at the same television shows. She realizes that her mother means the two of them and Paavo, or perhaps not Paavo, perhaps only the two of them. Daria tells the story again, spins a tale that is as long as anything she has said to her daughter in a year. She takes more time over it than her announcement to Nika that she'd signed with the agency, staked her hopes on finding an elderly Finnish man who had been too long alone. She fills in the details, the feel of the light, the smell of the water, the horror of seeing Matti disappear beneath the surface of the lake. Nika was the one who was there, the one who knows these things, yet she is leaning forward, hanging on the words of the story she will be expected to tell.

Nika nods. She doesn't speak, but it is a good nod, sharp and decisive. Daria can see the muscles move along her neck. Daria smiles, takes her daughter's hand without speaking. The silence will swallow them and it will save them whole. She thinks how exciting the story will be for the interpreter, how it will be a momentous task for the man with skin like the peels of new potatoes; how he will pause and lag and struggle to find a way to tell a family that their teenage son is dead and if it is anyone's fault it's his own. The interpreter will struggle for the words, and Daria wonders how many she and Nika already know: forest, lake, boyfriend, dark, I'm sorry. *Metsä, järvi, poikaystävä, pimea, pahoillani.* Daria could ask now, about *olen pahoillani,* whether Nika knows this phrase for a regret so extraordinary that daily language cannot hold it. She could ask, but doesn't. Even if Nika knows the word, it is not now or ever a thing she wants to hear her daughter say.

Ha Jin

The House Behind a Weeping Cherry

WHEN MY roommate moved out, I was worried that Mrs. Chen might increase the rent. I had been paying three hundred dollars a month for half a room. If my landlady demanded more, I would have to look for another place. I liked this Colonial house, before which stood an immense weeping cherry tree that attracted birds and gave a bucolic impression, though it was already early summer and the blossoming season had passed. In spite of its peaceful aura, the house was close to downtown Flushing, and you could hear the burr of traffic on Main Street. It was also near where I worked, convenient for everything. Mrs. Chen took up the first floor; my room was upstairs, where three young women also lived. My former roommate, an apprentice to a carpenter, had left because the three female tenants were prostitutes and often received clients in the house. To be honest, I didn't feel comfortable about that, either, but I had grown used to the women, and especially liked Huong, a twiggy Vietnamese in her early twenties, whose parents had migrated to Cholon from China three decades ago, when Saigon fell and the real estate market there became affordable. Also, I was new to New York, and at times it was miserable to be alone.

As I expected, Mrs. Chen, a stocky woman with a big mole beside her nose, came up that evening. She sat down, patted her dyed hair, and said, "Wanren, now that you're using this room for yourself we should talk about the rent."

"I'm afraid I can't pay more than I'm paying. You can get another tenant." I waved at the empty bed behind her.

"Well, I could put out an ad for that, but I have something else in mind." She leaned toward me.

I did not respond. I disliked this Fujianese woman and felt that she was too smooth. She went on, "Do you have a driver's license?"

"I have one from North Carolina, but I'm not sure if I can drive here." I had spent some time delivering produce for a vegetable farm outside Charlotte.

"That shouldn't be a problem. You can change it to a New York license—easy to do. The motor registration office is very close." She smiled, revealing her gappy teeth.

"What do you want me to do?" I asked.

"I won't charge you extra rent. You can have this room to yourself, but I hope you can drive the girls around in the evenings when they have outcalls."

I tried to stay calm and answered, "Is that legal?"

She chuckled. "Don't be scared. The girls go to hotels and private homes. No cops will burst in on them—it's very safe."

"How many times a week am I supposed to drive?"

"Not very often—four or five times, tops."

"Do you pay for the girls' meals, too?"

"Yes, everything but long-distance phone calls."

At last I understood why my female housemates always ate together. "All right, I can drive them around in the evenings, but only in Queens and Brooklyn. Manhattan's too scary."

She gave a short laugh. "No problem. I don't let them go that far."

"By the way, can I eat with them when I work?"

"Sure thing. I'll tell them."

"Thank you." I paused. "You know, sometimes it can be lonely here."

A sly smile crossed her face. "You can spend time with the girls—they might give you a discount."

I didn't know how to respond to that. Before leaving, she made it clear that I must keep everything confidential, and that she had asked me to help mainly because she wanted the women to feel safe when they went out. Johns would treat a prostitute better if they knew she had a chauffeur at her disposal. I had seen the black Audi in the garage. I hadn't driven for months and really missed the feeling of freedom that an automobile used to give me, as though I could soar in the air if there weren't cars in front of me on the highway. So to some degree I looked forward to driving the women around.

After my landlady left, I stood before the only window in my room, which faced the street. The crown of the weeping cherry, motionless and more than forty feet high, was a feathery mass against a sky strewn with stars. In the distance, a plane, a cluster of lights, was sailing noiselessly east through a few rags of clouds. I knew Mrs. Chen's offer would implicate me in something illicit, but I wasn't worried. By now I was accustomed to living among the prostitutes. When I first figured out what they did for a living, I wanted to move out right away, like my former roommate, but I couldn't find a place close to my job—I was a presser at a garment factory downtown. Also, having come to know the women a little better, I realized that they were not "bloodsuckers," as people assumed. Like everyone else, they had to work to survive.

I, too, was selling myself. Every weekday I stood at the table ironing the joining lines of cut pieces, the waists of pants, the collars and cuffs of shirts. It was sultry in the basement, where the air conditioner was at least ten years old, inefficient, and whined loudly. We were making quality clothes for stores in Manhattan, and every item had to be neatly ironed before being wrapped up for shipment.

Who would have thought I'd land in a sweatshop! My parents' last letter again urged me to go to college. Try as I might, I couldn't pass the TOEFL. My younger brother had just been admitted to a veterinary school, and I'd sent back three thousand dollars for his tuition. If only I had learned a trade before coming to the United States, like plumbing, or home renovation, or *Qigong*. Any job would have been better than ironing clothes.

The brothel had no name. I had once come across a newspaper ad in our kitchen that read "Angels of Your Dream—Asian Girls from Various Countries with Gorgeous Figures and Tender Hearts." It gave no contact information other than a phone number, which was the one shared by the women. I almost laughed out loud at the ad, because the three of them were all Chinese. Of course, Huong could pass for Vietnamese, speaking the language as her native tongue, and Nana could pretend to be Malaysian or Singaporean, since she came from Hong Kong and spoke accented Mandarin. But Lili, a tall college student from Shanghai, looked Chinese through and through, even though she spoke English well. She was the one who handled the phone calls.

Unlike most underground brothels, this one didn't change its women regularly. I guessed Lili would return to school when the summer was over, and then Mrs. Chen might hire another twenty-something who was fluent in English. I wasn't sure if my landlady was the real boss, however. The women mentioned someone called the Croc. I had never met the man, but I learned from them that he owned some shady businesses in the area and was also a coyote.

I liked having dinner with my housemates, usually around 8:00 p.m. Quite late, but that was fine with me, since most days I didn't leave the factory until seven. Often, I was not the only man dining with them; they offered free dinner to their clients as well. The meals were homely fare—plain rice and two or three dishes, one of which was meat while the others were vegetables. Occasionally, the women prepared seafood in place of a vegetable dish. There would also be a soup, usually made of spinach or watercress or bamboo shoots mixed with dried shrimp, tofu, or egg drops, or even rice crust. The women would take turns cooking, one person each day, unless that person was occupied with a john and another had to fill in for her in the kitchen. Some of their clients enjoyed the atmosphere at the table and stayed for hours chatting.

Whenever there was another man at dinner, I would remain quiet. I'd finish eating quickly and return to my room, where I'd watch TV or play solitaire or leaf through a magazine. But when I was the only man I'd stay as long as I could. The women seemed to like having me around and would even tease me. Huong was not only the prettiest but also the best cook, depending less on sauces, whereas Lili used too much sugar and Nana deep-fried almost everything. One day, Huong braised a large pomfret and stir-fried slivers of potato and celery, both favorites of mine, though I hadn't told her so. None of them had a client that evening, so dinner started at seven thirty and we ate slowly.

Nana told us, "I had a guy this afternoon who said his girlfriend had just jilted him. He cried in my room—it was awful. I didn't know how to comfort him. I just said, 'You have to let it go.' "

"Did he pay you?" Lili asked.

"Uh-huh, he gave me eighty dollars without doing anything with me."

"Well, I wonder why he came here," I said.

"Maybe just to have someone to talk to," Huong said.

"I don't know," Lili pitched in. "Maybe to find out if he could still do it with another girl. Men are weak creatures and cannot survive without having a woman around."

I had never liked Lili, who always spoke to me with her eyes half closed, as if reluctant to pay me more mind. I said, "There're a lot of bachelors out there. Most of them are getting on all right."

"Like yourself," Nana broke in, giggling.

"I'm single because I'm too poor to get married," I confessed.

"Do you have a girlfriend?" Huong asked.

"Not yet."

"So would you go with me if I wasn't a sex worker?" Nana asked, her oval face expressionless.

"Your taste is too expensive for me," I said, laughing, though it was only partly a joke.

They all laughed. Nana continued, "Come on, I'll give you a big discount."

"I can't take advantage of you like that," I said.

That cracked them up again. I meant what I said, though. If I slept with one of them, I might have to do the same with the other two, spending a fortune. Then it would be hard to keep a balanced relationship with all of them. Besides, I wasn't sure if they were all clean and healthy. Even if they were, I disliked Lili. It was better to remain unattached.

Then the phone rang, and Lili picked it up. "Hello, honey, how may I help you?" she intoned in a sugary voice.

I resumed eating as if uninterested, but listened carefully. Lili told the caller, "We have many Asian girls here. What kind of girl are you interested in, sir? . . . Yes, we do. . . . Of course pretty, every one of them is pretty. . . . At least one-twenty. . . . Well, that'll be between you and the girl, sir. . . . Wait, let me write it down." She grabbed a pen and began jotting down the address. Meanwhile, Huong and Nana finished their dinner, knowing that one of them would have business to take care of.

Lili said into the phone, "Got it. She'll be there within half an hour. . . . Absolutely, sir. Thank you, bye-bye."

Hanging up, Lili turned around and said, "Huong, you should go. The man's name is Mr. Han. He wants a Thai girl."

"I can't speak Thai!"

"Speak some Vietnamese to show him that you're not from China. He won't be able to tell the difference anyway, as long as you know how to charm him."

Huong went to her room to brush her teeth and put on some makeup, and Lili handed me a scrap of paper with our destination—a room at the Double Luck Hotel. I knew how to get there, having driven the women there several times. I clapped on my brown duck-bill cap, which kept my eyes hidden.

A few minutes later, Huong came out, ready to go. "Wow, you're beautiful!" I said, quite amazed.

"Am I?" She lifted her arms while turning a little to let me view her from the side. Her waist was concave at the small of her back.

"Like a little fox," I said.

She slapped me on the arm. She was wearing a beige miniskirt and had applied lipstick, but she seemed more like a teenager who had messed up her makeup, so that her face appeared older than her petite body, which was curvaceous but tight. As she walked with her denim purse hanging from her thin shoulder, her legs and hips swayed a little, as if she were about to leap. Together, we went down to the garage.

The hotel was on a busy street, and two buses stood at the front entrance, one still puffing exhaust out of the rear. Flocks of tourists were collecting their baggage while a guide shouted to gather them for check-in. I found a quiet spot around the corner and let Huong out. "Call if you need me to come up," I told her. "I'll be waiting for you here."

"Thanks." She closed the door and strolled away, her gait as casual as if she were a guest at the hotel.

My heart sagged as I lay back in the seat to take a nap. She was young and beautiful and shouldn't have been selling herself like this. For just $120, she would lie with any man in there. For sure she had to send her parents money regularly, but there were other ways of making a living. She wasn't stupid, and she could have learned a respectable trade. She had finished high school in Vietnam and could speak some English by now. But, from what I had gathered at the dining table, she was an illegal alien, whereas Nana had a Canadian green card and Lili held a student visa. They could make some money, definitely, but nothing like what the newspaper ads promised for the "massage" profession—"more than $20,000 a month." Usually, the women charged a john a hundred at the house, but they had to give Mrs. Chen forty of that. Sometimes a client would give them a tip, between twenty and sixty dollars. Nana was rawboned and on the homely side, with a slightly hollowed mouth, so her price for incalls was eighty dollars, unless the men were older and had more cash to throw around. On a good day, they could each make more than two hundred after paying our landlady. Now and then, an obnoxious client would not only refuse to tip them but also walk off with their belongings. Lili had once lost a pair of silver bracelets, stolen by a man who claimed to be from Shanghai, like her.

I had asked Huong about visiting hotels and private homes. She said she could make thirty or forty dollars more per client than she did at the house, though there were more risks involved. One night, I had driven her to see a john at the International Inn, but on arrival she had found two men in the suite. They dragged her in before she could back out, and worked her so hard that she felt as if her legs no longer belonged to her. She had to take off her high heels to walk back to the car. She wept all the way home. She was sick the next day, but she wouldn't go to a clinic, as she had no health insurance. I suggested she see Dr. Liang at Sun Garden Herbs. She paid ten dollars for a diagnosis fee. The old man put his fingers on her wrists to feel her pulse and said her kidneys were weak. Also, there was too much angry fire in her liver. He prescribed a bunch of herbs, which helped her recover. After that, I offered to accompany her into hotels and wait in the hallway, but she wouldn't let me, saying it would be too conspicuous.

I couldn't drift off to sleep in the car, thinking about Huong. What kind of man was she in there with? Was she all right? Did she like it if the john was young and handsome? Was she acting like a slut? Sometimes at night I couldn't sleep, and would fantasize about her, but when I was fully awake I'd keep my distance. I knew I was just a presser in a sweatshop, gangly and nondescript, and might never be able to date a nice chick, but it would be shameful to have an easy woman as a girlfriend. At most, I could be a good friend to Huong.

Tonight she returned in less than fifty minutes, which was unusual. I was pleased to see her back, though her eyes were watery and shed a hard light. She slid into the passenger seat, and I pulled away from the curb. "How was it? No trouble?" I asked, afraid that the client might have discovered she wasn't Thai.

"Rotten luck again," she said.

"What happened?"

"The man's an official from Beijing. He wanted me to write him a receipt, like I'd sold him medicines or something. Where could I get a receipt for him? Nuts!"

"Did he haggle with you?"

"No, but he bit my nipple so hard it must be bleeding. I'll have to put iodine on it once we're home. And now my clients will think I'm diseased."

I sighed, not knowing how to respond. As we were crossing Thirty-seventh Avenue, I said, "Can't you do something less dangerous for a living?"

"You find me a job and I'll take it."

That silenced me. She slipped a ten into my hand, which was the unspoken rule worked out by the women—every time I drove them, they tipped the same amount. Actually, only Huong and Nana did, because Lili didn't take outcalls, since she dealt with the phone calls and the johns who came to the house.

I thanked Huong and put the money in my shirt pocket.

The three women often compared notes on their clients. The best type, they all agreed, was old men. Older johns were usually less aggressive and easier to entertain. Many of them couldn't get hard and spent more time cracking dirty jokes than doing real business. Another strong point those old goats shared was that they could be more generous, having more spare cash in their "little coffers," unbeknownst to their wives. The older ones seldom ate dinner at the house. Some of them were friends of Mrs. Chen's, in which case the women would treat them like special guests, and even give them Viagra. I was surprised when I heard that.

"Viagra?" I asked Lili about Mr. Tong, a bent man in his mid-sixties. "Aren't you afraid he might have a heart attack?"

"Only half a pill, no big deal. Mrs. Chen said he always needs extra help."

"He pays you well besides," Nana said. "Lili, did he give you two hundred today?"

"One-eighty," Lili replied.

"Doesn't he have a wife?" I asked.

"Not anymore. She died long ago," Huong said, cracking a spiced peanut.

"Why wouldn't he marry again?" I went on. "At least he should find someone who can take care of him."

Nana let out a sigh. "Money's the root of the trouble. He's so rich he can't find a trustworthy wife."

Huong added, "I've heard he owns a couple of restaurants."

"Also your sweatshop, Wanren." Nana looked me straight in the face, as if forcing down a laugh.

"No, he doesn't," I shot back. "My factory is owned by a girl from Hong Kong named Nini."

That had them in stitches. Actually, the owner of my garment shop was a Taiwanese man who taught college before coming to America.

Many of the johns were married men who were reluctant to spend time and money on a mistress for fear of scandals and complications that might destroy their marriage. So they tried to keep up appearances while indulging in a sensual life on the sly. But there were always exceptions. One day, Huong said a middle-aged client told her that he hadn't had sex for almost two years because his wife was too ill. Huong advised him to come more often, at least twice a month, so that he could recover his sex life. As he was now, he was totally inadequate. "He's a good man," Huong told us. "He couldn't do anything with me at all, saying he felt guilty about his wife, but he paid me anyway."

"Then he shouldn't have come to a whorehouse in the first place," Lili said.

I could tell that Huong and Nana didn't really like Lili, either. She often bitched about misplaced things, and once accused Nana of using her cell phone to call someone in San Francisco. They had a row and didn't speak to each other for days afterward.

The story about the man with a bedridden wife made me think. If I were a policeman, knowing his family situation, would I have arrested him for visiting a prostitute? Probably not. I used to believe that all johns were bad and loose men, but now I could see that some of them were nothing but wrecks with serious personal problems that they didn't know how to handle. They came here, hoping that a prostitute might help.

I was in bed one night when a cry came from Nana's room. At first, I thought it was just an orgasmic groan she had faked to please a client. Sometimes I was unsettled by the noises the women and the men made, noises that kept me awake and fantasizing. Then Nana screamed, "Get out of here!"

I pulled on my pants and ran out of my room. The door of Nana's room was ajar, and through the gap I saw a paunchy man of around sixty standing by the bed, madly gesticulating at Nana. This was the first time I had seen an older john make trouble. I moved closer but didn't go in. Mrs. Chen had told me to give the women a hand whenever they needed it. She hadn't made it explicit, but I'd guessed that she wanted me to provide some protection for them.

"I paid you, so I'm staying," the man barked, and flung up his hand.

"You can't make a night of it. Please go away," Nana said, her face stamped with annoyance.

I went in and asked him, "What's your problem? Didn't you already get your time with her?"

He squinted at me. His face, red like a monkey's ass, showed that he was drunk. In fact, the entire room reeked of alcohol. "Who are you?" he grunted. "This is none of your business. I wanna stay here tonight, and nobody can make me change my mind."

I could tell that he thought this was like China, where it's common for a john to spend the night with a girl if he pays enough. "I'm just a tenant," I said. "You've been kicking up such a racket that I can't sleep."

"So? Deal with it. I want my money's worth."

As he was speaking, I glanced at Nana's bed. Two wet spots stained a pink sheet, and a pair of pillows had been cast aside. On the floor was an overturned cane chair. By now, both Huong and Lili were up, too, but they stayed outside the door, watching. I told the man, "It's the rule here: you fire your gun and you leave. No girl is supposed to be your bed warmer."

"I paid her for what I want."

"All right, this is not my problem. I'm going to call the police. We simply cannot sleep while you're rocking the house."

"Oh yeah? Call the cops and see who they'll haul away first." He seemed more awake now, his eyes glittering.

I pressed on, "All the tenants here will say that you broke in to assault this woman." I was surprised by what I said, and I saw Huong and Lili avert their eyes.

"Cut that shit out! I paid this ho." He pointed at Nana.

"She's not a whore. Nana, you didn't invite him here, did you?"

"Uh-uh." She shook her head.

I told him, "See, we're all her witnesses. You'd better get out of here, now."

"I can't believe this. There's no good faith in this world anymore— it's worse than China." He grabbed his walking stick and lumbered out of the room.

The three women laughed and told me that the old goat was a first-time visitor and that they felt lucky to have me living on the same floor. We were in the kitchen now, all wide awake. Nana put on a kettle to boil some water for an herbal tea called Sweet Dreams.

I wasn't pleased by what I had done. "I acted like a pimp, didn't I?"

"No, you did well," Huong replied.

"Thank God we have a man among us," Lili added.

Lili's words made me uneasy. I'm not one of you, I thought. But afterward I felt they were friendlier than before, and even Lili started speaking to me more often and with her eyes fully open. They'd ask me what I would like for dinner, and cooked fish three or four times a week because I was fond of seafood. My factory provided steamed rice for its workers at lunch, so I just needed to bring something to go with that. Whenever it was Huong's turn to cook, she would set aside the leftovers in a plastic container for me to take to work the next day. Nana and Lili often joked that Huong treated me as if I were her boyfriend. At first, I felt embarrassed, but little by little I got used to their teasing.

One morning in late July, I woke up feeling as if my lungs were on fire. I must have caught the flu, but I had to go to the factory, where a stack of cut pieces was waiting to be ironed. Unlike the sewing women, I couldn't sit down at the ironing table. The shop provided tea in a samovar, which tasted a little fishy, but I drank one mug after another to soothe my throat and keep my eyes open. As a result, I went to the bathroom more frequently. Some of the floorboards were crooked, and I had to be careful when walking around. By midafternoon, I was sweating all over and my pulse was racing, so I decided to rest on a long bench by the wall, but I tripped and fell before I could reach it. The moment I picked myself up, my foreman, Jimmy Choi, a broad-shouldered fellow of about forty-five, came over and said, "Are you all right, Wanren?"

"I'm OK," I mumbled, brushing the dust off my pants.

"You look terrible."

"I might be running a fever."

He felt my forehead with a thick, rough hand. "You'd better go home. We're not busy today, and Danny and Marc can manage without you."

Jimmy drove me back to Mrs. Chen's in his pickup and told me not to worry about coming to work the next day if I didn't feel up to it. I said I would try my best to show up.

I felt too awful to join my housemates for dinner. Instead, I stayed in bed with my eyes closed, forcing myself not to moan. Still, I couldn't help moaning through my nose occasionally, which made me feel better. Before dark, Huong came in and put a carton of orange juice and a cup on the nightstand, saying I must drink a lot of liquids to excrete the poison from my body. "What would you like for dinner?" she asked.

"I don't want to eat."

"Come on, you have to eat something to fight the illness."

"I'll be all right."

I knew she would be busy that evening, because it was Friday. After she left, I drank some orange juice and then lay back and tried to fall asleep. My throat felt slightly better, but the fever was still raging. I regretted not having gone to the herb store earlier to get some ready-made boluses. The room was quiet except for the faint drone of a mosquito. The instant it landed on my cheek, I killed it with a slap. I was miserable and couldn't help but miss home. Such a feeling hadn't visited me for a long time—I had always managed to suppress my homesickness so that I could make it through my daily routine. A busy man cannot afford to be nostalgic. But that evening the image of my mother kept coming to mind. She knew a lot of folk remedies and could easily have helped me recover in a day or two, but she would have kept me in bed for a few days longer to insure that I recuperated fully. When I was little, I used to enjoy being sick so that she could fuss over me. I hadn't seen her for two years now. Oh, how I missed her!

As I was dozing off, someone knocked on the door. "Come in," I said.

Huong came in again, this time holding a steaming bowl. "Sit up and eat some noodles," she told me.

"You cooked this for me?" I was amazed that it was wheaten noodles, made from scratch, not the rice noodles we usually ate. She must have guessed that, as a northerner, I would prefer wheat.

"Yes, for you," she said. "Eat it while it's hot. It will make you feel better."

I sat up and began eating with chopsticks and a spoon. There were slivers of chives and Napa cabbage in the soup, along with some dried shrimp and three poached eggs. I was touched, and turned my head away so that she wouldn't see my wet eyes. This was genuine homey food from my province, and I hadn't tasted anything like it for two years. I wanted to ask her how she had learned to cook noodles like this, but I didn't say a word; I just kept eating ravenously. Meanwhile, seated on a chair beside my bed, she watched me intently, her eyes shimmering.

"Huong, where are you?" Lili cried from the living room.

"Here, I'm here." She got up and left, leaving the door ajar.

I strained my ears to listen. Lili said, "A man at the Rainbow Inn wants a girl."

"Wanren's ill and can't drive today," Huong replied.

"The place is on Thirty-seventh Avenue, just a few steps away. You've been there."

"I don't want to go tonight."

"What do you mean, you don't want to go?"

"I should stay and take care of Wanren. Can't Nana go?"

"She's busy with someone."

"Can you do it for me?"

"Well," Lili sighed, "OK, only this once."

"Thank you."

When Huong came back, I told her, "You shouldn't spend so much time with me. You have things to do."

"Don't be silly. Here is some vitamin C and aspirin. Take two of each after the meal."

That night, she checked on me from time to time to make sure I took the pills and drank enough liquids and was fully covered with a thick comforter of hers, so that I could sweat out my flu. Around midnight, I fell asleep, but I had to keep getting up to pee. Huong had left an aluminum cuspidor in my room and told me to use it instead of going to the bathroom, so that I wouldn't catch cold again.

The next morning, my fever had subsided, though I still felt weak, not as steady on my feet as before. I called Jimmy and said I would definitely come to work that day, but I didn't get there until after ten. Even so, some of my fellow workers were amazed that I had reappeared so quickly. They must have thought I had caught something more serious, like pneumonia or a venereal disease, and would remain in bed for a week or so. I was glad there was not a lot of work piled up on my ironing table.

A week later, some sewers left the factory and we all got busier. There were twenty women at the garment shop, and, with two or three exceptions, they were all married and had children. Most of them were Chinese, though four were Mexican. They could come and go according to their own schedules. That was the main reason they kept their jobs, which paid by the piece, and not very much. Most of them, working full time, made about three hundred dollars a week. Like them, I could keep a flexible schedule as long as I didn't let work accumulate on my ironing table or miss deadlines. I must admit that our boss, Mr. Fuh, was a decent man, proficient in English and knowledgeable about business management; he even provided health-care benefits for us, which was another reason some of the women worked here. Their husbands were menial workers or small-business owners and couldn't possibly get health insurance for their families. Like the other two young pressers, Marc and Danny, I didn't bother about insurance. I was strong and healthy, not yet thirty, and wouldn't spend three hundred a month on that.

We had been getting more orders for women's garments lately, so I went to work earlier, around seven. But I took long breaks during the day so that I could sit or lie down somewhere to rest my back and legs.

Our factory advertised for some sewers to replace the ones we'd lost, and one evening I brought a flyer back to the house. Lili was busy with a client in her room, but at dinner I showed it to Huong and Nana and said I would try to help them get the jobs if they were interested.

"How much can a sewer make?" Nana asked.

"About three hundred a week," I said.

"My, so little—not for me."

Huong broke in, "Does your boss use people without a work permit?"

"There are some illegal workers at the factory. I can put in a word for you."

"If only I could sew!"

Her words made my heart leap. I went on, "It's not that hard to learn. There're sewing classes downtown. It takes three weeks to graduate."

"And lots of tuition, too," added Nana.

"Not really—three or four hundred dollars," I said.

"I still owe the Croc a big debt, or I would've quit selling my flesh long ago," Huong muttered. Besides smuggling people, the man also operated gambling dens in Queens, one of which had recently got busted.

I said no more. For sure, a sewer made much less than a prostitute, but a sewer could live a respectable life. However, I could see Nana's logic—her work here was more lucrative. Sometimes she made three hundred dollars in a single day. My housemates spent a lot of time watching TV and listening to music when they had no clients, but how long could they continue living like that? Their youth would fade someday. Then what would they do? I remained silent, unsure if I should tell Huong what I thought in Nana's presence.

A slightly overweight white man with wavy hair came out of Lili's room. He looked angry and muttered to himself, "Cheap Chinese stuff, fucking cheap!" Throwing a fierce glance at us, he turned and left. The women's clients were mostly Asian, and occasionally one or two Hispanics or blacks. It was rare to see a white john here.

Lili came out of her room, sobbing. She collapsed on a chair and covered her face with her long-fingered hands. Huong put a bowl of wontons in front of her, but Lili fell back in her chair, saying, "I can't eat now."

"What happened?" Nana asked.

"Another condom break," Lili said, gulping. "He got furious and said he might've caught some disease from me. He paid me only sixty dollars, saying I used a substandard rubber made in China."

"Was it really Chinese?" I asked her.

"I have no clue."

"It might be," Huong said. "Mrs. Chen always gets stuff from Silver City."

"But that's a Korean store," I said.

"I feel so awful to be Chinese here, because China always makes cheap products," Lili said. "China has degraded its people and let me down."

I didn't know what to say. How could an individual blame a country for her personal trouble?

That night, I asked Huong to come outside, and together we talked under the weeping cherry. The stringy branches floated in a cool breeze, while the leaves, like a swarm of arrowheads, flickered in the soft rays cast by the street lights. Fireworks were exploding in the west, at Shea Stadium—the Mets must have won a game. I nerved myself up and said to Huong, "Why can't you quit this sex work so we can be together?"

Her eyes gleamed, fastened on me. "You mean you want to be my boyfriend?"

"Yes, but I also want you to stop selling yourself."

She sighed. "I have to pay the Croc two thousand dollars a month. There's no other way I can make that kind of money."

"How much of your smuggling fee do you still owe him?"

"My parents paid up their fifteen percent in Vietnam, but I still have eighteen thousand to pay."

I paused, figuring out some numbers in my head. That was a big sum, but not impossible. "I can make more than fourteen hundred a month. After the rent and everything, I'll have about a thousand left. I can help you pay the debt if you quit your work."

"Where can I get the other thousand every month? I'd love to be a sewer, but that doesn't pay enough. I've been thinking about the job ever since you mentioned it. It would take a long time for me to get enough experience to make even three hundred a week. Meanwhile, how can I pay the Croc?" She swallowed, then continued, "I often dream of going back, but my parents won't let me. They say that my little brother will join me here eventually. They only want me to send them more money. If only I could jump ship."

We talked for more than an hour, trying to figure out a way. She seemed elated by my offer to help. But at moments her excitement unnerved me a little and made me wonder whether I was being rash. What if we didn't get along? How could we conceal her past from others? Despite my uneasiness, in my mind's eye I kept seeing her in a white cottage stirring a pot with a large ladle while humming a song—outside, children's voices were rising and falling. I suggested that we speak to the Croc in person and see if there was another way of paying him. Before she went back to the house, she kissed me on the cheek and said, "Wanren, I would do anything for you. You are a good man."

Great joy welled up in my heart, and I stayed outside in the damp air for a long time, dreaming of how we could start our life anew someday. If only I had more cash. I thought of asking Huong to share my bed, but decided not to, for fear that the other two women might inform Mrs. Chen of our relationship. A full moon was shining on the sleeping street, the walls and roofs bathed in the whitish light. Insects were chirring timidly, as if short of breath.

Two days later, I left work early, and Huong and I set out to meet with the Croc, who had sounded Cantonese on the phone. We crossed Northern Boulevard and headed for the area near I-678. His headquarters was on Thirty-second Avenue, in a large warehouse.

Two prostitutes, one white and the other Hispanic, were loitering in front, wearing nothing but bras and frayed jean shorts. Both of them seemed high on something, and the white woman, who had tousled hair and a missing tooth, shouted at me, "Hey, can you spare a smoke?"

I shook my head. Huong and I hurried into the warehouse, whose interior was filled with large boxes of textiles and shoes. We found the office in a corner. A strapping man was sprawled in a leather chair, smoking a cigar. He sat up at the sight of us and smirked. "Take a seat," he said, pointing at a sofa.

The moment we sat down, Huong said, "This is my boyfriend, Wanren. We came to ask you a favor."

The Croc nodded at me, then turned back to Huong. "OK, what can I do for you?"

"I need some extra time. Can I pay you thirteen hundred a month?"

"No way." He smirked again, his ratty eyes darting right and left.

"How about fifteen hundred?"

"I said no."

"You see, I have a medical condition and have to take a different job that doesn't pay as much."

"That's not my problem." He wagged his wispy mustache.

I stepped in. "I will help her pay you, but we simply cannot come up with two thousand a month for now. Please give us an extra half year."

"A rule is a rule. If someone breaks it with impunity, the rule will have no force anymore. We've never given anyone such an extension. So don't even try to get clever with me. If you don't pay the full amount in time, you know what we'll do." He jerked his thumb at Huong.

She looked at me, tears forming in her eyes. I patted her arm, signaling that we should leave. We got up and left the warehouse after saying we appreciated his meeting with us.

On the way back, we talked about what the consequences would be if we failed to make the monthly payment. I was mindful, know-ing it was dangerous to deal with a thug like the Croc. I had heard horrifying stories of how members of the Asian Mafia punished peo-ple, especially new arrivals who had offended them. They had shoved a man into a van and shipped him to a cannery in New Jersey to make pet food of him; they had cut off a little girl's nose because her father hadn't paid them the protection fee; they had tied a middle-aged woman's hands, plugged her mouth, stuffed her into a burlap sack, and then dropped her into the ocean. The Chinese gangs spread the Mafia stories to intimidate people. Some of those tales might just be rumors, and, granted, the Croc might not belong to the Mafia at all, but he could do Huong and me in easily. He had to be a gangster, if not the leader of a gang. Also, he likely had networks in China and Vietnam that could hurt our families.

After dinner, I went into Huong's room, which was clean and smelled of pineapple. On the windowsill was a vase of marigolds. I said to her, "What if we just leave New York?"

"And go where?" She sounded calm, as if she, too, had been toy-ing with this idea.

"Anywhere. America is a big country, and we can live in a remote town under different names, or move around, working on farms like Mexican workers. There must be some way for us to survive. First, we can go to North Carolina, and from there we'll move on."

"What about my family? The Croc will hold my parents accountable."

"You shouldn't worry so much. You have to take care of yourself first."

"My parents would never forgive me if I just disappeared."

"But haven't they just been using you? You've been their cash cow."

That seemed to be sinking in. A moment later, she said, "You're right. Let's get out of here."

So we decided to leave as soon as possible. She had some cash on hand, about two thousand dollars, while I still had fourteen hundred in my savings account. The next morning on the way to work, I stopped at Cathay Bank and took out all the money. I felt kind of low, knowing that from now on I couldn't write to my parents, or the Croc's men might hunt us down. To my family, I would be as good as dead. In this place, we had no choice but to take loss as necessity.

That afternoon, Huong secretly packed a suitcase and stuffed some of my clothes into a duffel bag. I wished that I could have said good-bye to my boss and some fellow workers, and got my three-hundred-dollar deposit back from Mrs. Chen. At dinner, both Nana and Lili teased Huong, saying she had begun working for me, as a cleaning lady. We two tried to appear normal, and I even cracked a few jokes.

Fortunately, there was no outcall that night. When the other two women had gone to bed, Huong and I slipped out of the house. I carried her suitcase while she lugged my bag. The weeping cherry blurred in the haze, its crown edgeless, like a small hill. A truck was rumbling down Main Street as we strode away, arm in arm, without looking back.

Paul Theroux

Twenty-two Stories

FRITZ IS BACK

I was born in Berlin in 1937. My mother was eighteen. She hid me from everyone for a year and a half. My father must have been someone who was hated, a Jew or a Gypsy: I never knew who he was. My mother got permission to emigrate in 1943 under "refugee status" and married a man named Wolfie. We sailed to Australia. None of us spoke English. We were put in a rural refugee camp, living in dormitories. After a year, we were sent to a suburb of Melbourne, where we were happy, but six months later my mother and Wolfie crashed their car. Mother was killed, Wolfie was so badly injured he could not care for me.

When the authorities came to put me in the orphanage, the next-door neighbor, Mrs. Dugger, said, "We could easily take him. He's one of the family. Fritz is no bludger." My name was Fred, but, being German, I was Fritz to everyone in Australia.

Mrs. Dugger didn't insist. She watched me get into the car. Then she reached through the window and patted me on the head. She said in a strange tone, "Bye, Fritz. Mind how you go."

I was put into the Fraser Boys' Home. I was happy there, oddly enough. The bigger boys protected me. And I was terrified when, after three years, Wolfie showed up, limping from his injuries, to take me away. He arranged for us to go back to Germany. We went by ship. He was abusive for the whole voyage. I had no idea why he wanted me to go with him; I still don't know. He abandoned me soon after we got to Hamburg. I was taken in by an old woman, and for the first time in my life I was held in the arms of someone who loved me. We both sobbed—the tears were endless. I was still young, but Germany was rebuilding, and I got a job in a restaurant. When I had saved some money, I went to hotel school, I worked in hotels, I became a manager, and eventually I became head of the company, a large hotel chain.

Our company was negotiating to buy a hotel in Melbourne. Forty years after I left that city, I returned. On my day off I went to the old neighborhood. I found Mrs. Dugger. She was blind, sitting on her porch.

"I used to live here," I said. "Long ago."

The moment she heard my voice, she began to cry. and said, "Fritz is back!"

She died soon after that. Her son told me that she talked about me constantly and it was only when I came back and she knew I was all right that she was able to let go. All those years of remorse for letting me be taken away by the authorities.

AN OBSTINATE CHILD

I have had an unusual life, so far, difficult in many ways, but not so difficult as that of my father, who is sixty-something. He was my tormentor for almost the whole of my childhood.

I had a bad case of measles at the age of four. I had developed normally before then, but after the measles I became disobedient and willful. I didn't listen. I didn't pay attention. I defied my father, who was a stern disciplinarian—Marine Corps, two tours in Vietnam. "Listen to me!" But I didn't. He spanked me, sometimes so hard I could still feel it days later. He smacked my hands, he twisted my ears, pushed me into a corner and forced me to stand. He made me call him "Sir." As I grew older, the punishments became more severe. The worst one was having to kneel on a broomstick. I did this for hours at a time. I was seven or eight years old, and it went on for years. I was rude, I was defiant, you name it—so my dad said. I was a wreck, but I couldn't cure myself of being an obstinate child. I was also terrible at school, where the punishments weren't as bad as my father's, though when he saw my report card he went ballistic.

When I was about thirteen, I was given an eye test at school. Everyone got one. I failed. The eye doctor gave me a prescription for glasses and also suggested that I get a hearing test. This hearing test was given to me many times over a lot of weeks. Some of the tests were administered by groups of doctors or with medical students watching. Sometimes they asked, "How'd you get all those bruises?" I said, "Fell down."

The results showed that I was extremely deaf, as a result of the measles. I was fitted with two hearing aids. My whole life changed, though I was still pretty rebellious. The other kids laughed at my "earphones." I improved at school, but my home life deteriorated.

My father became desolate and filled with guilt. Some days when I stop by I think he is on the verge of suicide, and it takes all the energy I have to reassure him and coax him into better humor, which is a pretty big burden for both of us. He still apologizes. I say, "How were you to know?"

MY PRIESTS

I was a Catholic in the 1950s, a student at an all-boys Catholic school, priests for teachers. I never heard of any of us boys being messed around with by a priest. I knew that I was afraid of them and probably would have done anything a priest asked me to.

But there was something else about them that impressed me and changed my life. In the ninth grade, we made weekly visits to the

YMCA pool, where all the swimming was done in the nude. I was embarrassed, but I was the only one. We were all naked. And I recall how the priests would come into the changing room and find a locker. They wore long black cassocks, they wore birettas and black socks. They would undress with us, carefully, folding their clothes and tucking them into the lockers.

Stark naked, they led us into the swimming pool, which stank of chlorine. They dived, they gave us swimming lessons. They taught us to pick up objects from the bottom of the pool—"surface dive." They showed us lifesaving maneuvers. "Never let a drowning man grab you. He'll take you with him."

What I remember of the priests were their naked bodies, big and pale without robes or cassocks. They were men, just white skin and hairy legs. After a while I did not believe they had any power at all, and certainly not spiritual power. As time passed, I liked them less and less—for their bodies—and as an adult, reflecting on their YMCA visits, I began to hate them for pretending to be powerful. I easily lost my faith.

SCHOOL DAYS

Like many boys of my generation, I was sent away to school. My father was an officer in the Indian Army, based in Bareilly, and he had the choice of sending me to a hill-station school—say, one in Simla—or to an English boarding school. He opted for England. There I went at the age of seven, accompanied by my mother, who left me at the underschool, returning every two years to check up on me. I know this seems extraordinary, but it was quite usual then. The period I am speaking of is the 1930s, for I was born in 1928, and my prep school days ended with the outbreak of war in Europe.

My mother died. This I was told by the headmaster, who took me aside and was very kind to me, his wife, Winnie—we called her Poodle—making me tea.

"Your father is coming to fetch you."

I was ten, but a small ten, a white weedy boy with bony bitten fingers and spiky hair. I was too nervous to be dreamy or lazy. I was a whiz at maths, chess, and Religious Knowledge, humiliated in all sports.

The day came. "Your father is in the foyer of Ashburnham." I ran. I was in a panic. I saw two men. I clutched one and began to cry.

"Neville, I am your father," the other man said.

This man I hugged was laughing: my uncle.

Nothing was right after that with my father. I began to think, Who is he? And maybe my uncle is my real father.

AUNTIE ROSEBUD'S JEWELS

My aunt Rosalind, whom we called Rosebud, had a fantastic collection of jewelry. She had two habits related to the collection. One, she was passionate about collecting, continually adding pieces, delving in markets, attending auctions and estate sales, and dealing privately. The other habit was her always announcing her finds and acquisitions. This meant that we were all keenly aware of what she had bought and what she owned. In so doing, she educated us. This is a topaz, this is a sapphire, this is a yellow diamond, and that's a black pearl. We learned the difference between white gold and platinum as settings, the virtue of one stone over another, the variety of hallmarks, the price of gold and diamonds—specific numbers and scarcity value.

Auntie Rosebud's collection continued to grow while we watched, from a few boxes to many chests of drawers, glass cabinets, and trays. We became knowledgeable ourselves. That close attention was a way of pleasing Auntie Rosebud. We felt that she needed us to take an interest, that she enjoyed educating us, and I suppose our knowledge linked us to this valuable collection and gave us self-esteem.

We were young adults, in the working world, when Auntie Rosebud sold her collection of jewelry. It was like a sickness and a death. An auction house swept down and valued the pieces, photographed them, and in a few months the whole collection was gone. She said, "You can bid for the ones you really like." But we didn't: we couldn't afford it. It wasn't the money she wanted. She had plenty. After the big auction she was more powerful than ever, and more of a mystery, and we felt so weak.

THE CHILD WITH THE CROOKED SMILE

I was in Central America, visiting schools for an aid project. Leaving one small school in a village, my guide, Ramón, said to me, "Did you see that small boy at the front desk, who was so slow? Alone, writing after school in his notebook?"

The boy with the crooked smile—I had seen him, and he had seen me, too.

"His story is so sad. His mother was only fifteen when she got pregnant. She had no boyfriend, no fiancé. She was just a schoolgirl. She gave birth, and afterward she moved out of the house and went to San Pedro.

"A few years later, visiting her parents, she saw her father hugging and kissing her younger sister, who was fourteen. She screamed at him to stop.

"Her father said, 'It's nothing. We're just being friendly.'

"She said, 'I don't want what happened to me to happen to her. Leave her alone!'

"But the father didn't. So the older daughter went to the police station and said, 'My father is having sex with my sister. He had sex with me, and this boy is the result.'

"The little boy looked at the policemen and smiled. They could see in his smile that there was something wrong with his head.

"The father was arrested. He went to trial and was given fifteen years and is in prison now. It's so strange. How do these things happen?"

A few days later we passed a small house in the forest near that village. Ramón pointed.

"That's the house of Señor Martin. He had seventeen children. Imagine! And now that I think of it, his second son was the one who committed incest with his daughters. He lived there."

"Seventeen children in that house?" I said.

"Two bedrooms," Ramón said. "Fantastic, eh, how these people can manage?"

THE SHADOW

I plan to retire soon. I have high blood pressure, yet my life has been uneventful—two children, both married; my wife is a real estate agent. I have spent my life in accountancy and tax planning. I used to think: I should get outside more. And then when my health issues prevented me, I was somewhat relieved not to have to get any exercise.

All my life there has been a shadow over me, one I could not identify, weighing me down.

I was at the supermarket—this was just the other day—and saw a young mother with her three children, one in a baby carriage, one holding her hand, and the third, the eldest, trying to help her. This big boy was about ten. He wore a baseball hat that was slightly too large for his head and tipping sideways. His eyeglasses were the cheap kind that make a kid self-conscious. He was pale, buck-toothed, very skinny, with an ill-fitting shirt and blue pants—not stylish, none of it. It was a poor family but an earnest one, conscious of decency and order. The boy was carrying a heavy bag, because his mother was burdened with the other children and the shopping. She chose each item very carefully, weighing the thing, looking several times at the price.

The boy was ugly, foolish-looking, really pathetic, trying to look anonymous but obviously what his schoolmates would have called a geek. His glasses were all wrong, he was weak, he was worried, he was trying to be helpful, but anyone could see he was miserably self-conscious and perhaps terrified. He knew what it was like to be mocked: he anticipated it every moment, glancing aside. I knew that his father was either dead or had deserted the mother. The father would have shown this boy how to dress and would have given him a manly example. But his mother nagged him. "You're the oldest!" He was in despair—I could see the shadow over him.

Later I examined my sadness and my pity. I realized he was me. I understood my life, after fifty years. I did not sorrow for myself but for that poor ugly boy.

THE MAN FROM SEVENTY-SEVENTH STREET

I was living on the Upper East Side. Every morning I walked down Lexington to Seventy-seventh Street and got the 6 train to Union Square, where I worked. I was at the station by eight, and without fail there was a man reading the *Wall Street Journal* just inside the turnstile. He always smiled at me, and I kept thinking that he would talk to me one day. He didn't, but he kept smiling whenever he saw me. This went on for about a year.

I moved to East Thirteenth Street, a short distance from my office, and never thought about the man again. But after my boyfriend and I split up, I kept the apartment, though I hated staying home at night alone. I was in the bar section of a café in Union Square and saw the man from Seventy-seventh Street. He smiled at me. I smiled back. We began talking. We were instantly on the same wavelength, as I had guessed we would be all along. I felt that I had known him for a year. We talked for about two hours—four drinks each—and then he said, "I want to make love to you in the worst way."

That struck me as funny. I even made a joke about it, that word "worst." We went to my apartment, and we devoured each other, making up for a whole year of eyeing each other and fantasizing. I was thinking how I would tell my ex-boyfriend how it was like a cannibal feast. The man from Seventy-seventh Street pounded me and twisted my body sideways and made a meal of one of my feet, while I watched, not aroused but fascinated.

I was exhausted, I fell asleep. When I woke up, I said, "I used to dream of you making love to me the whole time I saw you at the station on Seventy-seventh Street."

He stared at me. He said, "I've only been there a few times. I live in Brooklyn. I've never seen you before."

ENGLISH FRIENDS

My English friend Jane—very proper—gave me the name of this Englishwoman in London who would be glad to put me up for a few days until I got my InterRail paperwork sorted out. I just knew her as Victoria. When I called her from the airport, she said the best thing would be for me to meet her at her office in Westminster. I was totally impressed. She was a British civil servant, some kind of undersecretary in the Ministry of Health. These are the people who keep the British government running: the politicians and cabinet ministers come and go; these people stay. They brief the ministers on parliamentary bills and MPs' questions in the House of Commons. All this Victoria told me as she tidied her office before we left. She was drearily dressed and had greasy hair and was wearing a white shirt and a necktie, like a school uniform. She saw I was reading a framed certificate.

"That's my MBE," she said. It meant Member of the British Empire, a title. "I say it means My Bloody Efforts."

She then explained that she couldn't take any of the papers home, because they were secret.

"Lucky you," I said. "You can make an explicit division between work stuff and home stuff."

"Bang on!" she said, and she laughed harder than I would have expected.

We went to her house by Tube. Her husband answered the door. He was Jamaican, named Wallace. He wore a wool hat in the house. He was a carpenter, he said. He said very little. I tried not to look surprised. While Victoria made dinner, Wallace offered me a drink and showed me to my room. The room looked lived in, and I wondered where, in this small house, Wallace and Victoria slept.

After dinner, Wallace rolled a big fat joint and passed it to Victoria. She puffed and passed it to me. I didn't inhale much. I looked at her and saw the civil servant who had shown me her secret papers and her MBE certificate in Westminster.

"I'm tired," I said, but when I went into the bedroom they followed me. They looked pretty interested. I said, "I can't do this."

My English friend Jane said I really missed something.

THE UNIFORM BUSINESS

I am pretty conservative on the whole and have a sales-and-marketing degree, which my parents urged me to get so that I could help them with their business. They are also conservative, you might even say puritanical. That is one of the reasons they chose this business, which is school uniforms.

Mainly it is girls' uniforms, skirts and blouses, kneesocks and blazers. What is thought of as an old-fashioned line of clothes is actually very up-to-date, since many schools these days are switching over to uniforms, not just Catholic schools but all sorts. My parents chose this business because they believed it was virtuous and fair, that they were promoting modesty. Uniforms are made to order, in batches: a certain plaid for the pleated skirt, a certain blouse and blazer. A lot of the sewing is outsourced to factories in the Dominican Republic and Guatemala.

When I graduated, I was put in charge of mail orders, mainly orders from clients who found our Web site, or from schools or individuals we had not been in touch with before—random orders.

Many of these came from Japan, some from Great Britain and Germany, and quite a number from the United States. In most cases, they were single orders, apparently unconnected to any school. I knew this from the patterns that were chosen. An individual would get in touch, specify colors and fabrics and sizes, enclosing the payment.

By tracking these orders, I found out some interesting things. The sizes were usually large, as though for a school for big and tall girls, adult-size, and these made up at least 20 percent of our total orders. Some of the skirts were huge. The measurements did not make sense. Yet the customers were satisfied, and I found out that they were, most of them, repeat customers.

Where were these schools? Of course, there were no schools. A fifth of our school-uniform sales were to prostitutes and fetishists— men around the world involved with sexual role-playing, dominatrixes, sadists, transvestites, and closet pedophiles. I did not tell my puritanical parents my conclusions, or they would probably have shut down the business, and where would we be then?

MY BROTHER'S MASK

My father became wealthy importing timber from Southeast Asia, mainly teak but other hardwoods too. He was one of the first to farm it, which meant that when he died the company still prospered. My brother, Hank, and I inherited everything, the big company and a considerable income.

My visits to the plantations got me interested in Asian antiques, and when I began to sell them, I was so busy that I needed Hank to help me out. Soon I saw that he was taking trips to Asia purely to buy drugs. Like Dad, he was an innovator—an early smuggler of heroin inside little Buddhas and carved temple finials in small, hard-to-detect amounts, for his own use. His wealth ensured he'd never have to resort to dealing or relying on dealers in the States. He injected: his arm, his foot, his neck. He said, "I have it under control," meaning that he could afford it.

But over time the heroin ate up most of his money, and he borrowed from me for a while. A very expensive habit, and destructive, too, or so I thought.

I made him a promise. I said, "If you give up the heroin, I will hand over half my own inheritance." I had doubled my money with my antiques business anyway.

Hank said, "Leave me alone. I'm like a person with an illness. Just leave me to my illness. A lot of people are in worse shape than me."

But I begged him. Finally, he agreed. Here is the weird part. As soon as he gave up heroin—a long, painful process of rehab and treatment—he became very weak. As an addict, he had been full of life; as a clean straight guy, he was pale, feeble, prone to colds, and sometimes could not get out of bed. This went on for a few months. Very worried, I brought him to a specialist, who diagnosed cancer.

He said, "Your brother has had cancer for years, but his heroin use has masked it. If he had still been using it, he would have had a happy death—sudden anyway. Heroin has been keeping him out of pain."

The next weeks were awful. He died horribly a month later.

STERN MAN

A stern man is the helper fellow on a lobster boat, and he is at my dooryard at 4:30 every morning except Sunday, ready to go, and if he's not there, I'll go without him. He does lots of things—hauls traps, baits them, hoses rockweed off the deck, boxes the bugs, gets handy with the Clorox. When you haul in winter your stern man might say he's cold, and you say, "Goddamn, if you're cold, you're not working hard enough." The stern man gets 15 percent of the profit on the catch.

I have had them all, the drug addicts, the numb ones, the stealers, and one was crazy as a shithouse rat. A Christless little son of a whore from Belfast went off with my punt. Another one phoned me with death threats when I fired him, and he also talked about cutting the lines on my pots. It is a hell of a business.

But Alvin was the best stern man I ever had. Never late, not a talker, a good worker. God knows where he came from. I'd ask him where he came from, and he'd go all friggin' numb or else change the subject. Also, he went quiet when I talked about women. Mention a piece of tail, or a fellow's teapot, or a pair of bloomers, and Alvin just began scrubbing the deck or hosing rockweed.

I was talking about Vietnam one day. He was the right age. My son was there, one tour. But Alvin said, "I didn't join up."

"Why not?"

"Couldn't."

"Nothing wrong with you," I nagged him a bit.

"Warner, I was in prison," Alvin said after a while. First time he ever used my name, but all this time he never looked me in the eye.

"How long for?"

"Bunch of years."

" 'Bunch of years'! So what'd you go and do?"

"I killed my wife."

"She probably deserved it," I said.

I knew I was right, because he didn't say anything else, though he left me a month later. Damn, I never found a better stern man.

MY WIFE CHEYENNE

Everyone has always liked us. "Here come Mort and Irma." They'd see us holding hands. We are small of stature—Irma's barely five feet—like a couple of kids. We had no kids ourselves, so we never had to grow up. We considered ourselves good mixers and had lots of friends. But we went kaput, and here's how.

As I'm in restaurant supplies, I travel quite a bit, and it's no fun, those cheap hotels you have to stay in to keep the profit margins up and the overheads down. Many of my accounts are in Florida, so we relocated to West Palm. But Florida is a huge state, and I still had to deal with the hotels and lots of nights away.

Irma got a little blue on her own and talked of buying a dog, and she didn't even like dogs. One Friday I returned home from the road, assuming we were going out to dinner, as we usually did. But Irma said, "Can't. I've got my group."

Just like that, a women's group. She had joined it while I was away; some neighbor introduced her. It made her happy. Good. My turn to stay home alone.

The next week, same thing but a little worse. I say, "Hon, how about a juicy steak instead of the group."

"I'm a vegan." Just like that. "We decided."

They had all turned vegetarian, the group. It was wives of working guys and some divorcées, kind of a support group. I told her I'm all for it, and I am. Traveling and sales is no picnic, but if this made her happier while I was away, hey, great. Then the name issue came up.

"Irma," I say one Friday, and she stops me, makes a face.

"Don't call me that. I'm Cheyenne."

"And I'm Tonto."

I had to sleep on the couch. This was no damn joke. And that wasn't the end of it. How could I be so insensitive? She was Cheyenne. They were all something. She had new stationery printed. She says she can take or leave the holidays. Imagine that. I'm still traveling, but when I come home these days, I don't know this woman.

ROCK HAPPY

I had been married for twenty-two years, living on the windward side of Oahu in Hawaii. No children. Originally I had come to Hawaii, as a young salesman, to advise people on how to set up Jiffy Lube franchises, but when my consultancy work was done, I decided to stay. I got myself a franchise, realized this was where I wanted to live, and sent for Diana, my high school sweetheart. She had a lot of complaints about living in Hawaii—the rats, the cockroaches, the way people talked English like it was another language, the lousy food, the terrible traffic—and many more, which is maybe the point of this story.

I was happy. I would have done anything to make Diana happy. I hardly noticed her criticisms of me, although our whole being in

Hawaii was my doing, as she said. I was in kind of a daze, but so what? I never got rock fever, like they say. I was rock happy.

We were driving one wet afternoon over the Pali, and just beyond the tunnel there was one of these speed traps. Cop flags me down. I drive onto the shoulder and get out my license and registration.

The cop was a big moke, six something, way over two hundred pounds, hands like pieces of meat. But he was very polite, very professional. It was true, I had probably been speeding. I laughed and agreed with him while he wrote out the citation.

A horrible choking honk like an animal's sudden fury made him stop writing. But it was a familiar sound to me.

"Billy! You tell him we're going to court! You hear me, Billy!"

The cop took a step back and looked into the car, at Diana's pudgy purple face, the veins standing out on her neck, the spit on her lips.

"Is that your wife?" He said it in a disgusted and pitying voice.

I said yes, and I almost added, What's the problem?

He tore up the ticket. "I ain't giving you this. You got enough problems, bruddah."

After a few months we separated, and within a year were divorced. Diana's back on the mainland now.

THE BUS DRIVER

It was at the three-day wedding event for my eldest daughter, who was marrying a very nice man, Brian, a successful contractor in Oregon. Taylor said, "I want a huge bash. You only get married once." I kept my big mouth shut.

The bash was held at a resort in Hawaii and involved all the guests being shuttled to lunches, rehearsals, dinners, activities, and so forth, getting in and out of vans and minibuses, and doing lots of socializing. We were sent a three-page itinerary. Movable feast!

I went with Tim, my second husband. On the first afternoon there was an important cocktail party at a function room on the property. The van was parked where it should have been, near the porte cochere, but there was no sign of the bus driver. I walked up and down looking for him.

A gruff-looking man approached the van and waited at the front passenger door.

I was annoyed that he was late and not even apologetic. I said, "Are you the bus driver?"

He said, "No," and a second later seemed to change his mind about getting aboard. This really annoyed me, because I was sure he was the bus driver, and I muttered something, which I wish I could remember now. He walked away. I waited awhile, and then it hit me. That man, the gruff stranger I had spoken to, was my ex-husband, Taylor's father, to whom I had been happily married for sixteen years until he went off with a much younger woman, who I heard had dumped him, couldn't stand his drinking. I looked back and did not see him. Later, we said hello but not much else. We never discussed my gaffe, which I think says a lot.

BLACK RUNS

I was unhappily married and living in Connecticut, your typical bored housewife. Then I took a course: radiology. X-rays, CAT scans, MRIs. Two years. I got my diploma and left my husband and came here to Maine. There's a lot of work in radiology, and the hours aren't too bad. I chose Maine because of the winters.

I spend the whole winter skiing, except last winter, when I had some medical procedures. I have five screws in my shoulder and a permanently damaged rotator cuff that screams in damp weather. I've broken both arms, my collarbone, and my left ankle. I need to have my knees replaced. That'll be fun. Basically, they make lateral incisions, sever your legs, put in metal, and give you some kind of ID so you can go through a metal detector in an airport.

The ankle was something else. I read my own CAT scan and opted for ankle replacement. Basically, they got me an ankle from a cadaver, and they removed my bad ankle and fitted me with this donor ankle. But it's too small. I'm getting pain. They might have to redo it.

I hate cross-country skiing. My ex was huge on it. I hated hearing him say, "Oh, look at that yellow spruce," or, "Oh, look, a rose-breasted grosbeak," or, "Oh, gosh, let's sit on that log and have a bagel." Cross-country is for, I want to say, fairies.

He didn't understand that pain is pleasure, if properly applied. What I want is black runs, all day black runs. I want to ski straight down on black runs, with my legs banging and the tears streaming out of my eyes and freezing on my face. And snot pouring out of my nose and streaking on my cheek, and my whole face burning from the cold. I am hardly able to breathe on a black run, which no man I have ever known can understand, which is also why I fired my husband, I've fired every boyfriend I've ever had, and basically it's just me and my dog.

A REAL BREAK

Mother and Grace—let's just say they weren't best buddies. So as the elder daughter, and single, I began to look after Mother when she began to fail. And she was a wreck. Got confused in stores, left the oven on, real muddled about time. I made her stop driving, so of course I had to take the wheel. God, the hills. I wrote Grace that I was moving in with Mother. The big Polk Street house had been in Mother's family for years; Mother was lost in it. Grace understood completely and said she was relieved. She had been in a Minnesota convent since taking her vows, though she sometimes spent extended periods in Nevada and Florida as a hospital worker "and doing spiritual triage, too," on Indian reservations. We seldom heard from her, but mother sent her money now and then. Because of the strictness of her religious order, she was never able to visit us in San Francisco. "And just as well," Mother said.

It got so that Mother could only manage with my assistance. I resigned from my secretarial job, lost my retirement and my medical plan, and became Mother's full-time caregiver. I updated Grace on Mother's condition and mentioned the various challenges we faced. Grace wrote saying that she was praying for us, and she asked detailed questions because these infirmities were to be specified in the prayers, or "intercessions," as she called them.

About three years into my caregiving, Grace called. She said, "Why not take a few months off? My superior has given me special dispensation to look after Mom for a while. It'll be a break for me. And you can have a real break. Maybe go to Europe."

Mother wasn't overjoyed, but she could see that I was exhausted. Grace flew in. It was an emotional reunion. I hardly recognized her—not because she had gotten older, though she had. But she was dressed so well and in such good health. She even mentioned how I looked stressed and obviously could do with some time off.

I went on one of those special British Airways fares, a See Scotland package. It was just the break I needed, or so I thought.

Long story short, when I got back to San Francisco, the Polk Street house was being repainted by people who said they were the new owners. Everything I possessed was gone. Mother was in a charity hospice. She had been left late one night at the emergency room of St. Francis Hospital. There was no money in Mother's bank account. Everything she had owned had been sold. I saw Mother's lawyer. He found a number for Grace—the 702 area code, a cell phone. Nevada.

"I'm glad you called," Grace said. I could hear music in the background and a man talking excitedly, a fishbowl babble, aqueous party voices. I started to cry but she interrupted me with a real hard voice. "Everything I did was legal. Mother gave me power of attorney. I never want to see you again. And you will never undo it." Unfortunately for me, that was true.

GIULIO AND PAULIE: FATHER AND SON

Giulio was recommended to me as a hard worker, a good man, very skillful in all sorts of building. This proved to be the case. When I praised him, he said, "I come from Sicily. We build the whole house there—foundation, brickwork, framing, plastering, carpentry, roofing, shingles, tiling, plumbing." He could do anything. He worked one whole summer, first brickwork, then replacing shingles, then glazing the cracked windows, then painting—every job I'd put off at last getting done.

He was seventy-seven years old. He asked for $40 an hour—a lot of money, the weekly bills were high—but he earned it.

After the second week, he brought his son, Paulie, a big, boyish fellow of forty-three, tattooed, potbellied, very funny, not a good worker but strong. He could heave the big sacks of cement, he dug holes, he lugged the bricks. He was also to get $40 an hour, but some days he didn't show up. "He's goofing around," "He's sick," "He's sleeping," Giulio said, seeming both dignified and somewhat ashamed of having to make excuses.

One day: "Paulie's in jail." It turned out he'd been in jail before, spent several years inside for theft, credit-card fraud, and receiving stolen goods. What astonished me was the contrast between father and son: the honest old man, so talented and hardworking; the lazy son, who was a petty thief and a druggie.

Time passed, Paulie stayed in jail, but as I got to know Giulio better, I realized that he was cheating me on his time sheet, charging me for tools he bought or broke, not quite truthful about the work, carelessly hiding the scrap wood and the mistakes, a subtle thief. And I began to see, first faintly, then powerfully, how prideful Giulio the sly worker was more like Paulie the jailbird than anyone could ever guess.

BIGOT ON VACATION

I left my small village in Norway as a young man—I was hardly seventeen—and became a student in the USA, first in Michigan, where I had an aunt and uncle, then in Massachusetts, where I attended MIT and where I eventually settled. My life's work has been in developing radar sensitivity—defense work, but I justify it to myself by saying that I was creating a shield, not weapons of destruction. This was not entirely true. Missiles are guided by radar. In this work, my colleagues were from India, Pakistan, China, Korea, Japan, and many other countries. I must emphasize the diverse nationalities and how well we got along—it is important to this story.

I lived through the 1960s in the USA, working on defense projects. Of course, I was seen as one of the bad guys. I married an American, I raised two children. I am proud of the life I have made here. My interests are sailing, skiing, and gardening. I am now retired—a happy man.

Here is the strange part. About every four years I go back to my village, which is near Bergen. It is always a horrible visit. I become enraged when I see what has happened. It has gotten so bad that I dread going home. The visits disturb me, because I see that I am a bigot. My lovely village is now the residence of Pakistanis, Indians, Africans, Vietnamese—brown people, who have come there as refugees, so-called, because Norwegians are so happy to provide houses and welfare. When I was a boy, we had one religion, one language, one culture—one race. Now it's a filthy mess. Skullcaps, shawls, smells. There is crime. So many languages. A mosque! A temple! Not refugees but opportunists. I am so angry when I am there: my lovely village spoiled. I think I will never go back again. I know I am a bigot there, and I hate myself when I am home.

MRS. SPRINGER, OLD-TIMER

Mrs. Springer, who was a longtime resident of our facility, was born in 1900. She was vain about the date, being the same age as the century. She clearly remembered the First World War. "I was at school. The school bell rang when the war ended, and we were given the day off." She remembered talk of Al Capone and Prohibition, the Great Depression and Lindbergh's flight. She was married to a science-minded German, living in Munich when the war started. Her husband's family was wealthy—Springer was their name. She volunteered for war work, knitting socks. She told us all her stories. She had met Hitler. "He had very fine hands, small and pale, like a woman's."

She became a refugee after the war. She went to Los Angeles; her husband followed her later, and he became a metallurgist for Hughes Tool Co. He died. She lived alone a few years and then entered our facility.

We went to her ninetieth birthday party. We predicted that she would live to a hundred. She accomplished this, but it was a decade of failing health. She lost most of her hearing. Her sight dimmed. At her hundredth she needed to be steered to the cake. We shouted for her to blow out the candles, but she couldn't hear us or see the candles. Even so, she smiled and said it was a great day.

Her hundred-and-first she spent in her room. We were away a lot after that, and each time we got back, we were surprised to see her still alive. Her other friends were less attentive too, even a little irritated when they had to run an errand for Mrs. Springer. We missed her hundred-and-second birthday. That year I saw her once. It seemed inconvenient, and somewhat unfair, her living into another century. Her nurse called and complained that no one bought her medicine anymore. Her son died, not of any specific cause. "He was getting on," someone said.

We forgot about Mrs. Springer, we guessed she had died, and we were astonished to hear that she had a hundred-and-fourth birthday. We were not invited. Only her nurse, her cleaning woman, and—somehow—the plumber were there. She kept to her room. People said she was alert, that she asked about elections and the weather. No one visited her. We were embarrassed and, I'm sorry to say, a bit bored by her, and none of us saw her again until her funeral.

THE CRUISE OF THE *ALLEGRA*

It was my first winter cruise. I was a waiter on the *Allegra*, most of the passengers well-to-do people who spent part of the winter cruising in the warm waters of the Pacific, from Puerto Escondido to Singapore and back, including stops in Australia and New Zealand. That winter we stopped along the South American coast too, from Guayaquil to Santiago, and then to Hawaii via Easter Island. Often, the passengers did not bother to go ashore—just stayed on deck and looked at the pier and drank and made faces.

Ed and Wilma Hibbert avoided the others. They were in their mid to late seventies, from Seattle. Always dined alone, did not socialize, Ed very attentive to Wilma, who seemed the frail type. I heard whispers. "Snobs," "Stuffed shirts," "Pompous," "Cold." They must have heard them too.

Wilma fell ill at Callao, stayed in her suite, and was taken to a hospital in Lima, where she died. Ed Hibbert left the ship but did not vacate his suite. His table was empty until Honolulu, where he rejoined the ship.

And then the invitations began, one widow after another inviting him to dinner, to drinks, to the fancy-dress ball. They were not amateurs but persistent and alluring seducers.

Amazingly, Ed obliged. He seemed to welcome the attention, not like a bereaved spouse at all but like the most discriminating bachelor. The same women who had made demeaning remarks now praised him and competed for his affection. And I had the feeling that in obliging them, dallying with them, without committing himself, he was having his revenge, perhaps revenge on his wife too.

He was on two more cruises, same routine, didn't remarry.

EULOGIES FOR MR. CONCANNON

I did not know Dennis Concannon. I was invited to his funeral by a friend of his son's who needed a ride. As it was a rainy day and I had nothing else to do, I stayed for the service, sitting in the back. The whole business was nondenominational, according to Mr. C's wishes. The turnout was very large—the church was filled. A reading of his favorite poem, by Robert Frost, with the memorable line, "That withered hag." Several sentimental songs. Then the eulogies.

One man got up and said, "I never met anyone else like Dennis. I worked for him for almost twenty-five years, and in all that time he didn't even buy me a cup of coffee." He went on—people laughed.

A woman: "I used to tremble whenever I was called to his office. I never knew whether he was going to make a pass at me or fire me."

Another man: "The salesmen put in their expense reports that they'd had their cars washed. 'Salesmen have to have clean cars.' But Dennis said, 'This was the fourteenth of last month. I compared the car washes to the weather report. It was raining that day. I'm not paying.'"

Someone else: "His partner, George Kelly, would be sitting next to him at some of the meetings. One would talk. Then the other, but saying the same thing. It was terrible. We called it 'Dennis in Stereo.'"

There were more speakers, with equally unpleasant stories of this man. At the end of the funeral I knew Dennis Concannon as a mean, unreasonable, bullying bastard who had gotten rich by exploiting and intimidating these people, the attendees at his funeral—not mourners but people who were having the last word.

Judy Troy

The Order of Things

DURING THE first inning of the Worland Lutheran softball game Reverend Carl sprained an ankle and Lily Forrest, a wrist. Thus, they sat together in the small stand of bleachers, watching their spouses play the outfield. They were each in their early forties, married to teachers; they had each recently lost a sibling to cancer. And oddly, they looked alike: six feet tall, with pale eyes, angular features, and light hair. In the year since Carl had come to Worland with his wife and daughter, he had not been able to stop thinking of Lily. He had the sense that he and she had known each other before and had been waiting for this chance, which might never have come, and so he had tried to keep his distance. But now they were thrown together. In the August wind, with the afternoon sun slanting over the dusty softball field, they talked quietly to each other. And even when not talking their silence felt intimate.

Three weeks later they drove separately to the Super 8 on Highway 120, south of Cody, from where they could see Yellowstone Regional Airport with the small planes taking off and landing. Lily had arrived first, and stood in the sunlight in her jeans and canvas jacket. It was a weekday morning; afterward she would drive to her father's ranch, where she worked now in place of her brother.

"I registered for us," she told Carl. "I said I was Margaret Finch, from Sioux Falls, South Dakota." Margaret Finch was the gray-headed secretary Carl had inherited, who had worked at the church for thirty years. "Her name just came into my head," Lily said. "I don't know why. Guilt, I guess."

"Do you want to reconsider?" Carl forced himself to say, although he couldn't imagine getting back into his car now that he had come this far.

"No," Lily said. "I don't want to. You can talk yourself out of anything if you think about it enough."

Their room was on the east side of the motel on the first floor, and in the meadow behind it late-summer cicadas were buzzing. They stood in the open doorway, looking at the beige carpeting and off-white walls. The double bed was made up with a striped comforter.

"They asked if I wanted a king," Lily said. "Maybe I should have said yes. I mean, we're so tall."

"I don't think it applies to height," Carl told her. He had meant it to be funny but had said it so seriously that it was a moment before Lily smiled.

Inside, she took off her jacket, folded it in half, and laid it across the small table. Then she fingered the cuffs of her gray sweater. Her bangs were clipped to one side with a brown barrette, and she wore mascara—a detail Carl wouldn't have noticed had not his daughter, recently, against her mother's wishes, begun applying it each morning before leaving for school.

"What do we do now?" Lily said, which was a relief to him. The closest he had come to being unfaithful was with his sister's friend, Debra Harding, when his sister was at the hospice, and that had been just ten minutes of necking at the far dark end of a parking lot. At the funeral they were both too embarrassed to look at each other.

Lily pulled off her sweater, under which she wore a white camisole with lace along the edges. She undressed more quickly than he did.

He had always been self-conscious, and wanted to offer excuses: he used to be in better shape, he had been trimmer when he was younger, he was just about to join a gym. But he forgot those when she undid his belt and put her hand on his zipper.

They pulled back the comforter and got into bed. Lily's breasts were small and round, with delicate pink nipples, and her skin was white except for her arms and neck, still tanned from summer. For weeks afterward Carl would not be able to picture her body without getting an erection. And afterward when they lay back against the pillows they held hands, which was something he had never done with his wife—not because she wouldn't have liked to but because he had never until now been somebody who touched another person easily.

"We should go," Lily said quietly, and Carl nodded, but for an hour neither of them moved.

They met in Cody again, then farther north, near Powell—first at a Travelodge and then at the Summit Breeze Motel, in Ralston, which overlooked Heart Mountain. By then it was mid-October, a cold morning of intermittent rain. A week earlier snow had fallen in the Tetons and in western Montana, and only by luck had it not snowed yet in Worland. They were taking a chance, going that far from home. "Never take chances," Carl's father used to tell him. "Always be prepared for what's next," and Carl had grown up believing that was possible. Now, like Lily, he knew better. It was impossible to know the future and therefore impossible to prepare for it.

The Summit Breeze Motel was old and shabby, with small concrete-block bungalows, and in their small bungalow they did things with each other that Carl had not done since he was first married. Then in bed, with the sound of rain on the thin roof, they talked about their marriages.

Lily's was companionable enough in a way, she said, but lonely for her. Her husband did not—could not, she said—open up. "How much can you love somebody you don't know?" she said.

Carl and his wife had married too soon. "We thought we knew

each other better than we did," he told Lily. "And once we did it seemed too late."

The rain had turned to sleet without their noticing. They dressed and ran to their cars, and on the highway Carl stayed half a mile behind Lily, watching the lights of her car. He felt that as long as he could see them he could keep her safe. It wasn't true—it was childish thinking—but he had never wanted anything so badly.

Winter meant treacherous conditions and impassable roads. They couldn't leave Worland and they couldn't meet in Worland; inevitably someone would see them. And neither Carl nor Lily brought up the possibility of meeting at the church, despite the fact that it was isolated—two miles south on Laramie Road, separated from town by a large tract of land on which roads had gone in but nothing more. But the church was off-limits, Carl felt. It was a line he couldn't cross, though at the same time he couldn't bring himself to think of any aspect of their relationship as a sin. If the woman were anybody but Lily, he thought, he would judge what he was doing as harshly as the church would. In fact, he wouldn't have gotten involved in the first place. It was Lily who made the difference.

For the next month they talked daily but saw each other only on Sunday mornings, where there was the presence of their spouses and Carl's daughter, and the difficulty Carl had trying not to look at Lily during the service. In an effort not to, he would find himself staring at somebody else's face without realizing it, or paying so little attention to what he was saying that he repeated himself or lost his place. Even harder was trying to keep his face and voice neutral when he greeted Lily after the service. Either he failed, and imagined people noticing; or he succeeded, which felt like a crime he was committing against himself. And Sunday to Sunday the days grew progressively longer.

Then on a freezing December afternoon Lily appeared at the church. "I'm here for a legitimate reason," she said quickly. "I picked up the

newsletters for Margaret. She asked me to. She's home with the flu."
She stood in the doorway of his study, her face flushed with cold.

They locked the door and used the old brown leather sofa that the
pastor before Carl had bought as a self-indulgence but left behind.
Outside the window was just the hilly cemetery and empty fields
beyond it, and white clouds rushing across the sky. Nobody would
come by; most likely the phone wouldn't even ring; and, in place of
whatever Carl thought he would feel, was overwhelming relief at
being with her again. Afterward, when she was gone and he was alone
in the late afternoon, he drove out to Gooseberry Creek and walked
along its frozen length in the near darkness. He stayed out in the cold
until he was able to replace thoughts of Lily with everyday thoughts:
his car needing gas, his wife and daughter making pizza for supper.
But on his way home he turned left on Western Avenue instead of
right so that he could drive past Lily's house, hoping to catch a
glimpse of her in her kitchen.

From then on they met at the church as often as they could. Lily
would walk instead of drive the two and a half miles from her house,
and instead of taking Laramie Road she would cut across the fields
and the newly built roads. She walked for exercise anyway, she told
Carl. Now her exercise was determined by Margaret Finch's schedule,
and an hour before Lily was due Carl would start watching for her
from his study window, waiting to see her striped wool hat appear
over the rise of the hill in the cemetery, then her face, then her long-
legged stride. Each detail of her touched him; the sum of them was
what was knowable of her, it seemed to him, and the rest of her was
limitless—as was true for anyone, he now knew, finally able to see
that limitless quality in her.

Perhaps through her, he thought one morning, he could love the
world. Because the world did look different to him: the white peaks
of the mountains, the narrow streets of Worland, the snow starting at
midnight and falling early into the morning. Everything he looked at
was transformed by what he felt. Feeling was the preparation, he saw.
Feeling came first and thought came after; that was the order of

things. Was it the opposite of what his father taught? How had he lived so many years without knowing that feeling came first?

They talked now about the future. Carl's daughter had two more years of high school; once she graduated they could divorce their spouses and marry. They didn't talk in detail about where they would live or what they would do. There would be time to talk about that then compared to the little time they had together now.

They were like teenagers, Lily said one February afternoon. As long as they were together they believed that everything else would just work itself out. Snow had begun falling that morning and Carl had worried she wouldn't come, but she did come, shaking off the snow and leaving wet footprints in the vestibule. Now, as she dressed, pushing her bangs back from her forehead, Carl saw that her hair, like his, was beginning to gray along the hairline. It seemed that the more he saw of her, the more he saw of himself, even in small ways such as this. He helped her on with her parka and walked her through the church into the cold early dusk outside.

"Stay warm," he told her, then watched her set out. She turned back once to wave. The temperature had dropped and Laramie Road had an icy sheen to it. Carl had no presentiment, no unexplainable feeling he could have acted on, and by the time he heard sirens he was already home, eating supper with his wife and daughter. Lily had been less than half a block from home when a pickup skidding on the ice had jumped the curb.

There was no one but Carl to conduct the funeral. For two days he sat in his small office at home, coming out only at mealtimes and to lie in bed from midnight to five in a semiconscious sleep. His office was an add-on off the kitchen, and through the closed door he could hear his wife and daughter come and go. It was like hearing a play, he thought; they didn't seem connected to him nor did he feel connected to them. He was visiting after having been away for what seemed like the only real life he had ever had, and now that visit was supposed to be his life.

"There's no point to geometry," he heard his daughter say, and his wife answering, "Nobody sees the point of things until later."

By the second day the snow had stopped and the sun had come out. Outside Carl's window icicles under the eaves were dripping.

Lily was buried the following morning. After the viewing at the funeral home there was the long progression of cars winding through Worland to the church cemetery. The parking lot filled up, leaving everybody else to park along Laramie Road a quarter of a mile in each direction. Both Lily and her husband had grown up near Worland; more than the usual number of people would be looking to Carl for answers. That was how he was thinking of it. That was the part he was supposed to play, and perhaps that was why, standing in the snow in the hilly cemetery, waiting to begin, his own emotions seemed remote to him, like birds holding back in the trees across the road.

He conducted a brief graveside service, beginning and ending with a quotation: "She will rise and shine like the stars and the sun," and "How strange it is to know that she is at peace and all is well, and yet be so sorrowful!"

Only Margaret Finch recognized the source. "I always thought Luther was a bit of a madman," she said, "but he did know how to put things." She had come up to Carl and walked with him through the cemetery to the parking lot. He had never been comfortable with her, in the sense that he had never—except for Lily—been comfortable with anyone. But as he walked alongside her now he felt a connection and found it hard to say good-bye, even though he would see her in a few minutes. She was heading to the Forrest home, where Carl's wife and daughter already were, helping set things up, and where he would be soon.

Meanwhile he stood in the parking lot, watching it empty. He would have to walk away from the church, he thought. He had strayed too far from it. He didn't know what it meant anymore.

But when he opened his car door a sentence from Saint Theresa suddenly came to him: "The important thing is not to think much, but to love much."

He had read that in the seminary and not been struck by it. He had forgotten it. He had not understood it until now.

Nadine Gordimer

A Beneficiary

CACHES OF old papers are like graves; you shouldn't open them. Her mother had been cremated. There was no marble stone incised "Laila de Morne, born, died, actress."

She had always lied about her age; her name, too—the name she used wasn't her natal name, too ethnically limiting to suggest her uniqueness in a cast list. It wasn't her married name, either. She had baptized herself, professionally. She was long divorced, although only in her late fifties, when a taxi hit her car and (as she would have delivered her last line) brought down the curtain on her career.

Her daughter, Charlotte, had her father's surname and was as close to him as a child can be, when subject to an ex-husband's conditions of access. As Charlotte grew up, she felt more compatible with him than with her mother, fond as she was of her mother's—somehow—childishness. Perhaps acting was really a continuation of the make-believe games of childhood—fascinating, in a way. But. But what? Not a way Charlotte had wanted to follow—despite the fact that she was named after the character with which her mother had had an early success (Charlotte Corday, in Peter Weiss's *Marat/Sade*), and despite the encouragement of drama and dance classes. Not a way she could follow, because of lack of talent: her mother's unspoken interpretation, expressed in disappointment, if not reproach. Laila de Morne had not committed herself to any lover, had not gone so far as to marry again. There was no stepfather to confuse relations, loyalties; Charlie (as her father called her) could remark to him, "Why should she expect me to take after her?"

Her father was a neurologist. They laughed together at any predestinatory prerogative of her mother's, or the alternative paternal one—to be expected to become a doctor! Poking around in people's brains? They nudged each other with more laughter at the daughter's distaste.

Her father helped arrange the memorial gathering, in place of a funeral service, sensitive as always to any need of his daughter's. She certainly didn't expect or want him to come along to his ex-wife's apartment and sort the clothes, personal possessions to be kept or given away. A friend from the firm where she worked as an actuary agreed to help for a weekend. Unexpectedly, the young civil-rights lawyer with whom there had been a sensed mutual attraction, taken no further than dinner and a cinema date, also offered himself— perhaps a move toward the love affair that was coming anyway. The girls emptied the cupboards of clothes, the friend exclaiming over the elaborate range of styles women of that generation wore, how many personalities they could project—as if they had been able to choose, when now you belonged to the outfit of jeans and T-shirt. Oh, of course! Charlotte's mother was a famous actress!

Charlotte did not correct this, out of respect for her mother's ambitions. But when she went to the next room, where the lawyer was arranging chronologically the press cuttings and programs and photographs of Laila in the roles for which the wardrobe had provided, she turned over a few programs and remarked, more to be overheard by him than to him, "Never really had the leads she believed she should have had, after the glowing notices of her promise, very young. When she murdered Marat. In his bathtub, wasn't it? I've never seen the play." Confiding the truth of her mother's career, betraying Laila's idea of herself—perhaps also a move toward a love affair.

The three young people broke out of the trappings of the past for coffee and their concerns of the present. What sort of court cases does a civil-rights lawyer take on? What did he mean by "not the usual litigation"? No robberies or hijackings? Did the two young women feel that they were discriminated against? Did the plum jobs go to males? Or was it the other way around—did bad conscience over gender discrimination mean that women were now elevated to positions they weren't really up to? Women of any color, and black men—same thing? What would have been a sad and strange task for Charlotte alone became a lively evening, an animated exchange of opinions and experiences. Laila surely would not have disapproved; she had stimulated her audience.

There was a Sunday evening at a jazz club, sharing enthusiasm and a boredom with hip-hop, Kwaito. After another evening, dinner and dancing together—that first bodily contact to confirm attraction— he offered to help again with her task, and on a weekend afternoon they kissed and touched among the stacks of clothes and boxes of theater souvenirs, his hand brimming with her breast, but did not proceed, as would have been natural, to the beautiful and inviting bed, with its signature of draped shawls and cushions. Some atavistic taboo, a notion of respect for the dead—as if her mother still lay there in possession.

The love affair found a bed elsewhere and continued uncertainly, pleasurably enough but without much expectation of commitment. A one-act piece begun among the props of a supporting-part career.

Charlotte brushed aside any offers, from him or from her office friend, to continue with the sorting of Laila's—what? The clothes were packed up. Some seemed wearable only in the context of a theatrical wardrobe and were given to an experimental-theater group; others went to the Salvation Army, for distribution to the homeless. Her father arranged with an estate agent to advertise the apartment for sale; unless you want to move in, he suggested. But it was too big;

Charlie couldn't afford to, didn't want to, live in a style not her own, even rent-free. They laughed again in their understanding, not in criticism of her mother. Laila was Laila. He agreed, but as if thinking of some other aspect of her. Yes, Laila.

The movers came to take the furniture to be sold. She half thought of inheriting the bed; it would have been luxurious to flop diagonally across its generosity, but she wouldn't have been able to get it past the bedroom door in her small flat. When the men departed with their loads, there were pale shapes on the floor where everything had stood. She opened windows to let out the dust and, turning back suddenly, saw that something had been left behind. A couple of empty boxes, the cardboard ones used for supermarket delivery. Irritated, she went to gather them. One wasn't empty; it seemed to be filled with letters. What makes you keep some letters and not others? In her own comparatively short life, she'd thrown away giggly schoolgirl stuff, sexy propositions scribbled on the backs of menus, once naively found flattering, a polite letter of rejection in response to an application for a job beyond her qualifications—a salutary lesson on what her set called the *real world*. This box apparently contained memorabilia that was different from the stuff already dealt with. The envelopes had the look of personal letters: hand-addressed, without the printed logos of businesses, banks. Had Laila had a personal life that wasn't related to her family-the-theater? One child, the product of divorced parents, hardly counts as "family."

Charlotte—that was the identity she had in any context relating to her mother—sifted through the envelopes. If her mother had had a personal life, it was not a material possession to be disposed of like garments taken on and off; a personal life can't be "left to" a daughter, like a beneficiary in a will. Whatever letters Laila had chosen to keep were still hers; best to quietly burn them, as Laila herself had been consumed, sending them to join her. They say (she had read somewhere) that no one ever disappears, up in the atmosphere, stratosphere, whatever you call space—atoms infinitely minute, beyond conception of existence, are up there forever, from the whole world, from all time. As she shook this one box which was not empty, so that the contents would settle and not spill when it was lifted, she noticed some loose sheets of writing paper lying facedown. Not held in the privacy of an envelope. She picked them out, turned them face up. Her father's handwriting, more deliberately formed than Charlie knew it. What was the date at the top of the page, under the address of the house she remembered as home when she was a small girl? A date twenty-four years back. Of course, his handwriting had changed a bit; it does with different stages in one's life. His Charlie was twenty-eight now, so she would have been four years old when he wrote that date. It must have been just before the divorce and her move to a new home with Laila.

The letter was formally addressed, on the upper-left-hand side of the paper, to a firm of lawyers, Kaplan McLeod & Partners, and directed to one of them in particular: "Dear Hamish." Why on earth would Laila want to keep from a dead marriage the sort of business letter that a neurologist might have to write to a legal firm—on some question of a car accident maybe, or the nonpayment of some patient's consultation fee or surgery charges. (As if her father's medical and human ethics would ever have led him to the latter. . . .) The pages must have got mixed up with the other, truly personal material at some time. Laila and Charlotte had changed apartments frequently during Charlotte's childhood and adolescence.

The letter was marked "Copy":

"My wife, Laila de Morne, is an actress and, in the course of pursuing her career, has moved in a circle independent of one shared by a couple in marriage. I have always encouraged her to take the opportunities, through contacts she might make, to further her talent. She is a very attractive woman, and it was obvious to me that I should have to accept that there would be men, certainly among her fellow actors, who would want to be more than admirers. But while she enjoyed the attention, and sometimes responded with a general kind of social flirtation, I had no reason to see this as a more than natural pleasure in her own looks and talents. She would make fun of these admirers, privately, with sharp remarks on their appearance, their pretensions, and, if they were actors, directors, or playwrights, on the quality of their work. I knew that I had not married a woman who would want to stay home and nurse babies, but from time to time she would bring up the subject. We ought to have a son, she said, for me. Then she would get a new part in a play and the idea was understandably postponed. After a successful start, her career was, however, not advancing to her expectations. She did not succeed in getting several roles that she had confidently anticipated. She came home elated one night and told me that she had been accepted for a small part in a play overseas, in the Edinburgh Fringe Festival. She had been selected because the leading actor himself, Rendall Harris, had told the casting director that she was the most talented of the young women in the theater group. I was happy for her, and we gave a farewell party at our house the night before the cast left for the United Kingdom. After Edinburgh, she spent some time in London, calling to say how wonderful and necessary it was for her to experience what was happening in theater there and, I gathered, trying her luck in auditions. Apparently unsuccessfully.

"Perhaps she intended not to come back. But she did. A few weeks later, she told me that she had just been to a gynecologist and confirmed that she was pregnant. I was moved. I took the unlikely luck of conception—I'd assumed, when we made love on the night of the party, that she'd taken the usual precautions; we weren't drunk, even if she was triumphant—as a symbol of what would be a change in our perhaps unsuitable marriage. I am a medical specialist, a neurological surgeon.

"When the child was born, it looked like any other red-faced infant, but after several months everyone remarked how the little girl was the image of Laila, her mother. It was one Saturday afternoon, when she was kicking and flinging her arms athletically—we were admiring our baby's progress, her beauty, and I joked, 'Lucky she doesn't look like me'—that my wife picked her up, away from me, and told me, 'She's not your child.' She'd met someone in Edinburgh.

I interrupted with angry questions. No, she prevaricated, all right, London, the affair began in London. The leading actor who had insisted on her playing the small part had introduced her to someone there. A few days later, she admitted that it was not "someone," it was the leading actor. He was the father of our girl. She told this to other people, our friends, when through the press we heard the news that the actor, Rendall Harris, was making a name for himself in plays by Tom Stoppard and Tennessee Williams.

"I couldn't decide what to believe. I even consulted a colleague in the medical profession about the possible variations in the period of gestation in relation to birth. Apparently, it was possible that the conception had taken place with me, or with the other man a few days before or after the intercourse with me. Laila never expressed any intention of taking the child and making her life with the man. She was too proud to let anyone know that he most likely wouldn't want her or the supposed progeny of their affair.

"Laila has devoted herself to her acting career and, as a result, I have of necessity had a closer relation than is customary for the father with the care of the small girl, now four years old. I am devoted to her and can produce witnesses to support the conviction that she would be happiest in my custody.

"I hope this is adequate. Let me know if anything more is needed, or if there is too much detail here. I'm accustomed to writing reports in medical jargon and thought that this should be different. I don't suppose I've a hope in hell of getting Charlie; Laila will put all her dramatic skills into swearing that she isn't mine!"

That Saturday: it landed in the apartment looted by the present and filled it with blasting amazement, the presence of the past. That Saturday, coming to her just as it had come to him. Charlotte/Charlie (which was she?) received exactly as he had what Laila (yes, her mother—giving birth is proof) had told.

How do you recognize something that is not in the known vocabulary of your emotions? Shock is like a ringing in the ears; to stop it, you snatch back to the first page, read the letter again. It says what it said. This sinking collapse from within, from your flared, breathless nostrils down to your breasts, stomach, legs, and hands, hands that not only feel passively but go out to grasp what can't be. Dismay, that feeble-sounding word, has this ghastly meaning. What do you do with something you've been *told*? Something that now is there in the gut of your existence. Run to him? Thrust his letter at him, at her— but she's out of it now, she has escaped in smoke from the crematorium. And she is the one who really knows—knew.

Of course, he didn't get custody. He was awarded the divorce, but the mother was given the four-year-old child. It is natural, particularly in the case of a small girl, for a child to live with the mother. Despite this "deposition" of his, in which he was denied paternity, he paid maintenance for the child. The expensive boarding school, the drama and dance classes, even those holidays in the Seychelles, three times in Spain, once in France, once in Greece, with the mother. Must have paid generously. He was a neurologist, more successful in his profession than the mother was on the stage. But this couldn't have been the reason for the generosity.

Charlotte/Charlie couldn't think about that, either. She folded the two sheets, fumbled absently for the envelope they should have been in, weren't, and with them in her hand left the boxes, the letters, Laila's apartment locked, behind the door.

He could only be asked: why he had been a father, loving.

The return of his Saturday—it woke her at three, four in the morning, when she had kept it at bay through the activities of the day, work, navigating alone in her car through the city's crush, leisure time occupied in the company of friends who hadn't been *told*. She and her father had one of their regular early dinners at his favorite restaurant, went to a foreign movie by a director whose work she admires, and the news of that Saturday couldn't be spoken, was unreal.

In the dark, when the late-night traffic was over and the dawn traffic hadn't begun: silence.

The reason.

He believed in the chance of conception, that one night of the party. Laila's farewell. Even though his friend, the expert in biological medicine, had implied that if you didn't know the stage of the woman's fertility cycle you couldn't be sure—the conception might have been achieved a few days before or after that unique night.

I am Charlie, his.

The reason.

Another night thought, an angry mood: Who do they think they are, deciding who I am to suit themselves? To suit her vanity—she could, at least, bear the child of an actor with a career in the theater that she hadn't attained for herself. To suit his wounded macho pride—refusing to accept another male's potency, his seed had to have been the winner.

And in the morning, before the distractions of the day took over, shame, ashamed of herself, Charlie, for thinking so spitefully, cheaply about him.

The next reason that offered itself was hardly less unjust—confusedly hurtful to her. He had paid one kind of maintenance, and he had paid another kind of maintenance, loving her in order to uphold the conventions before what he saw as the world—the respectable doctors in white coats who had wives to accompany them to medical-council dinners. If he had married again, it would have been to a woman like these. Laila was Laila. Never risk another.

The letter that belonged to no one's daughter was moved from place to place, to a drawer under sweaters, to an Indian box where she kept earrings and bracelets, behind books of plays—Euripides and Racine, Shaw and Brecht, Dario Fo, Miller, Artaud, Beckett, and, of course, an annotated *Marat/Sade*. Charlotte's inheritance, never read.

When you are of many minds, the contention makes someone who has been not exactly what one wanted, who doesn't yet count, the only person to be *told*. In bed, yet another night, after lovemaking, when the guards were down, along with the physical tensions. Mark, the civil-rights lawyer, who acted in the mess of divorce litigation only when it infringed constitutional rights, said, in response, of the letter, "Tear it up." When she appealed (it was not just a piece of paper): "Have a DNA test." How to do that without taking the whole cache that was the past to the father? "Get a snip of his hair." All that would be needed to go along with a sample of her blood. Like whoever it was in the Bible cutting off Samson's hair. But how was she supposed to do that? Steal up on her father in his sleep somewhere?

Tear it up. Easy advice from someone who had understood nothing. She did not.

But a circumstance came about, as if somehow summoned. . . . Of course, it was fortuitous. . . . A distinguished actor-director had been invited by a local theater to direct a season of classical and avantgarde plays, taking several lead roles himself. It was his first return to the country, to the city where he was born and which he had left to pursue his career—he said in newspaper interviews and on radio, television—how long ago? Oh, twenty-five years. Rendall Harris. Newspaper photographs: an actor's expression, assumed for many cameras, handsomely enough late-middle-aged, a defiant slight twist to the mouth to emphasize character, the eyebrows raised together amusedly, a touch of white in the short sideburns. Eyes difficult to make out in newsprint. On television, alive; something of the upper body, gestures, coming into view, the closeup of his changing expressions, the deep-set long eyes, gray darkening with some deliberate intensity, almost flashing black, meeting yours, the viewer's. What had she expected? A recognition? Hers of him? His, out of the lit-up box, of her? An actor's performance face.

She couldn't ignore the stir at the idea that the man named by her mother was in the city. Laila was Laila. Yes. If she had not gone up in smoke, would he have met her again, remembered her? Had he ever seen the baby, who was at least two when he went off for twenty-five years? What does a two-year-old remember? Had she ever seen this man as a younger self, been taken in by those strikingly interrogative eyes, received?

She was accustomed to going to the theater with friends or with the lawyer-lover, though he preferred films, one of his limited tastes that she could at least share. Every day—every night—she thought about the theater. Not with Mark. Not beside any of her friends. No. In a wild recurrent impulse, there was the temptation to be there with her father, who did not know that she knew, had been *told*, as he was that Saturday. Laila was Laila. For him and for her.

She went alone when Rendall Harris was to play one of the lead roles. There had been ecstatic notices. He was Laurence Olivier reincarnated for a new—the twenty-first—century, a deconstructed style of performance. She was far back in the box-office queue when a board went up: "House Full." She booked online for another night, an aisle seat three rows from the proscenium. At the theater, she found herself, for some reason, hostile. Ridiculous. She wanted to disagree with the critics. That's what it was about.

Rendall Harris—how do you describe a performance that manages to create for the audience the wholeness, the life of a man, not just "in character" for the duration of the play but what he might have been before the events chosen by the playwright and how he might be, alive, continuing after? Rendall Harris was an extraordinary actor, man. Her palms were up among the hands applauding like the flight of birds rising. When he came out to take the calls, summoning the rest of the cast around him, she wasn't in his direct sight line, as she would have been if she'd asked for a seat in the middle of the row.

She went to every performance in which he was billed in the cast. A seat in the middle of the second row, the first would have been too obvious.

Though she was something other than a groupie, she was among the knot of autograph seekers one night, who hung about the foyer hoping that he might leave the theater that way. He did appear, making for the bar with the theater's director, and for a moment, under the arrest of programs thrust at him, happened to encounter her eyes as she stood back from his fans—he had a smile of self-deprecating amusement, meant for anyone in his line of vision, but that one was her.

The lift of his face, his walk, his repertoire of gestures, the oddities of his lapses in expression onstage that she secretly recognized as himself appearing, became almost familiar to her. As if she somehow knew him, and these intimacies knew her. Signals. If invented, they were very like conviction. At the box office, there was the routine question, "D'you have a season ticket?" She supposed that was to have been bought when the Rendall Harris engagement was first announced.

She thought of a letter. Owed it to him for the impression that his performances had made on her. His command of the drama of *living*, the excitement of being there with him. After the fourth or fifth version in her mind, the next was written. Mailed to the theater, it was most likely glanced through in his dressing room or at his hotel, among the other "tributes," and would either be forgotten or taken back to London for the collection of memorabilia it seemed actors needed. But, with him, there was that wry sideways tilt to the photographed mouth.

Of course, she neither expected nor received any acknowledgment.

After a performance one night, she bumped into some old friends of Laila's, actors who had come to the memorial, and who insisted on her joining them in the bar. When Rendall Harris's unmistakable head appeared through the late crowd, they created a swift current past backs to embrace him, to draw him with their buddy, the theater director, to a space made at the table, where she had been left among the bottles and glasses. The friends, in the excitement of having Rendall Harris among them, forgot to introduce her as Laila's daughter, Laila who'd played Corday in that early production where he'd been Marat; perhaps they had forgotten Laila—best thing with the dead if you want to get on with your life and ignore the hazards, like that killer taxi, around you. Charlotte's letter was no more present than the other one, behind the volumes of plays. A fresh acquaintance, just the meeting of a nobody with the famous. But not entirely, even from the famous actor's side. As the talk lobbed back and forth, the man, sitting almost opposite her, thought it friendly, from his special level of presence, to toss something to the young woman whom no one was including, and easily found what came to mind: "Aren't you the one who's been sitting bang in the middle of the second row, several times lately?" And then they joined in laughter, a double confession—hers of absorbed concentration on him; his of being aware of it or at least becoming so at the sight, here, of someone out there whose attention had caught him. He asked, across the voices of the others, which plays in the repertoire she'd enjoyed most, what criticisms she had of those she didn't think much of. He named a number that she hadn't seen. Her response was another confession: she had seen only those in which he had played a part.

When the party broke up and all were meandering their way, with stops and starts in backchat and laughter, to the foyer, a shift in progress brought Rendall Harris's back right in front of her. He turned swiftly, as lithely as a young man, and—it must have been impulse in one accustomed to being natural, charming, in spite of his professional guard—spoke as if he had been thinking of it: "You've missed a lot, you know, so flattering for me, avoiding the other plays. Come some night, or there's a Sunday-afternoon performance of a Wole Soyinka you ought to see. We'll have a bite in the restaurant before I take you to your favorite seat. I'm particularly interested in audience reaction to the chances I've taken directing this play."

Rendall Harris sat beside her through the performance, now and then whispering some comment, drawing her attention to this and that. She had told him, over lasagna at lunch, that she was an actuary, a creature of calculation, that she couldn't be less qualified to judge the art of actors' interpretation or that of a director. "You know that's not true." Said with serious inattention. Tempting to believe that he sensed something in her blood, sensibility. From her mother. It was or was not the moment to tell him that she was Laila's daughter, although she carried Laila's husband's name, a name that Laila was not known by.

Now, what sort of a conundrum was that supposed to be? She was produced by—what was that long term?—parthenogenesis. She just growed, like Topsy? You know that's not true.

He arranged for her a seat as his guest for the rest of the repertoire in which he played the lead. It was taken for granted that she would come backstage afterward. Sometimes he included her in other cast gatherings, with "people your own age," obliquely acknowledging his own, old enough to be her father. Cool. He apparently had no children, adult or otherwise, didn't mention any. Was he gay? Now? Can a man change sexual preference, or literally embrace both? The way he embraced so startlingly, electric with the voltage of life, the beings created only in words by Shakespeare, Strindberg, Brecht, Beckett—oh, you name them, from the volumes holding down the letter telling of that Saturday. "You seem to understand that I—we—actors absolutely risk, kill ourselves, trying to reach the ultimate identity in what's known as a character, beating ourselves down to let the creation take over. Haven't you ever wanted to have a go yourself? Thought about acting?"

She said, "I know an actuary is the absolute antithesis of all that. I don't have the talent."

He didn't make some comforting effort. Didn't encourage magnanimously—*Why not have a go?* "Maybe you're right. Nothing like the failure of an actor. It isn't like other kinds of failure. It doesn't just happen inside you; it happens before an audience. Better to be yourself. You're a very interesting young woman, depths there. I don't know if you know it, but I think you do."

Like every sexually attractive young woman, she was experienced with the mostly pathetic drive that aging men have toward young women. Some of the men are themselves attractive, either because they have somehow kept the promise of vigor—mouths filled with their own teeth, tight muscular buttocks in their jeans, no jowls, fine eyes that have seen much to impart—or because they're well known, distinguished, yes, even rich. This actor, whose enduring male beauty was an attribute of his talent—he was probably more desirable now than he had been as a novice Marat in Peter Weiss's play; all the roles he had taken—he had emerged from the risk with a strongly endowed identity. Although there was no apparent reason that he should not make the usual play for this young woman, there was no sign that he was doing so. She knew the moves; they were not being made.

The attention was something else. Between them. Was this a question or a fact? They wouldn't know, would they? He simply welcomed her like a breeze that blew in with this season abroad, in his old hometown, and seemed to refresh him. Famous people have protégés, a customary part of the multiply responsive public reception. He told her, sure to be indulged, that he wanted to go back to an adventure, a part of the country he'd been thrilled by as a child, wanted to climb there, where there were great spiky plants with red candelabras. She told him that it was the wrong season—those plants wouldn't be in bloom in this, his kind of season—but she'd drive him there; he took up the shy offer at once, and left the cast without him for two days, when the plays performed were not those in which he had the lead. They slipped and scrambled up the peaks he remembered, and, at the lodge in the evening, he was recognized, took this as inevitable, autographed bits of paper, and quipped privately with her that he had been mistaken in the past for a pop star he hadn't heard of but ought to have. His unconscious vitality invigorated people around him wherever he was. No wonder he was such an innovative director; the critics wrote that in his hands the classic plays, even the standbys of Greek drama, were reimagined, as if this were the way they were meant to be and never had been before. It wasn't in his shadow that she stood but in his light. As if she had been reimagined by herself. He was wittily critical at other people's expense, and so with him she was free to think—say—what she found ponderous in those she worked with: the predictability among her set of friends, which she usually tolerated without stirring them up. Not that she saw much of her friends at present. She was part of the cast of the backstage scene now, a recruit to the family of actors in the coffee shop at lunch, privy to their gossip, their bantering with the actor-director who drew so much from them, rousing their eager talent.

The regular Charlie dinners with her father, often postponed, were subdued; he caught this from her. There wasn't much for them to talk about. Unless she wanted to show off her new associations.

The old impulse came, unwelcome, to go with her father to the theater. Suppressed. But returned. To sit with him and together see the man commanding on the stage. What for? What would this resolve? Was she Charlotte or Charlie?

Charlie said, "Let's see the play that's had such rave reviews. I'll get tickets." He didn't demur, had perhaps forgotten who Rendall Harris was, might be.

He led her to the bar afterward, talking of the play with considering interest. He had not seen Beckett in ages; the play wore well, was not outdated. She didn't want to be there. It was late, she said. No, no, she didn't want a drink, the bar was too crowded. But he persuaded gently, "We won't stay. I'm thirsty, need a beer."

The leading actor was caught in a spatter of applause as he moved among the admiring drinkers. He talked through clusters of others and then arrived.

"Rendall, my father."

"Congratulations. Wonderful performance—the critics don't exaggerate."

The actor dismissed the praise as if he'd had enough of that from people who didn't understand what such an interpretation of Vladimir or Estragon involved, the—what was that word he always used?—risk. "I didn't feel right tonight. I was missing a beat. Charlotte, you've seen me do better, hey, m'darling."

Her father picked up his glass but didn't drink. "Last time I saw you was in the play set in an asylum. Laila de Morne was Charlotte Corday."

Her father *told.*

"Of course, you always get chalked up in the critics' hierarchy by how you play the classics, but I'm more fascinated by the new stuff—movement theater, parts I can take from zero. I've sat in that bathtub too many times, knifed by Charlotte Cordays. . . ." The projection of that disarmingly self-deprecating laugh.

She spoke what she had not *told,* had not yet found the right time and situation to say to him: "Laila de Morne is my mother." No more to be discarded in the past tense than the performance of the de Sade asylum where she had been Charlotte Corday to his Marat. "That's how I was named."

"Well, you're sure not a Charlotte to carry a knife, spoil your beautiful aura with that, frighten off the men around you." Peaked eyebrows, as if he were, ruefully, one of them—a trick from the actors' repertoire contradicted by a momentary, hardly perceptible contact of those eyes with her own, diamonds, black with the intensity that it was his talent to summon, a stage prop taken up and at once released, at will.

Laila was Laila.

When they were silent in the pause at a traffic light, her father touched the open shield of his palm to the back of her head, the unobtrusive caress he had offered when driving her to boarding school. If she was, for her own reasons, now differently disturbed, that was not to be pried at. She was meant to drop him at his apartment, but when she drew up at the entrance she opened the car door at her side, as he did his, and went to him in the street. He turned—what's the matter? She moved her head—nothing. She went to him and he saw, without understanding, that he should take her in his arms. She held him. He kissed her cheek, and she pressed it against his. Nothing to do with DNA.

Viet Dinh

Substitutes

IN 1974, we waited for the world to be ours. That fall, we were sixth graders, the top of the food chain at Vinh Xuong. Now our soccer skills were unmatched, and our bodies had grown in ways that we had not foreseen. If we had any fears, they were only of Mr. Hanh, who had taught at Vinh Xuong longer than anyone could remember. Even our parents had stories about his tight, pinched face. *He's lived on nothing but lemons his whole life,* they told us. He kept his white hair parted on the left, revealing a crisp line of liver spots along his scalp. *You have to watch out for his cane,* they warned us: a meter-long bamboo stick, thin as your pinkie finger. Upon command, a misbehaving student had to produce his hands, palm-side up if lucky, palm-side down if unlucky. No one dared watch the actual punishment. The sound of cane breaking the air like a sudden intake of breath, the deadening crack of wood against flesh: that was enough.

But that spring, even before Saigon fell, our town became awash in strangers. Can Tho had always been a port, but now its biggest export was desperation. The line of evacuees stretched down the riverside, along Hai Ba Trung Street, and into the alleys. They spread their belongings on the ground as if building personal forts and jostled for position, fighting to move two feet closer to the dock. Women pulled their hair and cried for mercy. They stood stooped, gold ingots dangling from cloth cradles around the necks, and bawling infants in their arms. In the market, those haggling for shrimp paste became indistinguishable from those haggling jewelry, silk brocade, money—anything they had—for safe passage down the Mekong.

Then there were us, the families who could not afford the tickets, who could not leave our houses, our livelihoods, our relations. Life had not changed for us: we went to the market as always, pulled our nets in from the river, fried the sprats until the bones were brittle, edible. We ate in silence, even as the Communists stormed Can Tho, filling the streets with drab olive uniforms, secondhand Kalashnikovs, indiscriminate trigger fingers. They came into our homes and sat with guns lengthwise across their knees. They asked if we'd been collaborators, if we'd abetted the ARVN. May as well admit it now, they said, because the truth would come out. Even as our parents insisted on neutrality, the soldiers gestured to us with their muzzles: *Do you want your children to grow up orphans?*

One day, the docks groaned under the weight of exodus; the next day, empty. The Communists had swept everyone out to sea, into corners even more remote than Can Tho. Our parents forbade us from picking through the abandoned belongings: *It's bad luck,* they said. Food jettisoned as unnecessary weight rotted in the gutters. Even the stray dogs refused to eat it. Those who had been captured were frog-marched through the streets, pleading with each step. To where, no one knew. Our parents urged us to forget the commotion. There was nothing to be done now.

All you have to worry about, they said, *is school.*

By September, Mr. Hanh had lost none of his fearsomeness.

"To your desks!" he barked. Strolling the aisles, he was a minesweeper, tapping out misbehavior with his cane. "Pens and paper out. Hands folded on top of your desk." His face was as shrunken and desiccated as a preserved prune, the effect more pronounced when he pursed his lips to scrutinize our work. "Who taught you how to write? Monkeys? Your parents should be ashamed."

After a month, Mr. Hanh still hadn't exhausted his stores of creative punishments: tardy students knelt at the front of the room, arms outstretched. Talking in class resulted in an oral recitation from memory; falling asleep earned you a mouthful of chalk dust from a well-aimed eraser. It was rumored that Mr. Hanh had been trained as a sniper against the Japanese.

"He's too old," someone said. "It was probably against the French."

Once, he knelt eye level to Minh. "Open your mouth! Lift your tongue." His bony fingers took a wad of chewing gum out of Minh's mouth and rubbed it into his eyebrows. "There will be no gum chewing. Understood?"

And the cane: every time he picked it up, our palms sweated. It was reserved for poor work, and woe to him who caught it across the knuckles. From that alone, we knew how arthritis must have felt and treated our grandparents with more respect. The red welts from a caning stayed all day, and no matter how sore your fingers were, how much they'd swollen, you had to continue writing, because if your compositions were illegible, that meant more punishment. This was something we had to survive, just as our parents had survived their own youth. Each day, we scratched our collars and crossed our legs in hopes that he'd misread the clock and dismiss us early. We thought our torture would never end. Then, three months into the school year, it did.

Miss Bui was Mr. Hanh's opposite: young, lovely, kind. Her *ao dai* cupped her hips, curved around her bust. At the start of the day, her long black hair caught the morning sun; lit from behind, it became the Mekong, red with silt. She trailed the scent of jasmine when she walked, and some of us made errors just so she'd correct us.

She must have recently graduated from teachers college, because although she was patient with our schoolwork, she didn't know how to discipline. She frowned when notes were passed (unlike Mr. Hanh, who made the recipient of the note read it out loud before the writer ate it), and when Minh and Truong's argument over a playground soccer foul spilled over into the classroom, she couldn't break it up.

"Boys," she pleaded. "Boys! Stop it!" We waited for her to take Mr. Hanh's cane, propped in the corner since his disappearance, and wield it like a martial-arts swordsmistress, but Minh and Truong continued to roll on the floor, swinging punches and kicking desks out of their way. Unwilling to surrender, they grunted and panted. Finally, Miss Bui ran out of the classroom, her slippers clapping against the floor, and returned with Principal Kim. In his gray polyester suit, Principal Kim pried Minh and Truong apart, holding each boy aloft as if they were unruly cats and carried them away, ignoring their howls. They were really in for it.

For the rest of the day, Miss Bui bowed her head, as if the swirls of dust where they had tussled were evidence of her own failure. The topic of our composition was "Why do people fight?" As we read them aloud—*we fight for honor, we fight for protection, we fight for justice*—she searched the sky beyond the window. The afternoon was blank: no birds, no planes, not even smoke from cooking fires. The world beyond the white plaster of Vinh Xuong, just past the low walls that enclosed the yard, seemed distant, imaginary, as if we had only read about it.

"I hope you have learned something today," she said.

After school, Principal Kim reprimanded Miss Bui. "It is your responsibility to stop fights," he said. "We cannot allow students to run wild."

Her reply was inaudible. We yelled at some nearby third graders to stop gossiping, but heard nothing further.

The next day, Miss Bui seemed normal. She had cut her hair

shoulder length, which we all agreed was a pity. The previous day lingered in Minh's black eye and Truong's split lip, but we'd already put it behind us. We returned to spilling ink across our homework so that she would walk toward us, smiling as serenely as Quan Yin, and we treasured the swish of her white pants, the tilt of her head as she approached.

She, too, vanished.

We had nothing but speculations, and these we traded like playing cards. Miss Bui's absence was made more acute by Mrs. Pham, who clipped her tightly bunned hair with rusty bobby pins. She carried age in her face, in her stooped posture, in the way she shrank from our loud voices.

The trouble started the second day.

We were doing recitations, and she called on Truong. When he didn't respond, she looked at him and asked, "Truong?"

The devil flashed in his eyes: "I'm not Truong, I'm Phuoc. He's Truong." And he pointed to Minh.

Minh immediately shouted, "Liar! That's not true. That's Truong." And Minh pointed to Quang. Within seconds, the room reeled with accusations and confessions: "That's Truong!" or "I'm Truong!" The demon inside Truong now possessed all of us; even students who had never gotten in trouble played along. When the accusations got ugly—"Truong is the stupidest boy in school," "Truong is the one who smells like fish!"—Truong slammed his fist against the desk like a gavel.

We had so much fun calling each other Truong that we'd forgotten Mrs. Pham. She stood at the front of the room, paralyzed. In a voice like dead leaves, she whispered, "Please be quiet. Please be quiet." She must have been saying it for minutes. We pitied her. But we didn't let her off the hook. We wondered if she had ever taught school before. If she had, it must have been very young children. More likely, she had been a housewife, maybe a shopkeeper. Every smile struggled against the wrinkles weighing down her skin. She threatened to go to Principal Kim when we grew too unruly, so we pulled back our antics until her face eased into neutrality. As long as we wrote our compositions, she ignored the ball of paper being kicked along the floor in an ersatz soccer game.

None of us knew where she came from. It seemed unlikely that she was from Can Tho or our parents would have known her. Khanh claimed that the Que family had taken her in. But perhaps she didn't have a home. That would explain why she always wore the same white blouse and black skirt. Each day, her clothes merged further toward gray.

Still, Khanh stuck by his story. She was a refugee from Saigon, he insisted. Her husband had abandoned her. That's why she always seemed so sad. He had a pass to take his family to America, but instead of taking his wife, he took his mistress. *I mean, who wouldn't have taken someone else?* Khanh took a drag off his cigarette. That's why she seemed so inexperienced, he continued. She had to find a way to make money.

We agreed: *How sad.* For our recitation, we chose the history of a Vietnamese emperor who executed his wife in order to save the country. We watched for a long sigh, a fist clenched in rage. Maybe she would tell us her story. And maybe this would have brought us closer, given us a pathway to understanding tragedy. But she only said, "We'll pick up the story tomorrow."

Maybe it's better that Mrs. Pham left. We all knew the ending: the emperor would marry a Mongol princess and still lose Vietnam to the marauding Chinese.

Mr. Luu was with us for a week. He kept a suitcase the size of a washbasin by the desk. The leather along the bottom had cracked and peeled away, the cardboard underneath spotted with water stains. We wondered what could have been in it; Minh said that it didn't move when he kicked it. Clothes alone couldn't have been that heavy. Gold bars, maybe. Or maybe his children. Two of us could have easily fit inside.

The roster still had Mr. Hanh's crisp, spidery handwriting on the cover, but Mr. Luu didn't bother to mark absences. Truong, who wanted to trick another teacher, yelled out "Here!" for every name except his, but Mr. Luu didn't glance once.

The first day, we were stupefied. We spent most of the day writing in our notebooks as Mr. Luu read *The Journey to the West*. Even the funny parts, like when the Monkey King tries to trick Pigsy into becoming a rich man's wife, were drained of laughter. Perhaps it was the gray February weather. The rain was cold, and the sun never dried the damp from our skin. After school, there was nothing to do besides play soccer: we were too old to catch fireflies and too young to kiss girls. The curfew kept us inside at night, listening to the radio with our parents, songs interspersed with victorious slogans.

Our rebellion started the next day. As soon as we were in our seats, he began what we thought was a dictation. But we could barely understand him; he was reading from a guidebook to New York City.

Truong passed a note across the aisle, but Mr. Luu didn't notice. Before long, paper went back and forth as if we were trading critical communiqués: "Hi," "How are you?" "I can't believe we're doing this," and "It's like we're not even here." Soon we got up to hand-deliver our notes, then, after a while, decided to stop wasting paper and began whispering. And, finally, we gave up whispering. Amid the cacophony, Mr. Luu ignored us and read to himself.

We admired his honesty: he'd soon be gone. He knew it, we knew it. He'd be sailing south down the Mekong with Mr. Hanh, Miss Bui, and Mrs. Pham toward . . . Toward what? We didn't care. We could do whatever we wanted. Here, in school, we were free of checkpoints, of soldiers, of guns.

The only time Mr. Luu spoke was when Truong and Minh's horse-play got rough, and Truong stumbled against Mr. Luu's case. "Clumsy!" he hissed. As he pulled the case toward him, the handle looked as if it might wrench free of its rivets. We were good until the silence became too unbearable and we remembered that, one way or another, he didn't care.

. . .

We weren't surprised to find Mr. Luu gone. But we were surprised by who took his place: an army officer—a general, judging from the pins and medals adorning his uniform—standing with hands held behind his back, his family name, Khang, embroidered above his colorful commendations. The red cloth band above the black rim of his cap was as bright as a new flag. But the scar bisecting his face from one ear to the other frightened us the most: it was as red as the band on his cap.

We sat with our backs straight, hands folded on our desks. Mr. Hanh would have been proud. He called out names as if we were conscripts, and Truong didn't dare contradict him.

"So," he said, after a few minutes of our squirming. "What are you studying?"

We each answered him differently. We'd had so many lessons in the past few months that we couldn't agree on one. The general sliced his hand through the air: "Enough!"

We trembled, the sweat cold on our backs.

"How many of you consider yourself scholars?" he asked. No one spoke, and he squinted as if he could discern the liars. "I thought so." He pointed to Khoi. "You! What do your parents do?"

"My parents build farm machinery." Khoi added "Sir," hurriedly.

"Farmers feed our people," General Khang said. "Tell me, do you need to go to school to build combines?"

"No, sir," Khoi replied.

The general chose another student. "And your parents? What do they do?"

"My father unloads fish at the docks."

"Good. Without him, I wouldn't have any *nuoc mam*. And yours?"

"My father sells snakes at Phung Hiep."

The general went around the room, asking about our families. We knew better than to respond *My father was a soldier,* even if it was the truth. General Khang asked again, "How many of you plan to be scholars?"

No one.

He pointed to Truong.

"Answer me honestly. Do you want to be in school?"

Truong hesitated. Then, taking the general at his word, replied, "No."

"Excuse me? I didn't hear your answer."

"No, sir," said Truong, louder.

"How many of you do not want to be here right now?" he asked. A smile crept onto his face. Even the scar seemed to smile.

Minh raised his hand slowly, as did a few others. Truong shot his into the air unequivocally.

"Vietnam needs people who serve the common good," General Khang said. "We must turn our backs on those who turn their backs on Vietnam. Now tell me—" He broke into a huge grin, and our fear passed away. He wasn't scary; he was on our side. The general clapped his hands, a firecracker's pop. "Who wants to be a part of their new country?"

Hands went up immediately. We felt joy returning, excitement returning. Truong and Minh shouted out, "I do!" and upon hearing them, the rest of us yelled, "I do!" We clamored for attention, and he chuckled. He raised his hands to quiet us.

"You are the future of Vietnam. It's on your shoulders that we will rise. So forget about school. Go help your mothers in the fields. Help your fathers on the fishing boats. Make our people strong."

General Khang picked up Mr. Hanh's cane, still in the corner. We'd almost forgotten about it. The wood was white from chalk dust. He held it up. "This," he said, "is the old world." He brought the pointer over his knee and broke it in two. We cheered. He tossed the pieces into the waste bin.

Outside, shuffling feet, chatter: other classes had already been let out. General Khang saw us glancing toward the door. "Go on," he said. "Join your comrades. Make your country proud."

And with that, we streamed out, our voices mingling with the others. In the yard, soccer games had begun, and we joined in, raising a cloud that settled in our hair, our clothes, our eyes. We walked out of Vinh Xuong dirty, our faces turned up to the sun, basking in freedom. The world opened up before us, and from here, nothing would ever be the same.

We would never return to Vinh Xuong. Soon afterward, the gates were replaced by guard shacks, and the soldiers, stone-faced, barked at us when we approached holding soccer balls. The walls doubled in height, stucco smothered beneath smooth concrete. On top, spirals of razor wire like a notebook's spine.

At night, Vinh Xuong was lit up as if from flares, and the speakers hung high on poles spat messages of liberation into the darkness. Word spread that people near other re-education camps were unable to sleep from the noise. From a nearby hill, we could see into the yard where middle-aged men sat in straight rows, cross-legged, writing on scraps of paper while a voice spoke of the new social order. They looked hungry, repentant.

Once a week, women stood outside the gates, cradling infants or rice wrapped in banana leaves. When the guards shook their heads, the women dispersed. Sometimes, the gates disgorged an emaciated man, and the women rejoiced. Sometimes, the guards brought out a list of names, and women crumpled as if crushed by the sky.

Someone swore that he saw Mr. Hanh in our classroom, and one afternoon, we gathered on the hill. The window was a dark rectangle, indistinguishable from the others.

He was right there.

Are you sure it wasn't a ghost?

Might have been. But it was Mr. Hanh, for sure!

We waited for a face to appear in the black space. We must have been there for hours before someone appeared. We pointed excitedly, squinted. And, like that, the person disappeared. Maybe it was a different man grown old and gaunt. Or perhaps it was Mr. Hanh, after all. From behind the wall, guards marched in formation. The prisoners, as well. Why would Mr. Hanh be there? We didn't understand, but we weren't afraid. After all, this was now our world. *It's good to be free,* we told each other—but even so, who among us had never dreamed of escape?

Karen Brown

Isabel's Daughter

ONCE IN a while I see Isabel's daughter. The last time, she was with old Neal and it was late at night. They came in the house and she looked as if she'd just woken up and her clothes were covered with dog hair from Neal's dog. It was the usual, friends passing her from one to the other. She had learned how to live out of Isabel's Louis Vuitton bag, the few things she owned always stuffed in it, as if someone had stood in a doorway and told her to hurry up. I remember her arriving at the house with the bag loaded with mismatched clothes and a few Barbie dolls. Back then, she spent a lot of time with her father, who moved to Miami without her when Isabel died. I saw she'd begun to look more like Isabel, in an awkward, leggy, preadolescent way, with her dark eyes and that same wavy black hair of Isabel's I used to put my hands in. I don't know why I didn't expect it to happen. I got her something to drink, and she perched on the couch and her hair fell over her face. Neal started rolling a joint, and it all seemed wrong.

Isabel was my first steady girlfriend, and by this I mean she was waiting for me at my house when I got off the road three times in a row. I managed a tour of heavy metal bands from the eighties, and I was gone for weeks on different legs—first Europe, then Canada, then the northern US. I had an eccentric great-uncle, a cultivator, who left me this house, a tiny bungalow with striped metal awnings and a jungle of vines and tropical plants that bloom and thrive in the backyard. I leave my key under the mat, and people drop by and crash if they need to, but they don't usually stay long, and they don't usually clean and decorate and move in their clothes, like Isabel.

She bought an air conditioner and had it installed in one of the dining room windows. She found furniture at tag sales—a desk and a rocking chair that look old and worth something, and a set of Dickens, which she arranged on the mantel, purchased for the color of the red leather binding, the gilt on the pages. She was dancing steadily at the same place, and the heavy metal tour was doing surprisingly well, some of the acts actually learned to play in their fifteen years or so out of the spotlight, and we were both bringing in a lot of money during the time we were together. We spent the money on cars—a Miata for her, an old Alfa Romeo for me—and at Bern's Steak House and Lauro's Ristorante, and at Neiman's, and I will say we were happy, that she was happy, that I was perfectly happy.

That first time I came home she was out back in a lawn chair that I had never seen before, in a spot where the sun managed to break through the jacaranda and bamboo, wearing just the bottom of a bathing suit. It was summer, and the yard seemed exceptionally dense and green. I stood in the doorway and looked at her, and at her breasts, and couldn't honestly remember who she was. Her hair spilled over the back of the chair, and she'd smiled up at me, but her eyes held that hint of fear that made me pretend to remember her. She had come inside and put her arms around my neck and pressed her breasts up against my shirt and kissed me, and we had sex before I could even recall her name and where I'd met her, all of that information suddenly incidental. I am still a little sad about this, because I think now maybe she knew all along, and her having sex was just part of the bigger game she always had to play.

We did not pretend to have anything like love between us, so at first, I couldn't understand why she wouldn't leave. But whenever she stopped what she was doing—making avocado sandwiches at the kitchen counter, stacking the laundry in neat, folded piles on the couch, brushing her hair, naked in the bathroom—and looked at me and asked, "You want me to leave, don't you?" with her eyes tragic and full of recognition, I could not say yes.

"I'm fine with you here," I'd say, which would make her eyes change from sad to doubtful. She would slit them at me and pout, considering me.

"You're lying," she'd say, going back to whatever she was doing.

"I don't lie," I told her. I had never been accused of lying before. She would not look up again, just continued slicing the avocados, or pulling the brush through her wild hair, or smoothing out the piles of towels on the couch. I was grateful I did not have to look into her face, to read whatever was there. In the beginning, I would force myself not to guess, to look away when her hand went to her eyes to wipe them, or to her mouth to hide its trembling. But there was something about Isabel that made her eyes, looking at me, impossible to ignore. Later, on the road, I came across an article about scientists studying people who could read faces, who could look at someone—a man pointing a gun, a psychiatric patient, and see the fleeting emotion that gave them away. By that time Isabel was gone, and their charts of expressions and meanings wouldn't have persuaded me that seeing things people wanted to hide wasn't a curse, that we don't just end up hiding ourselves from the things we see that we'd rather not have known.

I didn't meet her little girl until my third week home, just before I left for Canada. I pulled up to my house and a faded two-tone International sat idling at the curb. A huge brown dog of mixed breed lounged in the backseat, and an old gray-haired guy, who turned out to be Neal, sat on the driver's side. His hair frizzed out above his ears, and he smoked a cigarette he'd rolled himself, tipping his head out the window, blowing the smoke and the smell of tobacco up into the blue sky. I nodded at him, and he smiled, a wide, crazy grin.

"There you are," he said. He had a British accent I thought at first was a put-on. Isabel's daughter popped her head up in the back. "Here he is," she said.

She was only about seven or eight at the time, and her voice was high-pitched, almost shrill. She climbed over the dog and the back door swung open and her tiny legs, the knees bony and red, slid out of the truck. She had her bag with her, and she tossed it on the grass, turned around, and slammed the door closed with both hands.

"You all out?" Neal called from inside, his head behind a cloud of smoke. "All set there?"

I realized that he was putting the truck into gear, that he was leaving, and I had no idea who he was, or who the kid was, and hadn't yet made any connection to Isabel, her presence at my house so new in itself.

"Hey, hey!" I yelled. I banged on the passenger door. I might have sworn at him, I can't really remember now. I had a hangover and I probably looked deranged. Isabel's daughter shrieked and began to cry. The big dog in back bared its teeth and started barking, deep, guttural noises, dog saliva splattering the inside of the window.

"Oh Lord," Neal said. "Settle down there, settle down, Suzie!" He turned the truck off and got out and came around and placed his hand on my shoulder. He was trim and tan and wore khaki shorts and a misbuttoned shirt.

"So Isabel didn't tell you about us dropping by, did she?" Neal can be very calming, when the need arises. At this point, I realized the accent was real. He tipped his head to one side and looked into my face and introduced himself and the dog and the little girl, whose name was not Suzie, as I had imagined, but Aster, like the flower. He shook his head, ready to commiserate with me, his brown eyes wide. "Three bitches," he said, plopping down on the curb, pulling out his rolling papers and tobacco. "What are you going to do?"

Aster had wiped her eyes, leaving dirty streaks on her cheeks. "A bitch is a female, you know," she said, in that high, piping voice. "Not a bad word."

They ended up staying, the three of us sitting around in the backyard clearing in chairs that Isabel had acquired somewhere, waiting for Isabel to get home. Neal identified a mango tree and an avocado tree, and Aster found bananas, and did a few cartwheels and backbends, to entertain us. Eventually, Neal pulled out his pot, and rolled it up, and by the time Isabel got back we'd eaten mangoes and had come inside, and Neal was reading to us from *A Tale of Two Cities,* all of us taking turns improvising our own openings, even Aster, who chimed in, "It was the saddest of times, it was the funnest of times." Neal corrected her English, sternly, over his black plastic-rimmed glasses.

"You should say 'most fun' of times," he told her.

Isabel clomped past us in her platform shoes. Aster didn't jump up and run into Isabel's arms or even move from the floor by Neal's feet where she lay beside Suzie with her head in her hands. Her eyes followed Isabel through the room, into the dining room and on into the kitchen, where she thumped down a grocery bag on the counter and stood staring at us, as if we'd done something wrong.

"No one says hello?" she said.

Aster had learned that with Isabel, you had to make careful observations of her walk, her movements and expression, so you would know what might happen next, something Neal and I, on this day, hadn't bothered to do. The mango Isabel threw hit the wall behind Neal with a hollow sound, like a human head. We all startled. Suzie leaped to her feet. Isabel turned and left the room, went into the bedroom, and slammed the door, and the three of us stared at each other, openmouthed. I think I started to laugh first. Neal joined me, silently, just his shoulders shaking up and down. Aster, I saw, didn't know what to do, so I reached down and grabbed her ankle and tickled her bare foot until she laughed, too, rolling one way, then the other, trying to escape. Isabel had come out and stood in the doorway. I saw her mouth turn up at the corners, her eyes soften, but when she saw me looking, she glared.

"None of you wonder where I've been," she said.

Neal wiped his eyes. "You've been to the grocery, obviously," he said.

I knew she had worked this afternoon, covering for a girl who wanted to switch shifts. She hated dancing in the afternoons, hated the customers, the bright sunlight waiting outside the heavy metal door of the club. I saw she still wore her makeup. I realized her shift should have ended hours ago.

"I could be dead, and no one would know," Isabel said. Her bottom lip quivered. She had her arms wrapped around her chest, tight, holding herself. I hadn't become accomplished at consoling anyone yet, so I didn't realize I should have gone to her in the doorway and taken her in my arms. Instead, I patted the couch next to me.

"Come, sit," I said.

"Are you talking to Suzie, or to me?" she asked.

Neal started to laugh again. Aster stood up, her face pinched, and went to her mother and took her hand and led her to the couch, where Isabel sat down, woodenly, grudgingly, and began to cry. This had been the day they found Jeannie, the girl Isabel covered for, dead in her apartment. She had overdosed, the drug itself not a surprise to Isabel, but the mistake of taking too much, Jeannie's foolishness.

"What was she thinking?" Isabel sobbed. "How did this happen?"

Among the dancers, drugs became part of the identity they assumed. For me, too, working with musicians, they were always there on the sidelines, waiting to draw you behind their rosy curtain. Isabel had admitted to me her own days of addiction in Fort Lauderdale, the Lauderdale days, as she called them, referring to them in conversation with a solemn, shocked look.

"In the Lauderdale days," she might say, "I had a gray cat." And then the widened eyes and that shake of the head, so I knew not to ask its name, to remind her any further of whatever horror befell it. There had been a boyfriend then, too, whom she never discussed. I had asked her about him, curious, and she would answer at first.

"He was tall and gangly," she would tell me. "He had longish blond hair."

Later, I would want to know if he loved her, if she loved him, but I could never find a way to pose the question, the idea of love something unspoken and as dangerous as the drugs. In the end, this would work against me in a lot of ways.

You knew who to avoid to keep clean, and Jeannie had been one of those people. I had met her the one time I'd gone to the club while Isabel was working. It had been very dark, and the place had smelled of people's cologne, and the rock music blasted from high up near the ceiling, raining down bass and wailing guitars. The men wore dress shirts and ties, and Jeannie had come up to me and put her hands on my waist and rubbed her hips back and forth against mine—her way of getting my attention. She had thin, white-blonde hair, and her cheekbones stood out, and her skin was so pale she looked deathly, even then. I think I told her who I was, and I bought her a drink. It was her night off, and she was looking for something else, so she didn't stick around. Neither did I. I wasn't new to topless bars, but it was different with Isabel up there, her face flashing these looks in the light show, her eyes lost and sorrowful, and I never went back.

The night of the afternoon Jeannie died, Isabel's hair stuck to her wet face, and her eyes sought mine in bewilderment, and she clung to me and to Aster, the three of us huddled on the couch together. Neal gave his apologies and shook his head. He called Suzie to the door, and they left. I heard his truck start up outside and pull away from the curb and I wish I could have gone with him, removed myself from the circle into which I'd been enclosed: Aster's weightlessness; her fragile bones and skin, carried sleeping to the bed in the spare room; the spell of Isabel's sadness; the desperate sex; the way I told her I loved her afterward, my mouth buried in the hollow of her neck, her hair in my hands, smelling of apples.

"You don't owe me that," she said, smarter than I thought.

"What makes you think I feel indebted?" I asked.

Leaving the first time was not difficult. I told her I would call, and I did, every few days or so. Aster stayed with her at the house, and I think she found a babysitter in the neighborhood to come by and watch her on the nights she worked, and I began to imagine them there together—Aster starting at the school I drove past on my way to Publix, the two of them on the couch watching rented Elvis movies, Aster jumping up to dance on the couch arms, and Isabel, deadpan, shaking her head, telling her to get down already goddamn it, which always made Aster laugh, because she knew she was only pretending to be serious. I usually avoided imagining women in my life, but if you stare out of bus windows at unfamiliar roadsides long enough the only bright spot you know surfaces and fills you with hopefulness, and Isabel and her daughter were it. You begin to see your life like those colored ink swirls that hide 3-D optical illusions, looking at it from a certain distance until the miraculous image materializes, but glance away and back again and the whole thing disappears. How do you not become a little afraid?

When I came home it was fall and Isabel was still there, painting wooden stools brilliant colors, lining them up to dry in the backyard beside the flowering bougainvillea. She had paint on her clothes. Her hair was pulled up in a ponytail like a child's. There was a breeze now through the backyard leaves, and a brilliant orange vine threaded through the top of the neighbor's hedge. I stood in the doorway and we looked at each other, just like before. I didn't tell her I was happy to see her, and she didn't rush up to greet me. I may have said, "Well," pretending not to love her, and she may have shaded her eyes and grinned, saying nothing, the things we said still just clumsy and meaningless. The lives I'd dreamed up for us while I was gone did not exactly pan out. Aster had gone back to stay with her father, attending a school across town because Isabel couldn't wake up early enough every morning to take her. She came to us on weekends, and Isabel indulged her with presents and we brought her with us to restaurants where Aster would order lobster and salad with blue cheese dressing. She hung her drawings on the wall of the spare room, where the bed was covered with a comforter sequined with stars, and the dolls and clothes, the glitter makeup, the matchbooks from restaurants, the insect preserved in a plastic bag, its wings still golden and shimmering, lay scattered on the bureau top. Isabel would have good days and bad, and I managed the best I could, wanting to keep her there without crossing the lines I'd drawn around my life. I stayed off the road longer than usual, until the tour became too difficult to handle from home, with club dates canceled, and big-haired egos erupting, and I thought I'd lose the job.

I didn't want to go. Being with Isabel was more important than work, or money. I had grown used to her silences, her pile of laundry, her breathing beside me in the bed. By that time I could predict her every move, feel everything she felt. I had become more accomplished than Aster in reading the way she walked into a room, her glances, the way she stood, in a daze, holding her hair back from her face. I called her twice a day. After four weeks she stopped answering the phone at the house, and I called her cell phone, and then she stopped answering that. I imagine it was about this time that the Lauderdale man came looking for her, though I still pictured Aster making orange juice to sell at the curb, her toes blackened with the backyard dirt, or Isabel inside compulsively cleaning the old venetian blinds, the stereo playing music she swayed her hips to, a movement she had never meant to be seductive. When I came home after a month of not talking to her, I hesitated on my own porch, not wanting to open the door, but once inside I saw she was still living there, her clothes hanging in the closet, her razor in the shower, her jewelry and makeup spread out on the bureau.

I waited for her to return, wandering the vacated rooms of my house, feeling her absence in the disorder of her clothing on the bedroom floor, the molding contents of the refrigerator, the turquoise Barbie doll shoe I discovered in the cushions of the couch. It was three nights before she came through the door, wasted and thin, and trying to cover it all up. She fell into my arms and I could feel the bones of her back, her lungs under her rib cage expand and contract. She smelled of old clothes, not her own. She had on a man's shirt and a pair of baggy shorts. She had lost the cell phone and the keys to her car. She had been dropped off by Neal, who stood in the doorway, shaking his head.

"Good luck with this one," he said.

She frightened me so much I didn't want to be alone with her, and I asked Neal to stay, but he refused.

"She gave me bloody hell in the truck," he said. "She opened the door and jumped out. I told her if she wanted out she could stay out, just decide which." He pulled his tobacco from his pants and I saw his hand shake. "Lord," he said, under his breath. Isabel hung on to my arm, laughing.

"I thought we were here already," she said. "I thought we were in the driveway."

She pulled me with her onto the couch. She got up on her knees next to me and told me she missed me, that she was fired from her job.

"I hated that place," she said, a new honest Isabel emerging.

"I know you did," I told her.

She stared into my face, wanting to say she loved me, but I saw that she could not. Her eyes had dark circles underneath. She had the Jeannie pallor. I wanted to feed her and make her well. I felt a huge chasm open up around us where we sat on the couch. Neal left, smoking his cigarette, leaving the trails of it behind in the living room. I remember that from the last night, the smell of Neal's tobacco. We slept for a little while. Isabel woke up first and wanted to go into the backyard and check on the fruit. It was winter, and a few avocados were ripening on the ground, and the oranges weighed down their branches, but the yard seemed bare and unfertile, and the lawn chairs, some of them metal, were cold and covered with dew. We sat out there in the light from the back porch and I peeled Isabel oranges and she ate them and smoked her cigarettes, leaving a little pile of filters by her chair.

It was probably 2:00 a.m. when the Lauderdale man arrived on foot. He banged on the door, and when I'd opened it, had taken five or six giant steps back, so that he was on the curb, pacing. In the streetlight, his hair was greasy blond, with frosted streaks, parted in the middle. He hadn't shaved. He wore loose jeans and a T-shirt. He stood at the curb and looked up at the open door and raised his arms out from his sides like an airplane. In one hand he held a small blue-black gun. I had little experience with guns. Once on the road a guitar player pulled one out of his bag. He had held it with one hand and laid it out in the palm of the other, like an offering. I had told him he was an idiot, to put the thing away, and I think this is what I told the Lauderdale man, whose name, "Robin!" Isabel screamed from behind me in the doorway.

"Let's put that thing away, Robin," I told him. My voice was calm, almost amused. What's going on here? I remember thinking. Robin was very obliging. He set the gun by the curb and came up to the door, a foot away from me. The despair in his eyes made me sorry for him, so that when he tried to hit me, and I grabbed his arm to stop him, I was almost gentle.

"Let's sit down in here and talk," I said, and I stepped back from the doorway and pulled him by the arm into the house. He didn't fight me at all, just twisted his arm out of my grasp and jumped back from me to stand by the fireplace. Isabel swore at him, terrible language I had never heard from her before.

"I hate you," she screamed, her gaunt frame buckling at the waist with the exertion. She looked up at him with her wet eyes and I saw what she hated was the mess of loving him.

"I don't believe you," Robin said, nervously, watching her. There was a twitchiness to his limbs, a vulnerability about his hands with their long fingers and sore-looking knuckles. The floor lamp was beside him, and he went to step toward Isabel and one of his wayward arms knocked the lamp over. It hit the floor with unintentional violence. He bent to pick it up, the bulb still lit, and he glanced up at me, the halo of light around his face, sorrier than I have ever seen anyone since.

"I can't believe I'm doing this," he said.

Isabel turned and did her usual slam into the bedroom. Robin and I just looked at each other. I saw that once he and Isabel lived a life together, that she had done his laundry, decorated the walls of his house, left things behind to remind him of her, too—a painting of a mermaid on the concrete stoop, perfume whose fragrance reached him in his bed at night, wind chimes, pairs of high-heeled shoes.

"I think I should go," Robin said. His voice quavered. He held his hand out to me to shake, full of decency and some obvious upbringing. I didn't know what to say. Yes, he should leave, I thought. Isabel loved him. Neither of them were any good for each other, that was clear. I tried to work it all out in my head, quickly, while he stood there, shaking my hand. Once he left of his own volition, he would not be back. He would wander down the street in his rubber thongs and hit Bayshore Boulevard and wander down that, past the mansions with magnolias and ivy-covered brick. There wouldn't be anyone to offer him a drink or a cigarette or a bag or a hit, all of the residents long in bed. He would sit on a bench and get picked up, eventually, by the police, and they would take him in, maybe keep him for a few days in jail, an anonymous man in love with Isabel.

I nodded at him, tersely, agreeing with him. He went out the door and I watched him hesitate at the curb, deciding which way to turn. I had shut the door before I remembered he'd forgotten the gun. I couldn't leave it by the curb for anyone to discover, and though I knew by then she had not been to the house in a while I thought of Aster, leaping out of Neal's truck, stooping in the ragged grass to pick it up. I'd gone back out and brought the gun inside, holding it away from my body with two fingers, like a dead animal. I put it on the kitchen table. I went to check on Isabel. In the dark bedroom she lay flat on the bed in her clothes, staring up at the ceiling.

"Is he gone?" she whispered, full of dread.

"Yes," I said, knowing it would hurt her. And on cue she began to cry, quietly, trying to hide it from me, so I left the room and went out into the backyard to make her think she had.

There are things about that night that remain perfect and clear;

the cold metal lawn chair, the breeze that moved all the shiny leaves together, the smell of the backyard at sunrise, like ginger, the color of the light in the bamboo, the way the sun hit the kitchen window through the trees, throwing shadows on the house. When I decided to go back inside I found Isabel sitting at the kitchen table, and I pulled out a chair and sat down across from her. I had been up all night and wasn't thinking clearly. The gun sat there, foreign and oily next to the sugar bowl. But she was looking at me, and I was looking at her, and I admit I wanted her to say she loved me, that my need blinded me from anything else.

Sitting there, I should have been able to see how she felt about me, but her eyes were dark and unreadable and dry, and there was nothing in her face that told me anything, until she leaned over and pressed her mouth to mine. She pulled away, and I believed then, from her eyes, the way they softened, that moment of surrender that melted me any other time, in bed, across the room, that everything would be fine, but really, if you've fooled yourself all along, you don't know what she's thinking when she reaches for the gun.

In my living room, I watched Neal stub out the joint. He folded his hands in his lap and asked me if I had a beer, or something else to drink. Aster sat, still and silent on the couch, her arms grown lanky, her back slightly hunched in her small T-shirt. Neal had her for the night so one of Isabel's old friends who had taken the girl in could work. I told him to take her home so she could go to sleep, and she looked up at me and said, "I could just sleep here," and turned her head to glance down the hallway at the room where she used to do that, almost longingly. I pretended not to hear her, so she stared at me with those dark, brimming Isabel eyes. I must say, at least, she had learned to close them off from everyone, so that they didn't do any more than resemble her mother's. They didn't tell me her heart was breaking or anything.

Marisa Silver

The Visitor

T HE NEW boy was three-quarters gone. Both legs below the knee and the left arm at the shoulder. Candy spent her lunch hour lying on the lawn outside the VA hospital, sending nicotine clouds into the cloudless sky, wondering whether it would be better to have one leg and no arms—or, if you were lucky enough to have an arm and a leg left, whether it would be better to have them on opposite sides, for balance. In her six months as a nurse's aide, she had become thoughtful about the subtle hierarchy of human disintegration. Blind versus deaf—that was a no-brainer, no brain being perhaps the one wound in her personal calculus that could not be traded in for something worse.

It was sad. Of course it was sad. But she didn't feel sad. Sad was what people said they were in the face of tragedies as serious as suicide bombings or as minor as a lost earring. It was a word that people used to tidy up and put the problem out of sight.

The grass was making needle-like pricks through the thin material of her maroon scrubs, and she sat up, smoothing her matching V-neck over her chest and belly, feeling the familiar stab of self-consciousness as her hand rode over the unfashionable lumps. In photographs, Candy's mother, Sylvie, at twenty-two—Candy's age now—was as skinny as dripping water, but that could have been a result of the drugs. Candy had her grandmother's build, and she knew that with age her shape would settle into the short, hale block that was Marjorie, less body than space saver.

Candy glanced at her watch. She still had ten minutes until the end of her break.

She wasn't sure when she had last felt sad. She knew that she must have been sad when she was eleven and her mother had gone into the hospital for the last time. But she couldn't actually recall the feeling. She did remember being happy afterward, sitting at her grandmother's kitchen table picking walnuts out of their shells with the tines of a fork, while Marjorie made phone calls to let people know that Sylvie had landed on her final and terminal addiction: death. She listened to Marjorie say, "My baby *diiihd,*" the last vestiges of her Texas accent breathing so much air into the word that Candy could almost see it flying up toward the ceiling of the kitchen like a helium balloon. Sylvie's presence in Candy's life had been birdlike. She had swooped into Marjorie's apartment from time to time to drop a Big Mac into Candy's waiting mouth, but the enthusiasm that she'd carried with her usually dissipated quickly, smothered as much by Marjorie's insistence on behaving as if nothing were out of the ordinary as by Candy's abject need.

Candy recalled feeling another sort of happiness, too, when she had crawled over the railing of the hospital bed in order to lie next to her mother one last time. Marjorie had forced Candy to wear a new party dress she'd sewn the day before. The frock, made with leftover material from the flower-girl dress that Marjorie had been working on, was an embarrassing pink affair that grabbed at the tender buds of Candy's new breasts with tight smocking. What was the point, Candy had whined, as Marjorie finished off the hem, breathing heavily through her nose, her mouth a cactus of pins. But in the hospital, lying beside her mother, Candy had understood why she was so dressed up: she was there to act out the role of daughter in the hope that Sylvie would wake and finally take up her own part in the charade of parenting that Marjorie had insisted on whenever Sylvie showed up at the apartment—as if Sylvie had come back not for food or a shower or money but to French-braid Candy's hair or to explain menstruation to her. The metal guardrails on the bed had felt cold against Candy's thighs. The sensation was shocking in a pleasurable way that she couldn't name then, but it wasn't long before she discovered that the faucet in her grandmother's bathtub could be angled to hit her between the legs just so.

When Candy first started working at the VA, the other aides had said that it would take her a long time to become "used to it." They'd told her to look away from the wounds, to focus on the soldiers' faces as a way to protect the boys from embarrassment and herself from disgust. But she was not disgusted, even when she had to rewrap stumps or sponge gashes that were sewn up like shark bites. She found these molestations frankly interesting, the body deconstructed so that you could see what it really was: just bits and pieces, really, no different from the snatches of fabric that Marjorie wrestled into dresses for Mr. Victor of Paris, the tailor in Burbank who had employed her for thirty-seven years. The nurses praised Candy's bravery, but when she passed by a group of aides taking their break in the cafeteria one afternoon she knew from their covert glances that they found her strange. She once overheard a girl say that she had no heart.

Well, no heart was better than no brain, Candy thought, as she sucked on the last of her cigarette and stubbed it out in the grass, dismissing the notion that she might cause a brushfire in this hottest of seasons. She knew that hers was not a singular life, that she would not be the cause of anything monumental. Recently, the thermometer had topped out at 109 in the valley. The power had failed in her grandmother's apartment complex, where Candy had lived all her life. Marjorie, excited by the idea of a disaster that she might have some control over, had instructed Candy to gather her important papers, as if she expected the apartment to burst into spontaneous flames. Candy scanned the top of her dresser, where her community-college diploma sat in its Plexiglas frame, alongside assorted gift-with-purchase tubes of lipstick and miniature eyeshadow compacts. In a gesture that even at the time she regarded as TV-movie maudlin, she had put her mother's Communion cross around her neck and lain down on her bed. When she was woken by the sudden snap of lights turning on and the sound of her window fan whirring to life, she took off the necklace and placed it back in her dresser drawer. She showered and went to bed naked, letting the fan blow its slow, oscillating wind across her body.

The new boy's name was Gregorio Villalobos. Juana, the admitting nurse, told Candy that *lobo* meant "wolf" in Spanish. Down the hall lay a Putter and a Shooter, boys who clung to their jaunty monikers as though they were one day going to walk out of the hospital and back onto the golf course or the basketball court where they had earned those nicknames. Candy wondered if the new boy had been called El Lobo in the service. She could ask him, but he wouldn't answer her. He had not yet spoken. He watched her as she moved around the room, his eyes tracking her as if she were a fly and he was waiting for the right moment to bring down his swatter. Most of the boys looked at her when she brought them food or checked on IV bags, but their gazes were like those of old dogs: hope combined with the absence of hope. The nurses chattered at the boys as they went about their work, talking about the weather or whatever sports trivia they had picked up from their husbands. In general, the boys went along with this, and Candy often felt as if she were watching a play in which all the actors had agreed to pretend that someone onstage had not just taken a huge shit. Candy knew that the nurses were scared of silence, and perhaps the boys were, too. The truth hid in silence.

Before she left the room, she looked at El Lobo's chart. It wasn't her business to read charts, simply to mark down what he did and didn't eat, did and didn't expel. She'd received minimal training, most of which had to do with things that anyone who'd ever cleaned a house would know, and she couldn't understand much of what was written on the chart. But she did understand the phrase "elective muteness." She stared at El Lobo, feeling words crawling up inside her, pushing to get past her closed lips—that pathetic human need to communicate when there was nothing to say. She had been this way when her mother was alive. On the occasions when Sylvie was home, Candy had told her anything she could think of to tell: what had happened at school that day, what clothing the popular girls were wearing, how pretty she thought Sylvie looked, with her dark hair parted down the center and hanging on either side of her narrow face like a magician's cape. She'd talk and talk, and the more she suspected that her mother didn't care what she was saying, the more she'd fill the apartment with her desperate noise.

She replaced the chart on the hook at the foot of the bed and glanced at El Lobo once more before leaving the room. She could hold her silence longer than he could. He had no idea who he was dealing with.

That night, she woke to the sound of her grandmother yelling at the ghost.

"Get outta here *riii-ght* this minute!" Marjorie said, her accent always thicker when she was torn from her dreams, as if her unconscious resided in Beaumont, Texas, while the rest of her kept pace in LA. Water splashed noisily against the porcelain sink in the bathroom between Candy's and Marjorie's bedrooms.

Candy lay in her bed, which had been her mother's childhood bed, the headboard still bearing the Day-Glo flower stickers her mother had affixed to it. Candy tried to imagine Sylvie as a naive girl who liked stickers, but it was impossible. What she remembered most about her mother was the patchouli scent of her skin, underneath which hid a more elusive, dirty smell, an odor that Candy yearned to excavate whenever Sylvie was near. But Sylvie did not often let her daughter get that close. Even during the times when she was living at home, when she swore to Marjorie that she was clean, and Marjorie decided, all pinny-eyed, fidgety evidence to the contrary, to believe her, Sylvie kept herself apart. She'd take over her old room, leaving Candy to the foldout sofa in the living room, and Candy would spend the early-evening hours inventing reasons to walk past the bedroom door, hoping that it might open, that she might be invited in.

Candy listened as her grandmother hurried into the bathroom to turn off the faucet.

"Turn that water on again and I'll murder you!" Marjorie said, on her way past Candy's room to the kitchen. "It's quarter past three, for Lord's sake."

Candy got out of bed and made her way to the kitchen, too. Marjorie wore her quilted bathrobe, and her bulb of short graying hair was lopsided from lying in bed. She had already set the kettle on the stove. "Ah, she woke you up, too," she said, shaking her head ruefully.

"*You* woke me up," Candy said, sitting down at the table. "You probably woke the whole building."

"That ghost is running up my water bill. It has to stop."

"Maybe he's thirsty," Candy said.

"He's a she, and ghosts don't drink, darlin'. They have no bodies. She just turns on the tap to get my goat. *And in a dry season, no less!*" she yelled, shaking her fist in the air, as if the ghost were hiding just outside the kitchen door. The wattle beneath Marjorie's upper arm wavered and Candy remembered how she had played with that loose skin as a child. Something about her grandmother's excesses of flesh was comforting. On bad nights, when Candy felt an aching maw open up in her chest, she'd slip into Marjorie's bed. Her nameless dread was always calmed when her cheeks grazed the loose bags of her grandmother's nylon-swaddled breasts.

Marjorie set down two mugs on the kitchen table, then brought over the kettle and poured. "I'll tell you what, though. I'm tired of waking up in the middle of the night. I'm too old for it."

"Maybe we should have an exorcism."

"You don't believe in that foolishness, I hope. Oh, you're just teasing me, you bad girl," she added, when she saw Candy's grin.

"We got a new boy in," Candy said, changing the subject. "He's a mess."

"Ahh," Marjorie said, sympathetically, replacing the kettle on the stove.

"No one's come to visit him. It's been two days."

"Maybe he has no one."

"They're usually there at admitting with their balloons and those smiles. You can see them counting the minutes until they can get the hell out of there."

"You're harsh, baby girl. It's not easy to see something destroyed."

Candy looked at her grandmother's hands. Arthritis was beginning to shape them, like some devious sculptor, and it wouldn't be long before she could no longer work a sewing machine or hold needle and thread. What then? Could they survive on Marjorie's Social Security and Candy's pathetic salary? Candy remembered Marjorie's younger, stronger hands cupping Sylvie's cheeks as she tried to wake her, tried to get her to stand up from the living-room floor where she had collapsed sometime during the night. "Time to get your girl to school!" she'd say, her determination fending off the futility of her effort. Candy remembered, too, her grandmother's calloused grip around her own small hand when they made those hurried journeys to school together, more often than not leaving Sylvie behind, curled up on herself like a pill bug.

El Lobo was, of course, where Candy had left him the afternoon before, lying in his bed, gazing up at the ceiling. She raised the mattress so that he was facing forward, placed his breakfast tray on the rolling table, and swung it across the bed. She removed the lid of the oatmeal and the canned pears and peeled off the layer of plastic wrap covering the glass of water. The meal's monochromatic paleness was disheartening, but Candy dug into the oatmeal with a spoon and lifted it to El Lobo's mouth. He ate dutifully, but without affect, as if

some inner computer chip were responsible for the opening and closing of his lips and the gentle modulations of his throat. He made no
eye contact with her. Candy took the opportunity to go vacant as
well, a state she had perfected as a child. She'd found that she could
continue to do what was required of her—clean her room or go
through the motions of paying attention in class, even read out loud
if the teacher requested it, while her mind wandered. In that peaceful
oblivion, she felt swaddled in cotton, divorced from the feelings that
usually plagued her, unworried about what she looked like in her
homemade clothing or what others thought of the girl with a grandmother for a mother. The sounds of the other children came at her
muffled, harmless. Time passed. She disappeared.

She looked over to find that El Lobo's chin was covered with syrup
where she had missed his mouth. It irked her that he had let this happen without making any sound to alert her to the problem. She
wiped him clean, becoming even more irritated when he didn't seem
to register this help, either. She took a last, hard swipe at his mouth.
He finally looked at her, and his glance was sharp and full of menace.
The ease with which his expression resolved into hatred made it clear
that anger was his default position. The nurses talked about the
"sweet" boys or the "darling" boys, as if the upside of the physical
damage were that it turned a soldier into a feckless three-year-old,
thus ridding the world of one more potentially dangerous man. But
Candy knew that this boy was neither sweet nor darling, and probably never had been. She imagined him as a bored high-school shark,
moving slow and silent through the halls, heavy with his own power
and cravings. She had known boys like this, had fucked boys like this.

She marked on his chart the amount of solids and liquids he had
consumed, rolled the tray away from his bed, and carried the half-
eaten breakfast into the hallway. She spent the next seven hours of
her shift changing sheets and emptying bedpans, delivering food baskets that would be at the nurses' station by day's end, as most of the
patients had restricted diets or were fed through tubes. She wheeled
one boy to X-ray through the maze of hallways and elevators. Every

time the gurney lurched over a transom, the boy winced in pain. The first few times, she apologized, but then she stopped, because she knew that her regret, like a basket of muffins, was, in some way, an affront.

Later that day, after she had finished her shift, she returned to El Lobo's room. He was asleep, so she sat in the orange plastic chair in the corner and watched him. As he lay in his bed, covered in blankets, his wounds were invisible; his head, his nutmeg skin, his thick, dark eyebrows and generous, scowling mouth were untouched. A stranger might have thought him one of the lucky ones in this war. Only after his so-called recovery, when he would have to have special clothing made, when he would be assaulted by all the daily acts he could no longer accomplish, would he truly feel the extent of his wounds. She knew about collateral damage, knew that the injuries people saw were never the gravest. After Sylvie died, the school counselor had brought Candy into her office and handed her a pamphlet called *Teenagers and Grief: A Handbook*. She'd told Candy that, although it was against state regulations, she was going to give Candy a hug. She'd had no idea about the hard lump of rage that sat lodged in Candy's throat like a nut swallowed whole.

After fifteen minutes, El Lobo's eyes opened. For a second, his expression was soft and pliable, like that of a child waking from a nap, but then his mind took over and something calcified in his features, his muscles hardening against the invasion of thought. His gaze fell on her. She didn't move, but continued to stare at him. He stared back, his upper lip trembling in what she thought was the beginning of an insult. She felt a tingling in her gut, and her nerves were on alert, as if he had actually grazed her skin with that leftover hand. The second-shift nurse's voice cut through the silence as she entered and exited rooms along the hallway, announcing pain-relieving meds in a voice as bright and cutting as a laser. Candy stood and walked over to the bed. She reached under the cover and pinched El Lobo hard on his arm. She heard his sharp intake of breath, and slipped out of the room before she was discovered.

. . .

At 3:00 a.m., Marjorie tore into the bathroom.

"You leave me alone!" she yelled. "I've done enough for you already."

Candy decided to stay in bed. A few times, over the five years since the ghost had announced itself, Candy had tried to stay up all night. She thought that if she could just once catch Marjorie turning on the faucet—perhaps it was sleepwalking, or some early sign of senility— she would stop, and Candy could get some rest. But on those nights either the ghost had not appeared or Candy had dropped off to sleep, despite the cans of Coke littering her bedside table.

She heard the sound of the sewing machine clattering into action. The machine slowed and quickened, and Candy imagined her grandmother's bare foot playing the floor pedal. She knew that she had little chance of getting back to sleep. It was too hot to put on her terry-cloth robe, so, wearing only her T-shirt and underwear, she went into the living room, where Marjorie bent to her task.

"What are you making?" Candy said.

"Right about now, nothing," Marjorie said. She lifted the foot of the sewing machine and pulled the material out, snipped the threads with a pair of scissors, and set to ripping out what she had done. "Victor gives me two weeks to do a bride and four bridesmaids. Two weeks! The man is losing whatever brains he had to begin with."

Candy watched her grandmother's hands shake as she pulled out the tiny stitches with her seam ripper. Marjorie was no longer as adept as she had been when she was younger and able to unroll a bolt of cloth and see every seam and dart, every buttonhole and facing, when she could tell, even before putting one pin into the cloth, how it would all fall together. A dress form stood beside the sewing machine, draped in the raw ivory silk that Marjorie was working with. Headless and armless, the figure tilted slightly on its stand, as if leaning over to tell a secret.

"Expensive," Candy said, fingering the cloth.

"Hands off!" Marjorie ordered, batting Candy's hands away

lightly, as she had done when Candy was young. "Spend all this money on silk and then give me next to no time to do my job. This missy will be lucky if the whole thing doesn't come flying apart the minute she starts down the aisle."

"Where's the ghost?"

"Gone, that wretched thing. She'll be back, though. What I ever did to deserve a hauntin', I'll never know."

"Maybe she lived here. Before us. Maybe she wants her place back."

"And it's taken her thirty-five years to show up? Uh-uh."

"What, then?"

"Honey, I'm still trying to figure out the reason people do what they do when they're alive." She finished ripping out the stitches, sighed audibly, and fit the material into the machine again.

Candy went to the window and looked out over the apartment courtyard. The management had recently overhauled the space, taking out the grass and flowers that had required watering and replacing them with decorative pebbles. Only the concrete path that had wound through the garden remained. As a child, Candy had ridden her bike between clumps of impatiens and begonia and stands of banana trees, clumsy with their thick, waxy leaves. She knew every turn and straightaway by heart, but, still, there had been danger inherent in each corner, the thrill of heading into the unseen. She'd been eight when she'd made a turn around a bushel of bamboo and seen her mother lying asleep, across the doormat of Marjorie's apartment. Candy had parked her bike against the wall and squatted down next to Sylvie. She looked pretty lying there, like the illustration of Sleeping Beauty in one of Candy's library books. Candy watched her for a while, as if studying an insect, noting the little flutters of her eyelids and lips, her long, corded neck, the muscles of which seemed tense, even in sleep. Finally, she stepped over her mother and went inside.

"Mommy's back," she told Marjorie, who was hunched over her machine.

Together, they carried an incoherent and moaning Sylvie into the bathroom. Candy sat on the lid of the toilet while Marjorie ran the bath, undressed her daughter, and coaxed her into the water. Sylvie cursed her mother, calling her a bitch and a cunt, but Marjorie didn't react, only shushed her the way she shushed Candy when she was crying over a scraped knee, as if silence trumped pain. Once Sylvie was in the bath, she lay with her eyes closed, head back against the edge of the tub, while Marjorie gently soaped her body, lifting her arms one by one, cleaning between her small breasts and her legs. "Beautiful girl," she sang in an errant, unidentifiable tune. "Beautiful baby girl." Later, the three ate chicken with mushroom-soup sauce at the kitchen table and watched MTV on the twenty-one-inch Sony. In the morning, Sylvie was gone, along with the television.

The apartment was reduced bit by bit over the following years. The microwave followed the television, and then some of Marjorie's jewelry disappeared. Each time Candy came back to the apartment after school, she entered with trepidation, waiting to see what was missing. The relief she felt when she realized that Sylvie had not stolen anything new was always tempered by disappointment. When she and Marjorie arrived home from church one Sunday to find the space where the stereo had sat looking as vacant as a missing tooth, Candy had felt a rush of elation. Her mother had been in the apartment. Her breath, her dirty, pretty smell still hung in the air. Marjorie never got angry about the thefts. She'd just stand, hands on hips, facing the emptiness, and inhale deeply as if acquainting herself with the new geography of her life.

But when Candy was ten, and she and Marjorie returned from the grocery store to find that Marjorie's black Singer Featherweight, the hand-me-down from her mother and grandmother that she had oiled and massaged and kept going for years, was gone, she went to her bedroom and didn't come out until the following morning. Candy poured herself a bowl of Frosted Flakes and sat on the couch waiting for Marjorie to show her, as she always did, how to skirt this new boulder in her life, but she didn't open her door.

"Are you mad?" Candy asked the next morning, when Marjorie finally came out of her room, her face blotchy.

Marjorie fingered the thin pages of the phone book, looking for the number of a locksmith. "I'm just tired," she said softly. Two weeks later, Marjorie held Candy's hand at the kitchen table as they listened to Sylvie struggle to turn her key in the front-door lock.

"I know you're in there!" Sylvie yelled, pounding on the door.

Candy looked at Marjorie, who held her finger to her lips, and the two sat in rigid silence. Giving up on the door, Sylvie came to the kitchen window. She pressed her pallid and wild-eyed face up to the glass so that her nose and lips flattened and distorted.

"Let her in, Grandma. Please," Candy said.

"We don't want any visitors just now," Marjorie said.

For the next year, until her mother's death, Candy often had the feeling of being shadowed, as if a huge prehistoric bird were passing over her, but when she looked up, there was nothing there.

El Lobo had his eyes closed when Candy brought in his breakfast the next day, but she knew he wasn't asleep—there was something too effortful about his breathing. Noisily, she set up the tray table and dragged her chair to the side of his bed. When he finally opened his eyes, he stared, again, at the opposite wall. This time, she did not feed him but simply sat and waited for him to say something. He did not move or shift his gaze. The air in the room stiffened with tension, but neither one gave in. After ten minutes, she rolled the table away from the bed and took the uneaten food from the room. In the hallway, she met up with Tammy, the floor nurse.

"What happened?" Tammy said, eyeing the uneaten food.

"He's not hungry."

"He said this?" Tammy said, warily.

"He made it clear."

"He spoke?"

"He wasn't hungry," Candy repeated. "I'm not supposed to force-feed."

"Well," Tammy said, considering, "did you mark it down?"

Candy nodded. "Zero in. Zero out."

"It's bath time, anyway. Give me some help."

After gathering supplies and filling a small bowl with warm water, Candy came back into El Lobo's room. Tammy leaned over the bed and pulled El Lobo toward her. "Candy, get the tie," she said.

Candy put down her supplies and came around the bed. She saw El Lobo's dark skin where the hospital gown split open in the back. A fine down feathered away from his spine. She resisted the urge to touch that fur. She undid the tie and watched while Tammy gently laid El Lobo back against his pillows, then drew the gown down past his shoulders and chest. The dressing covering the wound where his arm had been was secured by white bandages that stretched across his breastbone, contrasting with his dark skin and his nearly black nipples.

"We're just going to do a little spa treatment!" Tammy said loudly. "How's that?"

El Lobo said nothing and Tammy chattered on, explaining that they would not be taking off his dressing but would just wash around it to freshen him up and that the doctor would be in later to see how he was doing, and wasn't he doing well, Candy? Good color in his face. Like he'd been to the beach! Have you been sneaking out of here and hitting the beach? Ha-ha-ha. All the while she sponged his chest, neck, and face, and then, reaching down under the blanket with the warm cloth, her head turned to the side as if to control her urge to look, Tammy cleaned him off below. Candy doled out fresh, damp cloths and took away the used ones, then held a bowl under El Lobo's mouth while Tammy brushed his teeth. Spit! Good one! Spit again! They dressed him in a clean gown. Hello, gorgeous!

Candy knew just what El Lobo, with his pliant body and immobile gaze, was up to. She felt a warm rush of anger start in her stomach and rise into her throat. She wanted to hit him. She wanted to hear him react.

"Candy. We have a situation here."

Candy looked over and watched as a stain spread across the sheet covering El Lobo's lower half.

"That's just a normal thing, honey," Tammy said to El Lobo. "You get that warm water down there and it makes you want to go, right?"

She began to remove the wet sheet covering El Lobo, but her beeper went off. She checked the readout and handed the sheet to Candy. "I'll call for an orderly," she said, and left the room.

Candy looked at El Lobo, whose head was turned away. She left the room, threw the dirty sheet in the laundry chute, and got a clean gown and fresh bedding from the supply closet. She looked down the hall for the orderly, but no one was coming. She waited next to El Lobo's door. After a few minutes, the orderly still had not come, and Candy was angry. Angry at the hospital for making her take care of this when it was not part of her job, angry because El Lobo had to lie there in his own piss and stink. She moved to the bed, thinking that she would change his tunic first. That would be easy enough to do alone, and by the time she was done the orderly would have arrived. But then she realized that if she did not change the bottom sheet first, his new gown would become wet, and she'd have to do the whole thing over again. So carefully, as if handling something breakable, she rolled El Lobo onto his good side. He was heavier than she expected a person with most of his body missing to be, and he did nothing to help her. When she stopped pushing, he fell back rather than staying on his side. Her frustration with him and his intransigence welled up and she was thinking of leaving, letting him lie in his own mess until the orderly arrived, when she noticed that his eyes were not simply closed but squeezed shut, like those of a child playing hide-and-seek.

Carefully, she pushed him onto his side again, this time bracing herself against his back as she inched the sheet out from under him. It was hard work, but she was careful not to make any sounds that would allow him to sense her frustration. She reached for a wet towel and quickly swiped it across the mattress, then shook out a clean sheet and managed to slip it underneath him just as he was becoming too heavy for her to hold where he was. She laid him back down and walked around the bed, working the sheet until it lay reasonably flat. Next, she undid his tunic and pulled it from his body. She plunged a washcloth into the bowl of now lukewarm water and gently cleaned him off. She wiped around his belly and his groin, reached under him to get at his backside. His soft, pale penis lay against his thigh, as bald as a newborn puppy, but she did not take her eyes away. This was his body. It deserved to be seen. She dressed him in a fresh gown, holding him against her chest as she tied the strings. She knew that she could not hold him by the shoulders to lay him back against his pillows because of his pain there, so she kept her arms around his ribs and leaned him all the way down as if she were embracing him. When she pulled away, his eyes were open, and she saw, for a brief second, the arrow of his hatred for her and for everything that had happened to him bending back on itself and aiming straight into his own heart.

Marjorie was sewing at the machine when the power went out. It was ten o'clock at night, and the darkness was sudden and blinding. For a moment, both Candy and Marjorie froze where they were in the living room.

"Oh, shoot. I'm just in the middle of something, too," Marjorie said, finally. "Get the flashlights."

Candy felt her way down the hall and into the kitchen, struck by how frightening real darkness was. For a brief moment, she felt panic rise up in her. What if the power never came back on? What if they all had to grope around in this darkness forever? She turned on the flashlights and brought them into the living room, glad to be near her grandmother again.

"It's getting hotter already," Marjorie said.

Candy opened the windows to the courtyard, but when she went to the other side of the room to open the street windows for a cross breeze Marjorie stopped her.

"Thieves," she said. "They just wait for times like this."

Candy could already feel sweat forming in the creases of her underarms and beneath her breasts. She took one of the flashlights and trained it on the thermostat.

"It's already eighty in here."

Marjorie went to her machine and slid the material out from under the foot. "I guess I'll have to do this by hand if I'm gonna be finished in time. Shine that light over here."

Candy stood above Marjorie and trained her flashlight onto the pearly white material. She watched as her grandmother struggled to thread a needle with fingers that were beginning to bend at odd angles, like old trees.

"I need glasses," Marjorie said, missing the eye of the needle and wetting the tip of the thread between her lips.

"Want me to do it?" Candy offered.

"I can thread my own needle, thank you. Been doing it half my lifetime."

She was successful on the next try, drew the thread out, and tied a knot at the bottom. She adjusted the material on her lap. Candy watched as Marjorie attempted to work the needle through the material in the seed-size stitches required for the seam she was sewing. The stitches were uneven, and Candy waited for Marjorie to stop, or get out her seam ripper, but she continued, her breath coming hard out of her nose as she pursed her lips. Candy felt heat rise in her face as she watched her grandmother's awkward, determined work.

"The power will probably come back on soon," Candy said, trying to keep her voice neutral.

"And if it doesn't? I've got a bride here who's not gonna care about my excuses if her dress isn't ready in time."

Candy tried to imagine the bride that her grandmother could see in this material bunched up on her lap. Was she short, tall? Full-breasted or flat? Was her grandmother conjuring up a beauty when the reality was far different?

"What's she like?"

"Who?"

"The bride."

"They're all the same, you know. Just girls. They don't know what's happening to them. Oh! Oh!"

Candy saw the spot of red and snatched the cloth off her grandmother's lap before the blood could spread any farther on the material. She reached for her grandmother's hand. "Don't move," she said. "I'll get a Band-Aid."

When she returned from the bathroom, Marjorie was standing and holding the wedding dress out in front of her with her good hand so that it fell into its bodiless shape.

"It's pretty," Candy said.

"It's beyond repair."

It was impossible to sleep. Even with the windows open, the bedroom was close, the heat making it almost hard to breathe. Candy lay on top of her covers, her arms and legs spread out so that her skin didn't chafe. Marjorie's bedroom door opened, and Candy listened as her grandmother went into the bathroom, then she got up quickly. If she was quiet, perhaps she could catch her grandmother turning on the water. But as her hand touched the doorknob she stopped herself and sat back down on her bed.

"Get out! Get out! *Come on, now!*" she heard her grandmother say, in the gentle, forgiving tone she'd used when she bathed Sylvie or when Candy touched her material with dirty hands, as if their transgressions didn't really bother her at all, as if she were grateful for the intrusion.

Paul Yoon

And We Will Be Here

Each day she woke before dawn and walked the grounds of the American hospital. She didn't go far. She kept to the footpaths that encircled the main hall, past the evergreens and the timber cottages now used as additional wards for the wounded.

It had once been a Japanese vocational school for the arts and she remembered the painter who had asked her and Junpei to model. They had been walking past the school that afternoon and the young man had called to them. He led them under the gate and to a tree, where she sat with Junpei between her legs. She pretended to read to her companion, though it wasn't a book she held. The painter had instead given her his hat and told her to imagine. It was made of wool and smelled of sweat and pine and the band inside had worn away so that strands of it fell onto her wrist. She had never been inside the school until then, though she passed it often and would later wonder behind which window the painter lived. The shadows of leaves moved across their arms. They kept still. Beside them was a stone garden. She never saw the young man again.

Her name was Miya and twenty-five years had passed since that day, though lately she found herself thinking about the painter as she took her walks around the hospital. Or not him exactly, but the painting, which she never saw finished. Perhaps it had hung someplace in the school's corridors. Or in someone's home or even at a museum, she thought, when she was feeling fanciful. Perhaps he had become famous and she was unaware of it. She wondered how many people had seen their image there, under that tree, and how many questioned who the children were, if they did at all.

She did not own any childhood photographs of herself and did not have anyone to tell her what she looked like then. She believed she was now thirty-four years old but wasn't certain. There wasn't anyone to tell her about that, either. She had been born in Japan, she knew, and had come to Korea at an early age, to this island south of the peninsula. But she had no memory of this journey or any time before that. Hers was a life adapted, she would have said, if someone asked.

The woman who raised her had passed away from sickness. Miya had brought her to the hospital and she remembered this as well, their kindness, Miss Hara among the soldiers. They had liked Miss Hara and a group of doctors once sang for her while she was dying. It was an American song. Barbershop, someone said, and she didn't know what that meant. Miss Hara smiled at them and gripped the footboard with her toes. This was two years ago.

She didn't know then that she would leave the orphanage and return to this place, assisting the nurses with the wounded. A volunteer, the doctor named Henry suggested, and she thought it a fine word. He was tall with freckled skin and a broad forehead. "Help is always needed," he said, and escorted her inside. On that first day he gave her a hospital gown and she was puzzled. He shrugged, embarrassed. They were low on supplies. The gowns were comfortable, he said, and even provided her with a nurse's cap so everyone could tell her apart from the others.

Every day she brought the soldiers water. She trimmed their hair if it tickled their ears. She scratched their backs. She made them fresh lemonade from the citrus grove. She spoke to them if conversation was what they desired. She wheeled them out of the wards for a bit of air. She worked until her body grew numb. A thousand beds and convalescents scattered throughout the buildings.

"What's your name?" she always asked. "Where are you from?" Australia, someone said. Another: Greece. She had met men from France, New Zealand, Thailand, America, and the peninsula. With every new arrival she searched their faces, pushing the gurney or the wheelchair through the corridors. A man's nose reminded her of someone she once knew. Someone else's lips curved downward the way hers did. She found the eyes of Miss Hara. Junpei's chin. The familiar touch of skin. A scar on the elbow.

I knew you once, she would think, moving through the wards as if she had done so all her life.

Her own room was on the second floor of the main hall, and when she wasn't occupied with a patient or when Henry told her to rest, she retired there. It wasn't much: a single bed, a desk beside a window. The walls were bare. She owned few possessions. She had a teacup, a comb, an extra set of clothes, and a sewing machine, all taken from the orphanage.

She sewed old gowns and soldiers' uniforms if they could be saved. She sipped water from the teacup for she wasn't sure if she could ask for tea. She kept the door closed. A bare lightbulb hung from the ceiling, casting a dome around her. Finished with her clothes, she would push the sewing machine aside and study the surface of the desk, where someone had painted what she assumed were landmasses, the texture of it thick and rising in places. Who did it or how long it had been there she didn't know. With her finger she traced the outlines of her imagined nations until sleep came to her and she lay on her bed and shut her eyes and felt the satisfaction of a day fulfilled.

These were her days. In their patterns she found comfort. Not once in two years had she left the hospital property. Instead, she kept watch over the grounds, pacing within its border and following the footpaths every morning before dawn.

On some days she climbed the tree beside the stone garden. From this distance she could see the campus in its intended symmetry. The main hall at the center, its roof of red tiles, weather-worn, and the eaves that shaded the stucco walls. The courtyard and the cottages. The citrus grove and the hills beyond which lay the orphanage. A horizon formed by coastal mountains, their peaks covered in the remnants of last month's snow. The color of the land muted.

None of it had changed, she thought. Any moment now the students would appear from the main hall, as they used to, she herself standing on the other side of the fence. She imagined this, repeating it in her mind, and waited for the sun to rise, her arms hooked around a branch, her legs dangling, the world, it seemed, not yet awake. The war was far.

And it was here one morning, up in the tree, that she witnessed the cargo trucks coming down the main road. She had grown accustomed to them, of course, but with every visit she felt her heart quicken. Headlights crowned the hill. There was the low pitch of a radio. She heard a woman's voice, singing, accompanied by a brass band that seemed to float across the fields, caught by the winds. The trucks grew closer, rumbling. In their approach they resembled elephants. Dust sprayed underneath their wheels. They turned into the driveway and parked in the courtyard, their engines idle, their headlights sweeping across the field.

All at once men tumbled out of the cargo holds, their bodies shadowed against the low sky. Scurrying like thieves. Some knelt on the grass and appeared to be digging. Then the air popped and the grass caught fire, first in one corner, then in another, and another, as if the ground had cracked open to illuminate the stretchers, dozens of them, already spread out on the lawn.

Miya climbed down the tree and brushed away dirt from her hospital gown. She tucked the loose strands of her hair behind her ears and put on her nurse's cap. She followed the path to the driveway, engulfed by the smoke of flares and the scent of the wounded. She helped a nurse lift a stretcher, shocked by the soldier's lightness. He was an American. His gaze lolled and his breath was sour. The nurse led them past the doors and into the main hall.

"What's your name?" Miya asked the soldier. "Where are you from?"

He looked up at her, seeing her upside down. He grinned. "Hi, doll face," he said. "I'm Benson from Boston."

"Hello, Benson from Boston," she said, and the American blinked and his smile vanished. When he was settled into a bed she took his hand.

Soon after, a patient was placed on the bed beside Benson's. She didn't go to him until later, curious, parting the curtain to reveal a young man with gauze wrapped around his head and bandages over his eyes. He was a mainlander, perhaps. Or an island native. He was comatose, she realized, and asked Benson whether he knew who the patient was. Benson didn't respond, staring up at the ceiling as he would for most of his time here. She checked to see if Henry was close by. He was at the end of the ward. She turned again toward the bandaged patient and shut the curtain behind her.

She leaned forward. It was as though layers of his body had been stripped. "Hello," she whispered, not yet recognizing him. The sun had risen and the ward blazed white for a moment before the clouds passed. She lifted the bandages away from his eyes, then quickly drew her hand back as if stung. She looked around, disoriented, clutching the bedsheet. *She knew him,* she kept repeating, though no one responded. *She knew him.* He was there, within this face, this aged body, she was certain of it. But her voice had failed her and so she spoke in silence about how long it had been and how he had come back, as she knew he would, this boy, whom she held under a tree, many years ago, while a man painted their likeness.

She was woken by the fading thunder of aircraft. Then the quiet returned and she lay listening to the sound of breathing. She was unsure of the time. Her eyes adjusted to the faint light from the windows, the convalescents lined up along the walls like dark monuments. She had fallen asleep on a chair beside Junpei's bed.

Benson was muttering, "I didn't do nothing. I didn't do nothing at all." She crossed over to him and massaged his temples with her fingertips. He was sweating. A fever. She went to the sink and soaked a cloth in cold water and then draped it over Benson's forehead. A nurse passed her, yawning. "Get some sleep, Miya," she whispered, heading to the quarters. Miya put on her coat. And then, looking back at Junpei, his shadowed body under a sheet, she stepped outside, breathing in the air.

At the stone garden she sat on the bench and took off her shoes. The garden's terrain was made of sand, raked to resemble currents of water running beside the stones. She placed her feet into the sand and felt the coolness of it and then the quick warmth, as though the earth were a hand tugging at her ankles. She looked up at the tree and then drifted into sleep once more, facing the dark windows of the ward.

In daylight she rose to the footsteps of convalescents and nurses. At the grove she plucked a lemon, slipping it into her pocket before returning inside. Junpei lay with his arms to his side. She leaned forward and inhaled his raspy breath and saw the child she remembered still there along the bottom half of his face. She brought the lemon to her mouth and bit into the rind, breaking away the flesh. She squeezed the juice onto a wet cloth and began to clean his chin, wiping away dirt and crusted blood.

"You'll need a proper bath, soon," she said. "Like everyone else here. It's no longer a school, you know. But there is still the tree. And the stone garden. Of course there is."

They found him beside the remnants of a house, she was told. "He wouldn't have gone inside first," Henry said, examining the patient's legs. "We'd have nothing left of him if he did."

She ran her fingers over his bandages, guessing where his eyebrows were hidden. "Where have you been, Junpei?" she asked him, cleaning his hands.

She had witnessed his first step, she recalled. At the orphanage's entrance. Once learned, he walked all throughout the day, the child's face filled with determination as he swayed his hips and his arms, shuffling past the dormitory, the classrooms, the barn—out toward the fences as well, ignoring Miya's pleas for him to slow. When she was doing her chores he would walk back and forth beside her, in circles, some form of fury in him, his body unwilling to pause until they were called for supper, where he would sit on her lap, his head bowed, as if catching up on a day's worth of breathing. "Messenger" the children called him.

The orphanage was still there, she knew, on the other side of the western hills. It had expanded over the years, housing children from the war. She did not go to it anymore.

She and Junpei had arrived at the same time. An earthquake had destroyed Tokyo. They had, along with hundreds of others, been airlifted to this island, which was under Japanese rule then. Solla, it was called. Their ages were guessed. Names were given. They had not known each other before. They were paired together and slept on a blanket on the floor, her arm tucked under his head. They lay on their sides, facing each other, their bodies in the shape of prayer. Junpei's hair caught in her teeth when she woke in the mornings.

In those early years she bathed him. She filled unused fuel barrels with water and lifted the boy into it. He would cling to her ears as she washed his chest. When he was older, she brought Junpei to Miss Hara's lessons, learning both Japanese and Korean to communicate with the local islanders. They were taught songs, mathematics as well. They helped with the house chores, wiping windows with newspaper, mopping the floors, taking breaks to duel with brooms in the yard. They took walks through the forest and up the hills to view the ocean. They walked to the school, counting all the artists they could see behind windows. Not once did they speak of Tokyo.

When the boy was nearly Miya's height, Miss Hara asked him whether he now preferred to stay with the other boys. He shook his head, clutching Miya's hand, and she felt the surety of his grip and

was convinced in that moment that they would grow old together—
that theirs was a shared life. She would, at night, tell him of this. A
house by the sea. They would fish. They would plant a garden.
"Horses," she would add, facing him, her fingers galloping across his
shoulders lit by the moon.

She would always remember that morning when he left her in the
yard to chase a crow. In memory there was his face and only that,
the open mouth, his wet eyes, his return, his hands picking at his
clothes, an animal-like cry erupting from the center of his body. How
he held her and she, unable to calm him, saw Miss Hara hurrying
to the barn. Miya followed. A crowd had formed. They were all gazing up.

It took her a moment to realize that what hung from the rafters
was in fact a person and not a doll, his limbs dangling, as if filled with
cotton. It was a boy, his face discolored from the rope around his
neck. And there was Junpei behind her, clutching her waist, pointing
at the floor where a shoe had fallen. No one else noticed.

After this, Junpei began to wander. She would wake to find that he
had already risen. Or she would be washing clothes and turn to see
that he had disappeared. He missed his lessons. In the evenings he
didn't show up for supper. She searched the dormitory and the classrooms. She searched the barn and the fields. She ran down the road
and saw at last his figure in the distance, standing there by the fence,
his hands rooted into his pockets.

"Junpei," she called one evening, taking hold of his wrist. "Where
have you been?"

It was growing dark. He wouldn't look at her, his eyes roaming
over the mountains. "Not far," he said.

"Miss Hara will be worried," she said, tugging on his arm.
"Come."

She turned and he followed her. At the orphanage they slept as
they always did, facing each other. Sometime later he woke her with
his voice. "I can't find it, Miya. I've looked everywhere. For the other
one. He was barefoot, you know. I saw his toes." He drifted, the

words slipping, and she dreamed of a boy who would not stop walking.

In six months' time, Junpei was gone. They had been at the orphanage for over a decade. It was the beginning of winter. Snow had yet to fall. She went to bathe. Upon her return, he wasn't there. The schoolbag they shared was missing, their pillow as well. Miya, wearing her nightgown, rushed to the road and called his name and waited. Her hair began to freeze. Miss Hara found her that afternoon, still waiting. With her hands she had torn the hem of her gown.

It was the year an American woman named Earhart had flown over the Pacific. From Hawaii to California. She recalled that she and Junpei had heard through the radio. That evening they climbed the hill behind the orphanage. They walked to the edge of the cliff. They raised their hands above their eyes and peered out at the horizon until the ocean faded.

All that week she remained beside him, vigilant. Benson ignored her, staring up at the ceiling. With her head resting on her hand she watched Junpei. The flat bridge of his nose. The curve of his cheekbones. His chapped lips. She dipped her finger in lemon water and placed it into his mouth, convinced that in his sleep it would sink into the soil of his tongue and he would dream of citrus. She felt his teeth, like crags, the one he had lost a mystery to her, this empty space near the front, an incomplete thought. The hair on his face was beginning to grow. He smelled of staleness and storage. She pressed her thumbs against the calloused skin of his feet, feeling for any traces of where he had been.

She spoke to him. Of her years. Of what he had missed. "You still have your youth," she told him. "You'll get used to things here."

She attempted to imagine his own years away but couldn't. They were an undecipherable map, with nameless cities and towns, borderless countries. She saw him forever on a boat following the routes along the Pacific, absent of history, invisible to it. He would have woken one day in a cabin, feeling the ocean shudder, great spires of smoke in the far distance in Japan, as if the entire country were evaporating. He would not have thought of her then.

And would he have ever gone to Tokyo? She wasn't sure. She didn't think so. She never believed he had gone in search of that. Instead, he had fled. Sure of this, she fell asleep beside him, speaking of gardens to his silent face.

She was startled from a dream she couldn't remember. Carrying a lamp, she wandered the hospital's corridors, as she did when she first arrived. In the hallways she brought the light up to the walls, pushing away the moonlight. On first glance the walls were bare, nondescript, the paint yellowed by age and dust. The longer she stared, however, bright rectangular shapes rose out of them, spaced out evenly along the walls like ghost windows.

She had searched for paintings before. She used to ask Henry about them but he shrugged, indifferent. All that night she looked again. First she explored the main hall, taking the staircase quietly. There were so many doors. She paused at each of them, listening to a patient's breathing. If she heard nothing, she slid the doors open and inspected the rooms now used to store equipment, cans of food, extra mattresses. She went outside and into the cottages, opening closets, waking the patients there. They looked at her perplexed, and she brought a finger to her lips as if sharing some kind of secret. She hunted with all that was left of her energy, releasing it in a great burst.

Exhausted, she headed to the stone garden. The moon hung over the crest of the hills, an even light spreading over the grass, the tree, and the sand that sparkled like diamonds. Midway there she stopped. One of the stones had moved. She squinted, then rubbed her eyes with her palms, shaking her head, feeling her limbs grow heavy. The stone moved again. It rose. It began to approach her and she clenched her fists, wondering to what world she had entered in these hours. Closer, it grew skin and then a face formed and she saw that it was a boy, no older than thirteen.

"Hey, miss," the boy said, in the island dialect. "I hear your footsteps. All over." He tapped his earlobes. He was dressed in dark pants, a button-down shirt, and rubber moccasins. His head was shaved and he had thin lips. A small leather pouch hung from his belt loop. He asked what Miya was looking for.

"Paintings," Miya replied. "Seen any?"

Laughter erupted from the boy's small mouth. "I see nothing," he said, and motioned for her to step closer.

She did so, bending forward. The boy's eyes were fogged, like porcelain. He reached up to touch Miya's face, extending his fingers along her jawline and then closing them over her nose. His palms smelled of cinnamon. He wrapped a hand around her pinky finger. "Come with me," he said, leading her to the stone garden.

Was he a patient? she asked. Another volunteer?

He didn't respond. He sat on the garden's edge and began to wipe the waves away in the sand until the surface was smooth. He opened his pouch and dug his fingers into it, lifting his hand to reveal dozens of marbles. These he placed in the middle of the sandbox, adjusting the cluster, each orb illuminating colors under the night sky. Satisfied, he offered another marble to Miya. She took it and lay on her stomach in the grass. She aimed. She flicked her thumb and followed the marble's path over the surface of the sand as it ricocheted against the others. The boy lay down beside her. His hands rested on his chin, his legs swinging in the air.

"What does it look like?" the boy asked.

She turned onto her back. Stars formed into shapes and then broke apart. The blinking dot of an airplane moved from left to right, vanishing behind the silhouettes of branches. She used to wait for Junpei to return. She would climb trees at the orphanage, the ground below shrinking. The forest canopy opened to her like the waves of the sea and a flock of birds rose out of it, spraying leaves. She waited for boats.

The boy nudged her, breathing into her ear, pointing at the marbles. "Hey, miss," he said, repeating his question.

"Fireworks," Miya responded.

. . .

The following morning the boy was gone. The day was warmer than the others. The sun had settled onto her skin. The ground was damp. When she rose from the garden she saw the land had created a cast of her body: grass folded pale to form her slightly parted legs, the curve of her shoulders, the sand indented where she had rested her head. Beside that was the shape of the boy, too, though it appeared he had been lying on his side, watching her. Or was it that? Her certainty, an instant before so sure, abandoned her. A wind came and stole the shapes. She looked for the marbles' paths but they had been erased as well, replaced by the waves that were always there. The rake lay under the bench like an old rifle. She brushed sand from her hair.

Inside, she found Henry tending to a soldier who was recovering from surgery. They were sending him to a rehabilitation clinic in Virginia, Henry told him. The soldier seemed pleased with the news. They shook hands. The doctor continued with his rounds. She stood in the ward's entrance for a moment and watched the soldier sit up in bed suddenly, stretch forward, fingers extended, and touch the space where his legs had once been.

She approached Junpei's bed. If she stared at him long enough it seemed he wasn't breathing. Or as if the entire room was, rising and falling. Henry was beside her now, making note of Junpei's vitals. He was holding the nurse's cap he had given to her. She must have dropped it somewhere.

"Junpei you said his name was?" Henry asked, without looking at the chart.

"There was a boy," Miya said. "He is blind. A native. Have you seen him?"

Henry kept his gaze on her and shook his head.

"Is he a volunteer?" she asked.

"Miya."

"He wore dark pants and moccasins. Perhaps he was a patient."

Henry looked over her shoulder and she saw the tiredness of his skin. He took her arm and led her outside to the corridor. They stood by a window and his brown hair speckled in sunlight.

"He carries marbles. In a little pouch."

"Miya," Henry repeated. "You aren't sleeping." He spoke in a whisper. "We've talked about this. Do you remember? You're of no use to me if you aren't sleeping."

She took her cap and put it on.

"There are others you could tend to," he continued.

She ignored him. She had known Henry for two years now. He had been one of the singers when the orphanage director was here. She avoided his stare and returned to Junpei and his stillness. She placed lemon juice onto his lips and then combed his hair with her fingers. She had done the same for Miss Hara and spent the days reading to her from a book of folktales, keeping her company as the woman drifted in and out of consciousness.

"Has he been bathed?" she asked Henry. "It's time, I think. Don't you agree? We could remove the bandages, also. From his eyes. It can't be good for him. He would wake to see nothing."

In Henry's hand was a tin cup filled with two tablets. "For your headache, Miya," he said.

Had she complained of that? She couldn't recall. She took the pills, slipping them under her tongue.

"Rest for an hour," he encouraged her. "You need your strength. Do you remember, Miya? Like we said. You need to rest."

He took her arm again and led her upstairs to her room. She didn't protest. After he left she spat out the pills and ground them on the floor with the bottom of her teacup. She then gathered the powder into her hand and blew it out the window, watching it scatter.

She turned to her sewing machine. At the base, written in English were the words *Little Betty.* "Hello, Betty," she said. "Where are you from?" From a basket on the floor she picked up a torn shirt and placed it on the tray. She couldn't recall to whom it belonged. She cranked the wheel and the spool on top rotated, unwinding the gray thread. The machine was rusting. The paint on the desk formed continents.

Through the walls she heard a man's voice on the radio. It was the news. There was to be a UN prisoner exchange with the North and the Chinese. Hill 255 was in the shape of a pork chop, another news segment explained. She wondered who had thought of that first, who called these things such names. Her window faced the front courtyard and beyond that were the main road and the hills that led to the orphanage. The hills were in the shape of ears, she thought, the sides of heads. Below her the main entrance opened and a soldier, discharged, stepped out onto the patio in uniform. He raised his hand to shade his eyes and looked around him as if he weren't sure where he was and how he had come here.

After Junpei left the orphanage, Miya turned silent. She performed her chores with a mechanical precision and then did more, relieving the other children of their responsibilities. They avoided her, unsure of what to say. She didn't notice. The weeks passed and she slept little, wandering the grounds and out to the field's edge where the forest began.

She was chopping wood behind the kitchen one afternoon when Miss Hara approached her. Together, without speaking, they carried the split logs to the furnaces. She had cut extra and brought them to Miss Hara's cottage, where she placed them at the doorstep. Miss Hara invited her inside. She was a slim woman with a receding hairline. She had long slender fingers that wrapped around her arms as she gazed down at Miya.

She had never seen the inside of the house before. It was sparse in its furnishings. A single tea table, a low desk beside the window where the woman kneeled and wrote letters. The walls were unadorned.

Miss Hara owned a single teacup and that evening they drank tea sitting on the floor, passing the cup back and forth as they watched the fire. Miya expected the woman would mention Junpei in some way but she didn't. She stood to retrieve a sheet of paper and a pencil. "Much to do," she said, and sighed. She told Miya of her plans for the next day. A list was drawn. She handed Miya the list and, smiling, lifted her hand and waved her off.

The next day Miya assigned chores to the younger ones: who would be picking vegetables in the garden, milking the cows, cooking, washing linen, cleaning the hallways and the dormitory. She made sure the mats were rolled and the floors swept. She enforced curfew. She led the children to the stable and fed the ponies, bringing their manure out to the field where she spread it over the soil.

She returned to Miss Hara, handing her the list. Miss Hara gave her another one. Again, she drank tea with the woman in silence. Another day came. Another list was given. In the years to come, she would, along with the others her age, begin to tutor the children.

She stayed, as did many. When a new child arrived, she was the first to carry them or take their hand, escorting them into the kitchen. The hours were quick and arduous. In her time, some, like Junpei, ran away, though this was rare. Even so, she grew used to this. And for those who approached her about leaving, Miya and Miss Hara assisted them in obtaining work with the local farmers and the fishermen. They would all gather in front of the orphanage and watch each child depart on a pony, their new employer guiding them down the road. There was even a marriage. They held a wedding ceremony. As a wedding gift the orphans built a house at the end of the field.

All the days ended at Miss Hara's cottage and a single cup of tea. Few words were spoken. Lists were no longer required. Some nights they ignored each other completely, Miss Hara writing her letters, Miya reading a book. At exactly the same hour each day Miss Hara would turn to her and wave her away by flicking her hand. "Good night, Miss Hara," Miya said, and the woman nodded, smiling.

It was in the summer, in the evening, that she saw the flicker of a lamp at the end of the road. A birthday had been celebrated, marking the day she arrived. She was, by Miss Hara's calculation, twenty-six. Japan was at war. Some of the island's residents had been enlisted to fight alongside them. She sat on the floor, gripping the windowsill, watching the light sway and grow larger. It beat in the rhythm of her heart. Then she saw the figure that held it. She rushed outside.

"Junpei!" she called, running toward him. "Junpei!"

The young man paused, perplexed, and looked at her, raising the lamp to Miya's face. "Aren't you pretty," he said, and drank from a bottle of wine. He stepped closer. He ran his fingers down the length of her hair. She didn't move away. He was sweating. He spat. "You are not from here," he said. He then grasped her hand and lowered it between his legs and she felt him and stood there, studying the shape of his body.

The broom appeared like a spear thrown across Miya's shoulder. She turned and there was the shadow of Miss Hara in the dark, raising her arms and beating the man. He had dropped the bottle and Miss Hara took it, shattered it on the ground, and stabbed the air with the broken bottle neck. She did this until the man was down the road and when he was gone she turned to Miya, who had begun to cry, and slapped her across the face and continued to do so until Miya fell. Miss Hara left her there.

In the middle of the night, after Miya had returned to the dormitory, Miss Hara came to her and took her back to the house. The woman washed the girl's face. They shared the mat, lying beside each other and looking up at the beams along the ceiling and the starlight that swept over them.

In the first week of August the bombs fell on Hiroshima and Nagasaki. And all the orphans woke one day to find that the Japanese army had left. The Americans came in their place. Cargo trucks could be seen on the roads and Miya kept waiting for the soldiers to take her and the others away. Instead, supplies were offered to them, including clothing, coffee, sugar, and toys. "Islanders," they were called, with affection, and she realized she had been here for over twenty years.

So the orphanage remained. The school across the hills, however, was abandoned. She no longer walked to it. At night she heard the distant engines of trucks and imagined the students leaving and the Americans carrying crates of artwork out of the buildings, sending them off on ships across the Pacific.

Miss Hara had begun to teach her how to sew, from a machine they were given by an American chaplain. They sat beside her desk and Miya pushed the fabric under the machine's needle while Miss Hara turned the wheel. A lamp was burning and the shadows of their arms loomed across the floor like birds. By then another war had started, this time on the peninsula.

All of a sudden Miss Hara spoke. "I have my vocation," she said, guiding Miya's fingers. "What will yours be?"

Miya didn't respond. She had never heard Miss Hara speak so many words outside of the classroom. The tapping noise of the sewing machine filled the room, as well as the woman's quick breathing. Her voice remained calm.

"I'm not the judge of this. But there is a world outside of this one. And someday they will go home. And we will be here."

She left to check on their tea. Miya spun the wheel herself. She heard the cup drop and looked back to see Miss Hara's outstretched arm on the floor behind a counter, the cup swiveling rapidly, then slowing. The sewing machine needle punched into Miya's finger.

She would, at times, attempt to recall those hours. It would only come to her in quick images. Her attempts at waking the woman. Running to the barn for a pony. Her own rapid breathing, the tremor of her heart. Her desire to shout, yet inability to. Her inexplicable strength in lifting the body onto the pony's back. Her galloping. Her ascent up the hills and crossing over them. Dusk.

For the second time in her life, she passed through the gates of the school. A young nurse, upon hearing the sound of hooves, stepped out onto the patio. Behind her, the faces of convalescents began to fill the windows, their eyes betraying curiosity and bewilderment, this girl on a pony, a woman's body slumped forward against the animal's neck.

The young doctor she would later come to know as Henry stepped forward, carrying a stretcher. Miss Hara was brought inside and placed on a bed. He thought at first the woman had been wounded. Blood streaked her face and clothes. Henry searched for the source. He couldn't find it. He turned to Miya and then saw her finger.

She returned to the orphanage after Miss Hara passed away. An American organization had decided to take over the institution. A married couple moved into Miss Hara's cottage. The husband translated. They were from the Midwest, they told Miya, and she didn't know what state that was. Each night they read the Bible before supper. They taught the children English and refused to allow the girls to bathe with the boys. Chaplains visited. Journalists, also. The dormitory filled with orphans from the mainland cities and towns.

Miya lasted there two months. The others stood in front of the orphanage to bid her farewell. She gathered Miss Hara's teacup, an extra set of clothes, a comb, her unsent letters, which Miya had hidden, and placed them all into a satchel. She carried this and the sewing machine to the car that was to take her back to the hospital.

Later, in the room Henry offered her, she would read over Miss Hara's letters. Most were requesting supplies, from the UN and Christian communities. The last stack, however, was a list: in columns were the names of orphans, copied onto dozens of sheets of paper in the woman's handwriting, all addressed to refugee camps in the mainland and towns in Japan. *Found,* it stated, at the top.

She looked for herself. She wasn't there, of course. She was nameless when she arrived, her age estimated. As was Junpei. She was about to put the letter away but then paused at the last person on the list. It was written as if it had been an afterthought, the handwriting less confident. She hadn't known Miss Hara's full name until then.

.   .   .   .

In the washroom she filled her teacup with water and then added salt taken from the kitchen. It was night, the room windowless. A light-bulb hung from the ceiling, giving off a dull glow. She covered the cup with her hand and shook the liquid mixture. She then rubbed the saltwater onto her teeth and along the base of her gums. What remained in the cup she swirled in her mouth and then returned to her room. She didn't bother with the light. Outside the hills faded into sky. She was wearing her hospital gown. She sat on the edge of the bed and combed her hair. The shirt she had sewn lay folded on her desk. Barefoot, she walked downstairs and into the ward.

Two nurses were making their rounds. They nodded to her and she returned their greeting. A weak light shone through the windows, touching the shoulders of the wounded. Someone coughed. Bed-sheets rustled. There was the scent of ether and iodine. She passed the curtain, leaving it parted, and stood above Junpei. She leaned over him, toward the window, and peered out at the tree and the stone garden. A bird lifted off a branch, a speck of shadow. She watched the stones for movement. "Where are you?" she said.

"Where is who?"

She looked down at Junpei. His face was motionless, his eyes still covered. She leaned down and placed her ear against his dry lips.

In the next bed over Benson lifted his arms. He was lying on his back, staring up at the ceiling. His chest was wrapped in gauze. "Where is who?" he repeated.

"Hello, Benson," she said, and asked if she could get him anything. He didn't respond.

She crossed the room to the sink and filled a bowl with warm water. She pumped powdered soap into it from the dispenser and then placed it beside Junpei's bed. "You stink," she said, laughing quietly, and patted Junpei's hand. "You've been neglected, you poor thing."

"What did you dream last night?" Benson called.

She didn't know. She unbuttoned Junpei's shirt and spread it out over the ends of the bed. There were bandages scattered across his chest and stomach, covering the sutures. She had watched Henry stitch the wounds, lifting the maroon thread and snipping the ends, closing the skin like shells.

"I dreamed of sand," Benson said. "Everywhere. And everyone was sinking into it except me. I walked right over it. Right to the end." He kept his hands raised, swinging them lazily in the air.

She dipped a sponge into the water and worked around Junpei's bandages, scrubbing his body. The soap smelled of dust. She hummed to herself, tracing the shape of his shoulders. She spoke of her day, the blind boy she had recently met. She told him he would have liked the marbles.

"I saw a house once," Benson continued while she washed Junpei's neck. "It had collapsed sideways like a tree. The whole structure. It lay in the middle of an unpaved street. You see. Like this." Benson tilted his arms over the bed.

Miya pressed the sponge against Junpei's cheeks, the water running down onto the pillow. She told him of the shirt she had made. For when he woke. She watched Junpei's mouth as Benson's voice came to her, hovering by the curtain.

"An older couple lived there," he said. "They had arranged the furniture to accommodate their new floor, which had once been their wall. They refused to leave. The husband was shaking a grenade. His wife stood by the sideways window. She had silver hair. She wore a brooch on her shirt, a flower, a star, I don't remember. I asked to take the wife. The husband refused. I motioned for her to leave. 'Come out the window,' I said. It was open, no glass. She reached through it and took my hand. She squeezed my fingers. Her palms were warm. I could smell her insides. And that's the last thing I remember."

Water droplets ran across Junpei's chest, carrying the light of stars. It was the nose, she thought, that remained from his boyhood. The flat bridge. His lips, too. The sharp angle of his jaw. She knew them well.

"You moved the stones," she said, rubbing the gauze wrapped over Junpei's forehead. "After the painter finished. You formed the shape of an arrow."

She took Junpei's fingers and placed them between her teeth. She trimmed his nails, which tasted of flour, and swallowed each crescent sliver.

"There," she said. "All better."

A light flashed across the ward then faded. The sound of a car passing the main road. The soft clatter of a nurse's footsteps approaching a coughing patient.

"Some nights I dream that house is still there," Benson went on. "It's grown roots. It's sunk. A window is used as a door. The couple's still there, way down below, waving." He turned his head in her direction for the first time. "Doll face," he said. "When you sleep next to that man. I don't know why you do. But you talk in your sleep."

She looked across at Benson. She waited for him to go on. The night had thinned and the floor of the ward shone. Benson returned to staring at the ceiling. He stretched his hands into moonlight, as if attempting to take hold of it, and then brought them down over his eyes. His lips moved but what he said she didn't hear. Her vision blurred. She wiped her face and looked down at the body she had just washed. "I never left," she said.

Someone touched her shoulder. It was suddenly morning, the light of day abundant. Her eyes focused on Henry standing beside her. And then she saw a woman at the foot of the bed. She had a receding hairline and long fingers. She wore a shirt that wrapped across her chest and a long skirt that billowed. She was running her hands over Junpei's toes. Miya smiled, thinking this a dream. "You're here," she said, taking Junpei's hand.

Henry was watching her but she thought little of it. The woman was crying, staring at the body on the bed.

"It's all right," Miya said. "I've kept your sewing machine."

"Miya," Henry said, and took her shoulder again. He leaned forward and spoke into her ear. "Miya. Are you listening?"

She nodded. "It's in my room. Little Betty, it's called."

"Miya. Listen to me."

His voice was steady. She looked to see if Benson was awake but he wasn't.

"Do I talk in my sleep?" she asked Henry, and he didn't answer. He pointed at Junpei. The blanket was pulled up to his waist and folded back. His shirt lay open and she apologized, reaching to button it.

Henry took her wrist. He spoke as if from a distance, though she could feel his breath against her cheeks, soft as wings. "The woman here. This is the boy's mother. She heard about her son and has come to visit him. Do you understand, Miya?"

"Which boy?"

Henry pointed at Junpei. "This one."

"He doesn't have a mother," Miya said. She smiled at him with patience. "Neither of us does. I told you, Henry. Ages ago. Remember?"

"It's time to stop," Henry said. "It's my fault. I'm sorry, Miya. His mother's here now. She'll be staying with him. You can help the others. Like we agreed." He gripped her arms. "Let's go," he said. "You need to rest."

Miya refused to move from the chair, placing her hands underneath her legs. She turned to the woman. "I kept it. Like you said. I make clothes now." She struggled against Henry's hands, twisting her shoulders. He called her name, a bit louder now, though the more he did so his voice seemed to fade and she stood quickly and leaned over Junpei and held his face. Then she tore away the gauze and lifted his eyelids and saw the emptiness there, a pair of tunnels. The mother began to shout. There were footsteps. She was embraced.

"Junpei," she whispered into where his eyes should have been. "Junpei. I have yet to find it."

She was pulled as if tied to a string and she fell backward, her legs giving way. She was caught and dragged across the ward. Her gown skimmed the floor. She watched Henry's body diminish, bending down to pick up her nurse's cap. She saw Junpei's feet, the woman still touching them. The faces of the convalescents passed by her, tall as trees. Out the window the hills swallowed clouds.

Later in the day, Henry visited her room. She had been using the sewing machine and he sat at the edge of the desk and placed his clipboard beside her. A small bandage covered her arm, her skin sore from an injection they had given her. She continued to sew, feeding the fabric through the machine. He looked down at her fingers. "Careful," he said, and smiled.

"You have lists," Miya said. "Like Miss Hara."

"That's right," he said. He showed her a piece of paper with her name at the top and a paragraph in his handwriting that he would not let her read. There were dates along the margins as well. *1951* was the first.

"You haven't been taking your medicine," he said.

"I don't have headaches," she said, cranking the wheel.

"Sometimes you have them without realizing, Miya. That's why you should take the medicine. It's for your health that I give them to you. I wouldn't do it if I thought otherwise. Over two years it's been. Since you came. Since we've known each other."

She finished a torn shirt and moved on to a pair of pants.

"You're a great help to us," he said. "You help the wounded. You always have. And always will. I am indebted. But it's getting worse, you see. I think you know that. Each time. Promise me you'll take them."

She listened to footsteps in the corridor. Henry rubbed his face and she saw his tiredness again.

"There should be paintings," she said. "In the hallways."

"There aren't any," he said. "I've told you this. And there isn't a blind child either. Now promise to take your medicine."

She hesitated, then agreed.

"Good," he said, and handed her a small tin cup. He watched her take them, swallow, and then he leaned down and carelessly sifted through her fabrics. "We wouldn't like it either," he said. "To be thought of as someone else."

He settled the nurse's cap on her head and tucked a loose strand of her hair behind her ear. He stood to go but paused at the door and watched her. She pretended not to notice. When the American couple had brought her here, she clutched the sewing machine against her stomach, unwilling to part with it. "A volunteer," Henry had said. "Help is always needed." Together they watched the couple leave by car down the road. "It isn't far," Henry said, and patted her shoulder. "Just across the hills."

One night after the woman came for her son, Miya saw the blind boy. She was in her room, unable to sleep, and heard a strange sound coming from outside the window, not unlike something being dragged across the dirt. She rose and placed her elbows onto the ledge and scanned the lawn, the footpaths, and the gate.

The boy was directly below her. He sat on a bicycle. Its frame seemed to engulf him. The handles were wide and his arms were outstretched, clinging to the bars. He circled the courtyard, the wheels creating a circle in the dirt, which he followed without error.

"There you are," she said quietly against the windowpane.

She undressed and slipped into the clothes she had worn when she first arrived here, a pair of old pants and a shirt Miss Hara had given her on a birthday. It was imprinted with flowers and she had said it came from England. Miya took out her satchel from under the bed and placed her comb and Miss Hara's teacup into it. She couldn't find her shoes, so she left barefoot and tiptoed down the corridor and down the stairs. At the ward she paused by the door and heard Benson muttering. Through a space in the curtain she saw the comatose patient lying with a blanket tucked under his chin. The man's mother was sitting on a chair beside him. Her posture was straight and she held a book out in front of her, reading under a lamp.

Miya left them and walked down the hallway to the main entrance. She pushed the door open and stepped outside, her body caught by a breeze. The entire courtyard was lit by a heavy moon above the hills. The snow on the far ridges had begun to melt. It was quiet, save for the gears of the bicycle. She approached the boy, who stopped pedaling and placed his feet on the ground. Tonight, he was wearing a cotton engineer's cap that drooped past his ears.

"Hey, miss," he said. "Want to ride?"

He waved his arm behind him. She raised a leg and sat on the seat. He took his cap off and placed it on her head. "Hold on to my waist," he said. He was thin and she felt his hip bones push up against her palms. Like before, he carried a pouch tied to his belt loop. She lifted her feet. He stood and began to pedal and the bicycle swayed from their weight. She clung to him. "Miss," he said. "Not so tight." She relaxed. Soon they were moving down the driveway.

"I pedal," the boy said. "You tell me where we're going."

They reached the end of the hospital property and passed under the gates. "Left," she said, and the boy swerved and she held him and began to laugh. "Stop!" she called. "Stop."

"You're not very good at this," the boy said, braking.

She got off the bicycle and walked to the fences. She twisted her hair up and hid it underneath the cap, lowering the brim to just above her eyes. A few of the windows of the main hall were lit and she could distinguish the silhouettes of the nurses walking through the wards. She used to take Junpei here, in those days after they had posed for the painter. She would help him climb the fence, holding his waist. They would shout, "Give us back our faces!" And if anyone approached them, they would run away.

The blind boy tugged on her sleeve. "We go on?"

"We go on."

They continued down the road, following the fences and the hills. The hospital began to shrink from view. Stars gathered along the crests of the distant mountains. They could smell the sea. He pedaled faster. Their bodies pulsed in the darkness. She wondered, as she did sometimes, whether her parents were still underground. A city rebuilt on top of them. It seemed possible.

"Hey, miss," the boy said. "War's ending." He tapped his earlobe. "Listen."

Andrew Sean Greer

Darkness

WHAT WERE THEY LIKE THE FIRST DAY?

The way we all were.

WHAT WAS THE FIRST THING THEY DID?

What we all did: opened the window. Helen opened it, the bedroom window: the lace curtain fluttered out into the cold air like a waving handkerchief, and they saw.

WHAT DID THEY THINK IT WAS?

A mistake of their clock; a power outage in the night; the work of Louise's diabolical sleeping pills (which felled her nightly like an ax to a tree, making her into a sleepwalking clock-changer); a cloud. They spent half an hour trying to figure out if they had lost their minds; they were old women, so it was not impossible; each of them had lost things before, had spent a secret hour in a hotel room searching for keys, only to discover them right in her pocket. But very soon the radio told them they had not gone insane. The sky had.

"How could particles in the air do this?" Louise wanted to know. She sat on the sofa, perhaps too frightened to look outside again. Every light in the house was on, a parody of morning.

Helen sat bravely by the window. "They say it happened after Krakatau, all those years ago," she said. "The ash was so thick that for three whole days it was utter darkness."

"But nothing's happened. They don't say anything's happened."

"They said it isn't dangerous. The sun just isn't out."

"Are you going to school?"

"I don't think so. Were you going to work today?"

"I don't know."

Helen stared out at the gloom, shivering. All down the street the young people wandered beneath the still-unlit streetlights, some with flashlights or lanterns, laughing. No old people out on the street at all, not in this kind of confusion, not with the sidewalks as loud as a carnival and the crash of police lights everywhere. In the apartment across the street, Helen could make out a couple sitting down to a candlelit breakfast. And below, in front of the building, stood an old Russian woman and her son, hand in hand, nearly indistinguishable in fur hats, looking straight up at the sky.

It was nine o'clock in the morning and as dark as the inside of an eye.

"It's nothing, I'm sure of it," Helen said. "It isn't time to worry yet."

But she looked over at Louise on the sofa, her dear Louise, her sweet white-haired girl, rubbing a spot out of the coffee table; and though it was not time to worry yet, she began to cry, because there was no helping it.

WHAT DID THEY DO THE SECOND DAY?

Called friends. They could not be alone—Helen said it felt like her grandmother's house in the war, with blackout curtains and the roar of military planes along the California coast and the threat of something happening—and so they invited friends over for lunch and made what they could from the pantry; for some nameless reason they did not dare go outside, though the city had put the streetlights on and the throngs of young people had lessened with the dimming novelty of it all. Louise made pasta by dropping eggs into the crater of a flour volcano. She did this in silence, flour puffing into the air as if she had burst the seeds of a milkweed. Helen thawed and roasted a chicken. Then, her hostess's instinct intact, she thawed and roasted another.

At noon, she heard a rattle from the living room, which was Louise drawing the curtains. She understood; they were not Aleuts; they could not bear constant night. Then she heard—like an exhalation of relief—the sound of a match. Candles.

Only two people came: an elderly colleague of Helen's at the college and a kindly, nervous painter Louise had met at an artists' colony. They were good, intelligent talkers at a party; neither was suitable that day. They had clearly come out of loneliness. Helen and Louise found themselves smiling and dutifully filling wineglasses and listening for a doorbell that never rang. What was meant as an afternoon of solace had become one of duty.

"I hear they are turning to rations," said the colleague, a professor of Victorian realism with a waxed gray mustache.

Louise wanted to know what kinds of rations.

"Gas," he said. "And fresh food and meat. Like in the war." He meant World War II. "Who knows? Maybe nylons, Helen."

Helen would not have it; "Ridiculous," she said, regretting the company of this pompous man. The curtains blew open to reveal the unearthly blackness, like the Roman servants who marched beside victorious generals and periodically reminded them of death.

Louise said she could not remember the war.

The painter spoke up, and what she said chilled them: "I think they've done something."

Helen quickly said, "Who? Done what?" Louise gave her a look.

The painter winced at her own thoughts, and her jewelry clanked on her wrists. "They've done something and they haven't told us."

The old man salted his chicken. The optimistic second chicken still sat in the kitchen, glistening and uncarved. "You mean a bomb?"

"An experiment or a bomb or I don't know. I'm sure I'm wrong, I'm sure—"

"An experiment?" Louise said.

Just then, they heard a roar. Instinctively, they went to the window, where in her haste to open it, Helen knocked a little terra-cotta pot over the sill and into the afternoon air, which was as red-dark as ever, but they could not hear its little crash above the din: the streetlights had gone out and now the city was alive with cries.

WHY DID THE STREETLIGHTS GO OUT?

It's unclear. Perhaps a strain on the system; perhaps a wrong switch thrown at the station. But it was a fright to people. That was when the blackouts began, the rolling blackouts, meant to conserve electricity. Two hours a day—on Louise and Helen's block it was at noontime, though it made little difference—with no lamps, no clocks, just flashlights and candles melting to nubs. It was terrifying the first few days, but then it was something you got used to. You knew not to open the refrigerator and waste the cold; you knew not to open the window and waste the heat. "Temporarily," the mayor said. "Until we can determine the duration." Of the darkness, he meant, of the sunless sky.

When he said this over the radio, Helen glanced at Lousie and was startled. As a child, she had noticed how sometimes, in old-fashioned books, full-color illustrations of the action would appear—through some constraint at the bindery—dozens of pages before the moments they were meant to depict. Not déjà vu, not something already seen, but something not-yet-seen, and that was what was before her: a woman in profile, immobile, her hair modern and glacially white-blue, her face old-fashioned as a Puritan's in its fury; her eyes blazing briefly with the demonic retinas of a snapshot; her hand clutching the arm of the chair in a fist; her lips open to speak to someone not in the room. A picture out of sequence.

"Louise?" she said.

Then it was gone. Her girl turned to her and blinked, saying, "What on earth does he mean by 'duration'?"

WHY DID THEIR GOOD FRIENDS NEVER COME?

They were afraid. They were all waiting for someone to come to them. They sat alone in the darkness, reading by candlelight, panicked as pigeons, waiting for someone to come, and yet they would not stir an inch. Young people will never understand this.

WHEN DID THEY DECIDE TO LEAVE?

After the riots, about two weeks later. Louise and Helen were out to dinner that night, Midtown, only the second time they had gone out to eat since the first day of the darkness, and they were still unsure if they were right to do so—if it was frivolous to be seen in a room with chandeliers and mirrors and poor people fussing over wealthier people. Louise felt everyone should be in mourning.

"The mirrors should be covered," she said to their dinner companions, who were Louise's agent, her husband, and their friend Peter. "Our garments should be rent. Don't you think? Shouldn't there be wailing somewhere?"

"If you covered the mirrors we'd have nothing," Peter said. He was an antique sort of comic type still seen only in old movies: the amusing bachelor. Despite his fastidiousness and absolutely secret private life, he seemed convincingly heterosexual; and despite the gray in his conical Victorian beard, and the lines now permanently tooled across his forehead, he appeared all the more boyish, as an adolescent actor appears all the more innocent costumed as an old man.

The agent shook her head. Light gleamed off her glasses. Light gleamed everywhere: off cutlery and plates and crystal, sequins and earrings and pearls; it was indescribably beautiful. Perhaps like the aviary of some rare bird, the last of its kind.

"We have a blind friend," the husband said. He was a scientist, a physicist working with lasers.

Helen found herself laughing. "Oh I hadn't thought about the blind! Aren't they lucky?" She absently drank from Louise's wineglass and Louise gave her a look.

The husband went on seriously; he was a very serious, very emotional man. "She says she can't help it but it's satisfying. She says she hates herself for feeling it, but it amuses her that the rest of us think the world is going to end. Because it's the same world for her."

"It can't be," Louise said. "She can tell there's no sun, and the plants—"

"For her, it's the same world."

Peter raised an eyebrow.

"That's stupid," Louise said. "I'm sorry, Frank. But it is."

Her agent put her hand on Louise's wrist. "Louise, don't be a bore."

Louise turned to her lover. "Helen?"

A moment later there was glass all around them in great shards and a hundred, much more than a hundred, young men running down the street, and . . . it seemed like torches, and lanterns, and certainly things were already set on fire in the street before the awestruck diners had the sense to stand up and run to the back of the restaurant. It happened all at once and yet took an extraordinarily long time; there was no way to remember it right. All Louise knew was that, when she awoke from the scurry of action, she found herself against the wall with Helen and all of them, her napkin in one hand and her fork in the other. Like the net and triton of Neptune, she would later say to others. *I am a useless woman,* she told herself.

They spent the night at her agent's place on an inflatable bed. Peter slept on the living room couch. Outside, they could hear the low moan of the rioting streets as if a monster were being tamed. "It feels like intergalactic warfare," Helen whispered, kissing her lover.

"I've never felt so much like an old woman."

"Enough. You're five years younger than me."

"Do you know the Byron poem?"

"Get some sleep. We'll see how things are tomorrow. If they've suspended classes, we can drive out to Nathan's." This was Louise's son.

" 'I had a dream,' " Louise said quietly, " 'which was not all a dream. The bright sun was extinguish'd, and the stars . . .' Something. I can't remember."

"Hush now."

" 'I had a dream, which was not all a dream . . .' Oh, what is it?"

"Hush."

In the morning, things were no better, and so they left.

HOW DID THEY MEET, HELEN AND LOUISE?

They met twice before they fell in love. The first time was when they were very young, in their twenties, and they both taught at an all-girls school in Connecticut; they had the brief kind of passion trapped young women have, kisses in the back room of the library, then it was forgotten. The second time was many years later, when Louise was married to Harold Foster, the composer, and they saw each other at a fund-raiser for Helen's college; Helen wore a black spangled pantsuit and stared at the woman in the pink dress who, although clearly in the midst of an argument with a tall, sour-looking man, smiled merrily; Helen stared at this woman as if called upon to perform a feat of memorization, and at last Louise turned, startled, and met Helen's eyes for a breathless moment—it was almost, for Helen, as if she held something bright and fantastic in her palm, a thimble of mercury—until the president began to speak. When it was over, Helen discovered that her former colleague had been taken home by her husband because she had not been feeling well. Only the sour old man remained.

The third time was on the street in New York City and it was winter, the air as cold and tense as the skin of an apple; the leaves had already brightened and browned and fallen, so the trees that had shaded the avenues in summer were now invisible—and this is how Helen thought of herself as she walked down Second Avenue, the kind of woman who could not seem to hail a taxi, was always leaping out of the way of trucks, getting knocked aside by young people racing down the street; this is how she thought of herself: an invisible old thing in a brown plaid coat.

The light changed; a car leapt right for her, and she braced herself. And then there was Louise.

She did not see Helen at first. Louise was standing on the corner in a long white wool jacket, with embellished little buttons, holding a bouquet of out-of-season irises and trying to hail a cab. Short little Louise, her tiny hand dangling from that great coat sleeve, like a butler ringing a dinner bell in a too-loud room, so hopeless.

Helen said her name.

Louise did not hear her or, more likely, didn't consider that anyone on Second Avenue could be talking to her.

More loudly: "Louise. I found you."

She turned. Astounding how life is, how it will shift ever so slightly and reveal something in the fold of its garment that you hadn't noticed before, something there all along, how it will turn just like a person turns and show you a face you once had memorized amid the chatter of a tedious party, memorized as if for a test, and here it comes, years after you expected it: the test.

"Helen," she said. With no surprise at all. A pale, polished face with the craquelure of age, that haughty upturned nose, the brightly colored lips no longer full as a boarding-school teacher's, and all of her gone soft with a little fat, a trick photograph of the woman to whom Helen had made a promise so many years before. She would no longer have cared to meet that young woman, that foolish young woman who turned away from her in a snow-bright room, married an older man, and wore a pink dress to a formal party like a fool;

Helen was too old to care about a woman like that. But of course that woman no longer existed. Only this woman existed, Louise, here on the sidewalk with a bouquet of flowers and no surprise in her face at all: "Helen."

"Who are the flowers for?"

"For me." She laughed. "No good reason."

A month later she moved into Helen's apartment. They did not explain themselves to anyone; when friends asked, in private, how they had met and joined their lives so suddenly, each acted as if it were something that had been decided long before.

And in these memories, of course, they would always later place one more object in the scene. Ridiculous to have thought of then; almost like remembering that your lungs filled and emptied themselves of air each moment, or that your heart dutifully pumped its ration of blood. Glowing dimly in every memory: the sun.

WHEN THEY LEFT, WHAT DID THEY LEAVE BEHIND?

Helen left her knitting, her records, her running shoes, her files, her research, her plants (already dying), her stones and shells picked up for no reason on foreign beaches and kept, lovingly, purposelessly, and every glittering necklace and earring and bauble anyone had ever given her. She could easily have taken these things, but the mood was rush-rush, and she was the kind of woman who prided herself on efficiency, fortitude, decisiveness; so many small, easily taken things were left behind in the too-proud spirit of the refugee.

If you asked Louise, years later, what she had left, she could have only stared at you angrily and said: "My books."

And the neat shoe boxes untidily crammed with photographs. And the nubbly, Ovaltine-colored couch that they had bought together before Louise had her teaching position and always meant to replace. And the jam in the fridge that a friend had made that summer: strawberry jam. And Louise's old wedding ring. And the art on the walls, made by friends in unfashionable artistic circles. And the mouse under the dishwasher. And the boy upstairs who had finally, loudly mastered "The Entertainer" on the piano. And the early morning shadow of the window falling across the bed, a neat cross with one broken pane, the first vision of every day, which they could have inked from memory on the coverlet. But of course shadows were already a thing of the past.

WHO DROVE?

Louise drove; it was her car, bought for a teaching stint at Yale that was accepted with fantasies of autumn drives during which she would make long speeches to her enemies, her parents, to people from her past who hadn't loved her; but the drives had been crowded and rainy; the stint lasted only a year; and the money, in the end, just barely paid for the car itself. It was German and plum yellow and she loved it.

They left early in the morning, not that it would have made a difference. That same shade of dim red at all hours, like a flashlight held inside a mouth. Stepping out of their apartment house into the gloom: every time, it was like a deep-sea dive.

"Where are we going?" Helen said at the first wrong turn.

"I talked to Peter while you were in the shower. He's in a state. He's all alone."

"He's across town, Louise, it's going to take—"

"Hel, I said we'd take him. I'm sorry."

"Phone him now and say no. We can't. Phone him now and say no."

They both knew this was nonsense; cellular service had stopped nearly a week before. Besides, they did not even own a cell phone.

It was an hour of traffic and police barricades until they reached Peter's building; his street itself had been a horror show of streetlights blinking in and out of sleep, shadowy crowds of young men smoking outside early-open bars—nightmare creatures to the no-longer-young—and, in the shifting spotlights of the lamps, things that looked like baseballs rolling along the pavement, which were simply rats with no daylight to fear.

It was all too much for Louise. She sat there with her face bruised by the dashboard light and said she couldn't get out of the car; Helen had to do it.

Helen said, "You goddamned old woman. You brought me here and now I've—"

"Oh Helen."

And of course she did; of course Helen kissed her dear Louise on the cheek and slammed the door and went inside; but Helen planned to remember this, to save it in her catalog of hurt.

It was only five minutes before she came down with Peter, who had not finished his packing. He insisted on bringing books, twenty of them, because he said the three of them were basically anchorites locking themselves in a holy room, taking vows, sealing the entrance, and they needed their bibles; and that took longer than Helen would have hoped. Still, it was only five minutes, yet so much was different. They could barely see Louise for all the broken glass.

WHAT HAD HAPPENED?

She wouldn't say. "Let's go!" she kept shouting, motioning them inside, huddled now in the passenger seat, unharmed except for a small cut below her eye and a wild look. It was her window that was broken. "Go! Let's go!" Helen tried to touch her, tried to coax a story from her, some version to explain the glass, pieces of which still clung to her like ice, the animal flush in her face, but Lousie would not answer. The lamplight shone in streaks through her thinning white hair, on her lips open in an unnamed fury, and it glowed in the bones of her face; she was like a painting, Helen thought later, a great beauty in a painting who will never tell, who will never reveal a thing. A brooch and a ring and a stark madness in her eye. Helen had loved this vain, private, exasperating creature for so long. They were wives, in their way. "Go!" Louise shrieked, "Go!"

So they went.

WHERE DID THEY GO?

Deep into Pennsylvania. It's impossible to describe how long it took to leave Manhattan, the eccentric streetlights, the stifled, bottled-up feeling of the traffic, the complete blackout of the Holland Tunnel as if their headlights were drilling (in slowest possible motion) into the diamond-hard center of the Earth—and Helen's eye was ever on the fuel gauge, a neon miniature pump, because it had already come over the radio that gasoline was to be rationed, along with firewood and vegetables, beginning the next day. And so that explained the crowds, the panic. Peter, smoking out the broken window, picking a piece of tobacco from his upper lip, said: "Oh it must be madness at the farmers' market." And on they went, mile after dark mile.

Three hours later they stopped at the brightest-lit restaurant they could find and ordered a gravy-soaked lunch, suffering the suspicious glances of a downy-mustached waitress who clicked her retractable pen like a switchblade. In the corner sat a silent family, dressed for church, and their teenage daughter (in flour-sack floral) with her eyes closed, wincing, as if recent events had happened just to ensure her personal humiliation.

Peter said, "You know what Gertrude Stein did?"

"What?" said Helen, dipping her fries into an impasto of ketchup. It was a relief not to care, not to pretend to care, about good food. Louise, on the other hand, looked childishly shocked at her sandwich.

Peter: "What she did in a time of disaster."

"I'm not sure I'd take Gertrude Stein's advice on disasters—"

"They lived in France when the Germans came in," he said, smiling at the waitress, who had brought his milk shake in a sundae glass, the leftover in a canister, in the old-fashioned pretense that she had made too much and was giving him the rest. The canister wore a shimmering chain mail of frost. "They would listen to the radio," Peter said, "and every Tuesday the announcer came on telling of some new city that had been taken, and it was horrible; she said it was so horrible that they laughed. Every Tuesday, it became comic. And what she did when the Germans did arrive, when she saw the planes, when the French boys all hid in the hills because they feared being taken into the German army and people left bread and cheese for them in secret places—when it was over, and they were occupied— what Gertrude Stein did was, she trimmed her hedges."

Helen noticed Louise eating just the bacon from her sandwich. "Metaphorically?"

"No, it wasn't poetic, it wasn't metaphor. She was done with metaphor," he said. "And with news. She wouldn't listen to the wireless. I think it was . . . the truth was a gorgon, and she could see it only reflected in others' faces, in Alice's, or in the girls' from the village who gave her illegal butter; but if she looked directly at it she would turn to stone. So she trimmed her hedges."

Helen looked away, to the teenage girl in the vinyl booth, who now seemed mortified almost to the point of sainthood.

"Then she was a coward," Helen said.

"We never hear what Alice did," Louise said softly.

Peter smiled and pulled on his beard. "She trimmed her hedges and she thought when she had finished trimming, then the Germans would leave."

Louise started to say something, but Peter opened his hands ecclesiastically: "She was very superstitious. She and Alice thought their car would take them to places it wanted them to go, places they belonged."

Helen's laughter rose in shining rings around them, and it was the carelessness of her voice—just as when she had laughed about the blind—that made the people stare. The gray-featured family, the anxious daughter, the waitress whose hair glowed from the light behind her. It was too wrong and strange, with the sky outside, and the world the way it was. It was a luxury. She might as well have brought out a diamond tiara and worn it just to spite them.

Louise entered loudly into the conversation: "I've been learning French."

Helen said, "You have?"

Peter said, "Their car had a flat tire and so that's why they didn't leave France."

Louise sat up very straight. Her eyes were on Peter, and with one hand she clipped and unclipped her Turkish earring (her ears had never been pierced). She said, "I've decided that when I learn to speak French, really speak it, then this will all be over."

Peter spoke to no one in particular: "Gertrude also had a prophecy book."

Helen said quietly, "I didn't know you were learning French."

The family in the corner folded in together, listening to their daughter, who had begun to whisper with one eyebrow cocked. She glanced only once at Helen, bitterly, cleverly, before joining back into her family.

And Louise, too, looked at Helen as if to say: *Yes. I have a stupid, secret belief, a magic belief. Yes. Aren't we vain, ridiculous creatures?*

TELL ME, WHAT HAPPENED TO LOUISE IN THE CAR, SURROUNDED BY BROKEN GLASS?

She never did say whether it was young men out with crowbars, or a stone thrown by rioters, though these explanations were very possible; perhaps she could not remember what happened, but Helen and Peter both wondered silently why the glass was outside the car and not inside.

DID THEY SPEND THE NIGHT IN THAT TOWN?

They could not imagine it—there was something hard and wary in the people's faces there, a look that Helen had seen only out west in desert towns—and the one motel sat uncomfortably far from the cluster of shops, two cars alone in its parking lot, its front office trembling with a purple glow that Peter identified as marijuana grow lamps. He also warned them that he was known to sleepwalk in strange places, ever since he was a boy. Any place would have been too strange, though, any motel or rooming house, with thin sheets and an amateur oil painting above the dresser, and brief-lived mayflies seeking the bathroom's incandescent sun, and the darkness poking in at every window like a burglar.

"I think," Louise offered once they were on the road again, with a plastic bag taped over the broken window, where it howled like a ghost, "I think we can make it to Nathan's."

Peter said, "I'm fine. I had too much coffee but I'm fine."

Louise said, "Maybe also we should—we should be careful."

"What do you mean?" Peter said.

She put up her hands to arrange her hair against the loud wind. "Maybe Helen and I shouldn't mention we're gay."

"Oh Louise," said Helen.

"You felt it. It's dangerous now, somehow. I don't know why. I don't know why just darkness would do that. But please."

"We'll get to Nathan's," Helen said. "We'll get to Nathan's in Pennsylvania and everything will be OK."

And no sooner had they crossed the state line, rounded a bend, than they came upon the incredible: a bright patch of day.

"Oh God!" Peter said. "Oh God!"

But not day—it had only the brightness, the clear ordinary delight of day, shifting and waving in the wind like a sheet pinned to a clothesline. What it was: it was a whole forest set on fire.

The cars moved in a sluggish row past this awesome thing, while helicopters busied themselves in the flames like bees in their flowers, and fire trucks sprayed long, gleaming fountains that turned, instantly, to smoke and to steam. Everything was bright and hot at last, and in some terrible way they were grateful; it was hard not to applaud whoever had done this. Peter was driving now, so slowly that he said, "Get out, you two, get out and look at it and I'll pick you up around the corner," and they did. They stood there with dozens of other people with their hands up in the air as if they were all ready to catch something, looking behind themselves and laughing at their shadows, which were back briefly from the dead and could wave at them; then the people looked at last on what their eyes could hardly bear to see: what Helen, smiling (while Louise groaned), called "the prodigal sun." It took a minute or two to make out, in that sublime light, hidden among the crackling pines, the cross-paned windows of a house.

YOU NEVER TOLD LOUISE'S VERSION OF THEIR MEETING.

If everything were saved from life, nothing forgotten, then she would have with her still the scent of Helen's hair in 1968, when they were both in their twenties and teaching at St. Margaret's—Helen history, Louise the language arts—standing very still in the back room of the library (lit only by one window and its fluorescent snow-glow) as Louise announced her engagement to Harold Foster. They were leaving for Harvard. The blonde scent of Helen's hair as they embraced. And of the room's airborne dust immobile in its web of static, and the odor of ancient, unread books and moldering maps of places that none of their students would ever visit and whose citizens would one day, not understanding why, awaken to a sunless sky. The watch in Helen's breast pocket, pressing like a tumor between them. The shiver of passion in that nubile body—gone, all of it, gone or misremembered now. But how could even an old woman forget what Helen whispered to her in that time when they were very young? What she hushed into her ear before she walked out the door—that she would find her one day—and Louise was left alone in that unused room, looking out at the snow's mounded brightness with the sensation of someone going blind.

And at the party: the feeling of someone tapping on her shoulder, and then a furious woman staring at her from across a room; it made her ill, and she had to feign a migraine to get her husband to leave.

And on the street after his death: windblown leaves scratching along the sidewalk, the wet scent of the flowers, the traffic light staring cyclops red, and, from behind her, a voice: "I found you."

DID THEY STAY AT THE FIRE?

They had to get to Nathan's, though it was hard to pull themselves away, even after they saw the burning house among all the burning trees. "Well aren't we all mayflies?" Helen whispered, giggling. Back in the car, they described the fire to Peter, what it felt like to walk a little ways down the hill to where the grass was dry and crackly, to have the hot wind on your face like a day at the beach—"God I always hated the beach," Helen added—and he nodded and they drove like that, in silence, for a long time until even looking back they could not make out the blaze except as a shimmer in the clouds, and ahead of them were blank unburned forests and the fistfuls of light they knew to be houses.

" 'I had a dream,' " Louise said softly after a while, " 'which was not all a dream.' "

Peter made a pleased noise in the front seat. Helen said nothing, only watched the black-on-black of the trees against the sky, and what she took for bats flying above, or perhaps birds, because they must wake up at last, mustn't they?

" 'The bright sun was extinguish'd, and the stars did wander darkling in the eternal space.' "

"I love that," Peter said. " 'Wander darkling.' "

Helen said, "Go on."

"Something . . . oh," Louise said. " 'Morn came and went—and came, and brought no day, and men forgot their passions in the dread of this their desolation; and all hearts were chill'd into a selfish prayer for light.' "

Helen said, " 'Men forgot their passions.' I don't see how that could be." There was not a single light on the road, nor anywhere in the landscape. Then they passed a darkened farmhouse and Helen thought she saw a woman in a white apron walking in a field of fallen corn; it seemed like everyone was a ghost now. But it was not a woman; it was a lung-shaped patch of melting snow on a hillside, and then it was gone.

Louise said, "I don't remember the rest. Maybe Nathan will have a copy."

Peter rolled down the window a bit, letting in the cold smell of trees. "I've been wondering, what will they do in New York when they're out of wood?"

"In the fireplaces, you mean?" asked Louise.

"I can't see men ever forgetting their passions," Helen said. "And I don't know what dread is anymore."

"When they're out of candles," Peter explained. From the back-seat, they could see just his eyes in the rearview mirror.

Helen told him: "They won't run out of candles. They don't run out of those things in New York."

"Eventually. They've run out of vegetables, haven't they? And gas."

She pulled her shawl around her. "I'm not worried about New York."

In that rectangle of mirror, they could see him blink in concern. "Do you think they'll set things on fire? Like the forest we saw?"

"I know what they'll do," Louise said quietly.

Helen took Louise's hand and shook her head, looking out at the shapes of things beyond the road, things unlit for days. "I'm not worried about that, New York can take care of itself. I'm not worried about dread, either. What did you say, honey?"

"I know what they'll do."

Louise took her hand away from Helen. She put it to her own cheek as if she had been struck by something. She looked into the hatchback where their things lay, piled and gathered, and Peter's things, and then the fingers of her other hand began to curl around the armrest in a fist. Her eyes went forward. A rare car, approaching from behind, lit up the interior and her hair went white.

Louise said, "They'll burn the books."

"Lo . . ."

Louise had a frozen look on her face. "Before they burn their furniture, they'll burn the books. Before the curtains or the sheets or their old letters. They always do."

She sat very regal in the backseat with the headlights illuminating her glacial hair, her furious jagged profile, her parted lips. The look was in her eyes again, a brightness that was not a reflection but its own light, the way the snow on the hillside was its own light, a lunacy, as if this old white-haired poetess were capable of something terrible, in which case we all are.

"They always do," Louise said loudly. "They'll take down the *Moby-Dick* they've had since high school, and they always hated how it sat on the shelf and gloated at them, and they'll throw it in the fireplace, there'll be a kind of . . . relief, satisfaction. They'll light it and put the kids around it and it won't matter." Her left hand gripped the armrest as tightly as a broomstick, but she would not look at either of them. "We are truly cannibals. *Don Quixote.* Or just a whole pile of them. *Huckleberry Finn.* Why not? If there's no light to read by anyway—"

"Lo, don't—"

Peter said, "You said that when you spoke French at last—"

She shook her head, talking almost in a shout. "I'm never going to learn it. I'm too old, and of course that's ridiculous. I'm ridiculous. These are the Dark Ages now, and it's going to come to that. All the books! And why not?"

"Louise!"

Louise was shrieking now: "The books! All the books!"

The car rushed by them and they were thrown into darkness again, that old darkness, and Peter could then hear only a movement

in the backseat; maybe a struggle of some kind, maybe someone crying, and then silence as his eyes strained to see the two old women in
the rearview mirror.

WHAT DID HE SEE?

A memory from his boyhood: Two objects in the darkness, fallen into
a quiet embrace. Just as he used to come upon his mother's hairbrush
at her vanity table, lying on its back, her silver comb nestled into its
bristles. A still life to which he often awoke after his sleepwalking
trips. An old woman and her lover, clutching one another, the sound
of one of them weeping, he could not say which, and nothing behind
them but a lightless window, a mirror, a reflection of his wide eyes
within it, a memory. A comb in a brush. If he watched them they
would wait. They would wait, the silver things, perfectly still until
dawn.

Junot Díaz

Wildwood

IT'S NEVER the changes we want that change everything.

This is how it all starts: with your mother calling you into the bathroom. You will remember what you were doing at that precise moment for the rest of your life: you were reading *Watership Down* and the bucks and their does were making the dash for the raft and you didn't want to stop reading, the book had to go back to your brother tomorrow, but then she called you again, louder, her I'm-not-fucking-around voice, and you mumbled irritably, Sí, señora.

She is standing in front of the medicine-cabinet mirror, naked from the waist up, her bra slung about her hips like a torn sail, the scar on her back as vast and inconsolable as the sea. You want to return to your book, to pretend you didn't hear her, but it is too late. Her eyes meet yours, the same big smoky eyes you will have in the future. Ven acá, she commands. She is frowning at something on one of her breasts.

Your mother's breasts are immensities. One of the wonders of the world. The only ones you've seen that are bigger are in nudie magazines or on really fat ladies. They're forty-two triple Ds and the aureoles are as big as saucers and black as pitch and at their edges are fierce hairs that sometimes she plucks and sometimes she doesn't. These breasts have always embarrassed you and when you walk in public with her you are conscious of them. After her face and her hair, her tetas are what she is most proud of. Your father could never get enough of them, she always brags. But given the fact that he ran off on her after their third year of marriage it seemed in the end that he could.

You dread conversations with your mother. These one-sided dressing-downs. You figure that she has called you in to give you another earful about your diet. Your mom's convinced that if you only eat more plátanos you will suddenly acquire her extraordinary train-wrecking secondary sex characteristics. Even at that age you are nothing if not your mother's daughter. You are twelve years old and already as tall as her, a long slender-necked ibis of a girl. You have her straight hair, which makes you look more Hindu than Dominican, and a behind that the boys haven't been able to stop talking about since the fifth grade and whose appeal you do not yet understand. You have her complexion, too, which means you are dark as night. But for all your similarities the tides of inheritance have yet to reach your chest. You have only the slightest hint of breasts: from most angles you're flat as a board and you're thinking she's going to order you to stop wearing bras again because they're suffocating your potential breasts, discouraging them from popping out. You're ready to argue with her to the death, because you're as possessive of your bras as you are of the pads you now buy yourself.

But no, she doesn't say a word about eating more plátanos. Instead, she takes your right hand and guides you. Your mom is rough in all things, but this time she is gentle. You did not think her capable of it.

Do you feel that? she asks in her too-familiar raspy voice.

At first all you feel is the density of the tissue and the heat of her, like a bread that never stopped rising. She kneads your fingers into her. You're as close as you've ever been and your breathing is what you hear.

Don't you feel that?

She turns toward you. Coño, muchacha, stop looking at me and feel.

So you close your eyes and your fingers are pushing down and you're thinking of Helen Keller and how when you were little you wanted to be her except more nunnish and then suddenly you do feel something. A knot just beneath her skin, tight and secretive as a plot. And at that moment, for reasons you will never quite understand, you are overcome by the feeling, the premonition, that something in your life is about to change. You become light-headed and you can feel a throbbing in your blood, a rhythm, a drum. Bright lights zoom through you like photon torpedoes, like comets. You don't know how or why you know this thing, but that you know it cannot be doubted. It is exhilarating. For as long as you've been alive you've had bruja ways; even your mother will not begrudge you that much. Hija de Liborio, she called you after you picked your tía's winning numbers for her and when you guessed correctly how old to the day she'd been when she left home for the US (a fact she'd never told anyone). You assumed Liborio was a relative. That was before Santo Domingo, before you knew about the Great Power of God.

I feel it, you say, too loudly. Lo siento.

And like that, everything changes. Before the winter is out the doctors remove that breast you were kneading and its partner, along with the auxiliary lymph nodes. Because of the operations, your mother will have trouble lifting her arms over her head for the rest of her life. Her hair begins to fall out and one day she pulls it all out herself and puts it in a plastic bag. You change, too. Not right away, but it happens. And it's in that bathroom that it all begins. That you begin.

A punk chick. That's what I became.

A Siouxsie and the Banshees–loving punk chick. The Puerto Rican kids on the block couldn't stop laughing when they saw my hair; they called me Blacula. And the morenos, they didn't know what to say; they just called me devil-bitch. Yo, devil-bitch, yo, *yo*! My tía Rubelka thought it was some kind of mental illness. Hija, she said while frying pastelitos, maybe you need *help*. But my mother was the worst. It's the last straw, she screamed. The. Last. Straw. But it always was with her. Mornings when I came downstairs she'd be in the kitchen making her coffee in la greca and listening to Radio WADO and when she saw me and my hair she'd get mad all over again, as if during the night she'd forgotten who I was.

My mother was one of the tallest women in Paterson and her anger was just as tall. It pincered you in its long arms, and if you showed any weakness you were finished. Que muchacha tan fea, she said in disgust, splashing the rest of her coffee in the sink. Fea had become my name. It was nothing new, to tell the truth. She'd been saying stuff like that all our lives. My mother would never win any awards, believe me. You could call her an absentee parent: if she wasn't at work she was sleeping and when she wasn't sleeping all she did was scream and hit. As kids, me and Oscar were more scared of our mother than we were of the dark or el cuco. She would hit us anywhere, in front of anyone, always free with the chanclas and the correa, but now with her cancer there wasn't much she could do anymore. The last time she tried to whale on me it was because of my hair, but instead of cringing or running I punched her hand. It was a reflex more than anything, but once it happened I knew I couldn't take it back, not ever, and so I just kept my fist clenched, waiting for whatever came next, for her to attack me with her teeth like she had this one lady in the Pathmark. But she just stood there shaking, in her stupid wig and her stupid bata, with two huge foam prostheses in her bra, the smell of burning wig all around us. I almost felt sorry for her. This is how you treat your mother? she cried. And if I could I would have broken the entire length of my life across her face, but instead I screamed back, And this is how you treat your daughter?

Things had been bad between us all year. How could they not have been? She was my Old World Dominican mother who had come alone to the United States and I was her only daughter, the one she had raised up herself with the help of nobody, which meant it was her duty to keep me crushed under her heel. I was fourteen and desperate for my own patch of world that had nothing to do with her. I wanted the life that I used to see when I watched *Big Blue Marble* as a kid, the life that drove me to make pen pals and to borrow atlases from school. The life that existed beyond Paterson, beyond my family, beyond Spanish. And as soon as she became sick I saw my chance and I'm not going to pretend or apologize; I saw my chance and eventually I took it.

If you didn't grow up like I did then you don't know and if you don't know it's probably better you don't judge. You don't know the hold our mothers have on us, even the ones that are never around— *especially* the ones that are never around. What it's like to be the perfect Dominican daughter, which is just a nice way of saying a perfect Dominican slave. You don't know what it's like to grow up with a mother who never said anything that wasn't negative, who was always suspicious, always tearing you down and splitting your dreams straight down the seams. On TV and in books mothers talk to daughters, about life, about themselves, but on Main Street in Paterson mothers say not a word unless it's to hurt you. When my first pen pal, Tomoko, stopped writing me after three letters my mother was the one who said, You think someone's going to lose life writing to you? Of course I cried; I was eight and I had already planned that Tomoko and her family would adopt me. My mother, of course, saw clean into the marrow of those dreams and laughed. I wouldn't write to you, either, she said.

She was that kind of mother: who makes you doubt yourself, who would wipe you out if you let her. But I'm not going to pretend, either. For a long time I let her say what she wanted about me and, what was worse, for a long time I believed her. I was a fea, I was a worthless, I was an idiota. From ages two to thirteen I believed her and because I believed her I was the perfect hija. I was the one cooking, cleaning, doing the wash, buying groceries, writing letters to the bank to explain why a house payment was going to be late, translating. I had the best grades in my class. I never caused trouble, even when the morenas used to come after me with scissors because of my straight straight hair. I stayed at home and made sure my little brother Oscar was fed and everything ran right while she was at work. I raised him and I raised me. I was the one. You're my hija, she said, that's what you're supposed to be doing. When that thing happened to me when I was eight and I finally told her what our neighbor had done she told me to shut my mouth and stop crying and I did exactly that, I shut my mouth and clenched my legs and my mind and within a year I couldn't have told you what he looked like or even his name. All you do is complain, she said to me, but you have no idea what life really is. Sí, señora.

When she told me that I could go on my sixth-grade sleepaway to Bear Mountain and I bought a backpack with my own paper-route money and wrote Bobby Santos notes because he was promising to break into my cabin and kiss me in front of everyone I believed her and when on the morning of the trip she announced that I wasn't going and I said, But you promised, and she said, Muchacha del diablo, I promised you nothing, I didn't throw my backpack at her or pull out my hair, and when it was Laura Sáenz who ended up kissing Bobby Santos, not me, I didn't say anything, either. I just lay in my room with stupid Bear-Bear and sang under my breath, imagining where I would run away to when I grew up. To Japan maybe, where I would track down Tomoko, or to Austria, where my singing would inspire a remake of *The Sound of Music.*

All my favorite books from that period were about runaways—*Watership Down, The Incredible Journey, My Side of the Mountain*—and when Bon Jovi's "Runaway" came out I imagined it was me they were singing about. No one had any idea. I was the tallest, dorkiest girl in school, the one who dressed up as Wonder Woman every Halloween, the one who never said a word. People saw me in my glasses and my hand-me-down clothes and could not have imagined what I was capable of. And then when I was twelve I got that feeling, the scary witchy one, and before I knew it my mother was sick and the wildness that had been in me all along, that I had tried to tamp down with chores and with homework and with promises that once I reached college I would be able to do whatever I pleased, burst out. I couldn't help it. I tried to keep it down, but it just flooded through all my quiet spaces. It was a message more than a feeling, a message that tolled like a bell: Change, change, change.

It didn't happen overnight. Yes the wildness was in me, yes it kept my heart beating fast all the long day, yes it danced around me while I walked down the street, yes it let me look boys straight in the face when they stared at me, yes it turned my laugh from a cough into a wild fever, but I was still scared. How could I not be? I was my mother's daughter. Her hold on me was stronger than love. And then one day I was walking home with Karen Cepeda, who at that time was my friend. Karen did the goth thing really well; she had spiky Robert Smith hair and wore all black and had the skin color of a ghost. Walking with her in Paterson was like walking with the bearded lady. Everybody would stare and it was the scariest thing and that was, I guess, why I did it.

We were walking down Main and being glared at by everybody and out of nowhere I said, Karen, I want you to cut my hair. As soon as I said it I knew. The feeling in my blood, the rattle, came over me again. Karen raised her eyebrow: What about your mother? You see, it wasn't just me—everybody was scared of Belicia de León.

Fuck her, I said.

Karen looked at me like I was being stupid—I never cursed, but that was something else that was about to change. The next day we locked ourselves in her bathroom while downstairs her father and uncles were bellowing at some soccer game. Well, how do you want it? she asked. I looked at the girl in the mirror for a long time. All I knew was that I didn't want to see her ever again. I put the clippers in Karen's hand, turned them on, and guided her hand until it was all gone.

So now you're punk? Karen asked uncertainly.

Yes, I said.

The next day my mother threw the wig at me. You're going to wear this. You're going to wear it every day. And if I see you without it on I'm going to kill you!

I didn't say a word. I held the wig over the burner.

Don't do it, she said as the burner clicked. Don't you dare—

It went up in a flash, like gasoline, like a stupid hope, and if I hadn't thrown it in the sink it would have taken my hand. The smell was horrible, like all the chemicals from all the factories in Elizabeth.

That was when she slapped at me, when I struck her hand and she snatched it back, like I was the fire.

Of course everyone thought I was the worst daughter ever. My tía and our neighbors kept saying, Hija, she's your mother, she's dying, but I wouldn't listen. When I hit her hand, a door opened. And I wasn't about to turn my back on it.

But God how we fought! Sick or not, dying or not, my mother wasn't going to go down easy. She wasn't una pendeja. I'd seen her slap grown men, push white police officers onto their asses, curse a whole group of bochincheras. She had raised me and my brother by herself, she had worked three jobs until she could buy this house we lived in, she had survived being abandoned by my father, she had come from Santo Domingo all by herself, and as a young girl she'd been beaten, set on fire, left for dead. (This last part she didn't tell me, my tía Rubelka did, in a whisper, Your mother almost died, she almost died, and when I asked my mother about it at dinner she took my dinner and gave it to my brother.) That was my mother and there was no way she was going to let me go without killing me first. Figurín de mierda, she called me. You think you're someone, but you ain't nada.

She dug hard, looking for my seams, wanting me to tear like always, but I didn't, I wasn't going to. It was that feeling I had that my life was waiting for me on the other side that made me fearless. When she threw away my Smiths and Sisters of Mercy posters—aquí yo no quiero maricones—I bought replacements. When she threatened to rip up my new clothes I started keeping them in my locker and at Karen's house. When she told me that I had to quit my job at the Greek diner I explained to my boss that my mother was starting to lose it because of her chemo, and when she called to say I couldn't work there anymore he just handed me the phone and stared out at his customers in embarrassment. When she changed the locks on me—I had started staying out late, going to the Limelight because even though I was fourteen I looked twenty-five—I would knock on Oscar's window and he would let me in, scared because the next day my mother would run around the house screaming, Who the hell let that hija de la gran puta in the house? Who? Who? And Oscar would be at the breakfast table stammering, I don't know, Mami, I don't.

Her rage filled the house, like flat stale smoke. It got into everything, into our hair and our food, like the fallout they told us about in school that would one day drift down soft as snow. My brother didn't know what to do. He stayed in his room, though sometimes he would lamely try to ask me what was going on. Nothing. You can tell me, Lola, he said, and I could only laugh. You need to lose weight, I told him.

In those final weeks I knew better than to go near my mother. Most of the time she just looked at me with the stink eye, but sometimes without warning she would grab me by my throat and hang on until I pried her fingers off. She didn't bother talking to me unless it was to make death threats: When you grow up you'll meet me in a dark alley when you least expect it and then I'll kill you and nobody will know I did it! Gloating as she said this.

You're crazy, I told her.

You don't call me crazy, she said, and then she sat down panting.

It was bad, but no one expected what came next. So obvious when you think about it.

All my life I'd been swearing that one day I would just disappear. And one day I did.

·   ·   ·

I ran off, dique, because of a boy.

What can I really tell you about him? He was like all boys: beautiful and callow and, like an insect, he couldn't sit still. Un blanquito with long hairy legs who I met one night at the Limelight.

His name was Aldo.

He was nineteen and lived down at the Jersey Shore with his seventy-four-year-old father. In the back of his Oldsmobile on University I pulled my leather skirt up and my fishnet stockings down and the smell of me was everywhere. I didn't let him go all the way, but still. The spring of my sophomore year we wrote and called each other at least once a day. I even drove down with Karen to visit him in Wildwood (she had a license, I didn't). He lived and worked near the boardwalk, one of three guys who operated the bumper cars, the only one without tattoos. You should stay, he told me that night while Karen walked ahead of us on the beach. Where would I live? I asked, and he smiled. With me. Don't lie, I said, but he looked out at the surf. I want you to come, he said seriously.

He asked me three times. I counted, I know.

That summer my brother announced that he was going to dedicate his life to designing role-playing games, and my mother was trying to keep a second job for the first time since her operation. It wasn't working out. She was coming home exhausted, and since I wasn't helping, nothing around the house was getting done. Some weekends my tía Rubelka would help out with the cooking and cleaning and would lecture us both, but she had her own family to look after, so most of the time we were on our own. Come, he said on the phone. And then in August Karen left for Slippery Rock. She had graduated from high school a year early. If I don't see Paterson again it will be too soon, she said before she left. Five days later, school started. I cut class six times in the first two weeks. I just couldn't do school anymore. Something inside wouldn't let me. It didn't help that I was reading *The Fountainhead* and had decided that I was Dominique and Aldo was Roark. And finally what we'd all been waiting for happened. My mother announced at dinner, quietly, I want you both to listen to me: the doctor is running more tests on me.

Oscar looked like he was going to cry. He put his head down. And my reaction? I looked at her and said, Could you please pass the salt?

These days I don't blame her for smacking me across my face, but right then it was all I needed. We jumped on each other and the table fell and the sancocho spilled all over the floor and Oscar just stood in the corner bellowing, Stop it, stop it, stop it!

Hija de tu maldita madre! she shrieked. And I said, This time I hope you die from it.

For a couple of days the house was a war zone, and then on Friday she let me out of my room and I was allowed to sit next to her on the sofa and watch novelas with her. She was waiting for her blood work to come back, but you would never have known her life was in the balance. She watched the TV like it was the only thing that mattered, and whenever one of the characters did something underhanded she would start waving her arms: Someone has to stop her! Can't they see what that puta is up to?

I hate you, I said very quietly, but she didn't hear.

Go get me some water, she said. Put an ice cube in it.

That was the last thing I did for her. The next morning I was on the bus bound for the shore. One bag, two hundred dollars in tips, Tío Rudolfo's old knife, and the only picture my mother had of my father, which she had hidden under her bed (she was in the picture, too, but I pretended not to notice). I was so scared. I couldn't stop shaking. The whole ride down I was expecting the sky to split open and my mother to reach down and shake me. But it didn't happen. Nobody but the man across the aisle noticed me. You're really beautiful, he said. Like a girl I once knew.

I didn't write them a note. That's how much I hated them. Her.

That night while Aldo and I lay in his sweltering kitty-litter-infested room I told him: I want you to do it to me.

He started unbuttoning my pants. Are you sure?

Definitely, I said grimly.

He had a long thin dick that hurt like hell, but the whole time I just said, Oh yes, Aldo, yes, because that was what I imagined you were supposed to say while you were losing your virginity to some boy you thought you loved.

It was like the stupidest thing I ever did. I was miserable. And so bored. But of course I wouldn't admit it. I had run away, so I was happy! Happy!

Aldo had neglected to mention, all those times he asked me to live with him, that his father hated him like I hated my mother. Aldo, Sr., had been in the Second World War and he'd never forgiven the "Japs" for all the friends he had lost. My dad's so full of shit, Aldo said. He never left Fort Dix. I don't think his father said nine words to me the whole time I lived with them. He was one mean viejito and even had a padlock on the refrigerator. Stay the hell out of it, he told me. We couldn't even get ice cubes out.

Aldo and his dad lived in one of the cheapest little bungalows on New Jersey Avenue, and me and Aldo slept in a room where his father kept the litter box for his two cats, and at night we would move it out into the hallway, but he always woke up before us and put it back in the room: I told you to leave my crap alone! Which is funny when you think about it. But it wasn't funny then. I got a job selling French fries on the boardwalk and between the hot oil and the cat piss I couldn't smell anything else. On my days off I would drink with Aldo or I would sit in the sand dressed in all black and try to write in my journal, which I was sure would form the foundation for a utopian society after we blew ourselves into radioactive kibble. Sometimes boys would walk up to me and throw lines at me like, Who fuckin' died? They would sit down next to me in the sand. You a good-looking girl, you should be in a bikini. Why, so you can rape me? Jesus Christ, one of them said, jumping to his feet. What the hell is wrong with you?

To this day I don't know how I lasted. At the beginning of October I was laid off from the French-fry palace; by then most of the boardwalk was closed up and I had nothing to do except hang out at the public library, which was even smaller than my high-school one. Aldo had moved on to working with his dad at his garage, which only made them more pissed off at each other and by extension more pissed off at me. When they got home they would drink Schlitz and complain about the Phillies. I guess I should count myself lucky that they didn't decide to bury the hatchet by gangbanging me. I stayed out as much as I could and waited for the feeling to come back to me, to tell me what I should do next, but I was bone dry, bereft, no visions whatsoever. I started to think that maybe it was like in the books: as soon as I lost my virginity I lost my power. I got really mad at Aldo after that. You're a drunk, I told him. And an idiot. So what, he shot back. Your pussy smells. Then stay out of it! I will!

But of course I was happy! Happy! I kept waiting to run into my family posting flyers of me on the boardwalk—my mom, the tallest blackest chestiest thing in sight, Oscar looking like the Brown Blob, my tía Rubelka, maybe even my tío if they could get him off the heroin long enough—but the closest I came to any of that was some flyers someone had put up for a lost cat. That's white people for you. They lose a cat and it's an all-points bulletin, but we Dominicans lose a daughter and we might not even cancel our appointment at the salon.

By November I was so finished. I would sit there with Aldo and his putrid father and the old shows would come on the TV, the ones me and my brother used to watch when we were kids, *Three's Company, What's Happening!!, The Jeffersons,* and my disappointment would grind against some organ that was very soft and tender. It was starting to get cold, too, and wind just walked right into the bungalow and got under your blankets or jumped in the shower with you. It was awful. I kept having these stupid visions of my brother trying to cook for himself. Don't ask me why. I was the one who cooked for us. The only thing Oscar knew how to make was grilled cheese. I imagined him thin as a reed, wandering around the kitchen, opening cabinets forlornly. I even started dreaming about my mother, except in my dreams she was young, my age, and it was because of those dreams that I realized something obvious: she had run away, too, and that was why we were all in the United States.

I put away the photo of her and my father, but the dreams didn't stop. I guess when a person is with you they're only with you when they're with you, but when they're gone, when they're really gone, they're with you forever.

And then at the end of November Aldo, my wonderful boyfriend, decided to be cute. I knew he was getting unhappy with us, but I didn't know exactly how bad it was until one night he had his friends over. His father had gone to Atlantic City and they were all drinking and smoking and telling dumb jokes and suddenly Aldo says, Do you know what Pontiac stands for? Poor Old Nigger Thinks It's A Cadillac. Who was he looking at when he told his punch line? He was looking straight at me.

That night he wanted me but I pushed his hand away. Don't touch me.

Don't get sore, he said, putting my hand on his cock. It wasn't nothing.

And then he laughed.

So what did I do a couple days later—a really dumb thing. I called home. The first time no one answered. The second time it was Oscar. The de León residence, how may I direct your call? That was my brother for you. This is why everybody in the world hated his guts.

It's me, dumb-ass.

Lola. He was so quiet and then I realized he was crying. Where *are* you?

You don't want to know. I switched ears, trying to keep my voice casual. How is everybody?

Lola, Mami's going to *kill* you.

Dumb-ass, could you keep your voice down. Mami isn't home, is she?

She's working.

What a surprise, I said. Mami working. On the last minute of the last hour of the last day my mother would be at work She would be at work when the missiles were in the air.

I guess I must have missed him real bad or I just wanted to see somebody who knew anything about me, or the cat piss had damaged my common sense, because I gave him the address of a coffee shop on the boardwalk and told him to bring my clothes and some of my books.

Bring me money, too.

He paused. I don't know where Mami keeps it.

You know, mister. Just bring it.

How much? he asked timidly.

All of it.

That's a lot of money, Lola.

Just bring me the money, Oscar.

OK, OK. He inhaled deeply. Will you at least tell me if you're OK or not?

I'm OK, I said, and that was the only point in the conversation where I almost cried. I kept quiet until I could speak again and then I asked him how he was going to get down here without our mother finding out.

You know me, he said weakly. I might be a dork, but I'm a resourceful dork.

I should have known not to trust anybody whose favorite books as a child were Encyclopedia Brown. But I wasn't really thinking; I was so looking forward to seeing him.

By then I had this plan. I was going to convince my brother to run away with me. My plan was that we would go to Dublin. I had met a bunch of Irish guys on the boardwalk and they had sold me on their country. I would become a backup singer for U2 and both Bono and the drummer would fall in love with me, and Oscar could become the Dominican James Joyce. I really believed it would happen, too. That's how deluded I was by then.

The next day I walked into the coffee shop, looking brand-new, and he was there, with the bag. Oscar, I said, laughing. You're so fat!

I know, he said, ashamed. I was worried about you.

We embraced for like an hour and then he started crying. Lola, I'm sorry.

It's OK, I said, and that's when I looked up and saw my mother and my tía Rubelka and my tío Rudolfo boiling out of the kitchen. Oscar! I screamed, but it was too late. My mother already had me in her hands. She looked so thin and worn, almost like a hag, but she was holding on to me like I was her last nickel, and underneath her red wig her green eyes were *furious*. I noticed, absently, that she had dressed up for the occasion. That was typical. Muchacha del diablo, she shrieked. I managed to haul her out of the coffee shop and when she pulled back her hand to smack me I broke free. I ran for it. Behind me I could feel her sprawling, hitting the curb hard with a crack, but I wasn't looking back. No—I was running. In elementary school, whenever we had field day I was always the fastest girl in my grade, took home all the ribbons; they said it wasn't fair, because I was so big, but I didn't care. I could even have beaten the boys if I'd wanted to, so there was no way my sick mother, my messed-up tíos, and my fat brother were going to catch me. I was going to run as fast as my long legs could carry me. I was going to run down the boardwalk, past Aldo's miserable house, out of Wildwood, out of New Jersey, and I wasn't going to stop. I was going to *fly*.

Anyway, that's how it *should* have worked out. But I looked back. I couldn't help it. It's not like I didn't know my Bible, all the pillars-of-salt stuff, but when you're someone's daughter that she raised by herself with no help from nobody habits die hard. I just wanted to make sure my mom hadn't broken her arm or smashed open her skull. I mean, really, who the hell wants to kill her own mother by accident? That's the only reason I glanced back. She was sprawled on the ground, her wig had fallen out of reach, her poor bald head out in the day like something private and shameful, and she was bawling like a lost calf, Hija, hija! And there I was wanting to run off into my future. It was right then that I needed that feeling to guide me, but it wasn't anywhere in sight. Only me. In the end I didn't have the ovaries. She was on the ground, bald as a baby, crying, probably a month away from dying, and here I was, her one and only daughter. And there was nothing I could do about it. So I walked back and when I reached down to help her she clamped on to me with both hands. That was when I realized she hadn't been crying at all. She'd been faking! Her smile was like a lion's.

Ya te tengo, she said, jumping triumphantly to her feet. Te tengo.

And that is how I ended up in Santo Domingo. I guess my mother thought it would be harder for me to run away from an island where I knew no one, and in a way she was right. I'm into my sixth month here and these days I'm just trying to be philosophical about the whole thing. I wasn't like that at first, but in the end I had to let it go. It was like the fight between the egg and the rock, my abuela said. No winning.

I'm actually going to school, not that it's going to count when I return to Paterson, but it keeps me busy and out of trouble and around people my own age. You don't need to be around us viejos all day, Abuela says. I have mixed feelings about the school. For one thing, it's improved my Spanish a lot. It's a private school, a Carol Morgan wanna-be filled with people my tío Carlos Moya calls los hijos de mami y papi. And then there's me. If you think it was tough being a goth in Paterson, try being a Dominican york in one of those private schools back in DR. You will never meet bitchier girls in your whole life. They whisper about me to death. Someone else would have had a nervous breakdown, but after Wildwood I'm not so brittle. I don't let it get to me.

And the irony of all ironies? I'm on our school's track team. I joined because my friend Rosio, the scholarship girl from Los Mina, told me I could win a spot on the team on the length of my legs alone. Those are the pins of a winner, she prophesied. Well, she must have known something I didn't, because I'm now our school's top runner in the four hundred meters and under. That I have talent at this simple thing never ceases to amaze me. Karen would pass out if she could see me running sprints out behind my school while Coach Cortés screams at us, first in Spanish and then in Catalán. Breathe, breathe, *breathe*! I've got like no fat left on me and the musculature of my legs impresses everyone, even me. I can't wear shorts anymore without causing traffic jams, and the other day when my abuela accidentally locked us out of the house she turned to me in frustration and said, Hija, just kick the door open. That pushed a laugh out of both of us.

So much has changed these last months, in my head, my heart. Rosio has me dressing up like a real Dominican girl. She's the one who fixes my hair and helps me with my makeup, and sometimes when I see myself in mirrors I don't even know who I am anymore. Not that I'm unhappy or anything. Even if I found a hot-air balloon that would whisk me straight to U2's house I'm not sure I would take it. (I'm still not talking to my traitor brother, though.) The truth is I'm even thinking of staying one more year. Abuela doesn't want me ever to leave—I'll miss you, she says so simply it can't be anything but true—and my mom has told me I can stay if I want to but that I would be welcome at home, too. Tía Rubelka tells me she's hanging tough, my mother, that she's back to two jobs. They sent me a picture of the whole family and Abuela framed it and I can't look at it without misting up. My mother's not wearing her fakies in it; she looks so thin I don't even recognize her.

Just know that I would die for you, she told me the last time we talked. And before I could say anything she hung up.

But that's not what I wanted to tell you. It's about that crazy feeling that started this whole mess, the bruja feeling that comes singing out of my bones, that takes hold of me the way blood seizes cotton. The feeling that tells me that everything in my life is about to change. It's come back. Just the other day I woke up from all these dreams and it was there, pulsing inside of me. I imagine this is what it feels like to have a child in you. At first I was scared, because I thought it was telling me to run away again, but every time I looked around our house, every time I saw my abuela the feeling got stronger, so I knew this was something different.

I was dating a boy by then, a sweet morenito by the name of Max Sánchez, who I had met in Los Mina while visiting Rosio. He's short, but his smile and his snappy dressing make up for a lot. Because I'm from Nueba Yol he talks about how rich he's going to become and I try to explain to him that I don't care about that, but he looks at me like I'm crazy. I'm going to get a white Mercedes-Benz, he says. Tú verás. But it's the job he has that I love best, that got me and him started. In Santo Domingo two or three theaters often share the same set of reels for a movie, so when the first theater finishes with the first reel they put it in Max's hands and he rides his motorcycle like crazy to make it to the second theater and then he drives back, waits, picks up the second reel, and so on. If he's held up or gets into an accident the first reel will end and there will be no second reel and the people in the audience will throw bottles. So far he's been blessed, he tells me while kissing his San Miguel medal. Because of me, he brags, one movie becomes three. I'm the man who puts together the pictures. Max is not from la clase alta, as my abuela would describe it, and if any of the stuck-up bitches in school saw us they would just about die, but I'm fond of him. He holds open doors, he calls me his morena; when he's feeling brave he touches my arm gently and then pulls back.

Anyway I thought maybe the feeling was about Max, and so one day I let him take me to one of the love motels. He was so excited he almost fell off the bed, and the first thing he wanted was to look at my ass. I never knew my big ass could be such a star attraction, but he kissed it, four, five times, gave me goose bumps with his breath, and pronounced it a tesoro. When we were done and he was in the bathroom washing himself I stood in front of the mirror naked and looked at my culo for the first time. A tesoro, I repeated. A treasure.

Well? Rosio asked at school. And I nodded once, quickly, and she grabbed me and laughed and all the girls I hated turned to look, but what could they do? Happiness, when it comes, is stronger than all the jerk girls in Santo Domingo combined.

But I was still confused. Because the feeling, it just kept getting stronger and stronger, wouldn't let me sleep, wouldn't give me any peace. I started losing races, which was something I never did.

You ain't so great, are you, gringa, the girls on the other teams hissed at me, and I could only hang my head. Coach Cortés was so unhappy he just locked himself in his car and wouldn't say anything to any of us.

The whole thing was driving me crazy, and then one night I came home from being out with Max. He had taken me for a walk along the Malecón—he never had money for anything else—and we had watched the bats zigzagging over the palms and an old ship head into the distance. While I stretched my hamstrings, he talked quietly about moving to the US. My abuela was waiting for me at the living-room table. Even though she still wears black to mourn the husband she lost when she was young she's one of the most handsome women I've ever known. We have the same jagged lightning-bolt part, and when I saw her at the airport, the first time in ten years, I didn't want to admit it but I knew that things were going to be OK between us. She stood like she was her own best thing and when she saw me she said, Hija, I have waited for you since the day you left. And then she hugged me and kissed me and said, I'm your abuela, but you can call me La Inca.

Standing over her that night, her part like a crack in her hair, I felt a surge of tenderness. I put my arms around her and that was when I noticed that she was looking at photos. Old photos, the kind I'd never seen in my house. Photos of my mother when she was young, before she had her breasts. She was even skinnier than me! I picked the smallest photo up. Mami was standing in front of a bakery. Even with an apron on she looked potent, like someone who was going to be someone.

She was very guapa, I said casually.

Abuela snorted. Guapa soy yo. Your mother was a diosa. But so cabeza dura. When she was your age we never got along. She was cabeza dura and I was . . . exigente. You and her are more alike than you think.

I know she ran away. From you. From Santo Domingo.

La Inca stared at me, incredulous. Your mother didn't run away. We had to *send* her away. To keep her from being murdered. To keep us all from being murdered. She didn't listen and she fell in love with the wrong man. She didn't listen. Jesucristo, hija—

She was about to say something more and then she stopped.

And that's when it hit with the force of a hurricane. The *feeling*. My abuela was sitting there, forlorn, trying to cobble together the right words, and I could not move or breathe. I felt like I always did in the last seconds of a race, when I was sure that I was going to explode. She was about to say something and I was waiting for whatever she was going to give me. I was waiting to begin.

Reading The PEN/O. Henry Prize Stories 2009

The Jurors on Their Favorites

Our jurors read The PEN/O. Henry Prize Stories 2009 *in a blind manuscript, that is, each story was in the same type and format with no attribution of the magazine that published it or the author's name. They also wrote their essays without knowledge of the author's name or the magazine. On occasion, the name of the author was inserted later into the essay for the sake of style.—LF*

A. S. Byatt on "An Ordinary Soldier of the Queen" by Graham Joyce

When I was young, we were told that a good short story conveyed a single impression, or a concentrated action—its essence was condensation and singleness. Stories I like don't necessarily conform to this model—they change direction, they surprise, they tell tales. It is true that in a short story every word must count—as it must in a poem. A novelist can get away with clumsy, or heavy, or skating passages, whereas a short story must make every word work, and each hold together with the others.

I enjoyed reading this selection of stories and almost didn't want to single out a favorite. I reread them after some time, paying particular attention to those that had persisted in my memory. I admired the ferocious energy of "Wildwood" and the complex shifts of feeling and information in "Purple Bamboo Park"—those two are still complete inside my head. But the story that haunted me, whose rhythms run in my mind, is "An Ordinary Soldier of the Queen."

This is the tale of an ordinary soldier—a decent man, a responsible man, a professional man, who looks after his men and understands his work. It is told in a completely convincing first person, which begins at ease in a known world—combat in the Falklands, in Northern Ireland, in Bosnia. The main action takes place in the desert in the first Gulf War. The British infantry is mopping up—the narrator tells his men to respect "the enemy" and not to sneeringly call them "ragheads." They come across strangely shrunk bodies in strangely spread man-size shadows. There is a dust storm, maybe the result of aircraft and vehicle action, maybe natural—"a dark thing, like a live creature, part smoke, part sand."

The tale moves into another kind of tale, always keeping the reasonable rhythm of the narrator's voice. He gets separated from his men. He hears a click, and realizes he is standing on an unexploded mine. He is visited by a butterfly—or maybe not—and an Arab in a red-and-white *shemagh* who has one blue eye and one horribly stitched up. He stands for hours on the mine, avoiding detonating it, and converses with the Arab.

The very practical, precise military tale becomes uncanny. The Arab is clearly a djinn or afreet. He has a courteous sardonic voice that the narrator—always straight with himself and the world—faithfully records. The narrator says his interlocutor would have to be a genie to help him. The Arab tells the narrator, "If I am a djinn I can summon up a wind. But if I help you, you will never be rid of me."

The narrator is blasted off his mine by friendly fire, and is found with the red-and-white cloth on his head.

Things do not go well for him thereafter.

The thing I admire most about this tale is the pace, the rhythm, the economy of incident and the accuracy of the words. Each sentence adds something to the world being described. It looks simple and easy, and is in fact controlled and crafted.

I think the greatest English short-story writer is Kipling, and this story has things in common with one of his—the ability to mix genres seamlessly, the familiarity with both the daily and the strange. It is about events in the world of action and politics. There is a brief—but telling—passing mention of depleted uranium in among the shrunken corpses and strange atmosphere in the desert, but it is not dwelled on. The fate of the ex-soldier in the last section—slightly out of his mind, working in "security," insecure, briefly in prison, disintegrating—is true to many lives of ex-combatants, and has a perfectly down-to-earth explanation. But the djinn or afreet is real, too. The phrase "friendly fire" is a compressed figure of speech—the djinns were made by God from smokeless fire when he made the world. Friendly fire blasts the narrator off the mine. The supernatural story is indivisible from the realist one. The colloquial dialogue and commentary can contain intensely, sharply poetic passages, which are still part of the plain, believable voice that talks to us. And tries to retain its dignity and goes mad.

A. S. Byatt was born in 1936 in Sheffield, England. Her novels include the Booker Prize–winning *Possession, The Biographer's Tale,* and the quartet *The Virgin in the Garden, Still Life, Babel Tower,* and *A Whistling Woman.* Byatt's story collections include *Sugar and Other Stories, The Matisse Stories, The Djinn in the Nightingale's Eye, Elementals,* and *Little Black Book of Stories.* A. S. Byatt was appointed CBE in 1990 and DBE in 1999. She lives in London.

Anthony Doerr on "Wildwood" by Junot Díaz

It was the burning wig. The wig stayed with me all night and into the next day, like one of those afterimages flash-burned into the retinas, the lights we see even after our eyes are closed. "It went up in a flash," Lola writes, "like gasoline, like a stupid hope, and if I hadn't thrown it in the sink it would have taken my hand."

Isn't that sentence a précis of Lola's entire struggle? The desperate prospect of her insurgency against the thermonuclear dominion of her mother?

In that moment the combustible space between Lola and Belicia, between obedience and rebellion, between wig and burner, between (as Lola's abuela would say) the egg and the rock, ignites, and the story catches fire.

"People saw me in my glasses and my hand-me-down clothes," writes Lola, "and could not have imagined what I was capable of."

"You think you're someone," says her mother, "but you ain't nada."

A dark, flummoxed, and deeply human heart beats beneath every sentence of "Wildwood." Its first sentence is a proclamation, almost a thesis statement. It then delivers its first fourteen paragraphs in second person and present tense, even though the rest of the story is in first person and past tense. It also wanders in time; shoehorns scenes into summary; dispenses with quotation marks; drizzles Spanish onto its English; strives toward a nearly unbelievable transformation (Lola runs the four hundred meters, Lola finally understands her mother); and the precipitating moment of the plot—"I ran off, dique, because of a boy"—does not occur until the reader is many pages in!

These are all formal risks, all chances the author has taken willfully and carefully, and these are all decisions that, had I been writing this story, I would have screwed up. And yet don't the risks of the story feel natural, inherent, and intrinsic? Don't they involve you more deeply in the charged intensity of Lola's voice?

I believe a good story writer is a *generous* story writer, generous in a sort of maniacal, foaming-at-the-mouth, Dr. Frankenstein way. A good story writer expends more than is expected—more than, perhaps, seems possible. She pours the full force of her intellect and energy into every paragraph, every dead end, every false start. And I believe the magic of a good short story comes from the compression of so many days of thought—a thousand afternoons of its writer thinking on things, wrestling with problems, noticing how light falls through leaves, or how a man wipes his glasses with a thumb and forefinger—compressing all those tens of thousands of hours into a space that can be experienced by a reader in an hour or so.

If it works, a good short story can show us something thorny and sublime and fabulously complex beneath the text, something trembling behind the little black symbols on the white page, some truth we can only feebly grasp, as if we are peering up at stars through thin clouds.

Writing stories is not, despite appearances, about spending lots of time with oneself. It's about learning to be able to look *beyond* the self, beyond the ego, to enter other lives and other worlds. It's about honing one's sense of empathy so that a story might bridge the gap between the personal and the communal.

Doing this well has to do with generosity, I'm certain of it. And "Wildwood," which is about Lola and Belicia first and foremost, and then and only then about sexual and psychological abuse, racism, misunderstanding, adolescent rage, and wig-burning, is a wildly generous story.

Here's Lola: "It's about that crazy feeling that started this whole mess, the bruja feeling that comes singing out of my bones, that takes hold of me the way blood seizes cotton."

Here's Mary Shelley: "It was already one in the morning; the rain pattered dismally against the panes, and my candle was nearly burnt out, when, by the glimmer of the half-extinguished light, I saw the dull yellow eye of the creature open."

Story writers don't fumble through so many lonely hours for money or glory. They write for love, to figure things out, to practice going after the truth, to investigate hurt, guilt, complexity. They do it to bring people like Lola to life.

You put in a thousand hours, you whittle away at a pillar of clay, and some rainy, electric midnight, when your candle is nearly burnt out, its eyes open.

. . .

Anthony Doerr is the author of a story collection, *The Shell Collector,* a novel, *About Grace,* and a memoir, *Four Seasons in Rome.* His work has won the Rome Prize, Barnes & Noble's Discover Prize, the New York Public Library's Young Lions Award, and inclusion in three previous *O. Henry Prize Stories.* In 2007, *Granta* put Doerr on its list of Best Young American Novelists. He lives in Boise, Idaho.

Tim O'Brien on "An Ordinary Soldier of the Queen" by Graham Joyce

"An Ordinary Soldier of the Queen" is a superb ghost story. It's also a survival story, a horror story, a bitterness story, a demon story, a class story, a trauma story, a miracle story, a tailspin story, and . . . yes, to be sure, a very wonderful story about war, though in exactly the same way and to exactly the same extent that "Bartleby" is a wonderful story about office life.

There is so much to admire, and so much to love, about "An Ordinary Soldier of the Queen" that I'm daunted by the task of doing justice to this beautifully shaped, immaculately pitched, and scarily convincing—as nightmares are convincing—short story. In the opening pages, we are carried along by the jaunty, no-nonsense voice of Seamus Todd, a worldly-wise color sergeant in the British infantry during the opening stages of the Gulf War. The voice alone is a literary accomplishment: tough, cynical, funny, wise, wiseass, courageous, down-to-earth, and rich with the lingo and flatly nuanced diction of a seasoned combat veteran. The first paragraph sets the tone: "I'm going to ask the Queen. I'm going to tell her what I know and ask her what is true, and if she winks at me, well, there will be trouble. This is me, Seamus Todd, born in 1955, ordinary soldier of the Queen and very little else, and this is my testament, which is honest, true, and factual. If I haven't seen it with my own eyes, then I have left it out."

In this cunning vein, Graham Joyce leads us to expect a realistic, even conventional tale about the terrors of modern desert combat—an account that is "honest, true, and factual." Twice in the first five paragraphs, Joyce reinforces our expectations by deftly injecting his prose with the numbing word "normal." For example: "War is normal. That's why it's a paid job. . . . You don't argue with the Queen. You form up. Move out. Press on." The events Seamus Todd sets out to recount, however, are anything but realistic or conventional, and his war experience is anything but normal. As a storytelling device, it is precisely the narrator's voice—so matter-of-fact, so wholly military, so *ordinary*—that gives heft and poignancy to an astonishing, even magical turn of events midway into the tale.

In the midst of battle, isolated from his comrades by a sandstorm, Seamus Todd steps on a pressure-release land mine. If he lifts his foot, he dies. As Seamus considers his predicament, in what is already a suspenseful scene, a "ghost" suddenly makes its appearance, smack in the vast Iraqi desert, a ghost both as real and as unreal as the land mine beneath the trembling foot of Seamus Todd.

Certain ontological questions arise, worthy of a color sergeant or a Queen: What exactly, or even inexactly, *is* a ghost? Is this one real? Can a ghost be unreal? (If so, what kind of pitiful ghost is *that*?) Oh, and how do you know when you're dead, or if you're dead, or if, years later, you're in fact still out there in the desert with your foot on an armed land mine? For that matter, how do you know it *is* years later? Minds malfunction, don't they? Clocks too? Is it all the hallucination of a corpse? (The surname Todd, remember, is only a consonant away from the German word *Tod*: death.) And what if the ghost, dressed as an Arab, offers to extract Seamus from this terrible mess, but with the proviso that "you will never be rid of me"? Is the offer credible? Is *anything* credible amid the upside-down, inside-out horrors of war? Is *everything* credible?

These are not the sort of questions we would have expected from Seamus Todd, which makes them all the more profound and all the more moving. In any case, let's hope the Queen has answers, because Color Sergeant Seamus Todd is not the type to put up with regal (or presidential) waffling. He wants the fucking truth.

Reading "An Ordinary Soldier of the Queen," I'm reminded that a good many fine war stories reach into the world of magic and ghosts and gods and angels and avatars and the awakened dead. Start with *The Iliad.* Move on to Ambrose Bierce's "Chickamauga," or to Kurt Vonnegut's *Slaughterhouse-Five,* or to Mark Twain's "The War Prayer," or to Ian McEwan's recent *Atonement.* To some temperaments, my own included, the systematic, sanctioned butchery of war does not always feel "real," and at times a so-called realistic story can seem to violate, or even demean, the essential unrealistic reality of the experience. Plenty of soldiers will testify that wars do not end with the signing of a peace treaty, that memory haunts just as a ghost might, and that in the middle of the night, decades after hostilities have ceased, a voice will murmur, "You will never be rid of me."

Tim O'Brien was born in Minnesota in 1946. His books include *If I Die in the Combat Zone, Box Me Up and Ship Me Home*; *Going after Cacciato,* which won the National Book Award; *The Things They Carried*; *In the Lake of the Wood*; and *July, July.* O'Brien's short stories have appeared in *Esquire, Harper's Magazine, The Atlantic Monthly, Playboy, Granta, GQ, The New Yorker, The O. Henry Prize Stories,* and *The Best American Short Stories of the Century.* The Guggenheim Foundation and the National Endowment for the Arts have awarded fellowships to O'Brien. He lives in Austin, Texas.

Writing The PEN/O. Henry
Prize Stories 2009
The Writers on Their Work

Karen Brown, "Isabel's Daughter"

Years ago a friend surprised us by showing up at our house with a little girl he was watching as a favor for someone. He was an unlikely
babysitter, an older British man whose usual company was an English
setter. He'd moved to the United States to be near his children, one a
famous rock star who seemed to want nothing to do with him, and
he often showed up at our house around dinnertime. He was good
company and a stern grammarian. He rolled his own cigarettes, leaving bits of spilled tobacco wherever he'd been sitting. I imagine he
might have thought the girl could play with my seven-year-old
daughter, or he thought that since I was a mother I'd know what to
do with her, but it was late at night and my daughter was in bed
asleep. The girl was near my daughter's age, tiny and dark-eyed, wearing clothes covered in dog hair from his car, and she sat on the couch,
valiantly trying to stay awake. This visit, the odd pairing of the man
and the girl, was just the sort of poignant situation that often
prompts me to write. I could not have foreseen that when I set out to
tell what I thought would be the little girl's story I'd create a narrator
who would inadvertently tell his own. It was a happy surprise—the

discovery of his voice. Something that doesn't occur that easily, or that often. When it does I am always grateful.

Karen Brown was born in 1960 and grew up in Connecticut. Her stories have appeared in *The Best American Short Stories* and *The O. Henry Prize Stories* and in journals that include the *Georgia Review, Epoch,* and *American Short Fiction.* Her first collection, *Pins and Needles,* won the AWP Grace Paley Prize in Short Fiction. She teaches at the University of South Florida, in Tampa, where she lives.

John Burnside, "The Bell Ringer"

Historically, bells have been rung to announce the outbreak of war and to celebrate the return of peace; to mark marriages and deaths, Sundays and feast days; to commemorate important political and social occasions; and to reinforce communal memories. It was this aspect of bell ringing—its importance to a community—that started me thinking about this story: once upon a time, each community was defined by the reach of its bells; anyone who could not hear the bells from a parish church was deemed to be outside that parish (beyond the peal, or pale), and everyone within the community would be able to "read" his or her local bells, knowing what they signified simply by the tenor of the sound they made. It occurred to me that, maybe, a seasoned listener might decipher all kinds of nuances in the peal of those bells, even discovering the secrets of individual bell ringers—their hidden wishes, their secret desires and fears, their private loneliness. So it was that my central character—a lonely woman in an unhappy marriage, with a fairly hopeless crush on the American student who has recently joined her bell-ringing group—conceives the fear, and perhaps the hope, that somebody, somewhere in her immediate community, will be reminded by the sound of her bell that, even if she seems to her neighbors no more than a quiet and somewhat downtrodden wife in a very traditional village, she is still capable of passion.

· · ·

John Burnside was born in 1955 in Dunfermline. He is the author of six novels, of which the most recent are *The Devil's Footprints* and *Glister,* as well as a memoir, *A Lie about My Father,* and a collection of short stories, *Burning Elvis.* He lives in rural Fife, Scotland.

Junot Díaz, "Wildwood"

For a Jersey kid growing up in the '80s, Wildwood was our very own local version of Sin City. From what I was told by the older kids everything was possible in Wildwood (at least during the summers) and that alone was probably the reason I wanted so desperately as a kid to run away there. I had a really abusive messed-up family life, and dreams of running away were endemic with all my siblings.

One of us did run away in the end: my oldest sister, who disappeared from the apartment and never came back.

I guess my fantasies about Wildwood and the painful reality of my sister's flight collided to give this story its earliest form. But what really made the narrative *hum* was my attempt to capture the powerful resentment that so many of the Dominican women of my generation continue to feel toward their complicated wounded problematic mothers.

Junot Díaz was born in 1968 in the Dominican Republic and raised in New Jersey and is the author of *Drown* and *The Brief Wondrous Life of Oscar Wao,* which won the John Sargent, Sr., First Novel Prize, the National Book Critics Circle Award, the Anisfield-Wolf Book Award, and the 2008 Pulitzer Prize. Díaz has been awarded the Eugene McDermott Award, a fellowship from the Guggenheim Foundation, a Lila Acheson Wallace Reader's Digest Award, the 2002 PEN/Malamud Award, the 2003 US/Japan Creative Artist Fellowship from the National Endowment for the Arts, a fellowship at the Radcliffe Institute for Advanced Study at Harvard University, and the Rome Prize from the American Academy of Arts and Letters. He is fiction editor of *Boston Review* and *Rudge (1948)* and is the Nancy Allen Professor at the Massachusetts Institute of Technology.

Viet Dinh, "Substitutes"

My family escaped from Vietnam the night Saigon fell: This is the start to my own immigrant narrative. In any violent conflict, friends separate and families split apart. For "Substitutes," I wanted to focus on the people left behind by those who leave—a nation dividing even as it "reunified." I had heard stories about the Communist reeducation camps—particularly from my uncle, who survived one—and I wanted to explore this idea of reeducation. Not of the adults who suffered in those camps, but of the children who found their education disrupted: children who, for whatever reason, were unable to start their own immigrant narratives.

Viet Dinh was born in Da Lat, Vietnam, in 1974, and spent his formative years in Aurora, Colorado. In 2008, he received a Fiction Fellowship from the National Endowment for the Arts. His work has appeared in *Zoetrope: All-Story*, *Threepenny Review*, *Five Points*, *Chicago Review*, *Fence*, *Michigan Quarterly Review*, and *Epoch*, among others. He received his MFA from the University of Houston and currently lives in Wilmington, Delaware.

Nadine Gordimer, "A Beneficiary"

Nadine Gordimer was born in Springs, Transvaal, South Africa, in 1923. She is the author of many books of fiction and nonfiction, including *July's People*, *The Essential Gesture*, *The Late Bourgeois World*, and *Beethoven Was One-Sixteenth Black and Other Stories*. She is a past vice president of International PEN. In 1991, Ms. Gordimer won the Nobel Prize in Literature. She lives in Johannesburg, South Africa.

Andrew Sean Greer, "Darkness"

"Darkness" is one of the few stories where I can pin down exactly where I was when the idea came to me, and what the precise influences were, though I worry these influences will seem like the too-obvious figures in a dream that dispel all of its mystery. It happened when I was teaching in New York City and living in the East Village. I had recently come from a reading at Symphony Space benefiting John Kerry, at which I read a piece from Gertrude Stein's "The Coming of the Americans" and Simon Schama read from Byron's poem "Darkness." I was on the corner of Seventh Street and Second Avenue when it occurred to me to connect the stories—to put the story of two elderly women in a time of war (Stein's piece) in the postapocalyptic world of Byron's poetry.

I had just finished reading William Maxwell's *The Château,* which ends with a catechism; I saw in Maxwell's storytelling a challenge to myself. Thus the question-answer format. I began the story the day after George Bush was reelected president of our country. I wrote it in a solid month, in one of the darkest moods I can remember.

Two final bits of trivia: first, that two different agents declined to represent the story, saying they "didn't get it," and I assumed it would never be published, until *Zoetrope: All-Story* approached me. And second: that originally "Darkness" had a happy ending. The last question was "Did they make it?" and the answer is "Somehow." My editor at *Zoetrope* offered that cut as his only edit of the story—the rest was virtually untouched—and I worried over the decision for many days. I think the version without it hits just the right emotional tone, and does not take it too far. Still, I am not sure which version I like better. Perhaps because, as I write this, I do not yet know how things will turn out.

Andrew Sean Greer was born in 1970 in Washington, DC. He is the author of four works of fiction, including *The Story of a Marriage* and *The Confessions of Max Tivoli.* His stories have appeared in such publications as *Esquire, The Paris Review,* and *The New Yorker.* He is the recipient of the Northern California Book Award, the California Book Award, the New York Public Library Young Lions Award, and fellowships from the National Endowment for the Arts and the Cullman Center at the New York Public Library. Greer lives in San Francisco, California.

Caitlin Horrocks, "This Is Not Your City"

I was working at an elementary school in Finland when a new girl showed up in the fifth grade. She spoke no Finnish and spent her days staring blankly at her books and warily at the other children. The teachers whispered in the staff room about the Russian woman and the much older Finnish man who had enrolled the girl, neither of whom could understand a word the other said. The girl eventually transferred to another school, but her profound loneliness, and my inability to lessen it, have stayed with me. The first drafts of "This Is Not Your City" were more or less about this real-life girl—problematically so, both since I knew so little about her and because the powerlessness that had made her so haunting was such a difficult quality to work with on the page. As I continued to write, the daughter became older, more able to express her frustration, in word and deed, with her situation. In the end, though, the story turned out to belong to the mother, the one who had resolved to uproot them. I wondered about the woman who made that choice, what her regrets and the costs of her decision might be, and how much determination it would take to see it through.

Caitlin Horrocks was born in Ann Arbor in 1980 and has lived in Michigan, Ohio, Arizona, Finland, England, and the Czech Republic. Her stories appear in *Tin House, The Southern Review, The Gettysburg Review, Epoch,* and elsewhere, and have been recognized by the Bread Loaf Writers' Conference. Her first book of stories, *This Is Not Your City,* will be published in Fall 2009. She lives in Grand Rapids, Michigan.

Ha Jin, "The House Behind a Weeping Cherry"

For several years I often went to Flushing, New York, to look at places and people for the stories I had been writing, all of them set in that immigrant community. Most times I would walk around and record details and peculiar things I saw. Once I stayed at a hostel for new arrivals, which was a three-story house on a busy street. I had planned just to see how new immigrants lived there, but the house, advertised as a family hostel, was very quiet in the daytime. At night, however, I found two women living on the same floor with me, and there were male visitors who made the place noisy. I wouldn't say that the women were prostitutes, but the racket made me sleepless and set my imagination flying.

I had always been fascinated by reports on how illegal immigrants survived once they landed in America. Among the jobs they do, prostitution and working in sweatshops are the two most common. I wanted to write stories about people working those jobs for survival. Now, in this big house, I imagined the place as an underground brothel where a man, a sweatshop hand in the daytime, lived among prostitutes and worked as their chauffeur at night. This was meant to combine both prostitution and the sweatshop as the setting for the story, so it could be more interesting dramatically. Of course, I planted the weeping cherry before the house.

The writing was a big struggle because I didn't know much about prostitution and sweatshops. At times I even doubted whether there was a story in this imagined material. Yet gradually, as I kept rewriting and revising, the story took shape.

Ha Jin was born in China in 1956. He has published five novels, three collections of short stories, three volumes of poetry, and a book of nonfiction, *The Writer as Migrant*. He has received the National Book Award, the PEN/Faulkner Award, the Hemingway Foundation/PEN Award, a Guggenheim Fellowship, and other prizes. His short fiction has been included in *The O. Henry Prize Stories, The Best American Short Stories,* and many other anthologies, and was chosen for *The Pushcart Prize* four times. Ha Jin teaches writing and literature at Boston University. He lives outside Boston.

Graham Joyce, "An Ordinary Soldier of the Queen"

"An Ordinary Soldier of the Queen" was written partly out of rage and partly from a desperate sympathy for our soldiers damaged in the

Gulf wars. In the UK we don't treat our soldiers returning from the Iraq disaster too well. I met an intelligent, uneducated, long-serving professional whose mind had been shredded, whether by trauma or exposure to depleted uranium from our own weapons I don't know. But the scale of casual evil into which he'd been recruited could, for me, only be expressed as demonic. The short story raised so many questions for me I went on to build a novel around it.

Graham Joyce was born in 1954 near Coventry in the United Kingdom. He's the author of eleven adult novels, three young adult novels, a collection of short stories, and has adapted his own work for the screen. He won the World Fantasy Award in 2003 for his novel *The Facts of Life* and the British Fantasy Award for Best Novel an unprecedented four times. Joyce teaches creative writing at Nottingham Trent University and lives in Leicester.

Kirsten Sundberg Lunstrum, "The Nursery"

"The Nursery" began with a news report I heard a couple of years ago about a teenage baseball player (rather than a wrestler, like David), who killed one of his teammates on the field. I don't now remember all of the details—nor even whether the incident was a freak accident or the result of a fight—but the story made me wonder how the parents of the boys involved must have felt. From there I had Beth, and a first draft of the story came together fairly quickly once I placed her in a fictionalized version of my hometown in Washington and gave her a nursery to run. Although I come back to the landscape of the Pacific Northwest again and again in my writing, I was particularly happy in this story with the way the overgrowth and lushness of that setting worked in contrast to Beth's withholding and reserve. She is a difficult character—not entirely likable. But at the heart of the story is the ferocity of her desire to protect, to nurture, which is why, regardless of her failures, I still feel so much sympathy for her.

. . .

Kirsten Sundberg Lunstrum was born in 1979 in Chicago, and grew up in the Seattle area of Washington State. She is the author of two books of short fiction, *This Life She's Chosen* and *Swimming with Strangers*, and is coeditor of *The Sincerest Form of Flattery*. Lunstrum teaches at Purchase College and lives in Connecticut.

L. E. Miller, "Kind"

I began writing "Kind" in 2005. My son was an infant then, and we were living, as we still do, on a small island on the North Shore of Massachusetts. As I wrote each week in my local café, I think I was trying to recapture some aspect of my footloose, single days in New York City: the freedom to try on different attitudes like hats, the malleability of the self during those years. All I knew about the story when I started out was that there was a timid young woman living alone in the city. She had neighbors, some not quite fully articulated ambitions, and a peephole mirror in her door.

Inspiring me were the writings of Mary McCarthy, Jean Stafford, and Dorothy Parker. I have always been intrigued by the way these writers capture urban life in the early and mid-1900s, the promise the city offered a woman hoping to shape her own destiny. Of course, in their stories, this promise was often fulfilled only halfway, or not fulfilled at all.

I wrote several drafts of the story. And then, as details will, the details began to present themselves. A photograph of a Sitka spruce became Hugh's painting. A trip to North Adams, Massachusetts, gave me the setting for Ann's hometown. A moment in Chang-rae Lee's novel *A Gesture Life* in which a character is described as being kinder to others than they are to her made me say, Aha! Edith! Readers of early drafts didn't *get* Edith, and I realize now that their bafflement reflected my own ambivalence about her. As I wrote on, I came to see more clearly how her kindness was at once a gift, a way to manipulate others, and a prison of her own making.

Finally, my mother worked briefly for Travelers Aid in the same capacity as Ann, and like Ann, she once confused Grand Central with Penn Station, much to the annoyance of a weary refugee. I am lucky that she lived in such interesting times and shares many of her stories with me.

L. E. Miller was born in 1963 in Boston. She has published short stories in *The Missouri Review, Scribner's Best of the Fiction Workshops 1999*, and twice in *CALYX*. Miller holds an MA in fiction writing from the University of New Hampshire. She lives in Newbury, Massachusetts, and works as a grant writer for several local nonprofit organizations.

Alistair Morgan, "Icebergs"

The story was sparked, in part, by real events. In 2004, Zimbabwe's former finance minister, Chris Kuruneri, bought a multi-million-rand mansion in Llandudno near Cape Town with "a suitcase full of cash." Kuruneri was arrested after the Sunday *Times* exposed his purchase of the Llandudno house. He returned to Zimbabwe to face charges of illegally siphoning foreign currency out of the poverty-stricken country. In 2007, he was acquitted by the high court of Zimbabwe. Although these events, upon which I embellished considerably, did help to drive the plot, they are peripheral to the main themes: loneliness and isolation. My attraction to these themes was helped along by the short stories of Richard Yates and Richard Ford, two of my favorite writers.

Alistair Morgan was born in Johannesburg, South Africa, in 1971. "Icebergs" is his first published story. His debut novel is *Sleeper's Wake*. Morgan currently lives and works in Cape Town, South Africa.

Manuel Muñoz, "Tell Him about Brother John"

This story had an easy beginning: I walked to work when I lived in New York, and every morning I would pass a homeless man who paced a small stretch of sidewalk at Eighth Avenue and Fifty-first

Street. Mostly he kept to himself, but some days he was boisterous and edgy; one morning, he approached me and said, "You'll tell him about Brother John, right?" I said I would, and kept walking. The phrase stuck in my head all day and refused to leave, so I wrote it down.

The homeless man gave me the two key tools for a story—a character and an action—but I could do nothing with them. Weeks later, when I was reading yet another article about the death of the "coming out" narrative, I realized my focus on that action—telling—was a great failure in the way I was thinking about stories. I was ignoring the listener. Every story needs a listener, and more often than not, we think of stories as being told rather than heard. Telling is a kind of selfish behavior, since listening is the act that brings about empathy. It was a lesson I thought I had learned a long time ago, but here it was again. And so the story began—the burden of telling, the responsibility of listening, and the consequences of not doing so.

Manuel Muñoz was born in Dinuba, California, in 1972. He graduated from Harvard, the first in his family to receive a college degree, and later received his MFA from Cornell. He is the author of two short-story collections, *Zigzagger* and *The Faith Healer of Olive Avenue*, which was shortlisted for the 2007 Frank O'Connor International Short Story Award. He was the recipient of a 2008 Whiting Writers' Award. He worked for several years in the managing editorial department of Grand Central Publishing in New York City before moving to Tucson in 2008, where he is now an assistant professor of creative writing at the University of Arizona.

Roger Nash, "The Camera and the Cobra"

Constantly, everyday life hits or tickles me on the nose with events that make people intriguing. Then writing a story seems the only way to rub my nose and work through the intrigue. We shape landscapes through our ideas for them (building another suburb, say), even shape them mindlessly. But I'm fascinated by how landscapes shape us. It seems, sometimes, as though they do their thinking through us. A landscape can awaken understandings in us that, at the time, we mistake as entirely our own, supposing we're in complete control of having them. Later, we realize that, but for being in that place, we'd never have arrived at those ideas. The place is to be credited with them too, certainly not us alone. Thoughts come to us best, in nature, if we're alertly open to receiving them. Paradoxically, nature speaks to us least when we're most attentive to it, but with the wrong kind of alertness. This happens when, as self-conscious, camera-wielding travelers, vividly excited by a new landscape, we view it within the frame of some of our narrowest, stay-at-home attitudes. Sometimes, these attitudes are encouraged by even the best-intentioned media endeavors, like *National Geographic.* "Look! Something's really happening now—a lot of animals moving around." As though nothing really happened in a quiet landscape. As nature speaks to us, awakening new mind-sets, we become more fully and richly ourselves. Then, like the doctor in my story, putting down his camera, we may have that feeling of "coming home" in our lives. We fully come home only as the fuller selves we can become: otherwise, an undiscovered, unexplored part of us is left wandering. Sometimes, to come home in this sense, we must leave our literal homes far behind, and meet radically different cultures and landscapes. And sometimes, like my doctor, you may come home in what seems, initially, the most unwelcoming of landscapes: a desert. We may worry that, in our technologized lives in North America, we're losing the ability to let nature speak and shape us creatively, rather than abruptly shaping it for our short-term economic gains. The danger is that nature will, indeed, shape us, and more and more, but through the painful and blind mechanisms of climate change (increased hurricanes, tornadoes . . .), rather than through our amazed and energized attentiveness to it. These concerns, too, led me into the story. They're not explored in it explicitly. Being indirect seemed the best way to avoid the creakingly dogmatic that can threaten writing that's explicitly "environmental lit."

Deserts have a hard time speaking to us today. They seem negativities, entirely. Our soldiers die in them. Or, we try, impossibly, to make them bloom perpetually, using nonrenewable water resources. I grew up as a child in the eastern Sahara. (My father was with the British forces there.) Perhaps my story shows how deserts still have things to say.

Roger Nash was born in 1942, in Maidenhead, England. In 1965, he moved to Canada. He's won the Canadian Jewish Book Award and, twice, the Confederation Poets Prize. His latest books are *Something Blue and Flying Upwards: New and Selected Poems* and a collection of essays on the psalms, *The Poetry of Prayer*. He teaches philosophy at Laurentian University, where he's director of the Humanities MA in Interpretation and Values. Nash lives in Sudbury, Ontario.

Mohan Sikka, "Uncle Musto Takes a Mistress"

If "Uncle Musto" is anything besides the story of a retired couple and the reverberation of an old infidelity, it's about the conflict between domestic restraint and the pursuit of self-satisfaction—what we as humans sacrifice to keep order at home and please our families, and what our lives could be if guilt and convention didn't curb our instinctual desires. The setting for my current writing is the changing Indian family, whose traditions are being buffeted by migration, economic dislocation, and new ways of loving and living.

The spark for Musto was a conversation with my father during travels in India. We were discussing an excellent social history by Prakash Tandon called *Punjabi Century, 1857–1947*—about the emergence of the Punjabi middle class in the nineteenth and early twentieth centuries. My father elaborated on a reference in the text about how, in the "olden days," extramarital entertainments for gentlemen were socially tolerated, if not sanctioned. In fact, an entire class of skilled women—musicians, dancers, sex workers—served the desires of middle-class men. I began to wonder what shape such desires at the edge of social sanction might take in a contemporary context, with its updated notions of propriety; how the acting out of these desires might relive and reflect historic mores; and what the consequences would be for the people, especially the women, involved.

The setting of the "colony," the Indian term for an urban neighborhood, will be familiar to anyone who has visited a North Indian town or city. My parents lived abroad when I was a child in India, so using a curious, lonely boy as the narrator was an organic and, I think, appropriate choice.

Mohan Sikka was born in Calcutta in 1966, and grew up in India and Zambia. His stories have appeared in *One Story* and the *Toronto South Asian Review* and in anthologies, including *Delhi Noir*. He now lives in Brooklyn, New York.

Marisa Silver, "The Visitor"

On the street where I have lived for nearly two decades, a fair number of residents believe their homes are occasionally visited by ghosts. As I have no information as to the existence or nonexistence of ghosts, and as I generally believe in the genuineness of belief, I accept their convictions. We talk about the things neighbors do—children, dogs, and the natural events that draw Angelenos into disaster-oriented fellowship: earthquakes, fires, heat waves, and the power outages that follow them. Occasionally, we talk about their unearthly visitors. So, I've spent a long time casually thinking about ghosts and those who believe in them. I think about the other kinds of ghosts too, the ones who don't rattle the chandeliers, but who haunt us all the same.

Most stories emerge for me as collages. Ideas and images take up residence in my mind around the same time and I trust that, because they are there, there is some connection among them. My job is to find those connections, not to assert them, but to excavate them. I'm usually quite surprised to discover what those connections are. In the case of this story, I had my neighborhood ghosts, and I had the strange netherworld that is the VA hospital. And I had heat and a blackout. Candy and her grandmother emerged, both shadowed by ghosts. And then there was the soldier, whose body had been turned partly into negative space by battle, and who had not yet made the decision whether or not to become a ghost himself, and so remained silent, forcing Candy to haunt him.

Marisa Silver was born in Cleveland, Ohio, in 1960, and raised in New York City. *Babe in Paradise,* her story collection, was a *New York Times* Notable Book of the Year and a *Los Angeles Times* Best Book of the Year. A story from the collection was in *The Best American Short Stories.* Her novels are *No Direction Home* and *The God of War.* Silver lives in Los Angeles.

E. V. Slate, "Purple Bamboo Park"

I happened to be living in Beijing when construction cranes seemed to be taking over the city but before anything new had emerged to take the place of what had been torn down. When I began the story, I was thinking about an old woman with a young, jealous heart who was constantly on the move but somehow in the wrong direction. The momentum of her on a bicycle seemed to give the story a push before I could think about it too much. As I wrote, her misplaced affection troubled me. Her remorselessness toward her daughter put me off. But I wrote as if from very far away, unable to alter the physics of what had started. After I had finished and submitted the story to my workshop, I subtracted some lines that I was told were unclear, but I didn't think I should add anything. ·

E. V. Slate's short stories have appeared in *Best New American Voices 2005, Crazyhorse,* and the *New England Review.* Slate currently lives and works in Singapore, and has spent time in San Francisco, Beijing, and Mumbai.

Paul Theroux, "Twenty-two Stories"

The essence of fiction writing—and travel writing too, is storytelling. I have been hearing such stories and reading folk tales my whole life, not just Grimm's but also the stories recounted by Africans, Indians, and others. I am speaking of the one-page story. I love the compression of them and the memorable events. In other hands, they could be novels or long stories. Many are the more dramatic for the spare detail. Quite a number of Jorge Luis Borges's tales are short and powerful. I invent them, I collect them, I adapt them; and I have many more than these twenty-two—indeed, I have about a hundred, which I think of as "Long Story Short," because that's an expression the teller often uses when recounting one. These perhaps represent the oldest form of literature in the world: the tale told at leisure by people sitting around a fire.

Paul Theroux was born in Massachusetts in 1941. He's the author of *The Mosquito Coast, The Great Railway Bazaar, The Old Patagonian Express,* and *The Elephanta Suite,* among many other works of fiction and nonfiction. He currently lives in Cape Cod and Hawai'i.

Judy Troy, "The Order of Things"

What made me want to write "The Order of Things" was coming across the St. Theresa of Avila quotation I use in the second to last paragraph: "The important thing is not to think much, but to love much." I wanted the main character to have reason to know the quotation and be suddenly moved by it, so it made sense for him to be a clergyman, and for him to be in love for the first time. I like bringing spirituality into a story—it raises the stakes and gives the story depth, and also it's interesting to me. I set the story in Wyoming because I spent time there once and the places I saw stayed in my mind. For me, it's always the setting as much as the characters that make a story real. As I was writing the story I didn't intend for Lily to die, but then it seemed inevitable, because it would be Carl's duty to conduct the service. What would that be like for him? I wondered, and finished the story in order to find out.

Judy Troy was born in 1951 in Whiting, Indiana. She is the author of a story collection, *Mourning Doves,* and two novels, *West of Venus* and *From the Black Hills.* Her short stories have appeared in *Epoch, The Kenyon Review,* and *The New Yorker,* among other journals and magazines. She is Professor and Alumni Writer-in-Residence at Auburn University, and lives in Alabama.

Paul Yoon, "And We Will Be Here"
"And We Will Be Here" began with an image I had of two children sitting under a tree, pretending to read a book as they posed for a painter. I imagined they were alone and did not have a family. And I thought of my grandfather, who, during the Korean War, took care of orphans and, later, started an orphanage in South Korea. I have always wondered what their—the orphans'—lives were like then and what happened to them when they were older, whether they stayed in the town or left, and whether they kept in touch with my grandfather, visiting him on occasion, or disappeared entirely. I don't know. My grandfather passed away a few years ago so he, and the children, were very much on my mind as I was writing this story.

Paul Yoon was born in 1980 in New York City. His fiction has appeared in *One Story, Ploughshares, TriQuarterly, Glimmer Train, American Short Fiction,* and *The Best American Short Stories,* among other publications. His first story collection is *Once the Shore.*

Recommended Stories 2009

The task of picking the twenty PEN/O. Henry Prize Stories each year is at its most difficult at the end, when there are more than twenty admirable and interesting stories. Once the final choice is made, those remaining are our Recommended Stories, listed, along with the place of publication, in the hope that our readers will seek them out and enjoy them. Please go to our Web site, www.penohenryprize stories.com, for excerpts from the stories and information about the writers.

Mary Carroll-Hackett, "Placing," *Alimentum*
Halina Duraj, "Terrible Driver," *Witness*
Mary Beth Keane, "Believers," *Antioch Review*
Owen King, "Nothing Is in Bad Taste," *Subtropics*
Rae Paris, "The Girl Who Ate Her Own Skin," *Indiana Review*

Publications Submitted

Because of production deadlines for the 2010 collection, it is essential that stories reach the series editor by May 1, 2009. If a finished magazine is unavailable before the deadline, magazine editors are welcome to submit scheduled stories in proof or in manuscript. Work received after May 1, 2009, will be considered for the 2011 collection. Stories may not be submitted by agents or writers. Please see our Web site, www.penohenryprizestories.com, for more information about submission to *The PEN/O. Henry Prize Stories*.

The address for submission is:

> Professor Laura Furman
> The O. Henry Prize Stories
> The University of Texas at Austin
> English Department
> 1 University Station, B5000
> Austin, TX 78712

The information listed below was up-to-date as *The PEN/O. Henry Prize Stories 2009* went to press. Inclusion in the listings does not constitute endorsement or recommendation.

AGNI Magazine
Boston University
236 Bay State Road
Boston, MA 02215
Sven Birkerts, Editor
agni@bu.edu
www.bu.edu/agni/
Semiannual

Alaska Quarterly Review
University of Alaska Anchorage
3211 Providence Drive
Anchorage, AK 99508
Ronald Spatz, Editor
aqr@uaa.alaska.edu
www.aqr.uaa.alaska.edu/aqr
Semiannual

Alimentum
PO Box 776
New York, NY 10163
Paulette Licitra and Peter Selgin,
    Editors
editor@alimentumjournal.com
www.alimentumjournal.com
Semiannual

**American Letters &
    Commentary**
Department of English
University of Texas at San
    Antonio
One UTSA Boulevard
San Antonio, TX 78749-0643

Catherine Kasper and David Ray
    Vance, Editors
AmerLetters@satx.rr.com
Annual

American Literary Review
PO Box 311307
University of North Texas
Denton, TX 76203-1307
John Tait, Editor
www.engl.unt.edu/alr
Semiannual

The American Scholar
Phi Beta Kappa Society
1606 New Hampshire Avenue
    NW
Washington, DC 20009
Robert Wilson, Editor
scholar@pbk.org
www.theamericanscholar.org
Quarterly

American Short Fiction
PO Box 301209
Austin, TX 78703
Stacey Swann, Editor
americanshortfiction.org
Quarterly

The Antioch Review
PO Box 148
Yellow Springs, OH 45387-
    0148

Robert S. Fogarty, Editor
review@antioch.edu
www.review.antioch.edu
Quarterly

Apalachee Review
PO Box 10469
Tallahassee, FL 32302
Michael Trammel, Editor
http://apalacheereview.org
Semiannual

Arkansas Review
Department of English and
    Philosophy
Box 1890
Arkansas State University
State University, AR 72467
Tom Williams, Editor
delta@astate.edu
www.clt.astate.edu/arkreview
Triannual

Ascent
English Department
Concordia College
901 S. Eighth Street
Moorhead, MN 56562
W. Scott Olsen, Editor
ascent@cord.edu
www.cord.edu/dept/english/
    ascent
Triannual

The Atlantic Monthly
The Watergate
600 New Hampshire Avenue
    NW
Washington, DC 20037
C. Michael Curtis, Senior Fiction
    Editor
letters@theatlantic.com
www.theatlantic.com
Monthly

Avery Anthology
Stephanie Firorelli, Adam
    Koehler, and Andrew Palmer,
    Editors
submissions@averyanthology.org
www.averyanthology.org
Biannual

Backwards City Review
PO Box 41317
Greensboro, NC 27404-1317
editors@backwardscity.net
www.backwardscity.net
Semiannual

The Baltimore Review
PO Box 36418
Towson, MD 21286
Susan Muaddi Darraj, Managing
    Editor
www.baltimorereview.org
Semiannual

Bateau
PO Box 2335
Amherst, MA 01004
James Grinwis, Editor
info@bateaupress.org
www.bateaupress.org
Biannual

Ballyhoo Stories
PO Box 170
Prince Street Station
New York, NY 10012
Suzanne Pettypiece, Editor
editors@ballyhoostories.com
www.ballyhoostories.com
Annual

Bellevue Literary Review
Department of Medicine
Room OBV-612
NYU School of Medicine
550 First Avenue
New York, NY 10016
Ronna Wineberg, J.D., Fiction
    Editor
info@BLReview.org
www.BLReview.org
Semiannual

Black Clock
California Institute of
    the Arts
24700 McBean Parkway
Valencia, CA 91355

Steve Erickson, Editor
submissions@blackclock.org
www.blackclock.org
Semiannual

Black Warrior Review
Box 862936
Tuscaloosa, AL 35486-0027
Alissa Nutting, Editor
bwr@ua.edu
http://bwr.ua.edu/
Semiannual

Bloodroot Literary Review
PO Box 322
Thetford Center, VT 05075
"Do" Roberts, Editor
bloodroot@wildblue.net
www.bloodrootlm.com
Annual

BOMB Magazine
80 Hanson Place
Suite 703
Brooklyn, NY 11217
Betsy Sussler, Editor in Chief
info@bombsite.com
www.bombsite.com
Quarterly

**Boston Review, A Political and
    Literary Forum**
35 Medford Street, Suite 302
Somerville, MA 02143

Deborah Chasman and Joshua
  Cohen, Editors
review@mit.edu
www.bostonreview.net
Published six times per year

Boulevard Magazine
6614 Clayton Road, Box 325
Richmond Heights, MO
  63117
Richard Burgin, Editor
ballymon@hotmail.com
www.richardburgin.net
Triannual

Brain, Child
PO Box 714
Lexington, VA 24450
Stephanie Wilkinson and Jennifer
  Niesslein, Editors
editor@brainchildmag.com
http://www.brainchildmag
  .com/
Quarterly

Briar Cliff Review
3303 Rebecca Street
PO Box 2100
Sioux City, IA 51104-2100
Tricia Currans-Sheehen, Editor
currans@briarcliff.edu
www.briar-cliff.edu/bcreview
Annual

Callaloo
English Department
Texas A&M University
4227 TAMU
College Station, TX 77843-4227
Charles Henry Rowell, Editor
callaloo@tamu.edu
http://callaloo.tamu.edu
Quarterly

**Calyx, A Journal of Art and
  Literature by Women**
PO Box B
Corvalis, OR 97339-0539
Beverly McFarland, Senior Editor
calyx@proaxis.com
www.calyxpress.org
Semiannual

The Carolina Quarterly
Greenlaw Hall, GB 3520
University of North Carolina
Chapel Hill, NC 27599-3520
Elena Oxman, Editor
cquarter@unc.edu
www.unc.edu/depts/cqonline
Triannual

The Chattahoochee Review
2101 Womack Road
Dunwoody, GA 30338-4497
Marc Fitten, Editor
www.chattahoochee-review.org
Quarterly

Chelsea
PO Box 773
Cooper Station
New York, NY 10276-0773
Alfredo de Palchi, Editor
www.chelseamag.org
Semiannual

Chicago Reader
11 East Illinois
Chicago, IL 60611
Alison True, Editor
mail@chicagoreader.com
www.chicagoreader.com
Daily

Chicago Review
5801 S. Kenwood Avenue
Chicago, IL 60637
Joshua Kotin, Editor
chicago-review@uchicago.edu
humanities.uchicago.edu/review
Quarterly

Cimarron Review
205 Morrill Hall
English Department
Oklahoma State University
Stillwater, OK 74078
E. P. Walkiewicz, Editor
http://cimarronreview.okstate.edu
Quarterly

The Cincinnati Review
University of Cincinnati
McMicken Hall, Room 369
PO Box 210069
Cincinnati, OH 45221-0069
Brock Clarke, Editor
editors@cincinnatireview.com
cincinnatireview.com
Semiannual

Colorado Review
Department of English
Colorado State University
Fort Collins, CO 80523
Stephanie G'Schwind, Editor
creview@colostate.edu
http://coloradoreview.colostate.edu
Triannual

Commentary
165 E. 56th Street
New York, NY 10022
Neal Kozodoy, Editor
editorial@commentarymagazine
   .com
www.commentarymagazine.com
Published six times annually

Concho River Review
English Department
Angelo State University
10894 ASU Station
San Angelo, TX 76909-0894

Mary Ellen Hartje, Editor
ME.hartje@angelo.edu
Semiannual

Conjunctions
21 E. 10th Street
New York, NY 10003
Bradford Morrow, Editor
webmaster@conjunctions.com
www.conjunctions.com
Semiannual

Crab Orchard Review
Southern Illinois University
   Carbondale
1000 Faner Drive
Faner Hall 2380, Mail Code
   4503
Carbondale, IL 62901
Allison Joseph, Editor
www.siu.edu/~crborchd
Semiannual

Crazyhorse
Department of English
College of Charleston
66 George Street
Charleston, SC 29424
Carol Ann Davis and Garrett
   Doherty, Editors
crazyhorse@cofc.edu
crazyhorse.cofc.edu/
Semiannual

Cream City Review
Department of English
Box 413
University of Wisconsin–
   Milwaukee
Milwaukee, WI 53201
Phong Nguyen, Editor
www.creamcityreview.org
Semiannual

**Daedalus, Journal of the
   American Academy of Arts &
   Sciences**
Norton's Woods
136 Irving Street
Cambridge, MA 02138
James Miller, Editor
daedalus@amacad.org
www.mitpressjournals.org/page/
   editorial/daed
Quarterly

Dappled Things
Mary Angelita Ruiz, Editor in
   Chief
dappledthings.editor@gmail
   .com
http://www.dappledthings.org
Quarterly

Denver Quarterly
Department of English
University of Denver

2000 E. Asbury
Denver, CO 80208
Bin Ramke, Editor
www.denverquarterly.com
Quarterly

Epiphany Magazine
71 Bedford Street
New York, NY 10014
Willard Cook, Editor
www.epiphanyzine.com
Semiannual

Epoch
251 Goldwin Smith Hall
Cornell University
Ithaca, NY 14853-3201
Michael Koch, Editor
www.arts.cornell.edu/english/
epoch.html
Triannual

Event
Douglas College
PO Box 2503
New Westminster, BC V3L
5B2
Canada
Rick Maddocks, Editor
event@douglas.bc.ca
event.douglas.bc.ca
Triannual

**Fantasy & Science Fiction
Magazine**
PO Box 3447
Hoboken, NJ 07030
Gordon Van Gelder, Editor
www.ffsmag.com
Monthly

Faultline
Department of English
University of California, Irvine
Irvine, CA 92697-2650
Devin Becker and Max Winter,
Editors
faultline@uci.edu
www.humanities.uci.edu/faultline
Annual

Fence Magazine
Science Library 320
University at Albany
1400 Washington Avenue
Albany, NY 12015
Lynne Tillman, Fiction Editor
fence@albany.edu
www.fenceportal.org
Semiannual

Fifth Wednesday Journal
PO Box 4033
Lisle, IL 60532
editors@fifthwednesdayjournal.com
www.fifthwednesdayjournal.com
Biannual

The First Line
PO Box 250382
Plano, TX 75025-0382
David LaBounty and Jeff Adams,
    Editors
info@thefirstline.com
www.thefirstline.com
Quarterly

Five Points
PO Box 3999
Atlanta, GA 30302-3999
Megan Sexton, Editor
info@langate.gsu.edu
webdelsol.com/Five_Points/
Triannual

The Florida Review
Department of English
PO Box 161346
University of Central Florida
Orlando, FL 32816
Jeanne M. Leiby, Editor
flireview@mail.ucf.edu
www.flreview.com
Semiannual

Fugue
University of Idaho
200 Brink Hall
PO Box 441102
Moscow, ID 83844-1102
Justin Jainchill and Sara Kaplan,
    Editors

fugue@uidaho.edu
www.uidaho.edu/fugue/
Semiannual

Georgia Review
University of Georgia
012 Gilbert Hall
Athens, GA 30606-9009
Stephen Corey, Editor
scorey@uga.edu, garev@uga
    .edu
www.uga.edu/garev
Quarterly

Good Housekeeping
Hearst Corp.
250 W. 55th Street
New York, NY 10019
Laura Mathews, Literary Editor
www.goodhousekeeping.com
Monthly

Grain Magazine
PO Box 67
Saskatoon, SK S7K 3KI
Canada
Kent Bruyneel, Editor
grainmag@sasktel.net
www.grainmagazine.ca
Quarterly

Greensboro Review
MFA Writing Program, English
    Department

134 McIver Building, UNCG
PO Box 26170
Greensboro, NC 27402-6170
Jim Clark, Editor
jclark@uncg.edu
www.uncg.edu/eng/mfa
Semiannual

Gulf Coast

Department of English
University of Houston
Houston, TX 77204-3013
Nick Flynn, Executive Editor
editors@gulfcoastmag.org
www.gulfcoastmag.org
Semiannual

Happy

46 St. Pauls Avenue
Jersey City, NJ 07306-
    1623
Bayard, Editor
bayardx@gmail.com
Quarterly

Harper's Magazine

666 Broadway
11th Floor
New York, NY 10012
Ben Metcalf, Literary Editor
letters@harpers.org
www.harpers.org
Monthly

Harpur Palate

English Department
Binghamton University
PO Box 6000
Binghamton, NY 13902-6000
Holly Wendt and Katherine
    Henion, Editors
hpalate@binghamton.edu
harpurpalate.binghamton.edu
Semiannual

Harvard Review

Lamont Library
Harvard University
Cambridge, MA 02138
Christina Thompson, Editor
harvard_review@harvard.edu
www.hcl.harvard.edu/harvardreview
Semiannual

Hayden's Ferry Review

Box 875002
Arizona State University
Tempe, AZ 85287-5002
Beth Staples, Managing Editor
hfr@asu.edu
www.haydensferryreview.org
Semiannual

Hemispheres

Pace Communications
1301 Carolina Street
Greensboro, NC 27401
Randy Johnson, Editor

hemiedit@aol.com
www.hemispheresmagazine
.com
Monthly

Hobart: another literary journal
PO Box 1658
Ann Arbor, MI 48103
Aaron Burch, Editor
www.hobartpulp.com

H.O.W.
112 Franklin Street
Fourth Floor
New York, NY 10013
Alison Weaver and Natasha
Radojcic, Editors
info@HOWjournal.com
www.HOWjournal.com
Semiannual

The Hudson Review
684 Park Avenue
New York, NY 10021
Paula Deitz, Editor
www.hudsonreview.com
Quarterly

**Hyphen: Asian America
Unabridged**
PO Box 192002
San Francisco, CA 94119
Melissa Hung, Editor
editorial@hyphenmagazine.com

www.hyphenmagazine.com
Triannual

The Idaho Review
Boise State University
Department of English
1910 University Drive
Boise, ID 83725
Mitch Wieland, Editor in Chief
english.boisestate.edu/idaho
review/
Annual

**Image, A Journal of the Arts &
Religion**
3307 Third Avenue West
Seattle, WA 98119
Mary Kenagy, Managing Editor
mkenagy@imagejournal.org
www.imagejournal.org
Quarterly

Indiana Review
Indiana University
Ballantine Hall 465
Bloomington, IN 47405-7103
Jenny Burge, Editor
inreview@indiana.edu
www.indiana.edu/~inreview/
Semiannual

The Iowa Review
308 EPB
University of Iowa

Iowa City, IA 52242-1400
David Hamilton, Editor
www.iowareview.org
Triannual

Jabberwock Review
Department of English
Mississippi State University
Drawer E
Mississippi State, MS 39862
David Johnson, Editor
jabberwock@org.msstate.edu
www.msstate.edu/org/
    jabberwock
Semiannual

Juked
J. W. Wang, Editor
www.juked.com
Annual

**Kalliope, A Journal of Women's
    Literature & Art**
Florida Community College at
    Jacksonville
South Campus
11901 Beach Boulevard
Jacksonville, FL 32246
Dr. Margaret Clark, Editor in
    Chief
maclark@fccj.edu
http://opencampus.fccj.org/
    kalliope/index.html
Semiannual

The Kenyon Review
Kenyon College
Walton House
Gambier, OH 43022
David H. Lynn, Editor
kenyonreview@kenyon.edu
www.kenyonreview.org
Quarterly

Lake Effect
Penn State Erie
5091 Station Road
Erie, PA 16563-1501
George Looney, Editor in Chief
gol1@psu.edu
http://www.pserie.psu.edu/
    lakeeffect
Annual

**The Land-Grant College
    Review**
PO Box 1164
New York, NY 10159
Dave Koch and Josh Melrod,
    Editors
editors@lgcr.org
www.land-grantcollegereview.com/
Semiannual

The Laurel Review
Green Tower Press
Department of English
Northwest Missouri State
    University

Maryville, MO 64468-6001
Brenda Lewis, Editor
http://catpages.nwmissouri.edu/
  m/tlr
Semiannual

Lilies and Cannonballs Review
PO Box 702
Bowling Green Station
New York, NY 10274-0702
Daniel Connor, Editor
info@liliesandcannonballs.com
www.liliesandcannonballs.com
Annual

The Literary Review
285 Madison Avenue
Mail Code: M-GH2-01
Madison, NJ 07940
Walter Cummins, Editor in
  Chief
tlr@fdu.edu
www.theliteraryreview.org
Quarterly

The L Magazine
20 Jay Street, Suite 207
Brooklyn, NY 11201
Jonny Diamond, Editor in
  Chief
editor@thelmagazine.com
http://www.thelmagazine.com
Annual fiction issue

The Long Story
18 Eaton Street
Lawrence, MA 01843
R. P. Burnham, Editor
rpburnham@mac.com
homepage.mac.com/rpburnham/
  longstory.html
Annual

Louisiana Literature
Box 10792
Southeastern Louisiana University
Hammond, LA 70402
Jack Bedell, Editor
lalit@selu.edu
www.louisianaliterature.org/
  press/
Semiannual

Low Rent
W. P. Hughes, Editor
www.lowrentmagazine.com

The Malahat Review
University of Victoria
PO Box 1700
STN CSC
Victoria, BC V8W 2Y2
Canada
John Barton, Editor
malahat@uvic.ca
http://malahatreview.ca
Quarterly

Mānoa
English Department
University of Hawai'i
1733 Donaghho Road
Honolulu, HI 96822
Frank Stewart, Editor
mjournal-l@hawaii.edu
www.hawaii.edu/mjournal
Semiannual

The Massachusetts Review
South College
University of Massachusetts
Amherst, MA 01003-7140
David Lenson, Editor
massrev@external.umass.edu
www.massreview.org
Quarterly

McSweeney's
849 Valencia Street
San Francisco, CA 94110
Dave Eggers, Editor
printsubmissions@mcsweeneys
 .net
www.mcsweeneys.net
Quarterly

Meridian
University of Virginia
PO Box 400145
Charlottesville, VA 22904-
 4145
Fiction Editor

meridian@virginia.edu
www.readmeridian.org
Semiannual

Michigan Quarterly Review
University of Michigan
3574 Rackham Building
915 E. Washington Street
Ann Arbor, MI 48109-1070
Laurence Goldstein, Editor
MQR@umich.edu
www.umich.edu/~mqr
Quarterly

**Midstream: Bi-monthly Jewish
 Review**
633 Third Avenue
21st Floor
New York, NY 10017-6706
Leo Haber, Editor
midstreamthf@aol.com
www.midstreamthf.com
Six issues annually

Minnesota Review
Department of English
Carnegie Mellon University
Pittsburgh, PA 15213
Jeffrey J. Williams, Editor
editors@theminnesotareview
 .org
www.theminnesotareview.org
Semiannual

Mississippi Review
The University of Southern
　Mississippi
118 College Drive
Box 5144
Hattiesburg, MS 39406-5144
Frederick Barthelme, Editor
fbx@mississippireview.com
www.mississippireview.com
Semiannual

The Missouri Review
357 McReynolds Hall
University of Missouri–
　Columbia
Columbia, MO 65211
Speer Morgan, Editor
www.moreview.com
Quarterly

**Natural Bridge, A Journal of
　Contemporary Literature**
Department of English
University of Missouri–St. Louis
One University Boulevard
St. Louis, MO 63121
Kenneth E. Harrison, Jr., Editor
natural@umsl.edu
www.umsl.edu/~natural
Semiannual

New Delta Review
English Department
15 Allen Hall

Louisiana State University
Baton Rouge, LA 70803-5001
Shane Noecher, Editor
http://www.english.lsu.edu/
　journals/ndr
Semiannual

New England Review
Middlebury College
Middlebury, VT 05753
Stephen Donadio, Editor
NEReview@middlebury.edu
go.middlebury.edu/nereview
Quarterly

New Letters
University of Missouri–Kansas
　City
5101 Rockhill Road
Kansas City, MO 64110
Robert Stewart, Editor in Chief
newletters@umkc.edu
www.newletters.org
Quarterly

New Madrid
Department of English
Murray State University
7C Faculty Hall
Murray, KY 42701-3341
Ann Neelon, Editor
www.murraystate.edu/newmadrid/
Biannual

New Ohio Review
English Department
360 Ellis Hall
Ohio University
Athens, OH 45701
John Bullock, Editor
noreditors@ohio.edu
www.ohiou.edu/nor
Semiannual

New Orleans Review
Box 195
Loyola University
New Orleans, LA 70118
Christopher Chambers, Editor
chambers@loyno.edu
www.loyno.edu/-noreview
Semiannual

The New Yorker
4 Times Square
New York, NY 10036
Deborah Treisman, Fiction Editor
fiction@newyorker.com
www.newyorker.com
Weekly

Ninth Letter
Department of English
University of Illinois, Urbana-
    Champaign
608 S. Wright Street
Urbana, IL 61801
Jodee Stanley, Editor

ninthletter@uiuc.edu
www.ninthletter.com
Semiannual

Noon
1324 Lexington Avenue
P.M.B. 298
New York, NY 10128
Diane Williams, Editor
www.noonannual.com/
Annual

North Carolina Literary Review
Department of English
2201 Bate Building
East Carolina University
Greenville, NC 27858-4353
Margaret Bauer, Editor
bauerm@ecu.edu
www.ecu.edu/nclr
Annual

North Dakota Quarterly
Merrifield Hall, Room 110
276 Centennial Drive, Stop 7209
Grand Forks, ND 58202-7209
Robert W. Lewis, Editor
ndq@und.nodak.edu
www.und.nodak.edu/org/ndq
Quarterly

Northwest Review
1286 University of Oregon
Eugene, OR 97403

John Witte, Editor
jwitte@uoregon.edu
darkwing.uoregon.edu/~nwreview/
Triannual

Notre Dame Review

840 Flanner Hall
University of Notre Dame
Notre Dame, IN 46556
William O'Rourke, Fiction Editor
www.nd.edu/~ndr/review.htm
Semiannual

One Story

The Old American Can Factory
232 Third Street, #A111
Brooklyn, NY 11215
Hannah Tinti, Editor
questions@one-story.com
www.one-story.com
Published about every three weeks

Ontario Review

9 Honey Brook Drive
Princeton, NJ 08540
www.ontarioreviewpress.com
Semiannual

Open City

270 Lafayette Street
Suite 1412
New York, NY 10012
Thomas Beller and Joanna Yas,
     Editors

editors@opencity.org
www.opencity.org
Triannual

Other Voices

University of Illinois at Chicago
Department of English, MC162
601 South Morgan Street
Chicago, IL 60607-7120
Gina Frangello, Executive
     Editor
www.othervoicesmagazine.org
Semiannual

Oxford American

201 Donaghey Avenue
Conway, AR 72035
Marc Smirnoff, Editor
oamag@oxfordamericanmag.com/
http://www.oxfordamericanmag
     .com/
Quarterly

Pakn Treger

National Yiddish Book Center
Harry & Jeanette Weinberg
     Building
1021 West Street
Amherst, MA 01002-3375
Nancy Sherman, Editor
pt2008@bikher.org
www.yiddishbookcenter.org
Semiannual

The Paris Review
62 White Street
New York, NY 10013
Philip Gourevitch, Editor
queries@theparisreview.org
www.theparisreview.org
Quarterly

Parting Gifts
3413 Wilshire Drive
Greensboro, NC 27408
Robert Bixby, Editor
rbixby@earthlink.net
www.marchstreetpress.com
Semiannual

Phantasmagoria
English Department
Century College
3300 Century Avenue North
White Bear Lake, MN 55110
Abigail Allen, Editor
Semiannual

Phoebe, A Journal of Literature and Art
MSN 2C5
George Mason University
4400 University Drive
Fairfax, VA 22030-4444
Nat Foster, Editor
phoebe@gmu.edu
www.gmu.edu/pubs/phoebe
Semiannual

Pilot Pocket Book
PO Box 161
Station B
119 Spadina Avenue
Toronto, ON M5T 2T3
Canada
Reuben McLaughlin, Lee
    Sheppard, and Bryan Belanger,
    Editors
editor@thepilotproject.ca
www.thepilotproject.ca
Semiannual

The Pinch
Department of English
University of Memphis
Memphis, TN 38152-6176
Kristen Iversen, Editor
www.thepinchjournal.com
Semiannual

Playboy Magazine
730 Fifth Avenue
New York, NY 10019
Amy Grace Loyd, Literary Editor
aloyd@playboy.com
www.playboy.com
Monthly

Pleiades, A Journal of New Writing
Department of English
Central Missouri State University
Warrensburg, MO 64093

Kevin Prufer and Wayne Miller,
Editors
pleiades@cmsul.cmsu.edu
www.cmsu.edu/englphil/pleiades/
Semiannual

Ploughshares
Emerson College
120 Boylston Street
Boston, MA 02116-4624
Robert Arnold, Editor
pshares@emerson.edu
www.pshares.org
Triannual

PMS poemmemoirstory
HB 217
1530 Third Avenue South
Birmingham, AL 35294-1260
Minda Frost, Editor
http://pms-journal.org
Annual

Post Road
PO Box 400951
Cambridge, MA 02140
Mary Cotton, Managing Editor
fiction@postroadmag.com
www.postroadmag.com
Semiannual

Potomac Review
Montgomery College
51 Mannakee Street

Rockville, MD 20850
Julie Wakeman-Linn, Editor
potomacrevieweditor@
montgomerycollege.edu
http://www.montgomerycollege
.edu/potomacreview
Annual

Prairie Fire
Artspace
423-100 Arthur Street
Winnipeg, MB R3B 1H3
Canada
Andris Taskans, Editor
prfire@mts.net
www.prairiefire.ca/
Quarterly

Prairie Schooner
201 Andrews Hall
University of Nebraska
Lincoln, NE 68588-0334
Hilda Raz, Editor in Chief
kgrey2@unlnotes.unl.edu
www.prairieschooner.unl.edu
Quarterly

Prism International
University of British Columbia
Buchanan E-462
1866 Main Mall
Vancouver, BC V6T1Z1
Canada
Claire Tacon, Fiction Editor

prism@interchange.ubc.ca
www.prism.arts.ubc.ca
Quarterly

Product
University of Southern
    Mississippi
118 College Drive, #5144
Hattiesburg, MS 39406-0001
J. W. Wang, Editor
Annual

A Public Space
323 Dean Street
Brooklyn, NY 11217
Brigid Hughes, Editor
editors@apublicspace.org
www.apublicspace.org
Quarterly

Quarterly West
University of Utah
255 South Central Campus Drive
Department of English
LNCO 3500
Salt Lake City, UT 84112-0494
Paul Ketzle and Brenda
    Sieczkowski, Editors
utah.edu/quarterlywest
Semiannual

The Rake
800 Washington Avenue North
#504

Minneapolis, MN 55401
Julie Caniglia, Editor
submissions@rakemag.com
www.rakemag.com
Monthly

Raritan
Rutgers University
31 Mine Street
New Brunswick, NJ 08903
Jackson Lears, Editor
http://raritanquarterly.rutgers.edu/
Quarterly

Red Rock Review
English Department, J2A
College of Southern Nevada
3200 E. Cheyenne Avenue
North Las Vegas, NV 89030
Richard Logsdon, Editor in Chief
Semiannual

River Styx
3547 Olive Street
Suite 107
St. Louis, MO 63103-1014
Richard Newman, Editor
bigriver@riverstyx.org
www.riverstyx.org
Triannual

Roanoke Review
221 College Lane
Salem, VA 24153

Paul Hanstedt, Editor
review@roanoke.edu
Annual

Rosebud Magazine
N3310 Asje Road
Cambridge, WI 53523
Roderick Clarke, Editor
www.rsbd.net
Semiannual

Salamander
English Department
Suffolk University
41 Temple Street
Boston, MA 02114
Jennifer Barber, Editor
http://media.cas.suffolk.edu/
salamander/
Semiannual

Salmagundi
Skidmore College
815 N. Broadway
Saratoga Springs, NY 12866
Robert Boyers, Editor in Chief
pboyers@skidmore.edu
http://www.skidmore.edu/
salmagundi/
Quarterly

Santa Monica Review
Santa Monica College
1900 Pico Boulevard

Santa Monica, CA 90405
Andrew Tonkovich, Editor
antonkovi@uci.edu
www.smc.edu/sm_review
Semiannual

Saranac Review
Department of English
SUNY Plattsburgh
101 Broad Street
Plattsburgh, NY 12901
Linda Young, Editor
http://research.plattsburgh.edu/
saranacreview
Annual

Sensations Magazine
PO Box 132
Lafayette, NJ 07848
David Messino, Editor
www.sensationsmag.com

Seven Days
PO Box 1164
Burlington, VT 05402-1164
Paula Routly, Editor
www.sevendaysvt.com
Weekly, fiction published
annually

The Sewanee Review
University of the South
735 University Avenue
Sewanee, TN 37383-1000

George Core, Editor
www.sewanee.edu/sreview/home
.html
Quarterly

Shenandoah
Mattingly House
2 Lee Avenue
Washington and Lee University
Lexington, VA 24450-2116
R. T. Smith, Editor
shenandoah@wlu.edu
http://shenandoah.wlu.edu
Triannual

Silent Voices
PO Box 11180
Glendale, CA 91226
Peter A. Balaskas, Editor
exmachinapab@aol.com
http://www.exmachinapress
.com
Annual

Sonora Review
English Department
University of Arizona
Tucson, AZ 85721
Jamison Crabtree and Michael
Sheehan, Editors in Chief
sonora@email.arizona.edu
www.coh.arizona.edu/sonora
Semiannual

The South Carolina Review
Clemson University
Strode Tower, Box 340522
Clemson, SC 29634-0522
Wayne Chapman, Editor
http://www.clemson.edu/caah/
cedp/scrintro.htm
Semiannual

South Dakota Review
Department of English
The University of South
Dakota
414 E. Clark Street
Vermillion, SD 47069
Brian Bedard, Editor
sdreview@usd.edu
http://www.usd.edu/sdreview
Quarterly

Southern Humanities Review
9088 Haley Center
Auburn University
Auburn, AL 36849
Dan R. Latimer and Virginia M.
Kouidis, Editors
shrengl@auburn.edu
www.auburn.edu/english/shr/
home.htm
Quarterly

Southern Indiana Review
College of Liberal Arts
University of Southern Indiana

8600 University Boulevard
Evansville, IN 47712
Ron Mitchell, Managing Editor
sir@usi.edu
www.southernindianareview.org
Semiannual

The Southern Review
Louisiana State University
Old President's House
Baton Rouge, LA 70803-0001
Bret Lott, Editor
southernreview@lsu.edu
www.lsu.edu/thesouthernreview
Quarterly

Southwest Review
Southern Methodist University
PO Box 750374
Dallas, TX 75275-0374
Willard Spiegelman, Editor in
  Chief
swr@mail.smu.edu
www.southwestreview.org
Quarterly

Spot Literary Magazine
PO Box 3833
Palos Verdes Peninsula, CA
  90274
Susan Hansell, Editor
susan.hansell@gmail.com
www.susan-hansell.net
Biannual

St. Anthony Messenger
28 W. Liberty Street
Cincinnati, OH 45202-6498
Pat McCloskey, O.F.M., Editor
samadmin@americancatholic
  .org
www.americancatholic.org
Monthly

St. Petersburg Review
Box 288
Concord, NH 03302
Elizabeth L. Hodges, Editor
submission@stpetersburgreview
  .com
www.stpetersburg.com
Annual

Subtropics
PO Box 112075
4008 Turlington Hall
University of Florida
Gainesville, FL 32611
David Leavitt, Editor
www.english.ufl.edu/subtropics
Triannual

Sun Magazine
107 N. Roberson Street
Chapel Hill, NC 27516
Sy Safransky, Editor
www.thesunmagazine.org
Monthly

The Sycamore Review
Purdue University
Department of English
500 Oval Drive
West Lafayette, IN 47907-2038
Rebekah Silverman, Editor
sycamore@purdue.edu
sycamorereview.com
Semiannual

Tampa Review
University of Tampa
401 W. Kennedy Boulevard
Tampa, FL 33606-1490
Richard Mathews, Editor
utpress@ut.edu
www.tampareview.ut.edu
Semiannual

Third Coast
Department of English
Western Michigan University
Kalamazoo, MI 49008-5331
Peter Geye, Editor
editors@thirdcoastmagazine
   .com
www.thirdcoastmagazine.com
Biannual

Threepenny Review
PO Box 9131
Berkeley, CA 94709
Wendy Lesser, Editor
wlesser@threepennyreview.com

www.threepennyreview.com
Quarterly

Timber Creek Review
8969 UNCG Station
Greensboro, NC 27413
John M. Freiermuth, Editor
Quarterly

Tin House
PMB 280
320 Seventh Avenue
Brooklyn, NY 11215
Win McCormack, Editor in Chief
robspill@ix.netcom.com
www.tinhouse.com
Quarterly

Transition Magazine
104 Mount Auburn Street
3R
Cambridge, MA 02138
F. Abiola and Tommie Shelby,
   Editors
transition@fas.harvard.edu
www.transitionmagazine.com
Quarterly

TriQuarterly
Northwestern University
629 Noyes Street
Evanston, IL 60208
Susan Firestone Hahn, Editor
triquarterly@northwestern.edu

www.triquarterly.org/index.cfm
Triannual

upstreet
PO Box 105
Richmond, MA 01254-0105
Vivian Dorsel, Editor
editor@upstreet-mag.org
www.upstreet-mag.org
Annual

Virginia Quarterly Review
1 West Range
PO Box 400223
Charlottesville, VA 22903-4223
Ted Genoways, Editor
vqreview@virginia.edu
www.vqronline.org
Quarterly

Weber: The Contemporary West
Weber State University
1214 University Circle
Ogden, UT 84408-1214
Michael Wutz, Editor
http://weberjournal.weber.edu
Semiannual

West Branch
Bucknell Hall
Bucknell University
Lewisburg, PA 17837
Paula Closson Buck, Editor
westbranch@bucknell.edu

www.bucknell.edu/westbranch
Semiannual

Western Humanities Review
University of Utah
English Department
255 S. Central Campus Drive
Room 3500
Salt Lake City, UT 84112-0494
Barry Weller, Editor
www.hum.utah.edu/whr/
Semiannual

Whistling Shade
PO Box 7084
Saint Paul, MN 55107
Anthony Telschow, Executive
    Editor
editor@whistlingshade.com
www.whistlingshade.com
Quarterly

Willow Springs
Eastern Washington University
501 North Riverpoint Boulevard,
    Ste. 425
Spokane, WA 99202
Samuel Ligon, Editor
http://willowsprings.ewu.edu
Semiannual

Worcester Review
1 Ekman Street
Worcester, MA 01607

Rodger Martin, Managing Editor
rodgerwriter@tds.net
http://www.geocities.com/wreview/
Annual

Witness Magazine
Black Mountain Institute
University of Nevada, Las Vegas
Box 455085
Las Vegas, NV 89154-5085
Amber Withycombe, Editor
amber.withycombe@unlv.edu
http://blackmountain.unlv.edu/
    programs/witness.htm
Annual

WLA: War, Literature & the Arts
Department of English
2354 Fairchild Drive, Ste. 6D207
USAF Academy
Colorado Springs, CO 80840-
    6242
Donald Anderson, Editor
editor@wlajournal.com
www.wlajournal.com
Semiannual

Words of Wisdom
8969 UNCG Station
Greensboro, NC 27413
Mikhammad Bin Muhandis
    Abdel-Ishahara, Editor
Quarterly

Workers Write!
PO Box 250382
Piano, TX 75025-0382
David LaBounty, Editor
couch@workerswritejournal.com
www.workerswritejournal.com
Annual

Xavier Review
110 Xavier University
New Orleans, LA 70125
Richard Collins, Executive Editor
rcollins@xula.edu
www.xula.edu/review/
Semiannual

**xconnect: writers of the
    information age**
CrossConnect, Inc.
PO Box 2317
Philadelphia, PA 19103
David E. Deifer, Editor
editors@xconnect.org
www.xconnect.org

Zoetrope: All-Story
916 Kearny Street
San Francisco, CA 94133
Michael Ray, Editor
info@all-story.com
www.all-story.com
Quarterly

Permissions

JOIN PEN!

ASSOCIATE MEMBERSHIP IN PEN AMERICAN CENTER IS OPEN TO EVERYONE WHO SUPPORTS PEN'S MISSION. MEMBERS PLAY A VITAL ROLE IN SUPPORTING AND FURTHERING PEN'S EFFORTS ON BEHALF OF WRITERS AND READERS BOTH AT HOME AND ABROAD. BENEFITS INCLUDE:

► A SUBSCRIPTION TO *PEN AMERICA,* OUR AWARD-WINNING SEMI-ANNUAL JOURNAL

► DISCOUNTED ACCESS TO THE ONLINE DATABASE *GRANTS AND AWARDS AVAILABLE TO AMERICAN WRITERS,* THE MOST COMPREHENSIVE DIRECTORY OF ITS KIND

► SELECT INVITATIONS TO MEMBER-ONLY RECEPTIONS

► DISCOUNTS TO PUBLIC PROGRAMS, INCLUDING PEN WORLD VOICES: THE NEW YORK FESTIVAL OF INTERNATIONAL LITERATURE

► FREE WEB PAGE AND BLOG ON PEN.ORG

ANNUAL DUES ARE $40 ($20 FOR STUDENTS). TO JOIN, FILL OUT THE REGISTRATION FORM ON THE OPPOSITE PAGE, AND MAIL THE FORM AND PAYMENT TO:

PEN AMERICAN CENTER
MEMBERSHIP DEPT.
588 BROADWAY, 303
NEW YORK, NY 10012

YOU CAN ALSO JOIN ONLINE:
WWW.PEN.ORG/JOIN

Associate Member Registration

NAME: _____

ADDRESS: _____

CITY/STATE/ZIP: _____

TELEPHONE: _____

E-MAIL ADDRESS: _____

I AM A(N): ❑ WRITER ❑ ACADEMIC ❑ BOOKSELLER ❑ EDITOR
❑ JOURNALIST ❑ LIBRARIAN ❑ PUBLISHER ❑ TRANSLATOR ❑ OTHER_____

❑ I AM INTERESTED IN VOLUNTEER OPPORTUNITIES WITH PEN.

❑ I ENCLOSE $40, MY ANNUAL ASSOCIATE MEMBERSHIP DUES.
            -- OR --
❑ I ENCLOSE $20, MY ANNUAL STUDENT ASSOCIATE MEMBERSHIP DUES.

❑ I ALSO ENCLOSE A TAX-DEDUCTIBLE CONTRIBUTION IN ADDITION TO MY DUES TO PROVIDE MUCH-NEEDED SUPPORT FOR THE *READERS AND WRITERS* PROGRAM AT PEN, WHICH ENCOURAGES LITERARY CULTURE THROUGH OUTREACH PROGRAMS AND LITERARY EVENTS, INCLUDING AUTHOR PANELS, WRITING AND READING WORKSHOPS FOR HIGH SCHOOL STUDENTS, AND THE WRITING INSTITUTE, WHICH INVITES TEENS TO INTERACT DIRECTLY WITH PROFESSIONAL WRITERS IN A SERIES OF WORKSHOPS. FOR MORE INFO, VISIT: WWW.PEN.ORG/READERSANDWRITERS.

❑ $50 ❑ $100 ❑ $500 ❑ $1,000 PRESIDENT'S CIRCLE
❑ OTHER $_____

TOTAL: $_____

(ALL CONTRIBUTIONS ABOVE THE BASIC DUES OF $40/$20 ARE TAX DEDUCTIBLE TO THE FULLEST EXTENT ALLOWED BY THE LAW.)

PLEASE MAKE YOUR CHECK PAYABLE TO **PEN AMERICAN CENTER.**

MAIL FORM AND CHECK TO:
PEN AMERICAN CENTER, MEMBERSHIP DEPARTMENT
588 BROADWAY, 303, NEW YORK, NY 10012.

TO PAY BY CREDIT CARD PLEASE VISIT **www.pen.org/join.**